RUINS AND REDEMPTION

ERIN P.T. CANNING

H.C. BROWN LLC

To my husband, the love of my life, who not only taught me what true, unconditional love looks like but also continues to be my best friend, my fiercest supporter, and the one person who truly sees me for me.

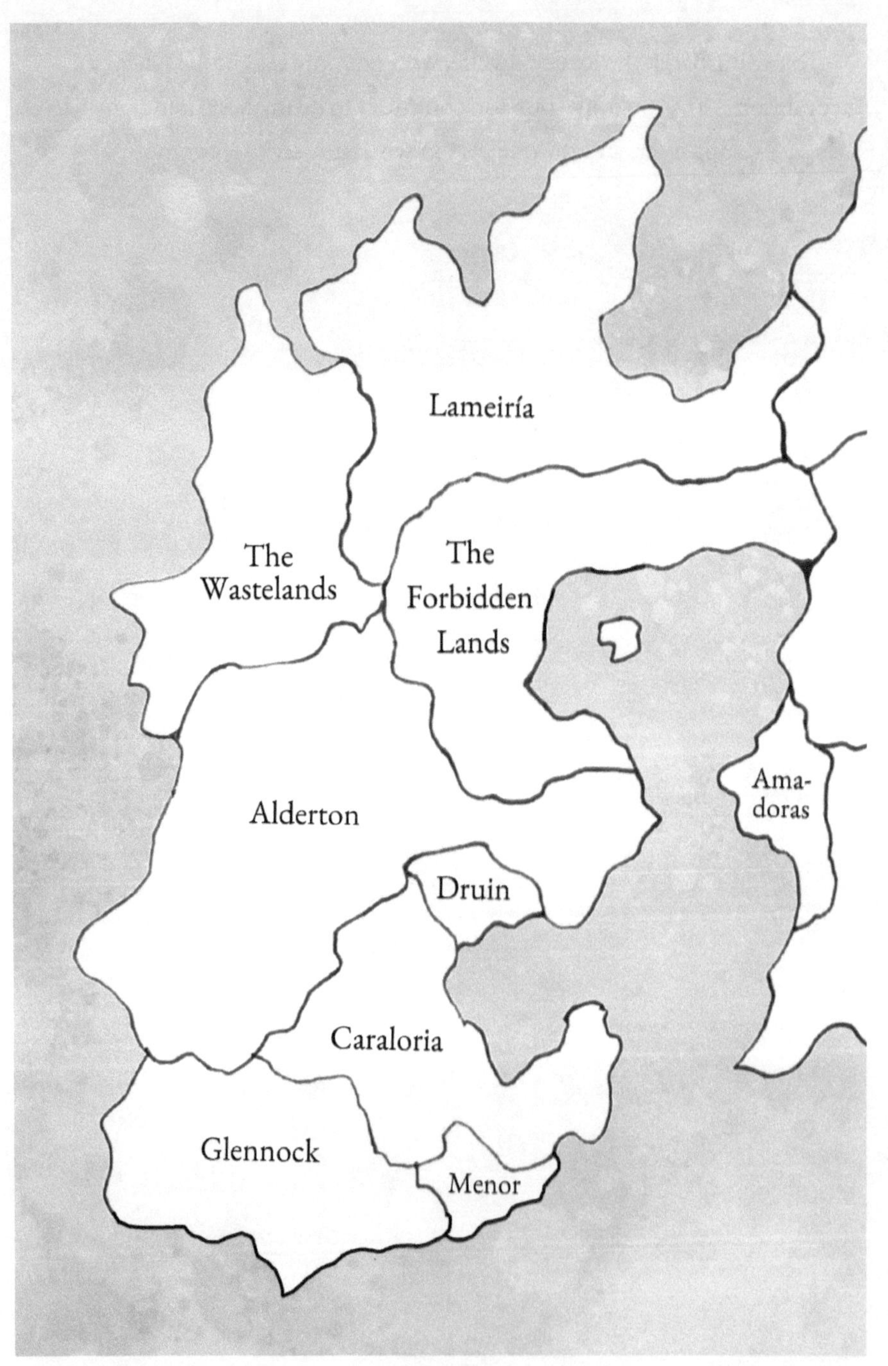

Lameiría
The Wastelands
The Forbidden Lands
Ama-doras
Alderton
Druin
Caraloria
Glennock
Menor

CONTENTS

CHAPTER ONE

THE CAVE

Turning her back on the Potomac River, Adaline rolls her shoulders to shed the memories that threaten to resurface. She locks her expression into neutral, ignoring the students' occasional glances from her to the rapids below, their roar masked as cars zoom by. She's done with sympathy. Sympathy won't change the past.

Upon receiving a thumbs up from her colleagues, she signals her three student interns to gather closer. "Okay, let's go. Don't forget to drink water as needed, and make sure your helmets are secured before we enter the cave. Once we reach the entrance, you'll want to stop talking. Unless you want to wake the bats."

She steps off the dirt road and climbs the rocky slope of the Maryland Heights Trail. As the tree branches coax her further into their fold, she glances over her shoulder to make certain her students are keeping pace. Behind them, her colleagues bring up the rear with Beccah taking photos of the trees and wildflowers. Ben just glares at the ground as if the leaves and roots intend to trip him and break his back.

Adaline smiles to herself. *Once a Grump, always a Grump.* She wouldn't change him though.

For a few miles, she focuses only on what lies ahead, on what's been calling to her since childhood, since her father started this research decades ago—only for the county to shut down the site. But she'd won. She'd found a grantor with enough funds and enough clout to convince the county to allow her and a small team admittance. She's about to survey the impossible.

Finally, I'm almost there.

The early summer sun peeking through the woods lights her path forward, as well as the knocked-over stone slab, broken at an angle, that points northwest. She pauses at the slab, fills her lungs with a fresh burst of satisfaction, and pushes the brush out of the way to lead her small team off-trail.

In front of the base of a hill, a line of staggered tree trunks conceals her destination. With one hand on a trunk, she climbs over the roots and threads herself between the trees until the mouth of a cave comes into view. Switching on her helmet's headlamp, Adaline ducks and steps into the darkness. The crisp, damp air envelops them as her team treks through the narrow tunnel. Their headlamps light the ground but not the dark abyss that lies ahead. When the tunnel slopes downward, Adaline tests the grip of her Timberland boots on the slippery cave floor and keeps going as if she's walked this path before.

"Don't forget to look at these," she whispers. Shining her lamp on the cave wall, she points to spiral petroglyphs that Native Americans carved into the stone, along with pictographs of deer and mountain lions.

Exactly where Dad marked them in his notes.

The student closest to her whistles in awe. "Are those Iroquoian?"

Adaline smiles. "Yes, they're part of the Monongahela culture that inhabited this portion of western Maryland between 1050 and 1635."

"Before European settlers wiped the Monongahela out with diseases?"

After a silent sigh, Adaline nods. "Most likely."

Facts are good. They help quiet her anticipation. When she first found her father's photos years ago, he's said this work was classified and sent her back to bed. But he never stopped studying this place, and she never thought she'd see the site with her own eyes.

At the end of the tunnel, she pauses to admire a pictograph of a figure with two side-by-side circles painted above a plump, oval abdomen. Based on the spiral inside the female's stomach, she must be a goddess of fertility and life. With her stick-like hands raised outward, she blesses the tribe below as a child plays, two women serve food, and a man builds a longhouse.

When they reach the cavern with the bats, Adaline shines her light on her hand and points upward. Her group walks slower, limiting the rattle of their backpacks and water bottles. After fifteen minutes, the tunnel opens up into a round, open chamber. A few cracks in the ceiling allow the morning sunlight to illuminate the site they've come to survey and study.

"Well done, everyone," she says. "Welcome to Maryland's very own underground Stonehenge."

Granted, the stone structures within the cave are nowhere near as plentiful as England's. Instead, this site comprises six pillars about two feet taller than Adaline and a barren center. Stalactites inch downward, reaching like fingers for the pillars.

"Whoa, Adaline. This is seriously impressive." Beccah meanders over, her feet nearly tripping over themselves as her eyes scan the pillars and the cave's formations. Layers of white, tan, and brown stripe the walls horizontally, and a pool of clear water glimmers beyond the thick stalagmites standing guard around the chamber's perimeter. "I can see why Eddie never forgot this place. Thanks for bringing me onboard."

Adaline breathes through the mention of her father's name. "Thanks for being an amazing geologist."

Between the students' wows and murmurs, Adaline slips her backpack off her shoulders, rests her messenger bag on the ground, and tugs the collar of her father's flannel to allow the chill in the air to cool her neck. She stretches her tank top away from her stomach and reties the flannel at her waist into a knot.

Shaking his head, Ben hobbles toward the opposite side of the chamber. When he passes in front of Adaline, he tosses his hands at the pillars as if they were nothing more than toy blocks. "Happy now?"

She smirks. "Obviously. Stop acting like you're still pissed the university said you have to help me."

"Humph!"

Okay. Continue ignoring the fact that my grant's allowing you to finish the work you and my dad started.

The sudden onslaught of grief crushes her lungs. She presses her hand into her chest, her fingers trying to massage away the pain. When she looks up, the Grump is still in front of her. Silently, he squeezes her arm and waits until her breath returns to normal. She releases a slow exhale and nods once, telling him she's fine and he can resume his Grumpy self, which he does. Quickly.

Rolling his eyes at the pillars, Ben crosses the length of the chamber, sets down his water bottle, and drops his bag on his foot. Once the Grump's done cursing under his breath, his colorful language echoing around the chamber, he tugs measuring tape and levels out of his pack.

"Alright, archeology first," he says, pointing to himself. Then he tosses his thumb in Adaline's direction. "Anthropology second. Let's set up our grid, starting with our datum point."

Adaline spends the rest of the morning grinding her teeth, forcing herself to slow down and reminding her students to follow Ben's directions. They measure two-meter square quadrants, push flags as markers into the dirt, and sketch the corresponding map they'll use to track the locations of their findings. With the tedious setup finished, the Grump sits down against a stalagmite, massages his knee, and hacks up a lung while Beccah preps her station for taking soil and rock samples.

The perfunctory work feels all wrong.

Adaline chugs half a bottle of water and stares at the structure out of the corner of her eye. Her bones are restless. If her students wouldn't think her crazy, she'd do a series of jeté leaps across the chamber and hug each pillar. Instead, she assigns the students to different grid quadrants and mentally leaps for joy as she pulls out her tools.

All concept of time vanishes from her mind. With a steady hand, she sweeps the bristles of her brush over four wavy lines, each as thick and deep as her finger. Someone engraved them into the side of a pillar, and her gut tells her to examine where they stop and start. Their eerie precision is almost laser-like. Unnatural.

Curiouser and curiouser.

She backs up to view the entire height of the stone structure, her arms crossed under her breasts, her head tilted to the side. Her gaze follows the path of light emanating from her headlamp. The horizontal waves measure the length of her palm, and a shelf protrudes beneath them.

It's a good spot to place an object of importance, maybe even something sacred. An offering, perhaps.

The air sizzles.

Behind the pillar, Adaline's team scrapes rocks, brushes aside soil, and rummages through their packs to retrieve different tools while they follow through with their assigned roles. One intern mumbles something that earns a high-pitched giggle from another.

Adaline tunes them out. From where she's standing, she can pretend she's the only one down here.

Drops of water echo from different directions throughout the cave system. Their calls oscillate between soft and loud, as if they're speaking to each other, as if they're reminiscing about the past. She listens to their tune, wishing they would retell stories of old, particularly how people managed to drag not one but six pillars into this cave hundreds of years ago and why they used stone not found within three hundred miles. The answer must be etched within these walls.

And yet this chamber is void of all signs of Native American influence. Not one indigenous pictograph decorates this section of the cave. And nothing about the structures' petroglyphs says indigenous.

Closing her eyes, Adaline inhales the damp, salty, mineral scent that tricks her into imagining she's near the ocean. The water's song encourages logic to wash away. Their melody hushes questions. Uncrossing her arms, she takes a few steps forward and presses her hands against the pillar, her fingertips rubbing against the gritty surface.

"What's your story?" she whispers.

Pressure builds in her ears as if she were on a plane accelerating into higher altitude. The drips of water and the interns' grunts fade into garbles until Adaline's left with deafening silence. As she scrunches her brow and leans her cheek against the pillar, she hears waves crash and break against a shoreline, as if she were holding a seashell against her ear.

A student's voice bursts her concentration. "Go tell her."

Adaline's eyes spring open. Shaking off the imaginary sound of the ocean, she laughs at herself, switches off her headlamp, and steps around the pillar to greet her best pupil. Masako dusts her palm with her brush. Her classmate pretends to focus on taking measurements between the third and fourth pillar, but he glances up every now and again, as if mentally encouraging his friend onward.

From mentoring Masako these past five months, Adaline's well acquainted with her student's can-do attitude and determination. But downcast eyes and an empty expression have replaced Masako's vibrant enthusiasm, a quality that reminded Adaline of her own excitement during her undergraduate studies—especially when she'd call her father, and they'd discuss for hours everything she was learning. *What's going on here?*

Adaline tucks the handle of her own brush into her back pocket. "Hey, how's it going by you?"

"Um, good. We have a lot of the measurements done on our side. But that's not...I have a question." She fidgets with her brush, pushing the bristles into her fingertips.

"Sure. Fire away."

"Do you think it'd be possible for me to pause my internship for a few weeks?"

"Why?" Adaline tries to keep the pitch of her voice even while she waits to understand why one of her best students would bail on her. She has only this summer to research the cave, organize and support her conclusions, submit her research for publication, and prove that resurrecting her father's work hasn't waisted her grantor's funding. Without publishing, she can kiss tenure goodbye. And without funding, she'll lose access to this cave. Just thinking of having to bat her eyelashes and dance around the fancy suits funding this project makes her stomach churn.

Adaline peers around a pillar and peeks at Ben to see if he's listening. As he scrapes away at a quadrant beyond the structure, he frowns and mumbles to himself no more than usual. She exhales. The last thing she wants is to hear her own mentor say *I told you so.*

Behind her back, Adaline pinches the pressure point between her thumb and index finger to alleviate the tension building around her temples. "What's going on?"

Masako looks down at her toes as she turns them inward. "It's just, I got a call from my dad last night, and I really want to go home next week. Spend some time with my mom. Take her to chemo."

The tension shifts from Adaline's temples to her chest where it settles fast and deep like a boulder dropped into the sea. "Absolutely. We'll work it out."

Masako's eyebrows tip upward as she manages a smile. "Thank you, Dr. Yates."

"Not a problem, really." Surely, she can find someone else eager to change their summer plans and abandon the idea of beaches for a cold, dank cave. "How's your mom doing?" Adaline's face wilts as Masako's eyes gloss over.

"Oh, you know. She says she's fine." Masako exaggerates the last word, her face twisting as if she's swallowed poison.

"I do know." *Fine is such a loaded little word.*

"Thanks again, Dr. Yates." She scurries away, only to pick up her clipboard and hide her face behind it.

Using both hands, Adaline massages the back of her neck and shoulders. Maybe while she attempts to unravel why nothing within this cave matches either early colonists' or Native American culture, she'll also think up how to tell the Grump about Masako. Of course, he'll understand, but he'll also use this as an opportunity to remind Adaline yet again why this particular project is nothing but a dead end.

The curse and blessing of having an old family friend for my own mentor.

Okay, get it together, Adaline. I won't let him in my head. I have only a few weeks to acquaint myself with every inch of this site and to coax the stone to speak to me. I can't afford setbacks, distractions, or doubt.

At the next pillar, a spiral marking reminiscent of an aerial whirlpool, cyclone, or maze draws her attention. To most ancient cultures, it's the spiral of life, but the indigenous version usually has a wobble to its design. This version is far too precise. Someone else must have made this.

But who? "You're not indigenous. You can't fool me."

After more hours of dusting, measuring, and surveying, her stomach growls. She crouches in front of her messenger bag and retrieves her mobile from the front pouch. Grimacing, she confirms her team should have paused for lunch over an hour ago, and her notifications remind her about the two texts she disregarded when she hopped into Beccah's car this morning.

The message from her best friend beams, "I'll miss you tonight. But I'm so happy for you!!! You're going to rock this!" followed by a rock and shovel emoji. Adaline grins. Still, her shoulders sag under the weight of knowing she's going to miss her friends' big night.

An approaching shadow stretches over her phone, making the notifications glow brighter. Adaline turns her phone upside down as Masako stops, leaving a few feet between them.

"Dr. Yates, you mind if we break to eat?"

"Good timing. You should go get some fresh air too."

"Do you want to join us?"

"Nah, you go on. I want to summarize my findings and theories from this morning. But do me a favor? Take Dr. Larson with you." Adaline nods in Ben's direction. "He needs some fresh air too." *And to stretch that knee properly.* "If you all go, he'll have to go with you."

Masako swings her pack onto her back and switches on her headlamp. "You're sure?"

Adaline's phone screen blares brighter. She flips it over again, holds down, and deletes both notifications. She doesn't need to read Derek's text that starts with *We need to talk.*

Because we really don't.

"I'm sure. You guys go ahead." Adaline slides her phone into her back pocket. "I'm fine."

Those last words make Masako flinch, but the intern does as asked. Before the Grump leads the students outside, he stares Adaline down as if his unyielding glare can force her to follow him. She flashes him a wide grin and waves her clipboard, and he cusses as he exits the chamber. Within a few moments, the echoes of her team dissolve into nothingness.

Beccah slips on her own backpack. "Whew, good thinking to get Ben out of here. What's it going to take for him to retire?"

"Don't let him hear you say that. Besides, he's still the best in his field."

"Uh-huh. And you're not biased in any way, considering he convinced you to study archeology during your undergrad years. I don't know how Eddie and you tolerated him."

At the mention of her dad's name, Adaline swallows the lump in her throat. "The Grump can be endearing."

"Yeah. Sure." Beccah pretends to gag. "Listen, I need to check in with the sitter. You okay down here for a bit?"

Adaline arches an eyebrow.

Beccah laughs. "Yeah, yeah. You're exactly where you want to be. Fine. But don't forget to eat too."

Adaline gives Beccah a thumbs up and holds her breath until her colleague disappears through the exit. Finally, Adaline has this local mystery all to herself.

Because the sun's rays have changed their angle, she clicks on her headlamp to better illuminate the side of the pillar concealed in shadow—not that less shadow reveals anything of significance.

"Secrets take time to earn," she says to herself, knowing full well that the very idea of patience makes her blood boil and her hands work faster.

This cavern has mesmerized her since she found her father's incomplete research paper detailing the chamber. Throughout her teenage years, she'd find him hunched over his field journals and pouring through history books, immersing himself in other religions and cultures, to see which might hint at the pillars' origins and purpose. Even when he came back from Japan, having lived among a small fishing village in Hokkaido for six months, he still attempted to apply his findings to understanding this cavern.

When she was fourteen, she sat at the top of the stairs and listened to him tell Nan that the local authorities had shut down access to the cave. His voice seemed to age twenty years within the span of a minute. Too many horny teenagers had found the cave system, and the county decided that *Access Denied* signs cost less than a dedicated security team—never mind the fact that Maryland had its own local henge.

At the sound of her stomach growling again, Adaline abandons her memories. Leaving her backpack and laptop for later, she carries her messenger bag to the center of the chamber, takes her phone out of her back pocket, and sits down crisscross. Removing her helmet and headlamp, she throws her curly brown hair into a messy bun, rolls up the sleeves of her red and black plaid shirt, and plunges her hand into the bottom of her bag where she retrieves a squished peanut butter and jelly sandwich, a broken protein bar, and another bottle of water.

She hides her phone in her bag. Out of sight; out of mind.

A cool breeze weaves its way into the circle, pushing loose curls off her neck. Enclosed by dripping water, she munches on her sandwich. Rather than scraping and dusting and prodding the pillars, she sits still and admires their circular perfection. Each pillar measures twenty point six feet apart from each other. The precision of their creators makes her chest swell. What she wouldn't give to see the tools they used to smooth down and place, not one, but six monuments identical in almost every way, aside from their unique etchings.

If only her father could see her now, sitting in his spot, following in his footsteps. If only she could have told him that the two years she spent convincing the grantor to secure permits, appease the local authorities, and fund the research had come to fruition.

Once again, the cave has a Yates studying it.

Not that she can call her father and tell him all about it. Not that her grandmother, the woman who raised her, will call tonight and ask her to detail how her first day went. Not that she has any family left to share her success with.

Swallowing a dried-up wad of sandwich, Adaline retrieves her clipboard from her bag. A keychain with a glass ballet slipper dangles from the metal clip's eyelet. She gently pinches the slipper and toggles it between her fingers, her heart weighing an ounce heavier as she drops the bobble behind her board and off her paperwork.

Again, she scans her notes. She needs to understand who and what created these pillars, and she needs evidence that justifies the significance of her work.

That justifies why her relationship with Derek failed. That justifies why she's missing her best friends' engagement party tonight. That justifies why she buried herself in her father's work after he died.

Adaline hugs her clipboard to her chest, as if she can block the flood of memories and the overwhelming desire to return to a time when school days ended with Nan's fresh-baked cookies permeating the house and her father playing guitar while telling her folktales from around the world.

Damn it. Why does grief have to last so long?

She blinks back the tears and takes long breaths to slow her chest from splitting open. When the aching subsides, she takes another bite of her sandwich and watches her fingers to make sure they stop shaking.

"Adaline," whispers a female voice as thin as the wind.

Not recognizing the lithe voice, Adaline rubs the tingling sensation out of her ears and scans the chamber for Beccah or Masako, but she doesn't see or hear anyone. The chamber is silent, aside from water dripping further in the cave.

She shakes her head and takes another bite of her lunch, but sudden yet brief shouts from multiple men cleave the peace of the cave in half. The bite in her mouth dries into a solid lump. She cranes her neck to see around the pillars, to discover the sources of those voices. But they vanished as quickly as they appeared. Hesitant to make any abrupt movements, she slowly chews and swallows another wad of sandwich.

Either I'm losing my mind, or I've pissed off some ghosts. Wait, do I actually believe in ghosts? If they want to tell me what this chamber was used for, then, yes, I most certainly do.

Adaline slots her clipboard, along with her half-eaten sandwich and the rest of her lunch, into her bag, unfolds her legs, and stands up, slinging her bag across her chest. She scans the cave one more time only to hear and see nothing. No men. No colleagues. No interns. No findings beyond her father's notes. No discoveries to justify her absence during Nan's last year.

Nan always said she was fine, and Adaline believed her. She chose to believe her. Just like she chose to dedicate the last two years of her life to accessing and studying this cave. Eight months have passed since the last funeral, and she has yet to return to her lifeless childhood home, to face the emptiness trapped between those walls.

But Nan had encouraged Adaline's studies. Like always, she told Adaline to follow her gut, to listen to that innate feeling that tugs her in different directions and acts like a compass, to trust the voice inside her head.

Granted, these voices had been outside her head. She's certain of that.

And that compass-like feeling has her staying put. Nothing is urging her to run from a haunted cavern. Perhaps the circular structure heard her plea. Perhaps those voices are here to help.

"I'm listening," she says, keeping her voice wispy.

She takes a few slow, small steps as she circles around the center of the structure. Goosebumps form on her arms, and her stomach tingles. She tilts her head downward, toward the tips of her toes, and scrutinizes the cavern's floor, expecting to see something other than dirt and sediment. Getting on her hands and knees, she swings her bag behind her back and digs her finger into the ground, pushing away handfuls of dirt, making her own piles of circles and swirls, and hoping to feel the bottom of the cave floor. At two inches deep, she sees nothing. But she can't stop. When she thinks about leaving this spot, her stomach sloshes sideways, and bile burns her throat. This place must hold something more.

I need a win. Please, I've had enough.

Snatching a nearby trowel, Adaline digs the tip into the floor and scrapes away more dirt until metal clangs against stone. She grabs her headlamp, slips it onto her forehead, and tilts the light sideways into the dirt. As she scoops sediment away, the light reveals the same stone as the pillars and the unmistakable edge of an etched curve, its sides as smooth as the waves and other designs on the pillars.

Holy shit!

Following the etching, she uses her trowel to remove the dirt from inside the curved groove imbedded in the stone floor. A bead of sweat falls from her brow, and the earth devours it as she continues to push growing mounds of dirt aside.

After thirty minutes and no sign of her team, she stands back to examine the intricate design she's uncovered on the stone floor. Its twists and turns are reminiscent of Celtic knots, although this pattern has a wider breadth. The curves and loops are airier and decorated with dots that could be stars or flower buds. The pattern might extend to the six pillars; they'll have to excavate the rest of the floor and remove the dirt.

Tossing her headlamp into her helmet, Adaline wipes her brow. *Look at what has been right beneath my feet.*

Once again, Nan was right. She'd always told Adaline that the best way to defeat doubt is to look to her feet for answers. She chuckles twice before the pattern blurs. Clutching the strap of her messenger bag slung across her chest, she closes her eyes to hold back the tears. If only she could call her father and Nan and tell them what she's found. If only she could go home. If only she still had family waiting for her.

A rumble in the distance makes Adaline lift her eyes and wipe away her tears. The cave floor shudders, and she stumbles backward only to fall forward onto her hands and knees, her bag trapped between her thighs. She reaches for her helmet and headlamp, but they dance and fall off the shifting dirt mounds. The pillars rattle, and dust falls from the ceiling. Outside of the circular structure, a stalactite crashes to the ground, shattering into large pieces, the sound so loud that Adaline covers her ears. Her headlamp flickers on and off, casting spurts of shadow and light onto the floor etching. Scurrying to her feet, she falls onto all fours again, the vibrations traveling up her arms and legs. Beneath her, the etching in the floor cracks and splits, revealing black stone underneath.

The quaking stops. The dust settles. She hears only herself panting, followed by distant waves breaking against a shore and leaves rustling in the wind. She should exit the cave as quickly and safely as possible. She should check on her team. But Maryland isn't prone to earthquakes. And the Potomac River doesn't sound like an ocean.

She inches forward to study the crack that split the etching, and the black stone pulls her hand toward it. She rubs her finger over the smooth, cool surface, but the jagged crack cuts her skin, and she yanks her hand away with a yelp. Before she can search for antiseptic, the black stone glimmers as if it's reflecting moonlight and turns iridescent.

I need to capture this on video.

Standing her messenger bag upright, she flips open the flap but pauses when men's voices echo and fade around her.

"Magnus, have your men found…"

"No, they seem to have evaded…"

"This jeopardizes…"

"That way!"

She doesn't know anyone named Magnus, but the pressure building around her temples and ears ruptures her thoughts, forcing her to squeeze her ears shut until they pop. The sound of waves cresting and crashing becomes clearer. A cool, salty breeze sweeps across her cheeks, causing rogue curls that escaped her bun to brush the side of her face. The silhouettes of trees and fallen columns superimpose themselves over the cave walls, while the shadows merge and take the form of one person running and two others punching each other. As if someone flipped a switch, all light within the cave snaps off, plunging Adaline into utter darkness.

CHAPTER TWO

ANOTHER WORLD

A s the cave ceiling dissolves overhead, stars peek through, only a few at first. Then billions consume the night sky. A full moon sagging heavily near the horizon casts a white sheen upon Adaline, the grass beneath her hands, and the trees shaking their tresses.

Stay calm. Stay calm. Stay calm. There's a reasonable explanation for this. Someone could have drugged me and ditched me in the woods. Let's try something less creepy. Oh, maybe a falling stalactite knocked me unconscious, and Ben and Beccah dragged me into the woods.

Adaline pushes herself up to standing, dusts the dirt off her hands, and feels around her scalp for signs of head wounds. Nothing. Her mouth falls open as the retreating shadows reveal the ruins of an ash-gray palace. Moonlight permeates the marble pillars, making them appear phosphorescent. The crumbled columns, partially collapsed roof, and zero interior lights accentuate the palace's tomb-like silence. Adaline shudders and staggers backward, clutching the strap of her messenger bag.

An owl hoots.

Toto, I don't think we're in Kansas anymore.

The person who had been running skids to a stop. His tall, slender frame casts a shadow that stretches past Adaline's toes. With his free hand, he rakes his fingers over his scalp, pulling his long, dark-blond hair away from his face so that nothing obstructs his vision. Like Adaline, his mouth hangs open, and the whites of his eyes widen so much that they resemble two more moons. In his other hand, he holds a sword against the backdrop of the full moon, its light outlining the blade's sharp tip.

"By the hands of the fae." His wonder reverberates through the night air.

Did someone drug me and ditch me in the middle of a movie set?

Adaline slides one foot behind her, ready to sprint away, but the blond sheaths his sword faster than she can blink and raises his hands as if they are white flags. She tilts her head to the side and waits a moment for her instincts to spring back to life and tell her to run. But her internal compass points to him.

Curiosity pulls her toward him. "Who, who are you?"

He doesn't hesitate either. "Ëólas." He moves closer to her, taking only four steps at first and keeping his hands raised in front of his long, rectangular torso covered with a tunic that fits him perfectly, as if it were custom made. His sword dangles from his belt.

So, I got knocked unconscious and woke up at Renn-Fest?

She inches closer until someone moans, and she whips her head toward the two men who had been fighting.

Spitting at his brunette opponent, the moaning man clutches a pole between them. His breaths turn rapid, expelling quick successions of smoke that drift toward the silent palace. "This is your doing."

The brunette doesn't seem to hear the moaning man. He stares at Adaline, his eyebrows stitched together and his mouth agape. His short, thick beard conceals half his face, like Ernest Hemingway, only with dark brown hair and a much younger face.

"Where did you...?" Hemingway yanks the pole—no, his sword—out of the stomach of the other man, who falls to the ground with limbs twisting at odd angles. The moaning man doesn't make any more sounds.

Adaline cups her mouth with her hands. "Oh god." She doesn't recognize her own voice and its high pitch. Her heart pounds in her ears, yelling at her to get the hell away from these people.

Ëólas steps toward her, more quickly now. "You're safe here," he says, his deep voice as sure and steady as the earth beneath her feet.

For no logical reason, she believes him. Even though he seems as shocked as her, there's a calmness to him that feels truthful.

She opens her mouth to ask where she is, but Hemingway hurries toward her. Ëólas picks up his pace too, and the distance between her and the two men on either side of her shrinks quickly. Her heart hammers down all thoughts, and her legs won't respond, that is until Hemingway pauses to wipe his blade with a rag. Red splotches bleed through the white cloth. Spinning around, Adaline sprints in the opposite direction.

"Wait," Ëólas calls after her, but she doesn't stop.

She bolts for the tree line, hoping to disappear within a forest beyond this grove. She thrashes between the trunks, avoiding the roots, but a garden greets her on the other side. Its flat, green expanse stretches toward the ocean with only bushes or broken statues to hide behind. With a quick glance back, she spies Ëólas and Hemingway running after her, their swords drawn. She pushes off the last tree and runs ahead, only for another man with red curly hair to block her path.

She screams and turns away as he swings his sword down at her. The clang of metal against metal rings in her ears. An arm, not a sword, catches her around the waist, preventing her from falling over while also moving her away from the redhead. She steadies herself against Ëólas's back, resting her palms on his cloak. His hair, falling to the bottom of his shoulder blades, conceals her hands.

Ëólas keeps his sword locked with the burly redhead's. "She's not one of them, Thoren," he says, pushing Thoren's sword away and forcing the brute to stumble backward and disengage. Looking over his shoulder, Ëólas flashes a soft, welcoming smile that could convince anyone to enter his home. His gold eyes catch her off guard too, locking her in place. "Please don't run off again. This area is not safe at the moment, though I assure you we will secure it once more."

Uh-huh. Okay.

Demanding her and Ëólas's attention, Thoren raises the tip of his sword level with Adaline's face. "She's wearing trousers and running around the ruins late at night, and you're telling me she's not one of them?"

As Thoren glares at her, his temples turn as red as his curls, which he's secured haphazardly in a half bun. His broad shoulders and thick neck resemble those of a linebacker, and Adaline has no desire to give him reason to tackle her. She nudges closer to Ëólas. If she might run into more people like Hemingway and this redheaded Goliath, she'd rather take her chances with Ëólas.

When she finds her voice, she's surprised she sounds so calm. "One of whom?"

Hemingway jogs over to them. "One of the men who attacked our people." He then speaks to Thoren with a low, gravelly voice that makes the Goliath listen. "She's not one of them, Thoren. Do as Ëólas said. Lower your sword."

The heft Hemingway adds to his words forces Thoren to lower his sword and his head, but he still grumbles.

Great, another Grump.

Ëólas and Hemingway position themselves so Adaline has room but not enough to run away from the three men surrounding her. When Hemingway turns to her, he unclenches his square jaw, and his entire upper body relaxes. A smile warms his face, and crow's feet hug his pale-blue eyes. When Adaline glances at his sword, he sheaths his blade and takes another step back. This time, his voice is gentle, like a father checking a child's scraped knee. "Are you unharmed?"

She nods but continues to clutch the strap of her shoulder bag and angles her upper body away from Hemingway and Thoren, not sure who's the bigger threat.

There has to be an explanation. "Why on earth are you using swords? Did Dax put you up to this? Did he send his LARPer friends to pull a prank? And interrupt my research…and make day turn to night…and make the cave disappear. Yeah, that makes sense." *I cannot disprove the absurdity of this situation with absurd thinking.* Besides, Dax would never jeopardize her career, and Cindy would murder him if he tried. "That's not what happened, is it?"

Ëólas furrows his brow. "What's a LARPer?"

A fourth man runs over to them and juts his chin in Adaline's direction. "You caught one!" He has dark skin with blue undertones and long, ash-gray hair parted in the middle. His deep voice and stoic expression remind Adaline of Morpheus from *The Matrix*.

"Oh my god. How many of you are there?" She steps closer to Ëólas, who once again puts away his sword.

Thoren looks her up and down and curls his upper lip. "They've caught something alright."

"Hey!" If her hands weren't shaking, she'd dig out her sandwich and throw it at his face.

"A female?" Morpheus looks at Ëólas and Hemingway for an explanation, which neither gives.

"Yeah, and?" Adaline juts her chin back at Morpheus, making the corner of his mouth turn upward.

"We'll explain later," says Ëólas. "Right now, we need to know the status of the others."

Morpheus nods. "I caught one, but I wasn't able to detain him alive. The third is yet unaccounted for."

Ëólas rubs his chin and grips his jaw. Dropping his arm, he tells Morpheus, "Gather the guards, set a perimeter around the palace, and fan outward. Send one to notify border patrol as well. I want him found this night. Alive." He emphasizes the last word.

After bowing to both Ëólas and Hemingway, Morpheus runs toward the palace. While the three remaining men discuss their next moves and whether Thoren should join Morpheus's search, Adaline slowly sidesteps away from the conversation.

Ëólas takes two large strides and halts beside her. "Please, we mean you no harm."

Her stomach flips, telling her he's being truthful. And something about his voice feels...familiar. *What the hell am I thinking? Form an exit strategy, Adaline.*

Thoren's freehand twitches beside his thigh where he's secured a dagger. "With all due respect, Your Majesty, I'm not leaving you alone with her."

Your Majesty? Seriously?

Adaline glances at Hemingway, waiting for him to laugh, but he doesn't. Instead, he hooks his thumbs over his leather belt and puffs his chest out, showing off his close-fitting doublet made of ornate gold and tan brocade. Beneath the short, decorative capped sleeves, he wears full-length fitted sleeves that end with a short, satin ruffle. The row of antique buttons down the length of his padded jacket matches the oversized buckle of his belt, and a thin gold circlet around his brow features a small, round garnet.

"I can handle a single lady, thank you," says King Hemingway. "And I'm not alone. Ëólas and I will escort her back to the castle."

Lady? Adaline shakes her head. "First, no thank you. No one's handling anything. Second, I'm not going with you. I don't even know you."

Thoren's puffy cheeks turn crimson, as if he tied too tight the band holding his red curls back. He pushes himself into Adaline's face and looms over her. His spittle flies toward her as he growls, "How dare you address the king in such a manner."

Adaline keeps her chin up and shoulders back. "A king. Yeah, okay," she laughs.

Thoren raises his hand, but when Ëólas steps in front of her, Thoren backs up immediately. It seems striking Ëólas wouldn't bode well for him.

Good to know.

Hemingway also steps closer to Adaline, making Thoren back up further. "I said I have this. Follow my orders and then meet us where we left the horses. That's an order."

Thoren glares at Adaline but runs after Morpheus while cursing under his breath. The moment he's gone, she breathes more easily, which doesn't make sense given she's still standing next to the one guy she's seen make use of his sword.

I need to call 9-1-1. "Look, whatever you guys are doing here, have at it. I just want to get back to the cave."

Hemingway tugs at the whiskers covering his chin. "Cave?"

"Yes, where I was doing research."

"Research?" Hemingway echoes.

"Why do you keep repeating me?" Adaline's tone again sounds three octaves higher than usual.

"You do not know how you came to be here?" Hemingway's words sound more like a statement than a question.

She nods. "I was just..."

"In a cave," he repeats, prompting her to nod again. "So your arrival here bewilders you as much as us. Forgive my friends. We are in the midst of safeguarding our city, and during our pursuit, you appeared like light through water. But now I think you might be human, correct?"

Ëólas's eyes widen. He circles around to look her over more carefully, from the bottom of her toes to the tips of her ears. His brows tilt together as he narrows his eyes, and the gold in his irises darkens to a smokey amber.

"You're human?" Ëólas whispers, as if saying that louder would cause the world to self-combust. He backs away, taking with him her only sense of safety.

No, no, no. You're the only one I trust here. Which makes no sense. So never mind.

She bites her lip to stop herself from asking Ëólas what's wrong, what's changed. His pensive mood pushes her to address Hemingway instead. "What do you mean I might be human? You ask that as if there's any other option. Look, I just want to know how I got here, who you people are, and what's with the damn swords."

The moment she says *damn*, Ëólas's expression twists into repulsion as if she hexed him personally.

Is cursing not acceptable here?

Hemingway, however, chuckles so hard that his upper body shakes. As he scratches the side of his beard, the corners of his lips spread into a grin, and his blue eyes sparkle.

How am I ever going to get away from these two? I can't read their hot and then cold attitudes.

Extending his arm, Hemingway offers Adaline his hand, his smile never wavering. She leans back, scrutinizes his open palm, and debates if he's waiting for her to hand him something. She shifts her shoulder bag in front of her like a shield and keeps his sword in her peripheral vision.

Ëólas, watching Adaline's every move, glides his hand to his hilt. "Magnus, why don't we—"

"Magnus?" She blurts Hemingway's real name so loudly that he pulls his lips upward, revealing dimples in the corners of his beard.

I heard his name in the cave. So, those ghostly voices belonged to Magnus and Ëólas. That must be why Ëólas sounds familiar.

Magnus inches his palm closer to Adaline. "Yes, I am King Magnus of Alderton, and the cautious one beside me is Lord Ëólas, who is serving as commander general of Lameiría. And you are?"

Alderton. Lameiría. Where the hell am I?

She could pull out her mobile phone right now, but her instincts warn her not to. As she stares at Magnus's hand, she purses her lips to one side. Then she releases them with a sigh. "Adaline."

She goes to shake his hand, but Magnus slips his fingers under her palm, clasps her hand, and pulls her knuckles to his mouth. He brushes his lips across the back of her hand, and her whole face feels like she's leaning over a boiling pot of water. Ëólas rolls his eyes, which makes her cheeks burn brighter. She tugs her hand away from Magnus's scratchy mouth, and, to her relief, he lets go.

"My apologies. That is how I'm accustomed to greeting a lady. I truly did not mean to upset you. I am honored to make your acquaintance, Lady Adaline. And from where did you come, aside from a cave?"

"Maryland." *And as a Marylander, I should know where I am.*

Magnus studies her plaid shirt, jeans, and Timberlands, but the dimples never fade away. When he looks at her shoulder bag, his eyes linger a bit longer. "I have not heard of such a kingdom. Nor have I heard an accent quite like yours. Your arrival, much like the rest of you, baffles us both."

Widening his stance, Ëólas tightens his features into a hard glare. "I've never heard of such a province or territory."

"I see." Magnus looks back at Adaline. "Then, as a human, I am responsible for your welfare."

"Why do you keep specifying human? Also, I'm not anybody's responsibility. I just want to know how to get back home."

"And I will endeavor to assist with that," Magnus says. "I will not leave a lady alone among the ruins as midnight approaches. Please, accompany me to the castle where we can explore this matter further."

"You can't be serious."

"Have you any other options at the moment? Any other companions to assist you?"

Adaline looks about her, willing Beccah or the Grump to appear from behind the trees. The owl hoots again, and the waves crashing against the cliffs warn her to move forward, not backward.

"You would be wise to accept Magnus's gracious offer." Ëólas clenches his jaw, accentuating his jowls. "Ingratitude will only endanger you."

"Ëólas, can you possibly refrain from scaring the lady? Please accept my apologies on his behalf, as well as for the circumstances under which you and I first met. I do not take a life easily, but that man took it upon himself to attack and injure my people. I take seriously the responsibility placed upon me to protect the people under my charge."

Well, I suppose that's something.

"Speaking of which," Ëólas says, "we need to return to the city and pacify the people. We've lingered here long enough."

"Ëólas is right. Please, come with us."

Adaline wrinkles her brow as she looks from Magnus to Ëólas, who no longer bears any signs of sympathy or concern. *What the hell am I going to do?* "What other options do I have?"

Magnus sighs. "The palace grounds are off limits. If you stay here without invitation, you will most likely find yourself a prisoner of Lameiría. If you travel south for a few days, you'll enter my kingdom, but traveling alone, without food or water or companions, would risk your personal safety."

"This is ridiculous." Ëólas runs his hands over his face, turns to Adaline, and closes the distance between them. "Magnus is your safest option. I understand your hesitation, but we have a city full of people who need our attention, now. So either choose to come with us, and we'll help you understand what's happened this night. Or start walking."

Maybe the moonlight makes his eyes appear gold?

When he arches his eyebrow, waiting for a response, Adaline releases a long sigh. Despite his direct manner and crisp words, she knows beyond a shadow of a doubt that he's telling the truth, which irritates her as much as it comforts her. "Okay. Where's this city?"

Magnus claps his hands together. "Wonderful. Though," he pauses and looks at her clothing, "I do not think it wise to share the origins of her arrival with anyone else. There's too much unrest and fear already."

"Hmmm, agreed." The moonlight emphasizes the sneer on Ëólas's face as he looks over her plaid shirt and Timberlands. He removes his cloak and in one quick motion drapes the light fabric around her shoulders. "Keep this shut."

She pulls the cloak tightly around her shoulders, and the faint scent of lavender and pine helps her muscles to release their tension.

Magnus flashes her a wide grin. "Lady Adaline, I give you my word that under my care, you will be safe, and I will lend you all of my resources to help you find your way home. These extraordinary circumstances cannot be for naught. I will not jeopardize that or you."

Forcing a small smile onto her face, she follows Ëólas and Magnus through the garden and around the outskirts of the palace ruins.

Okay, gut. You haven't been entirely reliable for the last two years, but I think that was more my fault. So don't fail me now.

Ëólas mumbles to Magnus, "How do we explain her arrival?"

"We may deal with that later," Magnus says.

On the other side of the palace, the streetlights of a city below flicker like candle flames. Near the palace's entrance, four horses wait for their group. Morpheus and Thoren have already mounted their steeds and seem relieved to spot Ëólas and Magnus again. Adaline follows Ëólas to his horse and mentally comforts herself that she doesn't have to steer that behemoth by herself. But after Ëólas climbs onto his saddle, he steers his white steed away and never looks back.

What the hell? Who dumped a bucket of ice water on him?

Magnus mounts his horse and tugs the reins closer to Adaline. He offers his hand, which she accepts, and pulls her up behind him. She debates where to hold on.

"My jacket, Lady Adaline. Hold on to my jacket. And stay close. If you squeeze my steed's flanks, we'll both be thrown."

Adaline scoots up against Magnus, repositions Ëólas's cloak to conceal her jeans, and turns her head to the side, wishing with every fiber of her being that she could have personal space right now. Being so close to a stranger, especially one who just killed a man, churns her stomach. But before she can change her mind and jump off, Magnus tugs the reins and follows after Ëólas. An instant later, the horse gallops forward, delivering Adaline quickly toward the city and a castle in the distance.

Chapter Three

THE CASTLE

Their group canters downhill for about a mile, and the landscape changes from meadows that dissolve into the night sky to staggered buildings no more than three-stories high. Adaline peers over Magnus's shoulder, keeping the hood of Ëólas's cloak past her forehead. Gaps between the buildings mean people can come and go whichever way they please, and the main road upon which Adaline now trots parallels a river that splits the city in half. The road leads directly to a castle with a tall outer wall surrounding large stone buildings with arched roofs, round towers topped with cupolas, and balconies ablaze with torches and interior lights emitting a soft glow.

Adaline restrains herself from scanning the faces in the crowd, even as more people gather and follow Magnus and Ëólas trotting side by side. "Okay, I'm definitely not in Maryland anymore."

Looking over his shoulder, Magnus whispers, "Certainly, though I recommend you say as little as possible for now. And make certain the cloak conceals your clothing."

She uses one hand to pinch shut Ëólas's cloak around her waist. With the other, she clenches Magnus's jacket, terrified of dirtying the brocade. When they cross under the castle's main gate, she throws back the cloak's hood to better see the inner courtyard. Arches contain shadows, and stairs lead upward and out of sight.

Magnus offers Adaline his forearm, which she grips as she slides off the horse's rump. She rubs her butt while soldiers or guards rush over to him and Ëólas, and Magnus instructs a guard to escort Adaline to his study.

Placing his hand on the small of her back, he turns her toward an open doorway. "We will join you shortly. First, Ëólas and I must address our people."

Our people? Not his people?

When Magnus follows Ëólas outside the main gates, Adaline leaves her escort confused as she inches along the wall and toward the gate so she can eavesdrop. More guards surround Ëólas and Magnus, and next to the king stands Thoren the Brute. Adaline hugs the wall so the redheaded Goliath won't see her when he pans around.

Magnus speaks first. "We have neutralized two of the assailants, but one is still at large. We are posting extra guards throughout the city."

When Ëólas's voice carries over the crowd, the murmurs that began to rise hush just as quickly. "The goals of the Neutral Territory will not falter because of the actions of a few. Everyone here is contributing to a new future. We will not be deterred."

Neutral Territory? Neutral to what? Are the lands beyond this city not neutral?

Magnus rests his hand on Ëólas's shoulder and looks at his people. "And anyone who seeks to disrupt the peace will answer to Lord Ëólas and myself."

The guard assigned to escort her taps Adaline's shoulder and pleads with his eyes that she follow him.

Fine. I don't want to get him in trouble.

Further into the castle, Adaline climbs stairs and travels through corridors, past several arches and doors, until they reach what she suspects is the heart of the castle. Once she enters the study, the guard excuses himself, leaving her alone in a room bigger than her condo. Two large desks made of heavy, dark oak or walnut face each other in the middle of the study. Beneath a row of arched windows, upholstered sofas with gold brocade beckon Adaline to have a seat. On the opposite wall, a fireplace wide enough for a loveseat dominates the center of the room, its roaring fire lighting every surface. Extending from both sides of the hearth, shelves line the rest of the wall. One holds a small collection of books that could fill Adaline's arms. The other shelves display swords, plants, and a wooden sculpture of a city's layout, perhaps this city, although the castle isn't included. Above the fireplace hangs a painting of the sea.

Adaline lingers on that image for a moment before taking her phone out of her bag and checking for cell service. Nothing. Not even one bar. She scans the walls for outlets, dragging aside one sofa and then another. Again, nothing. She hugs the phone to her chest, powers it off to save the battery, and slides it into her back pocket. She hugs Ëólas's cloak tighter around her.

Okay. Reality check. No cell service. No form of electricity at all. Everyone's wearing Renaissance-esque clothing. As fantastic as Maryland's Renn-Fest is, I've never seen a reenactment of this scope and dedication.

Adaline plops her butt on the paneled sofa, rests her elbows on her knees, and drops her head into her hands. Then she waits, uncertain if she should be grateful the room doesn't have a clock to tick her into oblivion or if she should bust down the door and find Magnus and Ëólas herself.

Leaning toward the latter option, she stands up and hurries to the door, but a young woman with light-brown hair enters the room. Wearing a long green dress, she carries with both hands a large tray with food, wine, and goblets that she places on a table against the back wall. On the crown of her head, she wears a thick band of ribbon from which a thick and loose-fitting net hangs, keeping her hair tucked neatly inside. The hairstyle is indicative of the Renaissance, but the sleeves that split at her elbow and drape to the ground are more medieval in style. She pours one cup of wine and carries it to Adaline, who accepts the goblet but doesn't take a sip.

"The king apologizes for keeping you waiting. He must deal with the unrest at the moment and is concluding an emergency council meeting." She curtsies and leaves without a sound.

Adaline puts the wine on the table, next to the empty goblets. Removing Ëólas's cloak, she drapes it over the sofa arm and rests her bag on the floor. She takes out her notebook and tries to sketch from memory the etching she'd seen on the cave floor. After an endless amount of time, she snaps her sketchbook shut, stuffs it in her bag, and flops backward against the stiff sofa.

Is this an interrogation tactic? Bore me to the brink of death?

Just when her inner voice is ready to scream, Magnus and Ëólas enter the study, followed by Thoren the Brute and Silver-Haired Morpheus, as well as two other men who cannot hide their confusion at her clothing.

Thoren takes one look at Adaline and growls. "How is she not one of the aggressors? Just look at how ridiculously she's dressed."

I could say the same about you, dickwad.

Retreating behind the furthest desk, she eyeballs a rock-like paperweight she could throw at him, then groans at the fact that six men stand between her and the exit. She cusses her naivety for trusting them. "Are you always so judgmental?"

"Are you always so disrespectful to your superiors?" Thoren snaps.

Adaline's nostrils flare, but before she can pick up the paperweight, Magnus and Ëólas place themselves between her and the four other men.

"Enough!" Magnus glares at Thoren. "Lady Adaline is a guest here and will be treated as such. Both Ëólas and I saw her arrival and vouch for her innocence."

Ëólas crosses his arms over his chest, and his face clouds over. "She appeared before us as if by..."

"Magic. Like an apparition turned solid." The awe in Magnus's voice makes Adaline curious, but the wonder he casts her way and the eyeballs that follow push her onto center stage. Alone.

She backs up and crosses her arms over her chest. *Magic. That word sounds more preposterous than the evidence piling up at my feet.*

Glancing at her defensive posture, Magnus strolls over to her and smiles warmly. "I apologize again for the scene you bore witness to upon your arrival."

She opens her mouth, but before she can utter a single word, Morpheus inhales sharply and looks to Ëólas for either confirmation or more details or both. "My lord, how can that be possible? I thought the young lady to be human. Is she not?"

Pursing his lips, Ëólas juts his chin in her direction. "She's certainly not an elf."

Adaline snorts. "Obviously." *Elves.* She shakes her head and laughs to herself. *I mean, if I'm losing my mind, we may as well go all out, right?*

Ëólas grinds his teeth and angles himself away from her. "The discussion of magic and the lady's arrival will not travel beyond the seven of us. Magnus and I are adamant about this."

"Precisely." Magnus rests a gentle hand on Adaline's arm and gestures at the men around the room. "My lady, if I may, allow me to better introduce our most trusted advisors. Lord Thoren is captain of the king's guard."

Thoren keeps one hand on the hilt of his dagger and the other on his sword's.

Ignoring him, Magnus points to Morpheus. "Similarly, Lord Merith is Lord Ëólas's personal guard. And the two in the middle are captains of the city guard, Lord Fólas of Lameiría and Lord Hamon of Alderton."

Tucking his hands in his pockets, Fólas suppresses a half grin like a comedian eager to deliver a punchline, but his tranquil, slightly triangular dark eyes give Adaline the impression that he's extremely patient and observant. Lord Hamon, the shortest of them all, runs his hand through his strawberry blond hair. When he lets go, his hair spills around his face like Westley from *The Princess Bride*. Hamon and Magnus are the only two with shoulder-length hair, and all the men wear variations of tunics made of rich fabrics, skinny trousers, leather boots, and thick belts from which they carry their swords.

"Hi." Adaline gives them a tired wave.

Fólas, Hamon, and Morpheus, aka Merith, nod hello. Thoren grunts.

"Lady Adaline, would you please share with us what exactly transpired before we met?" Magnus asks with a voice smooth as satin.

She bites the inside of her cheek until Magnus urges, "Speak freely."

With a loud exhale, Adaline drops her arms at her sides. "Okay." Time to put on her academic hat so she can think more clearly. Turning her back to Thoren, she paces in front of the fireplace as if it were a whiteboard and pinches her chin. "I was unearthing a design I discovered etched into the floor of a cave when I heard voices, your voices, Magnus and Ëólas. My headlamp went haywire, and the cave shook. And—"

"You mentioned the cave before. What cave?" Ëólas asks.

She had been avoiding his face since he walked into the room. Again, his irises glow gold in the flickering light of the fireplace. *Must be a trick from the fire.*

Instead of looking scornfully at her, he's plastered his face with indifference. She's not sure which expression is worse, the one that at least shows some sort of emotion or the one that indicates he cares for nothing. Regardless, he's erased any trace of the kind, empathetic face she first saw, the one that made her believe she was safe.

Move on, Adaline. "Fifty years ago, locals discovered a cave that concealed a circular structure comprising six stone pillars." When Ëólas glances at Merith and Fólas, a look passes between them that Adaline can't decipher, but she makes a mental note to not forget that. "The stone used for the pillars does not match the resources in the area, which means someone deliberately placed those pillars in the cave. Where they got the stone, how they carved them so identically and precisely, and how they managed to get them into the cave is, to say the least, puzzling. Anyway, I secured funding to explore the cave as part of my research, and—"

"Research?" Magnus interjects.

"Yes, my job requires that I continue researching—"

"Your job?" Thoren scrunches his nose. "Outside of your home?"

Hamon, who had been pacing in the background, stops mid-stride and pushes his strawberry blond hair away from his eyes to better see her. He cocks his head to the side as he considers her words. "Huh."

She bites her tongue and pinches the bridge of her nose. Usually, she has time to research and adjust to the cultural norms of the places she visits, and given the style of dress and pre-industrial revolution décor, Thoren's question is completely reasonable.

Wiping the irritation from her face, she clasps her hands in front of her. "Yes, I'm an assistant professor of cultural anthropology at The American University in Washington, D.C."

All six men glance at each other with raised or angled eyebrows.

The heat radiating from the fire makes her step further into the room, between the two massive desks, and she turns about so she can see everyone's faces. "Um, I'll back up further. I'm a scholar at an institution for higher learning where I research and teach about other civilizations, particularly their societies and cultures and their development. During the last three years, I've focused my research on socio-cultural anthropology. That's why I was in a cave. My colleagues and I are trying to figure out which culture created the circular structure in the first place and what purpose it served in their lives. Questions?"

Magnus scratches his cheek while his mouth forms the beginning of a question, and he leans against the back of his desk. "In truth, I have several, but please continue. You were examining a design on the floor, and then?"

Releasing a big puff of air, Adaline tosses her hands about as she speaks. "The ground shook, the design cracked open, and the cave sort of dissolved around me. Then I was standing outside, with you."

Her hands flop down to her sides, and she waits for everyone else to confirm what she already knows: Reality has flipped upside down. Everyone remains silent for a long while, each deep in thought.

Fólas is the first to break the silence as he looks at Ëólas. "And you saw this, my lord?"

Both Ëólas and Magnus nod. Everyone shifts uncomfortably in the room. Stealing glances at Adaline, Thoren stabs his cheek with his tongue and moves closer to Magnus. At the same time, Merith sidles closer to Ëólas, moves his feet to hip-width apart, and places his fists on his waist. While they both assess Adaline's threat level, Fólas and Hamon wander toward the arched windows and talk privately together. About what, she can't hear.

Yes, because I'm the dangerous one here. "You really don't know where Maryland is, do you?"

Magnus wrinkles his brow in concern and shakes his head. "I'm afraid not."

Strolling over to his desk, he grabs a rolled-up piece of paper that he unfurls across his other documents. When Adaline stands on her tiptoes, she sees land formations and division lines. She steps toward him, but Thoren's glare makes her stop. Magnus, however, seems used to ignoring Thoren and gestures for Adaline to come closer. Watching Thoren from the corner of her eye, she approaches Magnus, who points at the map.

"The kingdom below is Alderton, my homeland," he says. "The forest above comprises Lameiría. And the land in between the two is the Forbidden Lands, although Ëólas and I have recently renamed this portion the Neutral Territory, which is where you now find yourself."

"Neutral Territory? So, Alderton and Lameiría haven't gotten along in the past?"

Ëólas walks over to the desk and stands opposite her and Magnus, keeping the desk between them. He looks down at the map, and his expression darkens. "The history between human and elven kingdoms is rather sordid."

Adaline laughs to dissipate the unease building in her gut. "Elven. As in elves? As in real-life elves?"

Ëólas huffs through his nose and throws her words from earlier back at her. "You say that as if there's any other option?"

His retaliatory sarcasm isn't lost on her, but she can't fathom a reply. Her brain has lost the ability to further comprehend this bizarre day. She turns to Magnus, hoping for simple clarity, with her face frozen in a state of perpetual confusion.

Magnus arches an eyebrow. "You don't have elves in Merry Land?"

His ludicrous question makes her snort through her nose. "No. Elves are just fairy tales. Myths. Make believe. They're not real." *Why are they messing with me?*

Ëólas's lips pinch together, and his eyes darken the longer he scowls at her. When he speaks, his voice is quiet, but his words are sharp. "My people and I do not appreciate being dismissed so easily."

Adaline glances at everyone and waits for the punchline, but no one looks amused. In fact, no one seems capable of a smile. Neither Magnus, nor Thoren, nor Hamon move as they wait for the tension in the room to ease.

"Your...people?" Adaline's eyes wander from Ëólas to Merith and Fólas now flanking their boss's sides.

Fólas tightens his jaw and minutely shakes his head, and Merith glowers at Adaline like she just chose the blue pill. Rather than looking away, she opens her mind to the possibility and considers them more closely. Ëólas's golden irises demand belief, and from behind their long hair, the tips of slightly more pointed ears peek outward.

Holy shit. I've been talking to elves. And I've just pissed them off.

Chapter Four

THE . . . ELVES?

Adaline bites her bottom lip and wrings her hands. "I'm sorry," she says, pouring as much sincerity into her voice as possible. "I wasn't trying to be rude. I just. We don't. I mean."

"No matter." Dismissing her, Ëólas gives the map his full attention.

Adaline, looking down at her hands, clicks her thumbnails together and prays her face doesn't turn green while her undigested peanut butter and jelly sandwich sours in her stomach. How could she offend an entire species so quickly and so thoroughly? "I didn't mean to be presumptuous. I really am sorry. I'm just surprised."

Magnus rests one hand over hers and waits for them to stop shaking. "We all have much to learn from each other. And that's exactly why Ëólas and I formed the Neutral Territory, to bridge human and elf relations. Now, enough fretting." He removes his hand and jabs the map near the ocean. "This area to the east of our city is where we found you."

Despite a lingering sense of nausea, she blinks rapidly and tries to refocus. *Go back to academic mode, Adaline.* "Is this a map of your entire world, all the continents? One main land mass, and the rest is water?"

"Yes," says Merith. "Though we do have a few islands scattered about."

Adaline smiles at his kinder tone, and he drops his fists from his waist. His long silver hair and dark skin remind her of yin and yang.

As she studies the map, she turns her head sideways and traces imaginary lines across it with her finger. *Maybe. No.* She shakes her head.

"What are you thinking?" Hamon asks.

"Around two hundred or three hundred million years ago, my world used to be one large land mass, which we call Pangaea. But earthquakes caused the land to break and drift apart. I thought maybe, just maybe, I had traveled back in time," *or to a movie set*, "but Pangea never looked like this."

Adaline goes to her messenger bag and pulls out her field journal and a pencil. Sitting down on the sofa, she flips to a new page and draws a timeline starting at three hundred million years ago. "Pangaea broke up around one hundred fifty million years ago." She draws one tick mark at the beginning of the timeline and then draws a second. "Dinosaurs populated the earth about two hundred fifty to sixty million years ago, give or take. Dinosaurs were massive reptilian-like animals that were as tall as this castle."

"You mean dragons?" Thoren asks.

"Well, some of them did fly, but dragons from our mythology and literature are quite different."

"Like elves?" Ëólas asks, his tone curt.

When the three elves from Lameiría exchange glances again, Adaline shifts uncomfortably on the sofa, but she brushes away their agitation and focuses on facts. "Anyway, the first hominids, um, what we define as the first intelligent beings to walk on two feet, appeared only around six million years ago. And what eventually evolved into the modern human appeared only about three hundred thousand years ago. By then, Pangaea had broken into several separate continents." She shows them the timeline. "So you see, there's no way I'm in the past."

She flips her notebook shut and rests it on her lap. "That means I've traveled to a whole other planet or alternate universe or different dimension. I don't know. But, of course, that begs the question why you all speak English."

Again, they look at each other confused.

"We speak the Common Tongue," Hamon says, brushing his hand through his Westley-esque hair.

"Well, isn't that convenient," Adaline mumbles. Praise the powers that be for small favors when the impossible has just become possible. Adaline stuffs her notebook back in her bag, which Thoren keeps eyeballing. She slides her bag behind her legs and tries to look at anyone other than him so she doesn't have to witness him constantly watching her.

Thankfully, Merith provides Adaline with a distraction. Tilting his head to the side, he asks, "How do you know all this, about Pangaea and dinosaurs, if humans have populated your world for only a short time?"

"We have various methods, but the one best known is carbon dating. Um, when we dig up bones and other organic remains, we can test the rate of decay by…" Her words trail off as the six men, or rather males, guys, in the room look as though they didn't know they'd bought tickets to a horror movie until it was too late. "You know, the specifics don't matter. It's just one area of science. The short version is that the soil records our history, and I try to interpret those records."

With his mouth still hanging open, Magnus crosses his arms, leans back, and watches Adaline as she hugs her knees. A small smile appears, followed by a wide grin that spreads across his face. "A scholar, indeed."

Ëólas looks at Magnus as if he heard a completely different conversation. Arching an eyebrow, he shakes his head. "And yet we have learned little."

I don't see you offering any ideas. "Well, how else am I supposed to figure out how to get home if I don't explore every possible theory of where I am and how I got here? Do you have some ideas to contribute?"

She bites the inside of her bottom lip while she waits for him to look her in the eye again, waits for him to tell her what he knows about the circular structure, waits for him to clue her in on what he's really thinking.

Angling away from her, Ëólas cocks his head to the side. "Perhaps, but I'll need some time to consider those theories."

The fire in the hearth dims, making the room grow darker and colder. Adaline rises and grabs the strap of her shoulder bag. "That's fine. I'll be on my way then. I don't want to get in the way of your peace building."

Ëólas's slender nose, high cheekbones, and diamond-shaped jaw release their stiff, Grecian-statue-like indifference as his eyebrows rise and his lower lip hangs open. "And where do you plan to go?"

"Back to where you found me. If that's where I appeared, then it stands to reason—"

"That you'll get yourself killed." Magnus steps around his desk and walks over to her. "Adaline, please. We still have a dangerous man on the loose who's already killed this night. You're a woman of reason, a scholar. I'm certain you understand the risk of returning to the ruins in the middle of the night. I cannot believe your arrival is merely an accident, but the sun will rise soon enough, and we all need rest now. Please, give us time to figure this out. Together."

"How much time? Because I've already been missing for a few hours, and as much as the Grump, I mean, Ben and I disagree, he's going to report me missing."

"We can discuss this again tomorrow." The finality in Ëólas's voice tells Adaline that he's on the verge of walking out of the study, but Magnus glaring at him as though Ëólas has three heads convinces the elf general to soften his expression.

Turning back to Adaline, Magnus offers her a gentle smile that makes his blue eyes shine brighter. "In the meantime, you will remain under my protection in the Neutral Territory, where I too have planned to remain until early autumn."

Adaline's shoulders drop. *You make it sound like I'll be here all summer, not that I have any other options at the moment.* "Thank you. I appreciate the help."

"Your Majesty," Hamon says, "how do we explain the lady?"

"I'm a distant cousin?"

Magnus chuckles. "You wish for the status of a princess?"

With wide eyes, Adaline shakes her head fervently. "Oh, no. I'm not. I wasn't. I didn't mean."

Smirking, Magnus raises one hand to silence her. "As my cousin and myself unwed, you would become The Lady of the Castle, and I do not think that a role you would feel comfortable assuming."

Again, Adaline shakes her head. "Hell no. I have no idea how to run a castle."

"What about your ward," Ëólas offers, "from an extremely remote corner of the world?"

Fólas nods. "That would help explain the lady's unique accent."

As he thinks, Magnus pinches the whiskers on his chin. "That sounds acceptable. And being a foreigner will allow you many leniencies for not knowing our customs. What of your opinion, Lady Adaline? We could say your father recently passed, and I promised him long ago to look after you."

Even after traveling to another world, people will still think of her as an orphan. Adaline closes her eyes for a moment so she can measure her expression and keep it even. But the fact that her story's the same no matter where she goes reminds her she can't move on. Not yet anyway.

"Have I offended you?" Magnus asks.

Adaline takes a few deep breaths to push down the void that has been consuming her for two years, a void that grew wider over these last several months. "No. They say the best lie is built upon truth, so I suppose that will work." She's relieved her voice didn't crack.

Magnus's whole face melts in sorrow. "Your father passed?"

Adaline nods. Talking about her father's death still causes her throat to tighten.

"Recently?"

"About two years ago." She's used to people giving her the same pitiful look. But something about Magnus's transparent concern, the way he stares at his own empty hands until his gaze turns defiant, makes the void recede, just a smidgen, as if he's not only seen but also conquered the void himself.

"I'm truly sorry for your loss. Your mother must be beside herself. I'm sure you're eager to return to her." His voice is like a father taking on his child's pain.

"My mother passed when I was little." Even though she's able to say that matter-of-factly, everyone gives her the same look she's received since she was a child. Poor Adaline, the motherless. "It's okay. It's hard to miss something I don't remember."

"A husband then?" Magnus asks.

Adaline laughs out loud, remembering Derek's last message. Her laughter dies in her throat as she avoids the guys staring at her. *Why does there have to be six of them?* "I've got my work, which keeps me busy enough." She's always been a horrible liar, but they don't know her. *Surely, they can't tell.* "Anyway, aren't I too old to be your ward?"

The corner of Magnus's mouth turns upward. "Not as long as you are unwed. Here, that is," he adds as an afterthought. "Being my ward will also afford you extra protection."

"Protection from what?"

The guys glance at each other as though they're too gentlemanly or prudish to discuss unsavory ideas with a woman.

"Never mind," she says.

Hamon slaps his hands together, startling everyone, and throws his head back with a laugh. "Whew! This is going to be an adventure, isn't it?" He claps Thoren on the back, who growls in response and looks as though he'd like to punch Hamon in the face.

So, this is what I'm working with?

Adaline assesses her benefactors. The elves have rectangular frames, defined cheekbones, and narrow noses. They also look like England's finest for the World Cup. The humans, on the other hand, have broader shoulders, thick arms, and bodies ready for a professional wrestling match, granted that could be partially because of the padded jackets. Still, Adaline makes a note to not piss these guys off. At least, not any more than she already has. As for Thoren, well, he's merely a product of his time and job, which she can't fault him for.

I hope we can all trust each other.

As if reading her thoughts, Thoren steps forward and grabs her bag, dumping its contents onto the floor. "Given this matter is settled for now, what have you in here?"

"What the hell?" When her clipboard hits the ground, a shard of glass breaks off her ballet slipper keychain, and Adaline screeches. She drops to her knees and holds her clipboard to her chest.

Magnus narrows his eyes. "Was that necessary, Thoren?"

"I'm not letting her get so close to you without knowing what she has on her person. What is this?" Thoren holds up her plastic water bottle. "Poison?"

"It's water." She snatches the bottle from him, unscrews the cap, and guzzles the last two-thirds in seconds. "Man, I was seriously dehydrated." *I hope they have fresh water here.*

"My apologies," Magnus says, rubbing the center of his forehead.

Adaline shrugs. "As annoying as it is to be on the receiving end, it's understandable. Poison is a woman's preferred method for killing. Historically speaking. Research has proven that. But I don't go around poisoning people."

Thoren peers up at her, holding her trowel and other digging tools and pressing his finger on the tip to test the pointy ends of her pick collection.

"They're for excavating." She sits on the sofa to show the others she means to cooperate. "I literally dig stuff up."

Thoren picks up her red Swiss army knife and surprises her that he can read the inscription. "Edwin Yates?" He pulls out the first piece of metal and glowers at the sharp blade. "Yeah, this stays with me." He rotates the blade closed and pockets the knife.

Launching off the sofa, she lunges at Thoren. Her words rattle and end with a snap. "Give. That. Back."

Magnus grabs her arm and yanks her backward before she can reach Thoren, who has already pulled out his dagger and raised it level with her face. Thoren jumps to his feet, stalks toward her, and scoffs when Ëólas blocks his path. Again.

Wait, what? He's defending me?

Thoren points the blade in Adaline's direction. "I don't care if magic brought her here. I'll not have—"

Ëólas steps forward until the tip of the dagger presses against his chest. "Put. It. Away."

With a frown, Thoren sheaths his weapon. "The both of you are making my job much harder, you know?"

Adaline tears her wrist free from Magnus, more so to conceal the fact that her hands are trembling. When she finally looks at him, the disappointment on his face dissolves into a blur. "It was my father's."

Ignoring everyone's stares at either her or her other-worldly belongings on the floor, she stoops down and collects her stuff. Hamon drops to one knee and hands her the clipboard, which she carefully slides into her bag.

When she stands, she grips the shoulder strap with both hands. "Are we done for tonight?"

As soon as Magnus nods yes, she snatches Ëólas's cloak and extends her arm, holding it out to him. Keeping her hands, voice, and gaze steady requires the last of her energy today. She forces herself to look him in the eyes. His golden eyes. *I really have stepped into a fairy tale.* "Thank you for lending me this."

He looks at the cloak briefly and meets her gaze, but he locks all thoughts and judgment behind that stoic expression. "Keep it. Wear it until you reach your chambers."

Oh. Um.

The doors to the study open, and the same young woman who brought the wine enters the room and curtsies. The mesh snood confining her hair reveals small, round ears.

"Kayla," Magnus says. "I hear you are eager to be promoted from the kitchen to a lady's maid, yes? Good. My ward has had an arduous journey and arrived at a most unfortunate time. I do not want the condition of her arrival to spread like wildfire. Do I make myself clear? Good. Lady Marzella will make certain Lady Adaline has proper attire in the morning. In the meantime, see that Lady Adaline's needs are met."

As Kayla curtsies again, she smiles broadly.

Magnus drapes Ëólas's cloak around Adaline's shoulders and pulls the fabric shut. The hem swishes against her ankles. "Adaline, you must be weary from the shock this night has presented. Rest, and we will convene again tomorrow." He takes her hand and kisses the back quickly. Before he lets go, he presses the Swiss army knife into her palm. "You have friends here. I promise."

With her fingers wrapped around her pocketed knife, Adaline follows Kayla out of the study and down the hallway. Aside from a few guards posted sporadically, the rest of the castle's inhabitants must be asleep by now, which sounds ideal as she and her wobbly gelatin-like muscles are ready to collapse on a pile of dirt at this point.

But as they approach the end of the hallway, Adaline's back twitches, her eyes drift and turn her head to the side, and her curiosity spikes as if she's in the midst of research and knows she's on the verge of discovery.

Instead of turning left after Kayla, Adaline spins around. The doors to the king's study are still shut with all six men, elves, whatever, still inside and debating who knows what. But at the opposite end of the corridor, a pair of grayish-purple eyes lock with Adaline's. Even from so far away, Adaline can tell that the color is not normal, or rather, not human. Her eyes are too vibrant. Too ethereal. And the lady to whom they belong has long, straight platinum blonde hair and a small, heart-shaped face with pixie-like features that could lure men into traps. Adaline doesn't realize she's walking toward the lady until Kayla calls after her.

"My lady?" Kayla doesn't say anything more while she clasps her hands and waits.

Adaline twists back to give Kayla an apologetic smile. When she turns forward again, a swish of platinum blonde hair disappears around the corner. Only Adaline's heavy limbs and drooping eyelids prevent her from following after the blonde.

What is it with blonds today?

Too tired to keep track of which corridors and stairs and turns they make, Adaline's grateful when Kayla pushes open two arched oak doors and shows her the inside of a room with a four-poster king-size bed, and no king. Gold rope, knotted around the bedposts, ties back sheer Champagne-colored curtains. On either side of the bed, nightstands with several tiny drawers like a card catalog support candles emitting a soft glow. Opposite the bed, a small fire inside a wide, rounded hearth lights the other half of the room, including an upholstered loveseat and chaise in shades of maroon and gold and positioned beneath an arched window with sheer gold curtains. In the corner, two cushioned chairs surround a kitchenette table. The entirety of her condo could fit inside this one chamber. Overall, the warm tones and light-colored wood make Adaline feel as if she's booked a spa vacation hotel room—inside an Italian Renaissance castle.

Ambling over to the sofa, Adaline discards Ëólas's cloak and her bag and appreciates that Kayla doesn't question Adaline's clothing, granted that's most likely because of Magnus's warnings.

In an alcove beside the doors, Adaline undresses behind a partition while the doors to her room open and someone drags in a large object, but she's too tired to peek or ponder what that might be right now. Leaving on only her tank top and underwear, she folds each piece of clothing into small bundles, tucks her phone in between them, and rests the pile on top of her boots. Before standing up again, she caresses the stack, not knowing when she might wear them again.

I really shouldn't think about that right now. All I want is to slide into bed and be done with this day.

Guessing correctly, she opens the side door to the water closet, and using the wooden seat and metal bedpan beneath it isn't all that different from some of the more remote places Adaline's visited. The lack of stench, however, surprises her, especially because the people who constructed this castle didn't build out the wall so that waste would fall into a moat.

Huh. That's interesting.

After using silk cloths to clean herself, she leaves the closet. In front of her, a narrow console table holds a set of towels and a water pitcher, which she uses to clean her hands. *Maybe I can make my own soap?* She glances at herself in the round mirror above the pitcher. *Really? That's what I'm worried about right now?*

When she steps around the partition, she screeches and jumps backward, having not realized sooner that Kayla's been standing on the other side the entire time. Thankfully, no one else is in the room.

Kayla bows her head and worries her hands together. "Terribly sorry to have startled you, my lady. I've readied your bath."

"No, no. It's my fault. I'm just beyond tired and—wait, what?" *Holy shit. Is that a hot tub? I must have been really out of it to not hear them pouring buckets of water into that thing.*

Behind Kayla, steam rises from a wooden bath large enough to hold two people, and the sight of that promised warmth makes Adaline acutely aware that every muscle in her body aches to submerge itself. Her relief vanishes when Kayla walks over to the two portable wooden steps and waits for Adaline.

She's going to bathe me, isn't she? Oh god. What would a noblewoman say or do to make her lady's maid leave? "You must be tired. I can handle everything from here."

Kayla freezes and speaks so quietly that Adaline strains her ears to hear. "But, but the tub is slippery, my lady, and wh-who will wash the s-soap out of your hair?" Hugging a towel to her chest, Kayla keeps her eyes cast downward at the stone floor.

Well, shit. I didn't mean to make her feel unwanted. Adaline sighs. "You're right, Kayla. And I'm so exhausted that I could fall asleep in the water. Thank you for your help."

Kayla perks up and rests the towel on a side table with soap and herbs.

I guess this experience doesn't have to be all that different from when I visited a Japanese onsen.

Besides, those hot springs required Adaline to bathe naked with a whole group of women, so really this should be less embarrassing. Granted, Kayla's fully dressed. Adaline bites her lip. Taking that as her cue, Kayla steps aside and lowers her eyes, giving Adaline that last nudge to tiptoe across the cold stone floor, toss aside her remaining clothing, and climb the steps to the raised bath. The moment the hot water envelops her body, she relaxes against the curve of the tub. The water reaches just above her chest, and the heat untangles her thoughts and unwinds the craziness of the day.

Okay, I owe Magnus a thank you. And Ëólas, I suppose.

Although thinking about the elf, about the shift in his golden eyes from friend to foe, makes her body tense up again. *Forget him.* This bath is too good to waste on deep thoughts. Sitting forward, she focuses on the warmth wrapping around her limbs, and when Adaline closes her eyes, Kayla begins washing Adaline's hair. Eager to please, the lady's maid also turns down the bed, stokes the fire, and helps Adaline into someone else's nightgown. Only after Adaline's snug in bed does Kayla wish Adaline goodnight and excuse herself.

The moment the doors close behind her, Adaline shoves away her exhaustion and scurries out of bed. She grabs her pile of clothing and sets them down on the sofa, on the cushion nearest to the fireplace so she can see better. Retrieving her mobile phone, she powers it on, kneels backwards on the loveseat, and holds her mobile over the window ledge, her phone pressing against the glass window. After saying a silent prayer that this portion of the castle has wi-fi, she looks down. No signal. No connection. No option.

After turning off her phone, she gets onto her hands and knees and crawls along the walls, searching for power outlets or heating vents. Again, nothing.

Groaning to herself, Adaline climbs into bed, the soft mattress and cozy room an illusion of comfort. Silently, she tucks her phone and knife under the pillow beside hers, and as her mind toils away at what plans she might form tomorrow, she falls into a deep sleep.

CHAPTER FIVE

THE APPRAISAL

When the morning sunlight creeps over Adaline's face, she rolls over, turning her back to the window. The two wooden doors stand guard opposite her, their massive height hiding God knows what on the other side. Pushing the comforter off her chin, she sits up on her elbows. Near the partition, a white ceramic water pitcher and wash bowl rest on the vanity that sits low to the ground, squatting on stubby legs. Lush area rugs with grapevine designs distinguish the bed from the lounge and the changing area. Rather than getting up, Adaline throws the comforter over her head, counts to thirty, and slowly drags the blanket off her face as she sits up.

She's still in the room with the double doors, the squat vanity, and the loveseat under the window. Her eyes zero in on the sofa where she left her clothes. The clothes that prove she doesn't belong here. The clothes that represent home. The clothes that are now missing.

Adaline pulls her knees up to her chest and hugs them tightly until her hands slip off her shins. She wipes her sweaty palms on the bedsheets.

Research. I'm good at research. I just need to think of this like another project.

She wriggles out of bed, untwisting the nightgown from around her legs, and looks underneath the sofa to find nothing, not even dust. Only her bag and the cloak remain visible where she left them. The wardrobe holds an extra set of sheets and a bedpan, which makes Adaline scrunch her nose. On the bottom shelf, she finds her boots—not where she left them.

Someone entered my room while I slept.

Dashing to the bed, she thrusts her hand under the pillow. When her fingers hit her phone and knife, she exhales half the dread that had begun clogging her lungs. She closes her eyes, only for the memory of Magnus cleaning his bloody sword to come rushing back to the forefront of her mind.

He never clarified what crimes that man committed, that warranted the death penalty. What if I say or do the wrong thing?

For now, he seems protective of her, but history isn't in her favor. If she's stranded here long term and doesn't prove herself to be valuable, she needs a backup plan before he throws her in the dungeons or, worse, marries her off. Adaline shudders.

The sound of wood scraping against stone announces someone opening the door. How exhausted had she been last night for that to not wake her, unless there's another way to enter this room? Adaline twists her thumbs together and chips away at her nails. She can't let herself spiral like this. Emotionally driven analyses will lead her astray. She needs to switch off her nerves and focus on facts.

Kayla enters the room, carrying a tray of food with one hand and an array of garments draped over the crook of her other arm. "Good morning, my lady. I hope you slept well." She sets the tray down on the small table in the far corner, carefully hangs the dress in the wardrobe, and lays undergarments and other pieces across the bed.

My lady. Not milady. Interesting.

Adaline nods and sits down to eat, angling herself so she can see out the window and keep her pillow clearly within sight. A flock of birds enjoy their freedom in the far distance. Adaline's always been a night owl, but sleeping in after traveling to another world has eliminated her desire to hit the snooze button. Not that this room has a clock.

"Do you happen to know where my clothes are?" Adaline helps herself to the slices of meat, the cubes of cheese, and most of the fruit. The strawberries and blackberries she recognizes. But in all her travels, she's never seen the prickly magenta variety before. She rolls three around in her hand. "And what are these?"

"They're neccaberries, my lady. They grow all over Alderton, especially toward the end of summer. And I took your garments the first time I checked on you this morning. I washed them myself so no one else will see them. They're drying in my chamber, and I'll return them to your wardrobe by end of day." Kayla smiles but stares at the ground while she pinches the side of her dress.

Infusing her voice with appreciation, Adaline calls Kayla's name and waits for the girl to lift her head. The moment she looks up, a smile warms Adaline's face. "Thank you, Kayla. Truly."

The lady's maid lowers her eyes, but her cheeks turn rosy, and she stops fidgeting with her dress.

Oh, Kayla. I'm not who you think I am.

After breakfast, Kayla brings Adaline a small, rectangular piece of rough linen and three pinches of powder arranged in a row.

Adaline clicks her tongue a few times before making an educated guess. "To clean my teeth?"

"Yes, my lady. I wasn't certain of your preference, so I brought you sage, cinnamon, and tosium mixtures."

Tosium. Neccaberries. Adaline's fairly certain such an herb and berry don't exist back home, but now's not the time to ponder the similarities and differences between the two worlds.

"I'm sorry, Kayla. We clean teeth differently where I come from, so I'm a bit embarrassed. I'm not sure what I'm supposed to do here. Can you help me, please?"

Kayla eagerly demonstrates how to apply the powder and use the linen to rub her teeth, and Adaline's delighted that the mint-like tosium cleanses both her palette and her breath. After teaching Intro to Basic Hygiene, Kayla helps Adaline dress. At least she has privacy behind the partition while she secures the linen bra in front and the shorts around her hips with laces. Thank goodness she doesn't need to go commando and this world includes some sort of brassiere. Next come the layers, a breathable chemise that flows down to her calves, a corset that wrenches every breath out of her lungs, and two small padded rolls around her hips to encourage men to imagine her birthing their children.

Finally, Kayla has Adaline step into the satin dress and slip the bodice over her arms. When the burgundy fabric falls into place, Adaline holds the bodice against her chest so it won't crumble to the ground. "Whose clothes are these?"

"Lady Mercia's."

"Who?"

"Lord Thoren's daughter, my lady. His wife, Lady Marzella, gave this to me this morning."

Adaline forces herself to not gag out loud. The last thing she wants is for that man to see her wearing his child's clothes. Then again, maybe he'll be less eager to impale her.

Kayla pulls the laces in the back as tight as possible, but the dress still sags around Adaline's stomach, creating a ruching effect that undermines the corset's purpose of accentuating her breasts. But the strategic, wide square neckline and open-front chemise display her cleavage, and Adaline's cheeks flood with crimson. Thank goodness Ëólas left his cloak for her to hide under. After Kayla slips the matching sleeves over Adaline's arms and fastens them to the bodice's shoulder straps, she fetches the hairnet she had laid out on the bed.

Adaline twists one of her large curls around her finger. "Do all women wear a snood here?"

"Yes, my lady. All women older than twelve wear one beyond their home so no one mistakes them for ladies of pleasure. The snood will also better hide how short your hair is, my lady."

Adding this information to her collection of mental notes, Adaline sits down at the squat vanity so Kayla can smooth away the wavy curls that reach the bottom of Adaline's shoulder blades, and yet that length still qualifies as short here. Twisting her mouth to the side, Adaline runs her fingers over the back of the silver hairbrush, decorated with a sun overlooking a vineyard, while Kayla tames every curl beneath a wide hairband and a decorative mesh net, both of which sparkle with tiny gold gemstones that match the dress's gold thread along the seams and hem.

With reduced lung capacity, Adaline rises and approaches the full-length mirror. Instead of seeing herself, she sees a relic of the past. A pretty relic. But a fake. She glides her hands over the smooth burgundy fabric, and her hands stumble upon pockets hidden in the skirt's pleats.

Dresses with pockets! Score one for this world.

She tucks her smile inward to stop herself from cheering aloud and possibly scaring Kayla, who's standing off to the side and gleaming with satisfaction.

While Kayla opens the door and passes the food tray to someone outside, Adaline pockets her phone and knife and drapes Ëólas's cloak around her shoulders. Despite the warmth it offered her last night, the sage green material now feels as light and soft as satin. It's rather lovely with its gold trim and navy lining, and the simple but elegant fabric drapes effortlessly down her shoulders. On him, the length ended at his calves. On Adaline, it reaches her ankles.

Before exiting the room, she takes one last look at the stranger in the mirror. If she could send selfies to her best friends, the complete costume and its attention to detail would have elicited squeals of glee from Dax and an eye roll from Cindy. But she has no means of contacting her friends, who spent last night not running for their lives but getting engaged, and soon they would panic over Adaline's disappearance. She chose work over attending her friends' big night. Under no circumstances can she miss Cindy and Dax's wedding too.

I need to focus on what I can control.

As much as she's worried about her friends, she needs to learn as much as possible. Something brought her to this world, which means that same something should be able to send her home.

Once again, Adaline follows Kayla through the castle, although the closer they get to Magnus's study, the more Adaline's feet itch to steer her out of the main gate and into the city where she can observe a pre-industrial society, with elves no less, while they're making history.

What are the human's and elves' beliefs, norms, and customs? How do they differ? What economic system does the city use, and how do they form families? If only I had someone local to guide me, to explain what these two cultures expect and how the city works.

Kayla might be a good source of information, but she thinks she's caring for a proper lady. Adaline needs someone she can trust, someone with whom she can be mostly herself. But where can she find such a person? When she jams her fists into her pockets, the knife tumbles into her hand. The cool metal against her skin reminds her of Magnus's promise, of the six people who know the truth, even if only five seem friendly; she'll keep her distance from Thoren. As for those extinguished golden eyes, how quickly their light cooled, she imagines stuffing that memory into a box and dumping it out the window. Okay, so she has only four potential allies. She can work with that.

With or without a guide, her best course of action is to observe as much as possible and find opportunities in which to participate in society while disturbing their way of life as little as possible. She can do this. She can immerse herself in another culture, another world, for the time being. After all, she entered that cave with the goal of discovering something new.

If only I could include this experience in my research paper.

With darkness and exhaustion no longer pressing down on her, Adaline walks the spacious corridors with a skip to her steps despite her oversized slippers. Tall, arched windows permit the sunlight to wash the gray stone walls with a light-yellow sheen. The tapestries and draperies feature a gold and rich burgundy theme, which must be the signature colors of—where's Magnus from? Alderton? Yes, humans are from Alderton.

What about the elves? She expects each face she passes to belong to the blonde with the hauntingly lavender eyes. Even though the servants and guards are as physically diverse as any major U.S. city, they're all human and avoid Adaline's eye contact, though a few steal glances her way. Magnus called this region the Neutral Territory, so the elves must live and work somewhere.

Maybe they go back to the forest at night, or maybe they built residences here in the city?

A few feet ahead, two large doors propped wide open allow the chatter of women to spill into the hallway. The hurried flutter of their voices reminds

Adaline of her grandmother's social gatherings, when the women bragged about their children's successes and gossiped about neighbors while Adaline hid upstairs. When Kayla passes the doorway, Adaline edges along the wall, careful not to slip out of her shoes, and peers into the room. Within two seconds, a tall woman with a long neck and pointy nose waves for Adaline to enter. Before she can form a coherent thought or exit strategy, the lady strides over and loops an arm around Adaline's, trapping and directing her further into the ladies' parlor. She looks to Kayla for help or direction or information, but the noblewoman dismisses Kayla with a wave of her hand.

Shit.

"You must be Lady Adaline. I'm Lady Marzella, Captain Thoren's wife. My husband has not said a word to me about you except that you suffered a terrible fright toward the end of your journey. You poor dear."

Thoughts ricochet around Adaline's mind like pinballs. She's not yet prepared to play the role of the king's ward, and she didn't expect to end up in Thoren's clutches so soon, or rather his family's. Then again, Lady Marzella's narrow face bears the same sorrow Adaline's seen her whole life whenever another parent learned she was motherless, the kind of sorrow that hints at all the ordinary moments, all the conversations, and all the milestones she would never experience.

Adaline pushes the corners of her mouth into a smile. "Thank you. That's very kind of you."

The parlor has several sofas, all with end tables. Teacups and plates litter one large table, along with the remains of half-eaten bread, cheese, and fruit. Marzella steers Adaline toward the collection of sofas and chairs arranged in a large circle where at least fifteen other women, ranging from fifty years old to ten, sew bedsheets, pillowcases, and tablecloths. Their fingers never miss a stitch as they tug their strings tight and their needles dip down and up again like well-oiled machines. The ladies pause to nod at Adaline.

Their eyes assessing her from head to toe transport her back to Mrs. Weaver's ballet class, just after Adaline's family left England. Nan said dance lessons would help Adaline find friends and adjust to her new home in the States. She clung to her grandmother's arm as Nan led her into the mirror-lined room void of color and warmth. The girls gathered into established cliques that orbited around one girl in particular, Nicole, the quintessential prima ballerina. While Nan and Mrs. Weaver spoke, Nicole danced around Adaline and asked if she knew all the basic moves, demonstrating each. With her toes pointed out and her nose up, Nicole performed the role of the model student, and her tutoring announced Adaline's ineptitude.

If these noblewomen expect me to sew with them, my incompetence will give me away.

By the time Lady Marzella has rattled off most of the other women's names, Adaline's forgotten every one of them. But the last young woman's bright red locks, tucked neatly into her snood, give away her lineage.

"And this is my daughter, Mercia. She's my youngest and not yet wed, hence why she's come with us this season to the Neutral Territory."

Mercia sets down her embroidery and smiles at Adaline. Her cheeks and the tip of her nose match her red hair. "I'm pleased to make your acquaintance, Lady Adaline." The opposite of her father, Mercia speaks with a lightness that could lift a dandelion into the sky.

Adaline returns the smile, but Lady Marzella doesn't give them a chance to speak further before leading Adaline away from the women's circle. On a table along the wall, a row of baskets holds yarns, threads, and other such sewing items, along with piles of folded fabrics.

In front of this table, Lady Marzella halts and faces Adaline. "I'm delighted our daughter's dress accommodates you and that we could provide you with some comfort on this day, but rest assured I have summoned the seamstress so you will have new dresses."

"Oh. Thank you." *How am I to pay Magnus for those?*

She doesn't want to consider the possibilities. Instead, she glances at Mercia, at that docile face buried in her embroidery. Occasionally, the girl looks up and smiles at the other ladies' conversations but seems to keep her thoughts to herself.

I think I'll adopt Mercia's method for handling this situation.

When Adaline doesn't say anything more about the dresses, Lady Marzella plasters a smile on her face and turns away, grabbing an empty basket from under the table. After inspecting various balls of yarn, she selects two plain gray ones and drops them into the basket. Then she proceeds to the spools of gold and burgundy thread, heaped in a pile, and as she turns away from the items she gathered, she looks expectantly at Adaline, at her weak smile, at her lips pressed together tightly.

"Well, now," Lady Marzella says, breaking the silence between them, "Please let me know if you have questions about the Neutral Territory. I know how...unnerving living in such close proximity to the elves can feel at first, but, within time, you may feel at home here too."

"Thank you." Adaline clings to the hope that silence is golden, but after uttering the same words for a third time, she officially feels like a simpleton, and Lady Marzella's stifled expression indicates that she might think the same.

Thoren's wife returns to dropping several spools of thread into the basket, along with a thimble and pincushion. Leaning sideways, she spares Adaline her assessing gaze as she rifles through a large fabric pile. "I'm terribly sorry you lost your parents at such a pivotal age. How old are you, dear?"

The ladies closest to them stop talking. They never miss a stitch, even as they lean Adaline's way.

"Twenty-eight."

A young lady with copper-colored hair smirks, shifts away from Adaline, and resumes chatting with her friends as happy as a bird chirping on a spring morning. Unbeknownst to the lady, Adaline's relieved she's too old to be a threat to any of these women.

Lady Marzella, on the other hand, drops the fabric she's been holding. The linens cascade off the table and into a heap at her feet. "But, but you must have received proposals?"

To escape the long silence stretching between them, Adaline stoops down, gathers the fabric into her arms, and deposits them on the table. She focuses all her attention on folding a piece of fabric wide enough to cover a bed and planning her best course of action for excusing herself before she accidentally invites more speculation and judgment. The gossip mill would run at full steam if she shared details about Derek and the proposal that never was, and she'd rather bury those memories than give people reason to discuss them day in and day out.

Balking at the baskets, Lady Marzella scans the items she's gathered, having forgotten what she was doing. When Adaline sets the folded cloth down, Lady Marzella blinks, resets her brain, and rests one hand on Adaline's arm.

"Well, no matter. Being the king's ward will afford you many proposals soon enough, regardless of your age. Many of those in the king's command are eager to seek his favor." She offers Adaline a motherly smile that conveys not pity but promise. "No one will overlook your sweet face and smooth skin."

Adaline smiles but also drifts sideways toward the door, especially when Lady Marzella nods approvingly at Adaline's chest.

"We just need to make you a dress that better accentuates your assets," Lady Marzella says. "What are your other accomplishments?"

Certain her face now matches the burgundy of her dress, Adaline pulls Ëólas's cloak shut in front of herself. "My accomplishments?" *Oh my god, how do I make this stop?*

"Yes." Lady Marzella adds fabric to the basket. "Have you learned painting, hunting, embroidery, music—"

"Music." Adaline's eyes involuntarily jump from the basket to Lady Marzella's gaze, which continues to assess Adaline from top to bottom. "And reading," Adaline adds, taking a few more steps that bring her closer to the door.

"That's promising then." Lady Marzella raises her arms, offering Adaline the sewing basket, the invitation hovering between them. "Mercia and I are working on the tapestries for the dining hall. Why don't you tell us more about you?"

The polite choice would be to accept the basket. Adaline knows this, and she doesn't want more people thinking poorly of her and questioning her motives, but stitching for hours with a group of strangers and having to carefully select what to share or appear mute doesn't hold a candle to exploring a city brimming with life. With elves.

Summoning all her strength to squelch her nausea, Adaline smiles brightly at her new colleagues. "Thank you so much for the warm welcome, but I promised

Ma—the king—I promised the king that I would speak with him this morning. Can I leave that here for now? I look forward to our next chat."

Waving goodbye, Adaline backs out of the door. The moment the hallway swallows the parlor, she runs as quickly as her oversized flat shoes will allow.

CHAPTER SIX

THE CANDLEMAKER

Several wrong turns later, Adaline finds a corridor lined with guards, tipping her off that she's located the king. The guards, spaced six feet apart, follow Adaline with their eyes. Halfway down the corridor, she approaches the massive double doors that match the ones she entered last night, and, opposite the doors, towers the same archway she saw when she left with Kayla.

Yep, I'm in the right place.

All the guards in this corridor hold spears and wear padded jackets with leather armguards, but the similarities between them stop there. The clothing of the guards she just passed has the burgundy and gold she's come to associate with Magnus and Alderton as a whole. Their buckles feature ornamental grape vines and leaves, making Adaline curious to taste the quality of Alderton's wine, and their half helms and wide nose guards resemble a bullet.

Beyond the doors, the guards who occupy the second half of the corridor wear completely different uniforms. Their colors combine sage green like Ëólas's cloak, navy blue paired with a simple belt, and boots that stop short of their knees. Although Adaline admires the artistry of their nose guards and brow plates, how they resemble tree roots twisting around each other, it's the insignia on their leather breastplates that catches Adaline's eye most of all—three stars gleaming above a massive tree, its bough as full as an oak but its trunk as long as a redwood. Something about that combination invokes wonder.

Beautiful.

As much as she'd love to examine the guards, their authenticity, the lack of centuries of dirt coating their garments, she pauses in front of the doors, notes the muffled voices on the other side, and glances at the guards stationed beside the doors. Neither moves.

She clears her throat. "Good morning. Mag—the king said we would talk again today. Is he in there? Can I knock?"

No one speaks, just like the guards in front of Buckingham Palace, not that Adaline's ready to test their commitment with selfies and jokes.

"So...I'll just knock then?" She takes one step forward, and two guards tilt their spears across the door, blocking her path. "Or not. How do I make an appointment then?" Again, no answer. *This must be how Lady Marzella felt.* "I guess I'll just wait."

For twenty minutes, Adaline paces back and forth, hums the tune to *Wheel of Fortune*, and examines the opposite end of the corridor where, like the guards' uniforms, the color scheme transitions to blue and green. *That must be Lameiría's colors.* After casually strolling to the end of the corridor, she peers around the corner, and sure enough a female elf with ebony hair disappears into another room. *Elves!* Adaline circles the area and cannot find a single sign with any sort of writing that might read, *Do not enter.*

She dashes back to the two soldiers to test this theory. "I'm going to explore the castle. If Magnus needs me, I'll be about."

The guards remain silent. With a suppressed, eager smile, Adaline spins around and reaches the end of the hall when the doors to the study open and Merith calls her name. She halts mid-step and reminds herself that she's too old to feel like she's been caught with her hand in Nan's cookie jar, but something about Merith, perhaps his practiced calm, tells Adaline he's much older than he appears.

"Good morning, my lady. The king and my lord apologize for the wait, but they are preoccupied at the moment with important matters."

"Oh." Adaline clasps her hands together and meanders toward him, her scalp tingling with curiosity. What could be more interesting than a visitor from another world? "What are they discussing?"

Merith raises a single eyebrow yet keeps his expression indifferent. "That information is for council members only."

"Right. Of course. Should I wait then?"

"No, my lady. I expect this meeting to last half the day, but I can have a guard escort you to the ladies' parlor."

"No!" Adaline bites the inside of her cheek and takes a deep breath to slow her response, to not alert Merith to her trepidation. "That's okay. I can find my way."

"Alright, given you look the part now." Merith nods at her dress, still maintaining Morpheus's stoicism. "Go through that archway. When you exit the commons area, you'll find stairs that lead to the ground level. The gardens are particularly lovely. And my lady, the king requests that you actively avoid trouble today."

Frowning, she slams her hands on her hips. "He makes it sound like I had any choice in what happened yesterday."

Adaline exits the castle's main gate without a single guard paying her any heed. Once free of the stone walls, she exhales and walks along the riverbank, passing bridges and following the river that leads into the city. With each step, she inhales crisp, fresh air that fills her lungs and encourages long strides.

About a mile later, green fields give way to stone homes, but greenery still outlines the perimeter of each building. Vines rock climb toward the roofs. Next to each leaf, a tiny purple flower blooms and shimmers in the river's mist. The limited height of the homes and the wide lanes interspersing every few rows of buildings gives the city an open, airy feeling—the opposite of traditional medieval cities where buildings crouched on top of each other, and narrow alleyways bred crime and disease.

The further Adaline strolls into town, the more guards patrol the streets. Armed with swords across their backs or at their sides, they march in pairs, one from Alderton and one from Lameiría. The townsfolk go about their business, with elves to the left of the river and humans to the right, but the physical diversity of the peoples themselves means this world must have extreme climates, and the people at some point migrated around.

The path from the castle automatically drops her off on the elven side of the city. She contemplates crossing a bridge and walking along the human side of Front Street, but everyone Adaline passes either nods at her or keeps their eyes cast downward. No one calls her out for being on the wrong side of the river, so she continues along, curious to see how people might react further down.

On both sides of the river, the people sweep their steps, greet their neighbors, and haul their goods. Every now and again, she spies a citizen's tense twitch or nervous glance that melts away the moment they find guards patrolling nearby.

Several blocks later, shops line both sides of the riverfront with their doors wide open and goods on display. Hanging pots and pans, bolts of fabric, and barrels of spices and herbs add splashes of color up and down the street. She can't help but crane her neck as she passes by, peering over stalls and peeking inside the stores too, all of which boast a second or third story where the merchants most likely live.

Low stone bridges allow the guards to cross back and forth quickly. Further down, a covered bridge towering over the others reminds Adaline of the Rialto in Venice, minus the shops. The similarity causes her to yearn for a cappuccino. From both ends of the bridge, six rounded arch windows extend upward, supporting the bridge's roof and culminating in the middle with rectangular columns that frame a taller, gazebo-like center. A flat railing with wide, dense column balusters underscores the windows and cuts through the gazebo.

As she approaches the end nearest her, two detached columns, each capped with large spherical finials, announce the entrance. The bridge transitions smoothly to the cobblestone-lined street, making it convenient for carriages or horses, not that anyone's making use of the bridge today. The Venetian-esque bridge also marks the intersection of Front Street and Market Street, both of which continue as far as Adaline can see.

Overall, the city reminds Adaline of Maryland's Renaissance Festival, only the costumes are one hundred percent authentic, the swords are no doubt sharp, and tourists don't clog the streets, gawking and taking pictures. Adaline slips her hand in her pocket and grips her phone.

Oh, the evidence I could record.

And Dax, he'd squeal with delight and beg to be a metalworker's apprentice so he could compare his methods against the real deal. If anyone had a choice to be spirited away to another world, Dax would have been first in line and wearing his LARPer gear, if Cindy agreed to go with him. With a loud exhale, Adaline releases her mobile, finishes crossing the bridge's span, and continues straight ahead onto Market Street.

After she takes three steps, a woman's shouts pierce the din of merchants shuffling through the market. "Jemsin! Jemsin, you get back here right this moment!"

In front of a shop, the woman with a round, protruding belly tries to hoist herself out of her chair, knocking over rows of candles on a display table, while a little boy runs through the crowd with a grin as wide as the Cheshire Cat.

With one hand wrapped around her belly, the woman waddles after him. "Jemsin!"

Adaline ducks around a cart and snatches the toddler before he can dash past her. He tries to wriggle free, then pouts and tugs the cloak's clasp at the base of her neck. Chuckling, she holds his little hand as she shuffles him onto her hip and takes him to his mother, whose face burns with either anger, embarrassment, or both.

"Oh, my lady! I do apologize. Please, you needn't dirty yourself. Jem, you stop that at once," the woman snaps as Jem tries to yank off Adaline's snood while they cross the street and approach his mother.

"Don't worry. I don't blame him at all," Adaline calls ahead. She turns to Jem and wriggles her nose. "Does it look fun to play with? It's not fun to wear." Sticking her fingernail under the net, she scratches her scalp and pities her curls fighting their prison.

When Jem laughs his agreement, his eyes sparking with wild youth, she zips her finger as quickly as a bee to his nose before zipping her hand far off, beyond the both of them. Mesmerized, he follows her movements as her finger bobs back toward him, only this time, she lands on her own nose and crosses her eyes. Squealing, Jem grabs her hand, squishes her finger against his nose, and tries to cross his eyes, but they unscramble immediately. His giggles soothe Adaline's soul, reminding her of afternoons at Cindy's house when her youngest sister was born.

As they reach Jem's home, he reaches out for his momma, who transfers him to her swollen, almost nonexistent hip. Two seconds later, he slips down her side and runs inside the shop, oblivious to the two little girls picking up the candles their mother had knocked over and repositioning them on the display table. Beyond the store window, a young boy minds his own business as he dips candles into a vat of liquid wax. The entire family shares the same heart-shaped chin, bronze complexion, and chestnut brown eyes. Despite the commotion inside and outside the store, Jem's mother attempts to curtsy and gives another apology.

Adaline waves off the perceived inconvenience. "Really, it's no trouble. Cindy, my best friend back home, has three little sisters, and they were a handful. They used to run into my house, snatch treats from my grandmother, and run outside to play in my backyard."

Jem's sisters huddle together to hide their giggles. Their tan linen dresses match the wood railing that leads up the steps into their shop. In between picking up candles, the youngest daughter stares at the satin of Adaline's dress. Her big sister elbows her, and the little one retaliates by stomping her foot and pinching her sister's upper arm. When their mother sucks in her cheeks and narrows her eyes, the girls jump back to focusing on the candles.

The woman turns back to Adaline and lowers her head. "Please excuse my girls' behavior."

"It's okay, truly. Your girls remind me of home." Adaline's smile drains from her face. Once again, a single night has changed her life, and home is even further out of reach.

I shouldn't have ghosted Cindy's mom.

Doña Mariana used to call weekly, then monthly. But Adaline hasn't seen her surrogate mother, sisters, or abuela in almost a year, not since Nan's funeral. She's missed them, but visiting would have invariably concluded with Adaline having to face her lifeless childhood home. The home she and her father moved into after her mother's death. The home her grandmother infused with hot tea, warm biscuits, and endless conversations. The home that burst at the seams with her father's research, books, and treasures from adventures abroad. Her inheritance entombs everything Adaline's lost in the span of two years.

Worst yet, she'd taken for granted that the Seguar family would always be there, that she'd see them all soon enough, either at Liliana's quinceañera or Cindy's engagement party.

Will I ever see them again?

The candlemaker reaches toward Adaline, as if recognizing the look on her face, but quickly drops her calloused hand. "You must be homesick, my lady," she says quietly.

Adaline nods and bites the inside of her lip to stop it from quivering. "I'm so sorry. I'm Adaline."

"It's a pleasure to meet you, Lady Adaline. I'm Sallie." Looking over her shoulder, she points from the oldest daughter to the rest of her children. "My girls are Morie and Corra, and my eldest boy there is Adem. You've already met Jem. And this one here," she rubs her belly while resting one hand on the backside of her arched spine, "we haven't a name for yet."

Behind the glass window, the son pauses his work long enough to bow his head. When the girls curtsy, Adaline does the same and earns a broad smile from them both.

"I'm pleased to meet all of you." Adaline avoids saying their names, unsure if she's supposed to refer to all women as lady so-and-so or if that title is just for the gentry. *As a married woman, maybe she's referred to as ma'am or madam?*

Jem stumbles out of the shop and tugs Adaline's hem to follow him inside. At the sight of Sallie's face turning red, Morie runs out from behind the table, wraps both arms around Jem's waist, and hoists him away.

"May I come in," Adaline asks, "if I wouldn't be in the way?"

"Oh, please, my lady." As quickly as she can waddle, Sallie ushers Adaline inside. The shop has shelves upon shelves full of candles, from short stubby votives to tall narrow tapers for candelabras. In the corner, looking out over the market, Adem keeps dipping those candles. He couldn't be older than twelve. *He has strong arms for a tween.*

"Please, sit," Adaline says to Sallie, who refuses. "If you go into labor early because of me, I'll never forgive myself."

With a grateful smile, the candlemaker sits down at the table positioned toward the back of the shop and resumes her work, cutting off the bottoms of the candles to give them a flat base, while her youngest girl, Corra, trims the wicks.

The shelves, chock full of that creamy wax, nicely offsets the dark wood, but the only windows are at the front of the shop, meaning the inside relies heavily on daylight or the chandlers' own products. Drifting toward the oil lamps, Adaline trails her finger over one in particular, a simple bowl with a crevice for adding a wick. Its plain design must make it affordable, not that she could purchase one. *Do they use coins here?*

When Sallie indicates Adaline can have a seat, she does, carefully tucking Ëólas's cloak beneath her bum. "I hope I'm not intruding. I only just arrived yesterday, and I don't know anyone here."

"Has the lady not yet acquainted herself with the other ladies of the castle?" Sallie asks.

At the mention of the castle, Corra leans forward. Her sister must have heard that too, because a moment later, Morie nudges her little sister aside and busies herself with squeezing the finished candles onto the crowded shelves. Discreetly, she pushes her locks behind her ears so she can hear better.

Returning her attention to Sallie, Adaline nods. "I met a few this morning." She debates being honest, if she might give herself away, but she doesn't believe in building friendships on pretenses. "I'm afraid I don't have much in common with them."

Sallie dips her brows together in doubt, then nods politely while keeping her lips pressed together tightly.

Don't make this about me. Make it about her. "Do you ever decorate the candles?"

"Oh, no. Not really. I don't have time to make anything fancy."

Jem chases a ball around the shop floor. He's the only one allowed to play right now.

Adaline reaches for a candle in Sallie's stack. "May I try?" When Sallie gestures for her to do as she pleases, Adaline picks up the spare paring knife and cuts the wax bottom as evenly as possible. When she sets the candle on the table, it's still a bit crooked. Pursing her lips to the side in apology, she passes it to Sallie to fix.

Damn. She should leave this woman to her work, but the candle shop could provide Adaline the perfect opportunity to participate in society and observe daily life. Refusing to be a nuisance, Adaline picks up a pair of scissors. "Perhaps I'm better at cutting string. Would you and the girls mind if I took over for a bit?"

While the girls glance longingly at their mother, Adaline measures a wick with her thumb like they had done and snips one wick after another, their lengths matching the ones beside them. Sallie flicks her head toward the back door, and the girls don't wait for her to change her mind. They dash outside, taking Jem with them and allowing Sallie to sink more easily into her chair. The older boy watches his siblings until they disappear out of view, but he never falters in his work.

Sallie smiles at her eldest. "You can go out too, as soon as you're done with that batch. Just wake your grandmother first and ask her to mind the display table." Her words make Adem's eyes flicker with delight, and he dips faster. "Mind yourself! Don't burn your hand."

Adaline and Sallie work in silence while Adem finishes his last batch of candles, which he hangs to dry from the rafters. Sallie's mom handles the customers outside, but when one passes her and enters the shop, Adaline jumps up before Sallie can lean forward. The customer wears clothing similar to the lords of the castle. *But a lord wouldn't buy candles himself. Perhaps he's a servant.*

Regardless, Adaline holds her breath, praying the man won't ask why a lady of court is working in the candle shop, but he takes one look at her dress and keeps his mouth shut. Maybe she can find clothing more similar to the townsfolk. She'd be better able to blend in and participate in town life.

After the customer drops two hexagonal coins into Sallie's calloused hands, Adaline resumes her work and waits, giving Sallie the space she needs to feel at ease. When Adaline helped Japanese farmers pick edamame off the vines, the locals started talking freely within an hour, once they were certain Adaline wouldn't judge them. Sallie takes longer, but, sure enough, shared work loosens her tongue too. Initially, her stories focus on the city's growth and neighbors, especially those who are new and why they came.

Adaline stacks the finished candles on the shelves, next to their matching siblings, then fetches a new stack of dried candles near the vat. The lack of odor means the liquid is either beeswax or something other than animal fat. "Why did you move here?"

Scooting forward on her chair, Sallie spreads her legs so her belly can rest on the folds of her skirts and between her thighs. "Kian and I wanted to get away from his family." She peers out the open front door. "He should return with supplies soon."

When Adaline places the taper candles on the counter, Sallie rests her hand gently over Adaline's, the way Cindy's abuela always did whenever Adaline brought her a fresh cup of tea. "Thank you." Her voice reveals her exhaustion.

Adaline pats her hand in return, then picks up the scissors and returns to the wicks. "Do you mind me asking why you needed to get away from Kian's family?"

"They bossed us around and said Kian couldn't do anything without them. We came here to prove them wrong. After all, everyone needs light." She waves her hands at her family's hard work. "Being the first ones here, we set up shop quickly, which has proven advantageous, and we've been doing well."

Advantageous. Could Adaline do anything here that would prove advantageous? She'll need to find a means of supporting herself if she's stuck here and Magnus has already forgotten her.

Could this city use a professor with a background in archeology, religious anthropology, and socio-cultural anthropology? Adaline's posture wilts. "I don't think I'll ever fit in here."

"I felt the same when we first arrived, my lady. And we're still figuring things out."

Adaline smiles in gratitude.

"What of your father or husband?" Sallie asks. "Are you here for a brief visit, or does your family intend to invest in the city?"

Adaline rolls a candle back and forth between her hands. "I'm not married, and my father, well, he was a scholar. The king has taken me in. For now. I'm just an orphan playing dress up." She closes her eyelids and traps her tears, refusing to let even one escape. Not again. Crying doesn't rewrite history. Crying doesn't make her stronger. Crying doesn't resurrect the dead.

Sallie sets down her knife. "How long has it been, my lady?"

"Two years." Yet she still expects him to call her every Saturday morning and share something new he read, some discovery he made, no matter how small. Then he'd say, *Your turn, kiddo,* and Adaline would recite her post-doc research findings until she stumbled upon something he didn't already know. Sometimes those calls would last hours.

The challenges of following in my father's footsteps. I loved that challenge.

Adaline drops the candle, and it cracks in half. "I'm so sorry." Wiping her eyes with the back of her hand, she drops to her knees and scoops up the pieces.

"Not to worry, my lady. We can remelt the wax."

When Sallie's husband returns, Kian tries to sell Adaline candles, but Sallie tells him to leave Adaline be and relieve her mother instead. He places crates full of supplies behind the counter, and Adaline spies tufts of wool. A few moments later, Sallie's mom sits down with them but remains quiet while Sallie chats about the new bakery opening next week.

"Do you like living here?" Adaline asks.

Sallie hacks off the end of her last candle and rubs her belly. Each time she passes over the top, she opens her mouth to speak, then closes it again. Finally, she says, "Business is good."

"Will last night's events jeopardize that?"

"We don't know. We don't have the means to leave. But we fear..."

Adaline waits.

"We fear retaliation," says Abuela.

"From whom?"

Sallie and Abuela exchange a look, and Abuela shakes her head no.

Ignoring her mother, Sallie turns to Adaline and whispers, "We don't know what the elves really think. They don't speak much, not to us anyway. And rumor has it a human started the fight."

Adaline leans forward. "Did you see what happened?"

"No. I just heard screaming and saw people running away from the opposite side of town. When the shopkeepers started locking up early, I didn't ask questions. I pulled the children inside and did the same."

Adaline clasps her new friends' hands and asks the next question slowly. "Did you know anyone who got hurt?"

Sallie shakes her head. "Not personally. But I heard three died."

"The attackers?" That would add up to the numbers she heard last night, that Magnus killed one, Morpheus—no, Merith—killed another. And the last got away.

"No, townsfolk," Sallie whispers.

"The king must be pulling his hair out by now," Sallie's mom says. She even sounds like Cindy's abuela, both having a gravely texture to their voices.

"Why's that?" Adaline asks.

Abuela grabs a bunch of fine threads from behind the counter and sets them in front of her. As she plucks one free and then another, her hands tremble the entire time. But when she braids them together, her fingers are as nimble as a young woman's. "If you believe the rumors, half his council didn't want to invest in the Forbidden Lands, and if the elves abandon the city, we have to leave too. We're not allowed here without their permission. But we're the ones who won't recuperate, seeing as how the elves don't seem to want for much. Won't even buy our candles." She grumbles the last sentence.

"Do you really think the elves will retaliate?" Adaline asks Sallie. She recalls again the scornful looks Ëólas gave her last night, after he realized she's human, how that contradicted their initial meeting when her gut pushed her toward him, when he willingly approached her and dared to sheath his sword so she'd feel safer.

"I don't know. I don't know anything about them. They don't like to socialize with us."

Adaline leans back in her chair, rests an elbow on the counter, and rubs her chin with her thumb the way she usually does when hypothesizing. Her own experience thus far aligned with Sallie's observations, but Adaline hasn't actually tried socializing with elves yet. Nothing about last night lent itself to socialization.

"Well, there's only one way to test that theory. And now that I'm here, I can't *not* try." When Sallie and Abuela glance at each other in confusion, Adaline clarifies, "I'll go chat with some elves and see if I can make a friend."

Adaline goes to stand, but Abuela grabs her arm and looks her firmly in the eyes. "Be careful, dear girl." When she lets go, she abruptly rises, leaving her braided wicks abandoned on the counter. "I'll go prepare a meal for everyone. Lady Adaline, will you join us?"

An invite? To break bread? Adaline counts her blessings to have found such a welcoming, kind family. Placing a hand over her heart, she thanks them profusely. "As much as I'd love to stay, I've distracted you long enough, and I'm not certain when I'm due back at the castle." She can only imagine the work and cost of preparing food from scratch—and for such a large family. She can't possibly take their food. "Would it be alright if I came by again tomorrow?"

A genuine smile warms Sallie's tired eyes. "Whenever you wish, my lady."

Before Adaline can leave, Sallie pulls a hexagonal beeswax candle off the shelf with both hands and offers it to Adaline. "For your help today."

Adaline stares at the three-inch wide pillar, one of the thickest and finest candles in the shop, and clasps her hands around Sallie's. "Your company was more than enough payment. These past few hours were the least homesick I've felt since arriving here. Thank you."

As Adaline heads to the door, she glances back once to take in the family working and laughing together. Then she forces herself to leave them behind.

Chapter Seven

THE STONE CARVER

Once Adaline exits Sallie's shop, she takes a moment to breathe deeply and dust off any negative feelings. With determination guiding her, she springs back across the Rialto and strolls down the other half of Market Street, no longer able to resist exploring an elven market. Hints of music hum in the distance. The beats rise and fall away while she explores their display tables one by one. Anything made from fabric, wood, ceramic, or metal includes at least one decorative embellishment and swirls of calligraphy. The elves even carved into the edges of their tables, doors, and eaves designs of flowers, leaves, and branches interwoven. Her fingers itch to touch everything, and the elves continue their activities as if she weren't there.

She passes a row of baskets overflowing with nuts, figs, and a fuzzy purple fruit the size of apricots. Across the street, two elves, a male and a female, paint that same purple fruit on a ceramic vase and a bird inside a shallow bowl. Adaline wanders closer to the stall with purses and pouches hanging at various lengths from posts, and her eyebrows jump up at a sage messenger bag with no zippers and no magnetic clasps but plenty of pockets and a leather-like flap in the shape of a leaf.

Wow, I could hide my stuff better in that. And it's so pretty.

She reaches for the wide strap, anticipating the bag's weight and curious to discover how many pouches it might have inside too, when a young elf, no older than twenty, exits the shop, chuckling to himself, and stops short in front of her. He sucks in his breath and doesn't move a muscle until Adaline retracts her hand

and steps back. Only then does the young elf do an about-face and hurry back inside the shop.

Well, shit.

Adaline retreats to the middle of the street. Even though she doesn't catch their stares, she can feel the elves' eyes upon her, observing her every movement. She slows her pace and chews the inside of her cheek, and her shoulders crouch closer to her ears. Once again, she's the new kid in class, the transfer student with the funny accent who has no idea what a peanut butter and jelly sandwich is, let alone why anyone would want to eat such a combination—and on crustless bread no less. Granted, enough weekend playdates with Cindy lead to Adaline eventually adopting the quintessential American childhood favorite as her own.

Cindy never laughed at her. The moment Nan led Cindy's family to the backyard and her father lit the grill, her new home turned into a whirlwind of feet racing across the grass, legs jumping off the trampoline, and arms waving to each other. When Adaline brought her new friend into her bedroom, Cindy didn't ask why Adaline and her father left England, why she didn't watch the same cartoons, or why she didn't know any of the same songs. Instead, Cindy just tugged Adaline along, gave her space to find her voice in her own time, and let her ask as many questions as needed until Adaline couldn't remember life before Maryland.

I need someone like Cindy. In elf form.

Before Adaline can sink deeper into her concerns, a rectangular block of marble, taller than the elf standing in front of it and holding a chisel and hammer, catches her attention. The elf cocks his head to the side and rests his chin on top of the hammer while his eyes roam up and down the marble block. He takes one step back, then two more. Tilting his head toward his other shoulder, he circles the block to examine its side. His dark brown eyes widen when he discovers Adaline resting an elbow on top of his empty display table, her head resting in her hands.

"What are the triangles going to be?" Adaline points to the top where the stone carver began his work.

Aside from a few seemingly random shapes, the rest of the white marble reveals no other alterations. But given how long the elf had been staring at the block, he must see something more. He sees the hidden potential.

Without lowering his chisel and hammer, he angles himself so both his current work and Adaline remain within view. "I cannot yet say."

"Because you don't know, or because it's too soon?"

The corners of his mouth twitch upward. "It's too soon." Even though he speaks little, he keeps his tone gentle.

"I suspected as much. But you see it, don't you? What it's going to be?"

The stone carver pushes his shoulders back and stands taller as he studies Adaline from head to elbow, not in a creepy, predatory way, but rather as if to see her better too—that same artist's eye assessing what lies beneath. His gaze falls to Ëólas's cloak. Only when he's done inspecting her does he speak. "I try."

While the elf debates resuming his work, Adaline stares at the block, imagining the possibilities and if this person's work will wind up in a museum hundreds of years from now for generations to admire.

"I once saw a sarcophagus made of marble." Adaline omits the fact that she did so when her family vacationed in New York and spent a whole day at The Met. "The carvings on the side tell the story of Selene, the moon goddess, who fell in love with a shepherd from earth. The carver captured the moment she descends from her chariot to look up at her beloved Endymion fast asleep. He was granted—well, I'd argue, he was cursed—with eternal youth *and* eternal sleep. I stared at that carving for hours. The details, from Selene's curls falling over her shoulder to Endymion's sorrow…I don't know. It's just mesmerizing. That artist took his time too. He had to."

Adaline finally looks the elf in the eyes, hoping she hasn't scared him away. Instead, he's lowered his tools, and the smile he gifts her softens his oblong face and sharp chin. He nods once more and trusts her or the patrolling guards enough that he turns away from her so that Adaline sees only his light brown hair pulled back in a low ponytail. He takes one step forward, places the blade of his tool against the stone, checks the angle, and begins tap, tap, tapping the back of the chisel with his hammer. Dust and flecks of marble fall to the ground and coat his shoes. While he works, Adaline guesses where next he'll focus his efforts.

She waits to speak until he pauses again. "How long do you think this piece will take you?"

"As long as it needs." He doesn't turn around but speaks clearly so she can hear him.

Adaline laughs. "I've only worked with paint and clay. I'd be terrified I'd shatter the marble."

"That's why we must take our time. Never rush the process. The marble tells me when it's ready to shed the next layer."

As the elf continues his work, his hands move deftly, and the stone sheds its excess bit by bit, increasing Adaline's desire to unearth its secrets. Every time the elf steps back, she suppresses the urge to say, "It's hard to see things when you're too close," in her best Bob Ross impression.

After what feels like a half hour, maybe longer, the elf volunteers his own question. "What did you make with the clay?"

Standing up, she dusts off her elbow. "A garden. A secret garden. I'd just read the story. I covered the brick walls with vines, and inside I added a stone pathway, a miniature table and chairs, trees and bushes, and a fountain."

"Did it shatter when you fired it?"

"Ha! It would have, so I never did. It hardened well enough though, but it's forever a sad shade of dark gray. I wish I could have glazed it."

She had gifted the garden to Nan for Christmas their first year in the States, and Nan kept it on the bookshelf in her bedroom for the last twenty. As the nostalgia settles deep in her heart, she rubs her chest a few times to dislodge the discomfort.

The elf walks up to his display table, lays down his tools, and uses his dark tan apron with its hand-stitched floral pattern to wipe the chalky dust off his fingers. When his hands are pristine again, he places an open palm over the center of his chest and bows his head. "I'm Jósep."

Adaline's hands shake, but she pinches her dress and pulls off another curtsy without a wobble, her legs dipping with the muscle memory of a dancer. "I'm Adaline."

"A pleasure." Jósep squats down behind his table only to pop back up with a pitcher of crystal-clear water that he places on the table, along with a single mug. Adaline steps back to give him space, but Jósep exits his stall, crosses the street, and fetches another mug off the display table in front of the couple now painting trees and flowers on plates. After the three elves speak for a moment, Jósep returns, carrying the extra mug that he places in front of Adaline. He pours them both a drink while she bounces on her heels and bites her lip to stop her smile from growing too large.

They drink in silence. As she tilts her head back to drink the last drop, her eyes fall upon the block and the ground that has sunk beneath it. "What will you do with this piece when it's done?"

"Ah, I already promised it to the city gardener."

"Oh! The city has gardens?"

"Many." He winks as he lowers the pitcher and puts it away, out of sight.

"Is there one nearby?"

"Yes, in the city center."

Adaline looks back toward Front Street. She doesn't recall seeing a garden up ahead. She'll have to travel further tomorrow.

Jósep collects his tools. "My apologies. I meant the center of our community."

"Oh." Adaline's eyes widen, and she clasps her hands tightly to stop them from flailing all about. *An elven garden.* Given the nature-inspired décor and embellishments, this world seems to adhere to the same ideas about elven preferences. So an elven garden, where they would be more at home, more within their element, should be spectacular to see. "But I can go see the garden, right? I mean, there's not a law that says I can't?"

"You may go."

"Which way?"

He points down the street. "Follow the music. Someone's always playing something."

Adaline checks the sun's position in the sky. Its impending descent, along with an audible growl from her stomach, tells her she ought to head back to the castle. She needs to be patient. Tomorrow's another day—unless Magnus and Ëólas discovered how to send her home while she has been sightseeing. That thought alone makes her want to travel further into the elven side of the city.

"Thank you so much for letting me stay, Jósep. I hope I haven't interfered with your work too much. Can I come back tomorrow? To see what more you've revealed?"

With a single nod, Jósep returns to his task, but his brown eyes seem brighter, maybe even lighter.

Adaline meanders through the market and toward the castle, despite her curiosity yelling at her to find that garden. As accustomed as she is to traveling abroad, this adventure's proving to be the most fantastic. She tilts her face up to the sky and inhales deeply. Her body and spirit feel stronger, and the joy on her face catches the attention of the elves she passes along the way, many of whom seem to return her smile with their own.

As she nears the river, her steps slow down, and the little hairs on the back of her neck prickle upward. Her smile relaxes until it's dissolved altogether, and her shoulders squirm as if to shake loose someone's attention. Adaline pauses and spins around. She scans the crowd of busy elves going about their day, chatting with each other, and paying her no heed. Nothing seems out of place. Nothing appears wrong. Nothing hints at danger.

She shudders, and her heart picks up its pace. *Calm down. You're being silly.* Turning to leave, she catches sight of someone's backside disappearing between two shops, and everything inside her tells her to keep walking. Blend in. And act as if nothing's wrong.

As Adaline passes the last bridge, a long line of humans and elves alike outlines the road leading to the main gate. She slowly passes one after another. Despite the mixture of people in line, they create spaces and clusters that divide them by species, both side-eyeing the other and twitching nervously.

So this is what Magnus and Ëólas have been dealing with all day. Have all these people gathered to report their observations or to pay taxes or to announce their immediate departure from the Neutral Territory?

Her shoulders sag, and her mouth pulls the corners of her eyes downward too.

A human child who appears to be about five years old buries his face in between his father's legs, and the father pats the boy's head. The sweet scene turns sour when the man angles himself sideways and shifts his gaze so he can watch the elf behind them. He positions himself like a shield protecting his son.

Adaline sighs and walks over to the elf. "I'm sorry to bother you, but what's this line for?"

He blinks a few times and looks around to see whom she might actually be speaking to. When she doesn't look away, he opens his mouth, but before the elf can answer, the child's father interjects. "We're here to see the king, my lady. Once a week, we're able to bring our concerns directly to His Majesty."

"Oh." So the king interacts directly with his people. *Perhaps I should get in line so I'll actually see him today.* But when Adaline glances backward, ten more people extend the end of the line to over the bridge. She winces. She can wait till dinner. "So you're here to see Ëólas then?"

Again, the elf looks left and then right. The father can't possibly answer her question this time, so she softens her gaze and waits.

As the elf clears his throat, the freckles on his nose dance. "Yes, my lady. I am here to seek an audience with Lord Ëólas; however, we present our concerns to both my lord and the king. They decide jointly what's in the city's best interest."

"Huh." Adaline leans back and crosses her arms. *So they really do run the city jointly. Does that mean they're jointly avoiding me?*

The scornful look Ëólas gave her last night when she tried to give him back his cloak flashes in her mind.

If he thinks so poorly of humans, why is he even here? Does he really distrust me so much because some weird anomaly brought me here?

Adaline puts her fists on her hips and scowls, which makes the father and elf shift uncomfortably from one foot to the other. *Oops. I have to watch my body language here.*

The boy, who must not have noticed Adaline's momentary agitation, peeks out from between his father's legs and makes an O shape with his mouth when he sees the gold thread at the hem of her borrowed dress.

She smiles to herself and leans down, resting her hands on her knees so her face is level with the child's. "Have you ever heard of the story *Rumpelstiltskin*?"

The child shakes his head but turns one ear her way, just like many of the kids back home did when their parents dropped them off at summer camp. She loved that job during her high school years, how the children were eager for stories, how words could calm their heartache as they watched their parents rush off to work, how far-off adventures could distract them from their sorrow. She understood all too well. Stories had saved her too.

Standing up, Adaline clasps her hands behind her back and adds excitement to her voice. "Once upon a time, in a faraway land, a poor miller couldn't pay his king's taxes. Out of fear and desperation, he told the king his daughter could spin straw into gold thread."

The child peers up at his father to study his expression. When the man pats his son's curly head and sneaks a tickle behind his ear, the boy squirms closer to Adaline, his hand still gripping a fistful of his father's trousers. With a squeak, he asks, "What happened?"

Adaline grins. The more she talks, the more her voice captures the undulating mood of the story. Like Cindy's family, Adaline's hands move of their own volition too, adding emphasis and power to her words. "Well, the king demanded that the miller bring his daughter to the castle, and the miller cried he had doomed them both. The daughter knew they had no other option, so she went to the king to tell him the truth. But the king thought she was lying and wouldn't let her go. He locked the poor girl in a room full of straw and told her that if she didn't spin the straw into gold by morning, she'd be killed."

Another man further up ahead steps out of line. "What did she do?"

Adaline's cheeks turn red as she attempts to count the numerous heads that have turned her way. The man who spoke up has a toothy grin and a hole at the top of his shoe.

Thank goodness I didn't tell them about the elves and shoemaker.

She takes several steps backward so everyone can hear her better. Seeing Kian, the candlemaker's husband, Adaline waves at him, which prompts his peers to size him up and mumble around him. Kian blushes.

Biting her lip, Adaline angles herself slightly away from him and raises her voice so the whole crowd can hear her. While she finishes telling them the rest of the story, the gaps between the humans and elves shrink. At the end, everyone chuckles at the idea of the little man being so enraged that he tears himself in two.

Another man in the crowd waves his hand, announces he's a miller, and thanks Adaline for the warning. She laughs with the rest of the people, then asks others what they do, where they live, and why they've come to the Neutral Territory. Many express similar answers: to explore new possibilities. While she listens to their stories of long treks through forests and meadows, carts with broken wheels, or thunderstorms that halted their progress for days, she forgets the line inching toward the main gate. Within less than an hour's time, she learns about the various shops and businesses that comprise the city, including a few banks, a printing press, carpentry, textiles, and a hat shop. Her questions encourage more answers, and she quickly forms a mental map of the city.

When an elven couple with matching long dark hair mentions a tea shop they opened two days prior, Adaline skips nearer to them. "That sounds lovely. My grandmother and I spent evenings outside, counting stars and sipping tea." She briefly closes her eyes and inhales, as if she could inhale the memory itself. "Would it be alright if I come by soon?"

The lady returns Adaline's inquiry with a slight bow of her head. "Of course, my lady. We look forward to your visit."

"Thank you. I would like to—"

"Adaline, there you are!" calls a woman's voice over the crowd, her surprised tone telling Adaline that her fun has come to an end.

Chapter Eight

THE OTHER SIDE OF THE CASTLE

As Thoren's daughter emerges out of the front gate, Adaline silently thanks God, the fae, the source—whoever is listening in this world—that Mercia's crazy father or mother hen aren't with her. Still, the memory of Thoren swinging his sword at her pops into her mind, along with the following moments when a certain blond elf shielded her, only to later keep his distance as if she had transformed into a piranha.

Stop thinking about that. Let it go. It doesn't matter.

She presses her lips into a tight line. To not offend Mercia, Adaline uses one hand to massage the back of her neck so she has time to unlock her jaw.

Mercia's red locks match Thoren's, only she's managed to keep hers perfectly tucked under her snood. She lifts her skirt to avoid dirtying her hem, but as she rushes toward Adaline, Mercia seems unbalanced, as though she doesn't trust her own feet or the ground beneath her. When she reaches Adaline, the young girl smooths her skirt and brushes her hand over the rim of her snood, making sure no curls escaped. "Whatever are you doing?" She glances from the crowd to Adaline.

"Hi, Mercia. I was just getting to know some new friends."

Mercia and more than a few people in the crowd furrow their brows, then Mercia's eyes widen. She opens her mouth to speak, but before uttering a sound, she clamps her lips together and dims the light in her eyes. "The seamstress has been waiting. We must hurry."

Adaline cringes at the mention of the seamstress, especially in front of people who may have only one outfit that they most likely make and mend themselves.

After apologizing for leaving, Adaline tells everyone she hopes to see them around the city, all the while ignoring the grooves forming between Mercia's eyebrows as all reason and logic evaporate from her face.

Glancing at the crowd once more, Mercia hurries inside the castle with Adaline following behind and picking up her skirts to mirror her guide. As they head toward the sleeping quarters, a flash of platinum blonde hair yanks Adaline's attention sideways, causing her to halt mid-step. The elven lady, the one with the lavender eyes, the one Adaline has been subconsciously searching for all day, stands at the opposite end of the corridor. She remains so still that Adaline can't detect the rise and fall of the elf's chest under her pale blue satin gown, the fine fabric draping like a waterfall around her slight frame. Her hands hang limp at her sides, and her eyes stare off into the distance, past Adaline, but they contain flashes of emotion that make Adaline think the lady sees more, not less, than most. It's her stillness, though, that leads Adaline to question if the elf exists in this world—or if she's a remnant of a world long gone.

Within a single heartbeat, Adaline's feet take a step forward. When the lady doesn't move, Adaline takes another.

"Adaline?" Mercia's voice echoes down the hall.

Turning to announce her location, Adaline catches a glimmer of a smile from the blonde before she vanishes down another corridor. Again, Adaline's legs move of their own volition as she follows after the blonde, that is, until Mercia pops back around the corner.

Adaline halts and pinches her thumbs together, her voice unable to conceal her disappointment. "Sorry, Mercia. I thought I saw someone."

Mercia glances down the empty hallway. "An elf, I'm sure. That corridor leads to their side of the castle."

So, the castle is also divided.

Adaline swallows the lump in her throat, takes one last look at where the blonde used to be, and directs herself to face Mercia.

As blank as Adaline paints her face, a small smile edges across Mercia's mouth. But she doesn't say a word.

The seamstress orders Adaline to slip on a basic inside-out dress and stand on a pedestal in the center of her room. With pins sticking out from between her lips, the seamstress hovers around Adaline, jabs pins in the fabric to create a tighter fit, and takes measurements. The seamstress doesn't say much, but she does compliment Adaline's good posture.

After more than ten years of dance lessons, I would hope so.

Adaline stares at her wardrobe and daydreams about the moment she can retrieve her field journal and record all she's seen today. If she could buy that elven handbag, she could hide her journal in there. Maybe she could wrap the spiral binding in ribbon.

Which would pop off the moment I opened my book.

Unable to find a solution to anything these days, Adaline sighs loudly, and the seamstress measuring Adaline's chest sneers at her impatience. The offense punctures Adaline's daydreaming, and she finally registers Lady Marzella's words.

"Lady Adaline needs at least three dresses to start." She stands tall and lengthens her neck so much so that she resembles a swan rather than a mother hen.

Adaline met a few swans once on a school field trip to a farm. They were vicious. They squawked, flapped their massive wings, and chased anyone who dared to cross their path.

Adaline bites her lip. "Wouldn't one dress be sufficient?"

She doesn't need this poor woman spending weeks making several dresses when Adaline plans to go home as soon as possible. As soon as the king makes time to speak with her, that is.

Mercia, sitting at the small table in the corner, peeks up from behind her book while Lady Marzella stares Adaline down.

The vein near Lady Marzella's forehead pulses. "As the king's ward and currently his only family, one dress will not do. Two then, to start. One purple and one burgundy. Those colors should be appropriate for you." Lady Marzella looks down at the seamstress measuring Adaline from hip to ankle. "She needs undergarments as well and a proper fitting bodice. Keep the front-opening chemise sparse to show off her neckline."

Adaline grimaces. "I don't think—"

"You're twenty-eight, my dear. Trust me to do the thinking."

Fire burns in Adaline's chest and reveals itself in her cheeks, but she clamps her mouth shut and grits her teeth while she rattles off a string of curses in her mind. When the seamstress adjusts the fabric at the base of Adaline's lower back, she wipes her palms on the inside-out velvet holding her captive. A rich fabric Magnus must be paying for. To help her blend in. While she lives in his castle. Correction, his half of a castle. Because only he and five other people know her real story. And within the context of that fake story, Lady Marzella is helping Adaline the only way she knows how.

Adaline keeps telling herself this while she presses the meaty padding between her thumb and index finger to relieve the pressure building around her temples. She exhales, and her cheeks cool.

Apparently, Adaline's attempts to calm herself also hinder her ability to process the words exiting Lady Marzella's mouth. Adaline blinks, and Lady Marzella towers in front of her, waiting for Adaline to say something.

"I'm sorry. What did you say?" Adaline nibbles her bottom lip.

Raising her book higher still, Mercia conceals the entirety of her face.

Tossing her arms in the air, Lady Marzella exhales with exaggerated effort. She takes a few laps around the room, all the while making a tut-tut sound with her tongue. When she drops her arms from her hips, she walks over to Adaline and softens her gaze the way Nan would when using every ounce of her reserve to better understand her granddaughter's adolescent, larger-than-life problems.

"Adaline, my dear, you must still be in shock from last night's events. How dreadful to have been so close to the danger." She shudders. "How did you ever escape those barbarians?"

"I, I'd rather not discuss last night. I'm just lucky Magnus," she swallows hard, "and Ëólas found me."

Lady Marzella flinches and stills. Slowly, she tilts her neck, the odd motion and angle capturing Adaline's attention. With an icy stare, Lady Marzella peers into Adaline's eyes. Her nostrils flare thrice, but she evenly measures her next words. "Indeed. His Majesty is most magnanimous. You must have quite the history with our king, to know each other so intimately."

The seamstress, now at Adaline's feet, drops her pincushion, and the sound of Mercia turning a page fills the room. Fire consumes Adaline's cheeks, and she mentally curses herself. Every muscle in her body freezes as Lady Marzella's eyes lock onto hers.

When the seamstress pricks her finger on a stray needle, she jumps, massages the tip of her finger, and resumes her work undeterred.

Adaline's muscles thaw. She won't let a single prick deter her either. "We are still becoming friends, I hope. But I do owe them both my life."

When in doubt, choose honesty. The less I have to pretend, the more I can remain myself.

Lady Marzella blinks first, but her voice remains tart. "Your father would be doubly grateful as well, I'm sure."

Adaline nods but looks away. The mention of her father shatters all pretenses. A knowing look passes across Lady Marzella's face. She lifts her hand, as if to touch Adaline's forearm, but changes her mind and clasps her hands in front of her waist.

The seamstress pushes herself off the floor and readjusts her dress. "Pearls on the bodice, my lady?"

"I suppose so." Marzella turns to Adaline. "Did your father leave you an inheritance?"

Adaline chuckles to herself. "Nothing that would be useful here."

"Shame. I'll have to inquire with Thoren what the king plans to offer for you then. If your father knew His Majesty so well, then—"

"Magnus isn't planning anything," Adaline blurts out.

As Lady Marzella's neck and face turn crimson, the seamstress shakes her head, and Mercia looks up confused. Having received the go-ahead from the seamstress, Adaline dashes behind the partition to wriggle out of the fitting, taking care not to stab herself with hundreds of pins.

Out of sight, Lady Marzella decides to change the subject, sort of. "Adaline, I hope you'll heed my advice. You are now a member of the king's court, which is to your advantage. You must be cautious in how you encourage a man's affection. Use those skills wisely, as *noblemen* visit this castle daily."

Adaline rolls her eyes. *Ugh. She doesn't even attempt to conceal the innuendo.*

Stick with the truth, even if I pay for it later. "I almost had a proposal, but that's over now." *Last week's fight with Derek ensured that.* Adaline stretches her arms behind her back to tie the skirt around her waist. "You know, you're absolutely right, Lady Marzella. Yesterday was a lot, and today has been as well. Do you think I might be able to rest soon?"

Thankfully, Lady Marzella doesn't argue. Within five minutes, the seamstress leaves, her arms laden with fabric and a basket hanging at each elbow.

Lady Marzella heads for the door too. "The king has ordered we all dine together tonight to assuage the tension of yesterday's terrible events. Your lady's maid will see to it you're ready to dine. Mercia, dear? Coming?"

Abandoning her book on the table, Mercia jumps up. Instead of rushing to her mother's side, she helps Adaline by fastening the laces on the bodice. "I'll be along later, Mother."

Lady Marzella studies both girls for a moment and sighs. When she collects Mercia's book and excuses herself, Adaline sags her shoulders, and her limbs feel ten times heavier.

Two down, one to go.

"Please don't mind my mother." Mercia ties off the bodice, leaving the matching sleeves on the bed and sitting back down at the table. "Her sister never married and now relies entirely on my father's hospitality."

Adaline sits on the trunk at the foot of her bed. "I get that. But I've had to deal with a lot of changes these past few years. Honestly, I'm just trying to adjust to the last two days. Marriage isn't my priority right now." *Please spread that around, so no one thinks I'm sleeping with Magnus.*

Mercia rubs her thumb into the palm of her other hand. "I'm sorry for your loss."

"Thank you."

"I know acclimating to new surroundings and new people can feel challenging."

Adaline pinches her thumbs together.

Clearing her throat, Mercia adds, "But I find exploring helps me reorient myself faster."

Adaline's eyes snap to the girl's. "Me too." Holding her breath, she waits to hear what Mercia might say next.

"Have you explored the elven side of the castle yet?"

"No, but I hope to." Adaline slides her butt to the edge of the trunk.

Mercia leans forward and whispers, "I can show you around the castle."

"Is that allowed?"

Mercia's gray eyes twinkle. "It's not *not* allowed. Besides, Father's been busy all day dealing with the council and the ramifications of the attack. We won't be bothering anyone. And we have yet plenty of time before dinner."

Adaline stands up. "Lead the way."

Springing off her chair, Mercia heads toward the doors.

As they exit her room, Adaline pauses and runs back to her wardrobe. On the bottom waits her shoulder bag. She reaches in and pulls off the hanger Ëólas's cloak, which she spins over her shoulders and fastens at her neck. With the soft fabric shielding her, she hurries after Mercia and her next exploration.

Even though it's not *not* allowed, Mercia checks every corner before waving Adaline along to follow her. Whether they're sneaking into the elven side or out of the human side, Adaline's uncertain.

"Mercia, why do I get the impression this isn't allowed?"

The girl shrugs. "I don't want to risk running into Father." She looks back at Adaline and scowls. "He has a certain view on how a lady ought to behave, and I should be studying maths right now."

"Math?"

"Yes, so I'll be proficient at running my own household someday. But maths is easy and doesn't require an entire afternoon."

"Of course. I've had my share of prerequisite math classes too."

During their journey through the lower levels, the ladies pass the kitchen buzzing with servants preparing roasts and puddings and pies and breads. The smells make Adaline's nose want to drift toward them. As they pass through another corridor higher up, Adaline peers out an open-arched window, its glass panes left open wide to allow the late-summer breeze to cool the interior of the castle. In the side courtyard below, the washing ladies plunge their arms into sudsy water, use lean muscles to ring out the sheets, and stretch to hang the linens to dry while sweat drips down their brows. Adaline rubs the tip of her fingers together, feeling the remnants of her own calluses that have all but vanished during the last two years. Only her calluses aren't from hard work. They are from decades of playing guitar.

Once Adaline and Mercia pass the commons area and the king's study, the tapestries and carpets change from burgundy and gold to sage green and navy. The stone also appears whiter, and the doors and frames use a lighter natural wood trimmed with painted floral designs in gold. The elven servants walking through the corridors nod when they pass Adaline and Mercia. Just like along the riverbank, no one calls them out for being on the wrong side of the castle.

"Alderton and Lameiría built this castle as a joint effort when they agreed to create the Neutral Territory," Mercia explains. "The castle itself symbolizes the peace treaty."

The next corridors they enter remind Adaline of the one that leads to her own chambers, only the elves' rooms are further apart.

"Mercia, where are we going?"

With a mischievous smile, the redhead smiles widely. When they reach the end of the corridor, the hallway splits left and right with only a single set of double doors at either end. Mercia leads Adaline to the left. Thank goodness for the open windows letting light into the hallway, or Adaline would feel like she's being led to a dungeon.

Mercia halts outside the door, knocks once, and a small female voice on the other side tells them to enter. Mercia pushes the door open. Inside the spacious room, sheer lavender curtains surround a four-poster bed with a footboard and headboard of woven birch branches. The posts themselves are four young birch trees sprouting green buds that reach toward the top of the cathedral ceiling. The severed trunks sit evenly on the floor, which makes Adaline wonder if someone stitched fake leaves onto the branches up high or if those buds are forever preserved thanks to elven ingenuity. The rest of the white wood and lavender upholstery makes Adaline feel calm and ready to daydream.

Quite the accommodations.

In the corner, far from the private balcony, the blonde lady with the grayish-purple eyes lounges over the side of her chaise, her cheek pressing against the armrest as her own arm wilts over the chaise's side. Her hair rains down to the floor. The moment she sees Adaline, her eyes brighten and crystalize. In one fluid motion, she rises, swings her bare feet to the floor, and glides over to both ladies.

"Adaline!" The pixie-like elf's voice sounds like a flute's whimsical song. "You made me wait such a long time. But you're here now, and everything will be as it should. Welcome to Aerytol."

Adaline's mind races, trying to understand why the lady's words feel like they have more meaning to them. Had she seen Adaline arrive last night and had been waiting all day for them to meet? But the weight of her words feels heavier than that. And Magnus had said they are in the Neutral Territory. So, what's Aerytol?

Before Adaline can formulate a response, the blonde turns to Mercia. "Thank you so much for bringing her to me. Would you like tea?"

Adaline glances at Mercia, who wraps her arm around Adaline's. "She's very kind. You'll love her."

The blonde gestures to her balcony. Beyond the archway's matching sheer curtains, a table awaits with three place settings and a plate of pastries and biscuits. But as her eyes glaze over, the blonde tilts her head, and her expression slackens as if she's on the verge of falling asleep. "Mercia, I should warn you that the council meeting has concluded. You might wish to run back before Lord Thoren finds you."

Mercia's eyes go wide. She apologizes to both and turns into a flash of red running out the door.

The blonde shakes off her drowsiness and chuckles. "She's a sweet thing. But she'll need to become braver if she's ever going to fight for what she wants." Looping her arm around Adaline's, the elven lady guides them both to the table, and her next words sound like a sibling coaxing a younger sister to listen. "Come, Neir Nía. Come with me."

Near nee-uh?

Adaline parts her lips to speak but closes them again when the blonde sits down, pours Adaline's tea, and offers a bowl of sugar.

I'm not sure how to read her.

Once Adaline takes a seat next to the blonde and sips the tea, she decides to be blunt but keeps her tone gentle. "Who are you?"

The blonde laughs and turns toward the green fields that stretch into the horizon and conclude with the jagged line of a forest. The distance seems to draw her to it, so much so that Adaline's not sure if the elf still exists in the present, not mentally anyway.

Adaline rises, but the blonde tugs her hand. "Please stay. It's been so long." Her voice is laden with sorrow, and its weight pulls Adaline down.

Shifting in her seat, Adaline ponders asking what's been so long, but she doesn't have the heart to disturb whatever moment the blonde's trying to create, so Adaline copies her hostess. She sips her tea and stares into the distance. In the silence, she watches the sunset, the blue sky blending into indigo, the birds drifting lazily overhead, the wind brushing the boughs of that faraway forest.

For a moment, Nan's beside her again. They're on the back deck, sitting on the outdoor bench and rocking back and forth as they stare at the lake, at its pastel reflection. Neither speaks, each enjoying the comfort of the other's company and the knowledge that they're not alone, that they can put their racing thoughts and to-do lists aside for the time being, and that tomorrow promises a new day.

An ache cuts through Adaline's chest, a pain that hasn't yet dulled. But she's gotten so used to the discomfort that she's learned to ignore it most of the time, especially when teaching or researching or wandering through museums.

It has *been a long time*.

The blonde puts her hand on top of Adaline's, and she's grateful this elven lady knew exactly what Adaline has been missing most recently.

"Seira," the blonde says.

"Huh?"

"My name. I'm Seira."

The sound of her name, its sing-song lilt as Adaline repeats *sear-uh* to herself, eases a corner of her heart. "Nice to meet you."

The smile that blooms across Seira's face lifts her rosy cheeks and adds a depth to her lavender eyes that makes them seem hundreds of years older than Seira appears, older and wiser, as if she can see beyond the surface of everything and identify its core.

Within a few moments of being in her presence, Adaline's bones know that something far greater than chance brought her to this world.

Adaline exits Seira's chambers and meanders down the hallway, trying to sort through the mix of feelings and thoughts crashing into each other. Nothing about Seira's dance-like movements and selective words match the elves Adaline has met and observed thus far. She can't quite figure out how Seira fits into the picture of this world—much like Adaline herself.

That sudden connection lifts the corners of her lips upward.

Lost in her thoughts, she wanders toward the main corridor, her footfalls lighter. When she turns the corner, she comes face to face with Ëólas. As she gasps, both of them stop abruptly, inches away from crashing into each other, their bodies only an inch apart. His golden eyes and long dirty-blond hair replace her previous thoughts as she remembers him silhouetted in the moonlight, when his first instinct had seemed protective.

"Oh." Adaline takes a step back so they both have room to breathe and so her brain can function again. "Did you and Magnus—"

"What are you doing here?" He pushes his words through gritted teeth and clenches his jaw.

She takes another step back. Her momentary respite rolls off her shoulders and shatters on the ground. She narrows her eyes. "I was just—"

"Were you invited?"

"Not...exactly."

As quickly as a strike of lightning, his face hardens into a pointed stare. He glances down the hall toward Seira's room, then flicks his eyes back to Adaline. "You don't belong here."

Never were words truer.

Éólas moves to the side, distancing himself so that a chasm could separate them, and gestures down the hall, back toward the human side of the castle. "Go. And do not come back."

His eyes burn as he locks onto hers, and he refuses to let up, to look away, to consider her differently. He just waits for her to comply with his demand and glares at her as though she's polluting his side of the castle.

Adaline bites her lip to stop it from quivering. She shouldn't take his actions personally. She shouldn't allow emotions to compromise her indifference. She shouldn't feel her blood boil and heat rise to her face the longer he stares her down and doesn't flinch.

Lifting her chin, she strides over to him, removes his cloak, and hurls it in his face. "Then put up a sign!" Her voice echoes down the corridors.

His sharp inhale chips away at his stonelike features, but she leaves him carved into the background, holding his cloak and looking after her with raised eyebrows and mouth agape. Whatever he's thinking now, she doesn't care. She tramples heavily down the hallway, not bothering to look back. He's absurd to have expected her to know what's acceptable and what's not when he and Magnus have been busy all day.

It's not like they assigned me a guide. No, they just ignored the woman who wormholed to their doorstep. And why? Because they have to run a whole damn city and kingdom?

Adaline slows her steps.

Yes, they really do. Every day.

And they had to deal with the people who attacked the city yesterday. And help the citizens who lost loved ones. And listen to the concerns of their people who waited in line to see them all afternoon. Many of whom were scared. Unsure. Maybe even alone. Like her.

When she reaches the end of the corridor, she sighs and turns around, only to see Ëólas disappear toward Seira's room. She stares after his absence, and a cold sensation creeps up her arms, causing her to shiver. She reaches for the cloak, to pull it tightly around her, but her hands grab nothing but air.

The entire walk back to her own chambers, Adaline can't seem to swallow the lump in her throat. If only she could have a redo. If only he didn't look at her like she was a bomb about to explode at any moment.

She stops outside her room and leans her hands and forehead against the heavy doors.

He sees danger because he doesn't know her. And she's a stranger. From another world. Who plopped in the middle of a delicate situation. That she somehow just exacerbated.

Damn it.

Chapter Nine

A Dinner on Stage

When Adaline approaches the great hall for dinner, lords and ladies fill rows of tables and benches. Only a narrow path to the end of the room offers space. Perhaps she could walk along the wall and find a seat in the back where no one would notice her.

The moment she enters the great hall, a servant standing at the door announces her presence. All faces turn toward her. She contemplates backing out of the room and dissolving into the shadows, but the last thing she needs is to be the center of gossip. So, Adaline imagines the room to be another stage design. The guests are merely extras assigned to the background. Clasping her hands in front of her waist, Adaline pulls back her shoulders, lifts her chin, and follows the servant, placing one foot gingerly in front of the other. This event is not her first solo performance.

Show time.

Mirroring the city's layout, humans occupy one side of the dining hall, and the elves relax on the other. At the end of the aisle, Magnus and Ëólas sit side by side, facing their people, at a long, curved table. Each of them has an empty seat beside them, which must be reserved for their seconds in command or their spouses, that is, if they have spouses.

Wait, do they have spouses? Her eyes drift toward Ëólas, but she wills herself not to follow through.

Gathering her skirts, she climbs three steps to reach Magnus's table and stands in front of him. He leans back in his chair and smiles at her like an old friend meeting up over coffee, but the gray bags beneath his eyes droop as if weighed down, and his mouth hangs slightly open as if to allow his sighs to escape unnoticed.

"Good evening, Lady Adaline. I'm delighted to have you join us tonight."

Adaline tilts her head downward, crosses her ankles, and sinks into a curtsy the way Kayla showed her moments earlier. She holds the position for four heart beats and rises, steady on her feet. Even though Adaline nods at Ëólas, she doesn't lift her gaze beyond his navy-clad torso, the rich fabric cut perfectly to fit him.

The smile Magnus gives her causes the corners of his eyes to crinkle. Finally, she has an audience with him. He's right in front of her, wearing a long, dark burgundy jacket with a wide, gold brocade trim along the collar, his waist, and his cuffs. He's so close she could polish his jacket's coin-sized buttons so they'd shine in the lamplight.

She debates what to say but hesitates to speak as laughter erupts behind her because someone said something funny among the nobles.

With a deep breath, Adaline opens her mouth, but Magnus shakes his head, keeping the movement barely perceivable. "Not now."

She bites the inside of her cheek and clutches her hands together so she can't ask him when. So she can't suggest they go outside on the balcony. So she can't give him the middle finger. With an additional bow of her head, she turns to leave but halts when Magnus gestures at the chair beside him. She swallows hard. A servant pulls out the chair and waits. Adaline, forcing the corners of her mouth upward, walks around the table and silently takes her seat as the servant pushes in her chair, its arms locking her in place.

Welp, there goes my reputation.

The slight curve of the table enables her to see both Ëólas and the empty chair beside him. Instead, she faces forward, studies the crowd before her, and tries to picture the nobles naked or wearing chicken costumes. The image doesn't stick. The lords and ladies talk among themselves with ease, each knowing what to say, how to sound witty, and when to remain coy. Their bangles and rings jingle and clink as they gesture with practiced and perfected mannerisms.

Adaline worries the hem of her hand-me-down bodice and curls her toes in her floppy shoes while she waits and watches the nobles chat quietly among themselves. Food hasn't been served. Goblets are empty. And the conversation is quieting as the crowd waits for the king's cue. What he's waiting for, Adaline has no clue.

Magnus leans closer to Adaline's ear and, keeping his eyes on the crowd, whispers, "Relax."

Pulling her shoulders down from her ears, she releases her bodice and rests her hands on her lap.

Facts. I need facts.

The square silver plates feature a circular center that's sunk in about an inch. As Adaline anticipated, the place settings do not include forks, only a wide spoon and a thick knife that's more suited for killing people than being used to help feed them. As for the tablecloth, the embroidered hem displays green vines and tiny purple grapes and is most likely the handiwork of one of the women Adaline met this morning in the ladies' parlor. With her heart beating at a more even pace, she exhales.

At their table, two servants appear and pour the three of them wine. The moment the servants disappear, Adaline reaches for the goblet, but Magnus places his hand on her wrist to stop her and shakes his head once.

After retracting her hand, she buries her fists in her lap. "Shouldn't this seat be reserved for the lady of the castle?"

"I thought you would prefer my company to Thoren's."

Magnus juts his chin toward the front table where Thoren targets Adaline with his narrowed eyes. He doesn't look away from her, not even when he speaks to his wife or daughter beside him. Lady Marzella, to her credit, doesn't stare Adaline down. As for Mercia, Thoren's shadow reduces her to a small child, especially when she pretends to laugh at the conversation happening around her.

"Yep, you're right," Adaline says. "Thank you."

Magnus nods. Thoren's eyebrows knit together so tightly he could weld them into a steel unibrow.

"He didn't know you were going to have me sit here, did he?"

Magnus grins. "No."

She clamps her lips tightly together, but the corners of her mouth still turn upward, and her rosy cheeks announce her amusement. "Magnus, he's trying to keep you safe. He's just worried about you."

"I don't know which surprises me more, him not marching up here or you defending him." Despite the humor in his voice, the blue of his eyes darkens like sunset, and his shoulders sag ever so slightly.

Adaline leans toward him and keeps her voice below a whisper. "Are you okay?"

"Whatever do you mean?" Sitting up straighter, he forces his eyelids to open more.

"Nothing. You just seem—never mind."

"I'm fine, thank you. Today has been long, but tomorrow holds promise."

Adaline tries to decipher what he might mean or, more specifically, what that might mean for her. Before she dares asking him to clarify, Magnus's eyebrows shoot upward. Scanning the room to find whatever ended her conversation with him, Adaline glimpses Ëólas's stonelike face crumple and his full lips fall slightly open.

At the main entrance, Seira steps into the dining hall and drifts down the aisle toward the head table. Her small hands lift her dress, revealing bare feet that step lightly past the gentry as if they were only figments of her imagination.

With servants pulling out Ëólas's and Magnus's chairs, they stand to greet her. The tug on the back of Adaline's chair tells her she ought to do the same, but, being late to rise, she bumps the table. The wine sloshes out of their cups and soaks into the white tablecloth. Before she can use her napkin to sop up the spills, servants appear in front of her and quickly save the linens. She whispers an apology and thanks God the guests haven't noticed her blunder because they're all staring at Seira's arrival. Still, Adaline's pulse quickens when Seira twirls around the table and smirks at Ëólas, who hasn't yet shut his mouth.

A smile consumes Magnus's face. "Seira, we're delighted to have you join us this evening."

She nods and lowers herself into the seat next to Ëólas. Her long, slender fingers rest lightly at the edge of the chair arms. "Thank you, Magnus. You're too kind."

As everyone else takes their seats again, Ëólas purses his lips. When he speaks, his tone borders along cross and cautious. "Seira, I thought you had left for Lameiría."

She perks her lips into a sweet smile, closes her eyes, and takes a long breath. When she opens them again, her lavender eyes focus solely on Adaline. "Ëólas, why would I ever leave now when all the important moments are upon us?"

"Seira, I only..." Ëólas doesn't bother to finish his sentence when she refuses to look at him. He exhales loudly, leans back in his chair, and clenches his teeth.

"Well, now that we're all here, let's begin." Magnus raises his goblet, turns to the gentry, and gives a quick speech that reaffirms their goals here in the Neutral Territory. Ëólas praises everyone's efforts the last several years, and they both agree that everyone must work even harder now to prove to the rest of the world that their endeavor will last.

At the end of their joint mission statement, Magnus and Ëólas raise their goblets to the crowd and declare, "For Aerytol."

There's that word again. What or who is Aerytol? I thought we're in the Neutral Territory?

Everyone in the hall raises their cups in return. Everyone repeats the same phrase in unison. Everyone speaks with a resounding affirmation that echoes around the room. Everyone, except Seira, who leans her head against the back of her chair, and the vibrant purple of her eyes fades to dust while all emotion and consciousness evaporates from her body. Although her eyes are open, her head droops to the side, but no one seems alarmed at her behavior, at her pale color, at her blank expression.

Scanning the room again, Adaline searches for someone to call for help. Instead, everyone seems to actively divert their eyes from Seira. Before, no one could look away from her. Now, no one dares to look at her. Even Ëólas is preoccupied with drinking his wine and asking the bard to play songs while Magnus orders that dinner be served.

Adaline grips the arms of her chair to stop herself from screaming, from running to Seira's side, from checking her pulse and holding her hand. Even though Adaline met this woman only a few hours ago, seeing Seira catatonic twists Adaline's stomach and makes the bile rise in her throat.

Finally, Ëólas rests his hand on Seira's. The gesture is subtle, fleeting, but gentle. When he turns to face her, his face takes on that soft, careworn look he'd shown Adaline the first moment he saw her alone and confused among the ruins. While worry sears down Adaline's back, Seira's eyelashes flutter furiously. After a few moments, Seira sits up straighter in her seat. Her face warms again, and she smiles at Ëólas as if nothing had happened, as if Adaline had imagined the whole thing.

The servants fill the tables and the gentries' plates with various slices of roasted meats, minced pies, different cheeses, fruit platters, potato soup, and loaves of bread. As the savory scents permeate the room, Adaline's brain races to process the last few moments—that no one acknowledged Seira's condition and everyone's blatant inattention; that Seira's on a first-name basis with both Magnus and Ëólas and no one looked aghast; and that Seira took the seat next to Ëólas, who wants her to go home to Lameiría.

At first, Adaline thought Seira and Ëólas didn't get along, given the way she dismissed him when she entered the room, but that last moment between them, the way his touch brought her back, proves they have a bond.

Even though they're both different shades of blond, they look nothing alike, which means Seira is, might be, Ëólas's wife?

They're gorgeous side by side. But something about that guess feels completely wrong. Instead of that tingly sensation of discovery, that thought twists Adaline's stomach even more, as does watching Magnus eat everything off his plate with his fingers.

Then who is Seira? What's her role here? Why does no one question her? And why—Oh, the bowl of water is for washing our fingers!

Adaline continues to watch how Magnus and the others eat before mimicking them and attempting to settle her stomach with a thick slice of buttered bread.

Thankfully, Magnus provides a wealth of facts throughout dinner and points out the members of the city council, some of whom Adaline recognizes, like Thoren and Merith and the other two, Fólas and Hamon, who know her secret. The facts about the remaining council members make her head swim, and while she can't remember everyone's names, she does mentally record that both sides have captains of the city guard and masters of logistics. But those are the only overlapping roles. Whereas the elves have a city planner and historian, the humans have a treasurer, which makes Adaline ponder how their priorities may differ. Another interesting fact Adaline stows away is that three members of the elven council are female.

With Magnus tearing into a chicken leg, Adaline observes the four others she met last night. On the human side of the hall, Thoren and Lady Marzella speak politely to each other, but never do their hands meet. Hamon, however, runs his hands through his Westley-esque hair and manages to touch the shoulder, arm, or hand of every young woman near him.

Among the elves, Fólas has the attention of everyone at his table. He flings his arms outward and says something that must amount to a punchline because everyone bursts out laughing. But when he slaps Merith's shoulder, he abruptly stops laughing. Merith's single arched eyebrow makes Fólas raise both his hands in surrender, and the table erupts with laughter again.

Human or elf, they speak among their own with familiarity, the way Adaline and Cindy have always spoken to each other. With conversation nonexistent at her own table, she looks at her plate, telling herself to eat more to make up for her lack of lunch, and forces herself to take a bite of a meat-filled pastry puff.

"Oh," she moans and quickly takes another bite four times as large. Savoring the hints of rosemary and thyme, she can't identify the other major spice, but she doesn't care. The juicy delicacy of the meat filling has her reaching for another, along with some long strips of tender meat.

Wiping his mouth, Magnus leans her way. "I did not expect to spend the entire day caught up in council meetings and other affairs."

Perhaps that's Magnus's way of saying he's sorry for having left her waiting all day. Before she can think of an indirect way to ask him as much, he smirks and gestures with his chin toward the human nobles. "Thoren looks as though you're poised to assassinate me any moment."

Adaline drops the knife she'd been holding. Sensing he's not the only one watching her, she sneaks a glance at Ëólas, who immediately looks away and speaks with Seira.

Everyone thinks I'm a danger. Her eyebrows droop. "Trust is hard to gain here, huh?"

Magnus looks at the dining room, at its divided people. "Indeed."

"I suppose everyone's cautious of who might be a dog or a tortoise."

Magnus cocks his head. "I don't follow," he says, taking a big sip of wine.

"Oh, it's a Nigerian folktale." She waves him off, but Magnus waits for her to continue. "I'm not sure how well I remember it."

"I wouldn't know the difference." The corner of his mouth twitches upward into a challenge.

Adaline takes a gulp of wine, sets down her cup, and leans back in her seat. *Stories. I can always tell stories.* "Okay. Let's see. Once upon a time—Oh, back home, many folktales start with that phrase."

Magnus smiles widely. "We say 'in days of old.' And the elves start their stories with 'when the world was still new.'"

Different but similar. "I love that."

She takes another sip of wine and wets her lips before she begins. "Once upon a time, in days of old and when the world was still new, Mr. Tortoise, Mr. Dog, Mrs. Cat, and Mr. Rabbit all lived together on a farm. One night, Mr. Tortoise woke up and saw Mr. Dog sneak away. Because Mr. Tortoise was curious, he followed Mr. Dog and heard him say into the night air, 'Rope. Rope. Let me up. I'm hungry.' Magically, a rope appeared, and Mr. Dog climbed up. When he came back, he had food in his mouth, which he hungrily ate."

Magnus puts down his spoon and knife and shifts in his seat, propping an elbow on the table so he can better face Adaline. The patience and curiosity on his face encourage her to speak up. Just like her father, she keeps her tone even and unassuming as she continues.

"The next day, Mr. Tortoise said, 'Mr. Dog, I saw you get extra food last night. Will you show me how you did that?' Mr. Dog said he would, and, sure enough, when night came, Mr. Dog led Mr. Tortoise to the same spot. Once again, Mr. Tortoise watched Mr. Dog say into the night air, 'Rope. Rope. Let me up. I'm hungry.' Once again, the magic happened, and the rope appeared. Mr. Dog climbed up, and he told Mr. Tortoise to follow. As Mr. Tortoise was climbing up, Mr. Dog cut the rope."

"Humph," Magnus says, his eyebrows springing up.

Without revealing her thoughts about the story, Adaline picks up a slice of pie and takes a small bite, giving Magnus a moment longer to think about Mr. Dog's actions. Brushing the crumbs off her fingers, she clears her throat quietly. "Mr. Tortoise fell onto his back, shattering his shell. Mrs. Cat and Mr. Rabbit put Mr. Tortoise back together again, but from that day forward, Mr. Tortoise always had cracks on his shell, reminding him of what happened."

Magnus scratches the short, soft hairs covering his chin while Adaline takes a larger bite of pie, puts the rest down, and uses the napkin on her lap to wipe away the crumbs at the corner of her mouth.

After a long pause, he finally asks, "Who do you think was wrong? Mr. Dog for his actions, or Mr. Tortoise for his assumptions?"

Adaline shrugs. "I asked my father the same thing the first time he told me that story." They spent the last hour of every night reading, from her father sitting on the edge of her bed during her childhood to the both of them lounging on the sofa past midnight. Throughout her entire life, whenever she asked her father for advice, he'd simply tell her another story.

Magnus stops stroking his beard and leans forward. "And what did your father say?"

"That's for you to decide."

He smirks. "And what did you decide?"

"Me?" She exhales deeply but meets Magnus's stare. "That I should choose my friends based on their actions and not their words."

He narrows his blue eyes. As he leans back, he slowly nods his head as a broad smile fills his face. Crossing his arms in front of his chest, Magnus looks at Ëólas, who apparently had been listening to Adaline's every word, as well as the rest of the guests. Suddenly, her corset feels tighter.

She stares at her plate, at the juices of different foods pooling into the center, but from the corner of her eye, she watches Ëólas and Magnus stare at each other, Magnus with his grin, Ëólas with a suppressed smirk until he rolls his eyes and chuckles. With an arched eyebrow, Ëólas raises his glass to Magnus, who reciprocates, and turns to the rest of the nobles, who have given Magnus and Ëólas their full attention.

Ëólas smiles effortlessly as he projects his voice. "A toast to everyone here, whose actions prove every day our dedication to see this city succeed."

Magnus adds, "A success that we will continue to safeguard."

This time, Seira joins in the toast too.

So, Magnus and Ëólas are friends.

Even though Adaline doesn't know why, the sight of them mocking each other with whatever inside joke they share coats her chest with warmth. She sends a silent prayer up to her father, thanking him for telling her that story, and smiles to herself—until she glances up. Dozens of eyes stare at her, especially the human noblewomen. When Magnus pats her arm in gratitude, the ladies' glares and the occasional curled lip resemble her classmates after her first year of ballet, when her teacher kept complimenting her positions while needling the other students for their errors. She didn't have many friends then either.

Adaline shifts in her seat, the corset locking her waist and ribs in place and forbidding her from sitting comfortably. If only she could toss on her jeans and an oversized, light knit sweater, but Mercia's thumbs up allows Adaline to exhale a little.

She's never had to be on stage for so long. *How long do these dinners last?*

While Magnus and Ëólas chat with each other, Adaline pulls her shoulders back and finishes her pie in silence. One by one, the ladies turn their heads away from her, thanks to Seira drawing their attention with a magnetic force. Seira stares them down, tilts her head, and raises her chin. Not once does she blink. Even though her small face remains emotionless, she stares at them as if she were cursing their entire family for generations to come. One by one, ladies' glares quiver and shatter. They lower their eyes to their plates.

Adaline blinks. A lot. She waits for any of the ladies to look at her again. But none do. She turns toward Seira, who laughs at something Ëólas said.

Wait, Ëólas can make people laugh?

"Adaline." Magnus pushes away his plate, which a servant immediately collects.

At hearing her own name, she jumps.

Magnus cocks an eyebrow. "Are you alright?"

"Yep. I'm fine. Totally fine." *Everything's normal here. Completely normal.*

"Good. I do hope you enjoyed your first day in the Neutral Territory."

As she recalls Sallie and Jósep, the dining hall and audience fade into nonexistence. She straightens her back, and the lively lilt in her voice reveals her preference. "The city is amazing, Magnus. Truly."

"I'm glad you think so." His voice softens at her approval, but one disapproving look from Ëólas turns Magnus's next words into steel. "But the next time you venture into the city without first seeking permission, make sure you do not venture beyond Front and Market Street."

What the fuck? Adaline parts her lips, ready to unleash the words screaming in her mind, ready to remind them that they left her to her own devices today, ready to call them out for not assigning her a guide of some fucking sort. Spinning sideways in her chair, she ignores the corset trying to hold her back and faces Magnus head on. "Why the hell are you now—"

"Neir Nía," Seira calls so loudly that Magnus's expression shifts from fury to confusion.

Both he and Ëólas search the room for whomever Seira's referring to. When they realize she's focused on Adaline, Magnus rounds his lips into a question, and Ëólas locks his own deadly gaze onto the woman who invaded his world. Adaline yelps internally.

Seira smacks the back of Ëólas's hand, making him jerk backward and look at Seira as if she has turned into another person altogether. She shakes her head at him. "No, no, Ëólas. That won't do." Again, with her eyes settled on Adaline, Seira lowers her voice to a half whisper. "Unkindness leads to danger."

Adaline glances back and forth between the two men, males, guys, whatever, who hold her life in their hands. With Magnus and Ëólas studying her more cautiously, she shakes her head fervently. "No, I would never hurt anyone."

Her voice is too loud. Within seconds, Thoren stalks toward the table. He halts mid-step only because Magnus raises his hand and waits for Seira to speak again.

"Haven't you already, Neir Nía?" Seira lifts her gaze toward the ceiling as if the answer were floating above her. "If not, then you will." She shrugs her shoulders as if she just reported tomorrow's weather.

Silence fills the dining hall, but Adaline can't turn toward the guests. She can't face them. These three in front of her, they're the ones who matter.

"I, I..." Adaline tucks a few strands of hair behind her ear, as if doing so will reboot her mind. But Ëólas's hatred and Magnus's distrust blur her vision. "I can't stand anyone getting hurt. Really. I couldn't even hurt the carpenter bees that occasionally got stuck in our home. I would catch them in a cup and release them outside." Kindness. Nan always talked about kindness.

Seira rests her elbows on the table and leans forward. "What about spiders?"

Both Magnus and Ëólas exhale. Thoren rolls his eyes and trudges back to his wife, and the rest of the tables resume their chatter. But Seira doesn't look away from Adaline. She smiles as she waits for the results of whatever test she's initiated, and neither Ëólas nor Magnus dare to interrupt her.

Adaline parts her lips to protest but snaps her mouth shut again. Then she huffs loudly. "Okay, fine. I don't show spiders mercy." She wrinkles her nose and shudders. "But only when they invade my territory! When I'm on their turf, I leave them alone."

Seira grins, and her eyes glow dark purple. "Exactly."

Chapter Ten

THE ELVEN TAVERN

When dinner ends, Kayla escorts Adaline back to her chamber, and the nighttime routine mirrors yesterday's. Lying in bed, Adaline stares at the ceiling, unsure if it's past midnight or nearly dawn. She tosses and turns, fluffs her pillow ten times, and grunts at the ceiling. Swinging her feet onto the floor, she retrieves her field journal from her messenger bag and slumps down onto the sofa. Her pencil flies across pages as she sketches Sallie's candles, Jósep's carving tools, the hem of the wine-soaked tablecloth, and tonight's dinnerware. Adaline grimaces.

Please, don't let formal dinners be a regular occurrence here.

Snapping her journal shut, she spins around on the sofa and climbs onto her knees to peer out the window. The cool ledge sends a chill through her body as she rests her arms across the white stone. In the far distance, lamps flicker below, and dots of shadow come and go through the streets, especially throughout the elven side of the city. The night wind carries the sound of laughter. Laughter that originates from far beyond Front and Market Street. Laughter that draws her attention to the faint outline of the palace ruins illuminated by the moonlight. Laughter that taunts her to get the hell out of this castle, away from women like Lady Marzella, away from Ëólas's judgmental stare, away from Magnus's shallow promises, away from Seira's...

She clasps her hands together and closes her eyes. Absentmindedly, she rubs her chest. Something about Seira, about the energy that hovers around her—a mix of instability and inherent comfort—makes Adaline contemplate going back to bed.

But a bellow of robust nightlife cheer bursts her thoughts.

She hurries to the wardrobe and yanks Mercia's skirt over her undergarments. After shimmying the bodice over her head, she reaches behind for whichever laces she can reach and pulls as tightly as possible. The dress may still hang loosely around her torso, but it feels more comfortable, more familiar, without the bone-lined corset. She ignores the detached dress sleeves, certain the undergarment's long linen sleeves will keep her warm enough. When she pulls on her socks and boots, her feet wiggle and rejoice at the arch support. Last, she throws open her messenger bag and stuffs her pants and shirt inside. Forget the snood. With her bag draped across her body, she swings the pouch behind her.

Mentally, she apologizes to Mercia for taking her dress, but Adaline has a better chance of not drawing attention in these clothes. Once more she looks out the window, at the ruins glowing like a beacon. Surely she can handle herself. She's done solo field work before.

Once again, leaving the castle proves easy enough. The guards don't question her, so she marches onward, down the same path as that morning. With each step, her heart grows lighter and beats faster. Several blocks past the main Venetian-esque bridge, music and merriment burst into the night air, drawing her eyes to the elven side of the city.

"Keep moving forward," she whispers to herself. *An elven garden doesn't matter right now.*

But her feet turn sideways and pull her toward the music. The soft tune of the strings and wind instruments lull her to them, back to Market Street, only much further down than she had ventured earlier today. As she gets closer, the melody becomes clearer, louder. The water rushing downstream fades into a murmur along with all other sounds that inhabit the city. When she stops at an intersection, she searches for a park, but the music pours out of a well-lit building.

She looks back toward the ruins, now concealed by the shops and homes around her, and wanders up to a window. Sitting on wooden stools at the back of the room, a flutist, harpist, and piper finish their song. The elves applaud loudly and pass around metal pitchers while talking to each other and urging someone else up onto the small stage to share a story or song.

A guitarist takes to the stage, along with a lady. They bow and begin their song, a livelier tune that encourages most of the elves to abandon the tables along the perimeter of the tavern. People converge in the center where they dance in circles, flowing from one partner to the next as they spin around each other, occasionally with one foot up in a pirouette.

Adaline presses her face closer to the window. A massive grin inflates her cheeks, and she bounces on her toes in tune with the music.

"My lady?"

The male voice behind her causes Adaline to jump. As she spins around, she knocks over a stack of empty crates that tumble beside her and discovers Jósep, the stone carver, without his work smock covering his green and tan clothing now absent of chalky dust.

"I'm terribly sorry, my lady. I didn't mean to frighten you. But ought you not be inside the castle at this hour?"

She bites her lip and blurts out, "I'm leaving."

Jósep's eyes widen. "Oh." He breaks eye contact, and his shoulders slump downward. "Why, my lady?"

"Because I, I need to go home." Her voice is quiet. As the silence grows between them, she glances over her shoulder at the people dancing, and her heartbeat aligns with the rhythm of the music.

Jósep offers her a small smile, his soft features so unlike the hard stone awaiting his touch. "Do you know the way?"

She turns her back on the tavern's fun. "No. Maybe."

"I see. Well, before you leave us, why don't you join me inside?"

Adaline's throat squeals, but she bites down on her lips to stop her grin from returning. "May I really?"

Jósep walks over to the door, pulls it open, and waits for her. "Yes, my lady."

That's a bad idea. A really bad idea. But Adaline hurries inside.

At the sight of her, people near the door pause mid-sentence or mid-drink, but once Jósep declares her a guest, the elves turn around and resume their evening entertainment. The interior of the tavern has several tall windows open at the back of the building, allowing the night air to swoop in, circulate around everyone, and carry the echoes of their laughter into the world. The dim lights, natural wood décor, and lack of sticky surfaces make this tavern perfect for not only socializing but also curling up in a corner to read a good book.

Taking a deep breath, Adaline follows Jósep to a table in the back corner and tucks her bag underneath against the wall. He orders them food, insisting she need not worry about money here, and as she takes her first bite of a berry tart that she wishes she could save the recipe for, a bard jogs onto the stage and tells a story about a doe who watched the first elves enter Lameiría's forest. The nostalgia he crafts pulls the few lingering eyes away from Adaline. For his second song, he tells everyone about a bird who kept flying into the wrong nest, and his absurd lyrics fill the tavern with laughter.

After a few more songs and a few more drinks, Jósep's friends come over to say hello and fill out their table. When the tavern grows quieter in between sets, Adaline listens to Jósep and his friends discuss their craftsmanship and plans for growth, as well as the mischief they sought during their youth in Lameiría. Apparently, Jósep streaked at the summer moon festival—more than once, from what Adaline gathers.

While his friends retell the tale, Jósep stares down the well of his goblet, until the young lady with russet wavy hair asks him to dance. With a bouncy nod of his head, he scurries off the bench, but before he follows her onto the dance floor, he glances back at Adaline. He then turns back to his pretty elven savior and asks if she might return tomorrow night.

Oh, no. "Don't give up this opportunity because of me." Adaline pushes his arm. "I'll be here when you get back, Jósep. Go dance."

"Why don't you join us?" His eyes have a wine-induced twinkle that makes Adaline chuckle.

Still, she shakes her head. "I don't think I have nerves strong enough yet. Dance for me."

Jósep nods once but firmly. When the two flirts merge with the other dancers, Jósep's friends resume their debate about raw materials and the challenges of mining the underground quarry. Adaline tunes them out and listens to the music, her feet tapping to the rhythm that makes the floorboards vibrate beneath her. Alone with her thoughts, she watches this community, how they pat each other's shoulders, how one smile begets two more, how they sing and dance fearlessly and cheer each other on.

Interrupting Adaline's observations, the barmaid leans over and places a goblet down where Jósep had been sitting. With him dancing, Adaline pulls the cup closer and takes a peek. Instead of wine, his cup contains an amber-like liquid. She sniffs hints of cedar. No, eucalyptus? Maybe even cherry. All fairytales warn to never eat their food. But these are elves. With a shrug, she takes a sip. The moment the thick, velvety liquor wets her lips, her eyes sparkle. As she tilts the cup further upward, she searches the crowd for the server to ask for more.

A cool wind brushes against her cheeks that glow like hot coals, and her body sways with the music. She hiccups twice. Her feet tap faster, livelier, beneath the table, matching the choreography she's memorized from watching Jósep. Her legs bump the table as her lower half dances, so she spins around, hops off the stool, and flings herself into the fray, into the dancing, into the spinning. The whole tavern spins too as the dancers twirl past each other, a blur of faces, arms, and locks of hair flying freely.

Every inch of her body embraces the music like a long-lost friend. She extends and stretches her arms, lifts her chin, closes her rib cage, and rotates her body from pliés into chaîné turns over and over again as if she had returned to her contemporary dance classes where every bottled-up emotion tossed itself over the edge of the world.

With an unbridled grin, Adaline spins herself toward her next partner, but the arm that loops around hers tugs her off the dance floor. That same arm leads her toward the tavern door. When they stop walking, the room continues to spin, forcing Adaline to fix her gaze onto her new dance partner's torso and pecs.

How hard does one have to work to get such bumpy pecs?

As Adaline's head falls backward, she follows the bumpy torso to a long neck that supports Merith's face. His dark-silver eyes stare down at her.

"Merith!" Adaline laughs over the cheers and singing and points behind her. "The dancing's that way!"

"What are you doing here?" He opens and closes his mouth a few times until his brain seems to catch up with his voice. "I thought you retired after dinner?"

"You know what you need? A cool pair of sunglasses and a long trench coat. Do you have trench coats here? You could totally rock *The Matrix* look."

The intensity of his gaze makes Adaline's eyelids droopy, so she waves him away and skips back to the dance floor. At least her feet are moving, but she's still in the same place. She's become a cartoon character walking on ice and not getting anywhere. Turning back to Merith, she drops her head onto her shoulder and studies him. Only the room also turns on its side, which makes her giggle.

With exasperation laced through every word, Merith asks the crowd, "Who allowed her to drink spirits?"

Adaline gasps. "I drank ghosts?"

A laugh bursts open his pursed lips, but he shields his mouth with his large hand. "Wrong spirits, my lady."

"Whew."

From between two circles of dancers, Jósep peels himself away and hastens over to Adaline and the tall, dark tower beside her. He halts in front of Merith and lowers his head.

"Good evening, my lord. Surely, the lady hasn't—" Jósep glances at Adaline and inhales sharply. His eyebrows gather together, and his mouth turns downward. "My apologies, my lord. I was not aware. Does she not know—"

"No, she doesn't. You let her in here?"

Jósep looks down at his feet. "The lady needed friendly company, my lord."

Squeezing his eyes shut for a moment, Merith sighs heavily. "Clarify."

The elves continue speaking—at least, their lips move, but Adaline can't hear a single word of what they say. She squints to see through the haze that hovers around their faces and leans in closer, which causes them both to pause and take two steps away from her, although Merith hasn't yet released her arm. At one point, Merith presses his lips together in a small grimace and rubs his brow as if to dispel a headache, all while keeping Adaline firmly in place with one hand wrapped around her arm. Time passes, and no sound escapes their moving lips.

"Fine." Merith's sudden statement makes Adaline stagger backward and Jósep smile. "She's already here, and now might not be the best time to return her to the castle. How much spirit did you drink, my lady?"

Adaline pinches her thumb and pointer finger together, indicating less than an inch.

Merith sighs. "Thank the fae. No more tree spirits, my lady. Our liquor isn't made for humans. Let's get you water. And bread. A lot of bread."

Adaline winks and tugs him over to their table. Four glasses of water and three baguettes later, her stomach cannot hold another crumb. She still can't erase the smile from her face even though her cheeks now ache. Her grin widens when Merith gets up and tells a story about an elf who, in a drunken stupor, broke fae law and woke up the next morning sprouting a stag's horns.

While Adaline laughs wildly, Merith calls for a volunteer to sing next. Only when he pats her shoulder and pulls her up to standing does Adaline realize she had raised her hand as high as she could stretch upward. With all eyes on her, she forces her brain cells to reconnect so she can place one foot in front of the other and step up onto the stage with only one wobble. Maybe two. With her back to the crowd, she takes a deep breath. The musicians wait for her cue.

A memory of her father teaching her the guitar pops into her head, his massive hands placing her tiny fingers on the right chords. Years later, she taught him the first song she wrote. She can do this now, in a tavern full of elves. She cracks her neck and walks over to the elf playing an instrument similar to a guitar. He offers her the instrument, and she strums a few breezy, uplifting, fast chords, starting with a D major. The elf smiles and repeats them, and Adaline nods. When she turns to the crowd, most of the faces leaning forward reveal a spark of curiosity in the corners of their eyes.

She takes a deeper breath, mentally praises the tree spirits, and claps her hands to establish the beat. Merith joins in, followed by Jósep, and she cues the musician. She takes in the peppy melody, letting the rhythm fill her to the brim so she has no room to think. Tossing her cares over the edge of the world, she sings. She sings for herself. And she sings for her dad.

When the music plays,
don't think about your day.
Just let your body sway,
and sing eh oh eh!

Let's show what we can do
when it's just me and you.
We'll get the world singing too.
That's right, eh oh eh!

Because life is better when we're dancing,
and life is better when we're singing,
Eh oh eh! Eh oh eh! Eh oh eh!

The elves' stares and murmurs evolve into head nodding and grins, not that Adaline fully registers the shift in their demeanor. Her arms, legs, and feet that became looser and lighter as the night progressed have her floating on that stage.

By the third verse, the tavern echoes with a chorus of *Eh oh eh*, their joy like rays of light breaking through the clouds that have been accumulating since the day the police called, since they found her father's car in the river. For the first time since Nan's funeral, she can feel in her bones that life can still gift her wondrous surprises.

There's nothing we can't weather
when we come together.
This life is a treasure,
so sing eh oh eh!

Come follow my lead.
Our passions will exceed
as we plant the seed
to sing eh oh eh!

Because life is better when we're dancing,
and life is better when we're singing,
Eh oh eh! Eh oh eh! Eh oh eh!

When she finishes the song, the crowd's applause and awe make her cheeks glow brighter. Merith's and Jósep's vigorous clapping and proud smiles make her eyes turn glossy. She had been wrong these past two years: The music within her didn't die the day her father did.

As she skips off the stage, a few elves ask if she'll be back tomorrow. She smiles politely but hurries past, before she can identify the different feelings swirling in the pit of her stomach at the thought of being here another night. Pushing those emotions down, she dances to the side of the room and leans against the wall so her stomach can settle. She should have had more baguettes. Without music to guide her, her brain feels fuzzy, and her body isn't sure whether to dance or collapse in a heap.

Still clapping loudly in approval, Merith strolls over. "I've never heard a song quite like that before. It was brilliant."

The corners of Adaline's mouth turn upward, until Merith's smile vanishes.

He knits his brows together, forcing all frivolity to leave his face. "We should go."

Adaline tilts forward and cranes her neck to see what he's looking at, but the ground rushes up to meet her. Thankfully, his arms steady her, and she floats beside him, out of the tavern. When they cross the threshold, the fresh air hits her face, along with Ëólas's stiff posture, square shoulders, and rigid expression. She inhales so sharply that she sways backward. Ëólas catches her arm this time, keeping her upright. His grip is as sturdy as a building, and when he releases her, Adaline pokes his bicep to test that theory.

Whoa. Solid steel.

Ëólas glares at Merith. "You encouraged this? Including the spirits?"

Merith puffs his chest outward and mirrors Ëólas's stern tone. "That was an accident. The lady wasn't aware of the potency of our liquor."

Leaning forward, but not so much that she'd fall over, Adaline waves her hand in front of Ëólas's face to get his attention. "That was the best drink of my life."

Ëólas keeps his words crisp. Short. Non-negotiable. "The evening is through."

Meh. There's always room for negotiation. "I think you're wrong. We're having fun. You should come on inside. It's your turn to sing." She tries to tug him inside. He doesn't budge, but she doesn't stop trying.

Is all of him made of stone? She studies his feet. They look normal. *Why's Merith trying to hide his laugh?*

Ëólas peels her fingers off his silky soft tunic. "It's nearly daybreak. It's best we return you to your chambers before the other ladies notice your absence. Merith, send word for her maid to meet her in her quarters. I'll escort her myself so no one assumes anything untoward."

She pouts as she studies Ëólas, from his dark gold hair to his sculpted torso to his athletic legs. As her eyes linger southward, his cock twitches beneath his tight trousers, and she licks her lips. "Why won't anyone think anything *untoward*?" Peering up at him, she repeats that last word mockingly. "Elves and humans don't—"

"No." He won't look at her.

Her shoulders curl inward. She spins around two times to find Merith, to walk with him instead, but the third time she faces forward, Merith's sprinting ahead, taking all the fun with him. And her bag.

When did he retrieve my messenger bag?

As she stumbles along, she keeps her eyes down so she doesn't have to witness Ëólas recoil again, no matter how much he tries to contain his reactions.

Thank you, tree spirits, for not leaving me alone with him.

As the colors in the sky fade from black to crimson, Adaline's impressed her limbs can feel both loosey-goosey and heavier at the same time. With each step, her brain feels foggier and her eyelids heavier. The moss and vines along the homes would make a rather soft mattress. She yawns loudly and drifts toward nature's bed, but Ëólas uses her elbow like a joystick and steers her back toward the castle. She scrunches her nose at him. He ignores her and keeps walking.

How can someone with such warm eyes be so cold?

She wipes her hand over her face to rub away all emotions. If she has to walk next to an emotionless statue, then she can be one too. But she can't forget the look of disgust that flashed across his face when she asked about elves and humans, and her stoicism crumbles. The species here are so thoroughly divided.

Aside from some unusual eye colors and the shape of their ears, everything else about elves and humans appears to be similar. She looks Ëólas up and down again, his lean arms, his thick thighs flexing under his trousers, his Adam's apple defining his neck, his angelic features, and the hint of a large package hidden beneath his long shirt and coat. Yep, he's definitely all male. Granted, she can't verify what exactly is under his trousers—not that she wants to.

He's probably one of those guys who doesn't even realize he's attractive, in an annoyingly charming and cliché way. Or he knows he's gorgeous and thinks he's above everyone else. Yep, has to be the second case, given that icy glare he's perfected. Anyone who can lift their chin while looking down at people has a superiority complex. And Adaline's not one to tolerate men, or elves, like him.

Nope. Nada. Never.

For the hundredth time, she glances at Ëólas's placid face and stumbles over her feet. He flicks his eyes up to the heavens but makes sure she's steady before they resume walking—the never-ending walk that's taking years off her life to climb uphill.

"Your feet are dragging." He points at her dusty shoes. "You wore your boots? Did you stuff your clothes in that bag of yours too?"

Adaline can feel him stoking her inner fire, so she imagines dumping a bucket of water over her head to smother the flames. *Just ignore him.*

But he can't take a hint. "What were you think—"

She stops short and puts her finger on his mouth to silence him. The shock of her actions works. He's frozen solid with her finger smushing his full lips shut. "No. You're not allowed to judge me. I'm not the party pooper."

He parts his lips, then pauses. Wrapping his hand around hers, he draws her finger away from his mouth. For a moment, his expression reveals an inkling of amusement. "A party pooper?"

She shakes off his hand and tucks her finger into her fist. "Yes, a party pooper. I was having fun, the most fun I've had since I got here. And you took that away with that sour puss of yours."

Looking to the stars, he says, "May the queen of the fae grant me patience."

"The queen of the fae?" Adaline says far louder than she intended. With wide eyes, she almost swings into his chest, and he holds both her arms to keep her standing. *He's such a solid wall. Quite convenient. And warm. Why's he so warm?* "Is she real?"

"Yes."

"Do you know her?" she whispers with awe.

Éólas releases a loud exhale. "No."

"Oh. Where is she?" Adaline pouts.

"In the Immortal Realms."

Éólas nudges her to turn around and walk, but that only makes Adaline sway sideways, forcing him to use his hand to brace her waist and keep her upright. She places her hands on her abdomen to stop the sudden tingly sensation swelling down there.

Something he said was important.

Looking into his eyes, she imagines drawing information out of those golden orbs. Instead, they pull her in, and she sways again.

Stop, Adaline. Think, think, think. The fluttering in my gut is telling me something.

She leans closer to him until her nose bumps his chin. "Realm. As in another world?" *Ha! Go brain!*

"Yes." Ëólas backs up, his cheeks turning pink.

She made him blush. Adaline giggles. *So many discoveries today.*

"Do you know how to get there?" She leans in closer, resting her hands on his chest to keep herself upright, grounded, focused. He can't look away from her. He can't dodge her question. She won't let him. She tilts her face upward, and the pink dusting his cheeks deepens into red. *He must be warm too.* The night certainly did get warmer. So much warmer. Her whole body tingles now. "Do you know—" What was she asking?

"No, I don't know. No one knows how to get to the Immortal Realms."

He spins her around and pushes her forward, and her mood deflates as the cold air hits her face.

"Enough of this. Off to bed with you. Now."

"Bed?" she asks. "Which bed?"

Ëólas stiffens.

Oh right, the guest room I'm staying in. Her bedroom is in another world. But not the Immortal Realms.

"By the fae!" Ëólas pulls her left and right and up a flight of stairs, her own personal puppeteer. "You're the tortoise, you know."

Adaline's laugh echoes down the corridor until her voice vanishes. *He listened to my story.* She lifts her chin higher and swings her arms forward as she attempts a march. "I'd rather be a naïve tortoise than a cynical dog."

"I'm not—"

"I didn't say you were."

"Yes, well, be glad no one else can see you right n—"

Adaline attempts to silence his mouth with her whole hand, but he catches her wrist this time, and she frowns. "Stop. I demand you be chivalrous." *Like the way you are with Seira, the way you make certain she's okay.* "I know you're capable of being nice. Show that version of yourself. Now."

He arches an eyebrow. "You demand? You're lucky you—"

Adaline nods, and the whole castle nods with her, shifting the ground beneath her feet. When the room stops spinning, her gut doesn't, and the spirits turn her stomach into a bubbling cauldron. A bead of sweat rolls down her temple. She rests her forearm against Ëólas's upper arm and takes several slow, deep breaths. Lavender. She smells lavender. Her head is so heavy. Too heavy. Thoughts hurt now. Words hurt too. There's not enough room inside her brain, inside her chest. What's this feeling?

Ëólas searches her face until she's able to look at and focus on him. "Can you stand on your feet?"

Adaline narrows her eyes. "I am on my feet."

"No, you're on my feet."

She glances down and laughs loudly. "It's like learning to dance."

We could start waltzing here in the hallway.

"We're ballroom dancing, Ëólas!" Her face relaxes with the memory of helping couples learn to dance before their wedding day. "I used to teach dancing."

She tugs his arms down the hall with a one, two, three, but he refuses to follow her lead. Slipping an arm around her waist, he rests his palm on the small of her back to push her forward while she drapes her arm over his shoulder.

He's comfortable to hang on. But only in the silence.

He guides her to her door and extricates himself, taking several steps back.

A chill sweeps through the hallway, and the tree spirits make her lips move. "I wish you didn't hate me."

His features soften, making him far more handsome than he has a right to be. Like the night they met, he takes a confident step forward, only to pause, reset his chiseled indifference, and stow his arms behind his back. "I don't hate you, Adaline. I don't know you. And I don't trust you. You're an impossibility. A problem."

Her face turns green, the spirits sloshing around in her stomach and threatening to come up. "And you're an asshole!" She storms into her room so she can scream into a pillow and pass out.

CHAPTER ELEVEN

BOUNDARIES

Light invades the room despite Adaline's efforts to conceal her face with her pillow. She groans once, rolls over, and shadows soothe her again. A lithe, lyrical chuckle announces someone in her room. Adaline's eyes flutter open, and she uses her hands to push herself to sit up, which isn't easy with her limbs heavy as steel. Last night's liquor burns her stomach, making her grimace. From the foot of her bed, a pair of lavender eyes look down at her.

"Good morning," Adaline moans. Despite all her years of university and graduate school, this is by far the worst hangover. Actually, it's her first hangover. And there's no greasy bacon to take off the edge.

Seira prances to the corner table, loads a plate with food, and returns to Adaline, spinning like a ballerina at least twice on her way back without dropping a single item from the plate. With dainty hands, she passes her offering to Adaline, who accepts the assortment and lets it plop onto her lap.

Adaline rubs the blur from her eyes and studies the selection.

"Eat this first." Seira points to slices of meat cut so thinly that Adaline can see through them.

Too tired to argue, Adaline picks up a long slice, rotates it once to verify it's cooked, and drops the slice into her mouth where it folds like a ribbon on her tongue. The burst of flavor pops her eyes open. As the juice coats her throat and stomach, she groans contentedly and stuffs more in her mouth, torn between eating as many as possible and savoring each bite.

With a content grin, Seira climbs onto the bed and sits beside Adaline, snatching strawberries off the plate. A few moments later, Mercia comes in and sits on the edge of the bed as well. Seira passes her a strawberry.

"Care to join us in the ladies' parlor this morning?" Mercia nibbles the berry to hide her smirk.

Adaline drags her hands down her cheeks. "You're better off without me. I have no idea how to stitch."

Mercia jerks her head backward. Her movements freeze as she searches for the right words. After a few minutes, she brushes the wrinkles out of Adaline's comforter and chooses not to comment.

Seira pokes Adaline's arm. "I'll teach you." Without another word, she scampers off the bed, flits over to the sofa, and picks up fabric too pale and shimmery to belong to the seamstress—fabric that hadn't been there yesterday. Humming a tune oddly similar to "Over the Rainbow" and causing Adaline to do a double take, Seira threads a needle, oblivious to Adaline and Mercia watching her and the sunlight behind her that illuminates the crown of her head. Adaline half expects to see Glinda emerge and finish the dress for Seira.

With a loud grunt, Adaline climbs out of bed while bracing her stomach that, thanks to the meat and bread, doesn't do any more somersaults. When the area rug hugs her toes, Kayla enters, helps Adaline shimmy into Mercia's burgundy dress, and carries away the empty food trays. Afterward, the three ladies spend the rest of the late morning gathered around the table, with neither Mercia nor Adaline wishing to crowd Seira alone on the sofa. Ignoring the sewing basket Mercia placed between them, Adaline listens to the ladies' stories about the comings and goings of the castle, along with indirect updates from Thoren himself.

"They found the third assailant," Mercia whispers, having left her own sewing untouched. "They brought him to the dungeons late last night."

Wait, wait, wait. The killer was still on the loose while I explored the city, thought to run away, and spent the evening at the tavern far down Market Street?

Is that what kept Magnus and Ëólas busy yesterday? And Ëólas had been rather pissed off when he found Adaline at the tavern, but he still insisted on walking her back to her room. To keep her safe? And she threw his cloak in his face earlier that day too. Adaline puffs up her cheeks and releases the air like a deflating balloon.

Seira rests her hands in her lap and tilts her chin up, her eyes having that faraway look. "He's already dead. I think."

"Dead?" Adaline glances from Seira to Mercia.

"I'm not surprised. Father has said more than once that King Magnus won't allow anyone to threaten his reconciliation efforts."

Hadn't Ëólas described the history between humans and elves as sordid? "You mean between elves and humans, or between Alderton and Lameiría?"

"Well," Mercia leans back in her chair and sticks her legs out in front, crossing her feet at the ankles, "the former should lead to the latter. At least, that's what King Magnus and Lord Ëólas hope."

Tapping her fingers on the table, Adaline bites her bottom lip and debates waiting for more details or rushing forward with questions. "Why do elves and humans have so much—"

"Animosity?" Mercia asks.

Outside, a cloud blocks the sunlight and snuffs out Seira's halo while another shadow passes over her face too. Adaline holds her breath.

Tilting her head to the side, Seira's face droops like a weeping willow, and her voice sounds hollow, like a whisper from a ghost. "The war that left Aerytol in ruins."

Sitting upright, Mercia clasps her hands together in an act of contrition.

Adaline traps further questions inside. The sight of Seira's eyes misting over like a wave ready to crash against the shore lifts Adaline from her seat. She pats Mercia's shoulder as she passes by and sits on the sofa next to Seira. Picking up an extra needle already threaded, Adaline pulls a layer of the sheer periwinkle fabric over her knees too. "So, how do I not mess up your perfection?"

Nan always said that, above all else, the world needs more kindness. She also said asking questions isn't enough; one also needs to seek understanding.

As Adaline follows Seira's instructions, an increasing sense of guilt makes her hands shakier over time and the length of her stitches uneven. When she tells her friends she needs to find Magnus and Ëólas, they don't ask questions. Mercia merely agrees she ought to find her mother by now and leaves with a friendly smile while Seira collects her items.

Adaline discretely goes to the wardrobe, pockets her mobile and Swiss army knife, and stares at the empty hanger that used to hold the sage-green cloak. Without the extra layer around her shoulders, she feels paper thin, as if everyone will see through her today. She releases a heavy sigh.

"Neir Nía." Seira, appearing silently behind Adaline, makes her jump back and bump the doors to the wardrobe shut. "Here, I thought you might need a new one." Lifting her arms, Seira holds up a light-bluish-periwinkle cloak made of a silky satin. Along the decorative hem, a woven vine links beaded purple flowers like the ones Adaline saw climbing the buildings as she walked into the city.

Adaline reaches toward the soft material, then retracts her hand. "I can't possibly."

"You can, and you will." Seira wraps her fingers around Adaline's wrist and pulls her to turn around.

While Seira drapes the cloak over her shoulders, Adaline nibbles her lip, wondering if Seira overheard Adaline shouting at Ëólas yesterday—the first time. Of course, he could have told Seira what happened. But based on his reaction at discovering Adaline in the elven side of the castle, she can't imagine a scenario in which he would have suggested that Seira visit the human side, let alone offer Adaline a new cloak, and an elven one at that. But she doesn't have enough evidence to judge Ëólas fairly. After all, she forgot a killer was on the loose.

"Lovely. It suits you perfectly." Seira smiles from cheek to cheek as she looks at Adaline. "If only you'd let your curls down. Oh, wait." She dances to her sewing basket and returns with a beaded purple flower that she wraps around the headband portion of Adaline's snood, just above her ear. "Now they match, Neir Nía."

Adaline cocks her head to the side and quietly repeats to herself *near nee-uh*. Seira had called her that yesterday too. Rather than risking another question that might upset Seira, Adaline squeezes her friend's hand as they part and heads toward the king's study. The decreased number of guards and the silence within tells her she's missed them.

When she asks the guards where they might be, not a single one speaks.

"You guys are so helpful."

The doors open, and out steps an elf who immediately turns his back to Adaline as he closes the study doors without crushing the stack of rolled-up scrolls he cradles. His long hair, tucked behind each leaf-shaped ear, shimmers like black ice and reflects the corridor's candlelight. The wispy tips of his hair pat the small of his back as he shuts the doors to the study and faces Adaline. His dark hair contrasts with his pale skin, just like Merith, only in reverse. But when this elf settles his soft gray eyes on Adaline, his round facial features make him less like another yin and yang symbol and more like a cuddly panda.

"My lady," he says. "If you're looking for the king, he and my lord are tending to other matters at the moment."

Executing people? "I see." Adaline looks down and closes her eyes for a moment to allow her frustration to drain away.

"But your arrival at this moment is fortuitous. His Highness tasked me with relaying a message to you. Please return here in the early afternoon to meet with my lord and the king."

"Oh!" Adaline perks up but remembers Ëólas's displeasure at catching her running away last night. She swallows hard. "Thank you."

The panda nods his head and hurries off, leaving Adaline to return to her room. Mid-step, she stops. *Yeah, no. No way I'm wasting this opportunity.* Instead, she hurries into the city.

As Adaline climbs up the Rialto's incline, she trails her hand along the flat surface of the balustrade that serves as the ledge for the covered bridge's arched windows. Even though the bridge's width could accommodate four lanes of cars, or rather carriages, it's empty of traffic, despite the hustle and bustle surrounding her.

She sighs but continues exercising her glutes as she approaches the bridge's gazebo-like center. Here, she pauses. On each side, the rectangular columns frame a semicircular alcove suited for café chairs and tables, rows of benches, vendors pushing small carts on wheels, or any other sort of intimate social setting. Alone, Adaline strolls into the barren alcove and stands over the river that splits the city in half.

Maybe next time I should invite Seira and Mercia to join me.

Beneath her, the river rushes away from the castle, past the riverfront shops, and toward the edge of the city, beyond which rests the palace with its fallen columns. The sight makes Adaline's brain tingle. She reaches for her field bag, only to remember she left it hidden in her room, and she's not wearing denim and flannel but a full-length gown.

Peeling her eyes away from the ruins, she observes the humans and elves coming and going on either side of the bridge. To her right, human shoppers haggle human merchants and dash from one establishment to another. The merchants restock within seconds, carrying more items than they can handle, and cuss when stacks fall over. The women wear snoods and aprons in front of their linen dresses while everyone labors to earn their living, hoisting and heaving and huffing about.

To her left, the elves pause to watch the gulls fly overhead. They laugh with friends and share their breakfast with customers. They squat down to view their work at eye level and rotate each item to examine its every angle before choosing which step to take next. The ladies' long, loose, unrestrained hair billows in the breeze as they drift past each other. Their girdles dance around their knees, and they twist at the waist and laugh with their whole bellies in ways a corset would never permit.

As Adaline debates which way to exit the bridge, she recalls Magnus's decree: No going past Front or Market Street. With a grumble, she heads toward Jósep's shop.

When Adaline approaches his stall, he greets her with a slight bow and a bright smile. "My lady, you've returned." He sounds surprised.

"I have."

Resting her hands on his table, Adaline peers at the marble block. Even though Jósep has shaved more off the sides, making his project thinner, the block's future remains a mystery, including how anyone delivered such a massive amount of marble here in the first place.

"Do you mind me asking where such an enormous piece of marble came from?"

"Ask freely, my lady. As for the answer, there's a quarry between here and Lameiría."

"Oh. And how many people does it take to get that here?"

"Many. However, carting the marble isn't the hard part. Cutting and hoisting it out of the quarry is the challenge. But do not worry; I have a strong back." Jósep winks, and his casual demeanor encourages Adaline to shed any lingering worry that she's bothering him.

His shop stall is no longer empty. A few stone-carved pieces stand to the side, including a miniature stone bridge, a fisherman, an elven lady, and a tree with a luscious top. Each of them would fit in the palm of Adaline's hand.

She points to the fisherman first. "May I?"

When Jósep nods, she rotates the man between her fingers. His leaf-shaped ears remind her not to call him a man. As she studies the miniature yet thorough details, she rubs her thumb over his eyes, which, though small, are wide and open as he waits for his patience to pay off.

"Wow," she says, putting him down next to the lady. "I wanted to stop by and thank you for your kindness yesterday evening."

Jósep bows again. "I hope I didn't get the lady in trouble."

"No. Ëólas and I are still...struggling to understand each other."

The corner of Jósep's mouth perks up. "But all of us came here to make that effort, haven't we, my lady?"

Adaline nods. How strange that the people who know the truth about her are the ones she understands least of all, and the people who don't know the truth have been the most welcoming. Adaline pulls her cloak tightly closed. Seira...

"Jósep, what does neir nía mean?"

"It's a term of endearment, my lady. The literal translation is little sister, but ladies use it among close kin or dear friends."

"I see." *A dear friend. Huh.*

They chat more while Jósep works on his block, but Adaline keeps turning her head toward the music drifting down the street. Its origin must be far beyond Market Street, where she's not supposed to go. And why not? To be fair, Magnus issued his warning *before* they caught that third attacker, and all the elves on Market Street seem much more relaxed around her today. Surely Magnus's warning isn't necessary anymore. Plus, Adaline works and spends all hours of the night in D.C.; she knows when something feels off, when to turn back and seek a public setting.

Adaline bids Jósep farewell but pops back over to his table one more time. "Jósep, how does one say big sister?"

Jósep's eyes glimmer with gratitude, and Adaline knows instinctively that he's one hundred percent a kind soul, a kindred spirit.

"Tíer nía, my lady."

As Adaline waves goodbye, she repeats *tea-ear nee-uh* in her mind, noting the accent on the first syllables of each word.

Music guides Adaline down the street and around several corners. The uneven surface of the cobblestones and the thin bottoms of her oversized flats cause her feet to throb, but a few blocks away from the riverfront, moss fills the gaps between each stone and stretches over the street, not only adding cushioning but also indicating that these roads are older than those by the riverfront. The music lures her deeper into the city until the buildings give way to the elves' own Central Park, complete with bridges arching over rivers and ponds, rock gardens doubling as seating and tables, and floral nurseries blooming in every direction—nothing extraordinary except for the fact that nature contains its own magic.

The moment Adaline steps onto the grass, a vibration runs through her body, from the tips of her toes to the crown of her head. Shuddering once, she rubs her arms to relax the goosebumps forming under her long sleeves. She braves another step, then another, each one causing her blood to pump harder and adding to the pressure building inside her chest, not an uncomfortable sort of pressure but the type that precedes new experiences and discovery.

The music fades mid-song.

The elf playing the mandolin lowers his instrument, and the singer reduces her voice to a whisper while they watch Adaline. But the lyre player continues strumming, continues making himself heard, continues preserving the garden's melody. The eyes following Adaline as she enters the garden remind her she needs to take her time, keep her movements slow and predictable, and not rush introductions. When elves locate a pair of guards nearby, the musicians reposition their instruments and hesitatingly resume playing. The singer takes her time to find her voice again and continue the story of the first elves.

For a moment, guilt washes over Adaline for invading their safe space. But the music returning to full volume and vigor calms her nerves and relaxes her facial muscles until she closes her eyes and tilts her head toward the sun that's begun its descent in the other half of the sky. Without her vision, the breeze rustling the flowers, the chitchat of friends, the gurgling of the center fountain, and the music binding all the sounds together bring her back to Dupont Circle, minus the low drone of cars driving around the traffic circle. Countless times she had taken the metro to Dupont and sat on the benches while grading papers, eating lunch, and closing her eyes to better listen to the city's life and the music bubbling around her.

Her stomach rumbles so loudly her eyes flash open. Her lunch thus far included a single crescent roll and cup of water. She presses her hands into her stomach as if to silence another, lower growl and frowns at the thought of having to make her way back to the castle when she only just found this corner of heaven. With a sigh, Adaline turns to leave, but an elven lady blocks the exit. The elf gasps and drops the bundle she's carrying, and bread, yellow apples, and cheese spill onto the ground between them.

Adaline stoops to stop the apples from rolling away. "I'm so sorry. I didn't mean to startle anyone." She opens the elf's crumbled pouch, abandoned on the ground, and places the apples inside, then drops to her knees and stretches forward to repackage the cheeses wrapped in colorful cloths with different patterns.

Having regained her faculties, the elf kneels down and collects the rest of her scattered food. When she speaks, her words are barely louder than a whisper. "Thank you, my lady."

"No worries, really. I can only imagine how peculiar my being here must seem to you. I'm sorry to have intruded."

Adaline hands another apple to the elf, who stares at the yellow fruit for a moment and the periwinkle material draped around Adaline's shoulders. A look of recognition passes across the elf's face. When she finally accepts the fruit, she does so with a sweet smile. Both ladies stand. Only Adaline dusts off her palms and knees, as the elf's dress bears no hint of dirt. Neither does Seira's cloak.

Elven magic?

Adaline's stomach growls again, and her embarrassment makes her chuckle awkwardly. "I suppose I should head back." One glance at the sun, she estimates the time to be past one o'clock. "When I heard the music and Jósep told me about the garden, I had to find it. It was worth the walk. How did you build such a massive fountain?"

As the lady shifts and cradles the bundle in her arms, her silky strawberry-blonde hair dances around her chest. "It's a natural spring, my lady."

"Oh. Of course."

"You like the music, my lady?"

Adaline's nodding matches the music's beats.

"Then you should stay. We've all brought more than enough food." The elf gestures to a group of people sitting in one of the rock gardens and adding their own food to the center of a table for everyone to enjoy.

Oh wow! She never dreamed she'd gain an invitation to participate so soon. "May I really? I'd love to."

The lady smiles and leads Adaline to the gathering. The ten or so elves reserve their smiles but nod or wave hello. Adaline's too hungry to be shy. Sitting down, she observes the people selecting their fruit and cheese, the way they use a square cloth to hold their snacks and make certain not to touch the food they don't plan to eat, and she does the same, hoping she's impressing upon them her trust in them and not committing any cultural faux pas. The elves nibble a little at a time, so Adaline does the same, despite her stomach desiring the whole snack pile.

By the time she's no longer starving, her feet are tapping a choreographed dance that would have blended ballet with the freedom of folk music. A male elf with eyes greener than the plants surrounding them watches her feet, which she had removed from her shoes so she could feel the grass crunch beneath her.

"The lady enjoys dancing," he says. "I enjoyed your song last night."

Adaline locks her feet to the ground, and her muscles tighten. "Oh, you heard that." She pops two more cubes of cheese into her mouth so she can't speak more on the topic and prays she didn't look as drunk as she felt.

"The lady's a natural," he says to his friends. "I hope we'll hear more."

Adaline nods. "I'm, I'm not sure. I think last night was a fluke. Singing and dancing were another lifetime for me." *And I have no intention of drinking tree spirits again.*

Something about what she said makes the elf smirk, but he never clarifies. Instead, he listens to the music, closing his eyes and turning his face toward the sun.

The familiar gesture makes Adaline grin, and that one similarity is enough to encourage her to ask the elves what brought them to the city. Some came with family. Some came to lend their talents and help Ëólas. But they all primarily came because of their curiosity.

"I completely understand that," Adaline says.

The elves nod in agreement, and the conversation continues even when the musicians join them. Everyone takes turns sharing stories about their lives, about what they miss back home and what they find fascinating about their new lives here—the seemingly small anecdotes that don't change lives but connect them. And here in this park, far away from the castle, Adaline feels at home.

Chapter Twelve

A Trial and a Hard Truth

When Adaline arrives back at the front gate of the castle, Hamon, the human co-captain of the city guard, rushes over to her. "Finally! The king has been waiting for you. Hurry along now."

Adaline stares blankly at him for a moment, replaying what he said to make sure she heard him correctly. With a humph, she picks up her skirts to better match his long strides.

Who's been waiting for whom?

Hamon runs his hands through his blond hair. "I thought I'd have to order all of my guards to tell me where you'd run off to. Lord Jorrel said he spoke with you. Why did you not wait inside the castle?"

Lord Jorrel? Oh, that must be the panda. "I went for a walk." *And not that much farther than Market Street.*

"We do have extensive private gardens behind the castle. You could walk there next time, rather than exploring the city. And on your own, no less."

"Why wouldn't I explore the city? I thought being the king's ward would afford me extra protection?"

"Yes, but not all men in the city are gentlemen."

"Well, everyone I met outside the castle was very kind."

Hamon scoffs. "I'm glad, my lady." When they enter the courtyard, he halts and faces her, giving Adaline a moment to catch her breath. "Please, do be careful. The city is more restless than ever, and your miraculous arrival—well, you're our responsibility. I'd hate to see you hurt."

Adaline purses her lips. As much as she wants to argue about her ability to take care of herself, she can't bring herself to accost his sweet Westley-like smile. He must win many ladies with that boyish charm. God forbid if he ever actually says *as you wish* to whomever he's courting.

"Thank you, Hamon."

"Any time," he says sincerely and leads her to the dining hall, now empty, except for Magnus, Ëólas, and the other three she met the night she arrived.

Finally, we're alone. What's the chance they figured out how to send me home?

She follows Hamon down the center aisle toward the group. This time, Magnus and Ëólas stand on the raised platform with the curved head table pushed back far behind them, Magnus with his hands clasped together and Ëólas with his arms crossed in front of his chest. Thoren, Merith, and Fólas flank their sides. Not a single one of them offers a friendly expression.

Adaline lingers at the end of the aisle, near the last table filled with a buffet spread. The stack of plates remains untouched. Scents of roast chicken and quartered potatoes waft beneath her nose. She draws Seira's cloak tighter around her front and wraps her arms around her stomach to hide its growl.

Halting in front of Magnus, Hamon folds one arm across his chest and bows. "I found her just outside the castle, Your Majesty." He climbs up the three steps and takes his place next to Thoren, completing the towering row of stern faces looking down at her.

Even Merith, who sang and danced with her last night, keeps a stoic expression. *Why do I suddenly feel like I'm on trial?*

Thoren rolls his eyes and rests his meaty hand on the hilt of his sword. "Of course that's where she went. I suppose she plans to keep us waiting too. No manners at all. Get over here, girl."

Girl? Adaline scowls.

Slowly, she walks toward them, noting the balcony on the far side of the room that promises fresh air. And freedom. Hadn't she wanted to see them this morning? To apologize for being impatient. And trying to run away while they hunted a killer. And getting drunk. And throwing a cloak in Ëólas's face. And calling him an asshole.

Crap. I'm a terrible guest.

Taking a small breath, Adaline stops in front of Magnus and curtsies. She nods at Ëólas, but he looks past her, probably because no matter how much she tries to mimic a noble lady's mannerisms, she can't erase what he witnessed last night.

Maybe he doesn't understand the concept of carefree fun. Whenever I see him, he tends to look miserable. Maybe his king ordered him to come here. I mean, his reactions can't always be because of me. That's just ridiculous.

Ëólas's eyes flick to her and jump to her cloak where his focus settles. Despite his trained indifference, he tightens his jaw, cracking his marble-like gaze.

Maybe that's not so ridiculous.

Adaline hides her hands behind her back and clamps down on the pressure point on her hand. The sharp pain clears the dense fog permeating her brain.

Magnus rubs the bottom of his beard. "Out enjoying the city again, I see. And where to did you venture today?"

Adaline swallows. A grown woman shouldn't be made to feel like a teenager caught climbing into her window past curfew—not that she had ever done such a thing. Nan would have stared at her for hours until the guilt made her crumble into a sobbing mess of confession. None of these people are her parents. Well, legally. Magnus is technically acting as her guardian. But she's a grown-ass woman who's been on her own for a long while now. She should ignore that disappointed paternal look on his face.

How much older could he possibly be anyway? A few years at best.

"Did you not hear the king?" Thoren growls. "Speak when His Majesty addresses you."

Magnus side-eyes Thoren, who grumbles but doesn't speak again. When Magnus returns his attention to Adaline, his eyes wrinkle at the corners. Even though his words sound flat, his eyes appear amused. "I am not fond of having to repeat myself."

Pulling her shoulders back, Adaline clasps her hands in front of her waist, invoking her grandmother's habit when addressing crowds. "I strolled down Market Street and found the elven gardens, where I listened to music and—"

"Why were you on my side of the city?" Ëólas's golden eyes could drill through steel.

Adaline's heart thumps loudly in her ears. "Your side? I thought you said you were trying to bring people together? Again, I didn't see a sign saying *No Humans Beyond This Point*. No one stopped me, and my friend—"

"Friend?" Ëólas arches an eyebrow.

Adaline clamps her mouth shut. *Did I just get Jósep in trouble? No, that can't be.* These guys must know everything that goes on in this city. "Jósep and I were just talking about the differences between working with stone versus clay. Our conversations were completely harmless, and I never would have spoken with him if I thought I'd get him in trouble, and he was just—"

"I already know this." Ëólas disappears inside his head.

Ha! I knew it. Wait, then what upset him?

Magnus grins. "You think of Jósep as a friend?"

Oooooh. He's mad I made an elven friend?

Jósep not only let her ask countless questions but also invited her into that tavern, either to keep her safe or change her mind about running away. Regardless of his motives, he never made her feel small or out of place. "Yes, I do. Isn't that a good thing?"

Magnus releases a loud chuckle. "Indeed." But his laugh fades, and the corners of his mouth turn downward, dragging Adaline's relief with them. "However, I told you not to venture beyond Market and Front Street, and you chose to disregard my orders. Openly. Willfully."

Adaline looks down. *Crap.* "I thought—"

"Defying the king's orders is grounds for imprisonment," Thoren says.

Hearing the smile in his voice, she clenches her jaw and stays silent, because she's alone, outnumbered, and at their mercy.

Magnus releases a slow breath, drawing her eyes up toward him again. He pinches the bottom of his beard one more time and rests his hands on his hips. Looking her over, he knits his brows together. "Do you habitually undermine the rules of your king back home?"

"My country doesn't have a king." She cusses herself the moment she lets those words slip out. The last thing she wants is to be responsible for introducing the idea of revolution. *What's the least I can reveal?* "We have a different system of government."

Thoren throws his hands up in the air. "No wonder she has no sense of propriety."

Merith smirks and flicks his chin sideways, silently telling Adaline to keep her eyes on Magnus. Still, Merith grants her a half-smile before resuming his official, guard-like expression.

That slight gesture bolsters her enough to look at Magnus, whose grin surprises her. But when Ëólas whispers in his ear, Magnus gives up his amusement. "Lady Adaline, you seem accustomed to having the freedom to do as you please, and I have gifted you with the space to continue moving about freely. Within reason."

Except for his flaring nostrils, Ëólas remains immovable. "And with that privilege, you chose to disobey your benefactor, discard his assistance, and venture far into the elven side of the city while knowing that elf-human relations are fragile at the moment, especially given the recent attack."

Adaline squeezes her hands into fists. "I was just listening to music."

Ëólas glowers. "Just? The elves on Market Street have more exposure to humans than the more residential sections of the city, and your presence most likely alarmed many. I will not tolerate you frightening my people and—"

"I didn't frighten—"

Within three strides, Ëólas looms over her, casting a long, cool shadow that snuffs out light and warmth. His words, though quiet, are as sharp as icicles. "Do. Not. Interrupt. Me."

Merith shakes his head ever so slightly, looking more disappointed than angry, maybe even hurt.

Adaline's stomach sinks.

Ëólas unfolds his arms and tilts forward, only a few inches but enough to make the room shrink around them until the world comprises only the two of them. His breath sends a chill that rolls through her body. "While you live here, listen to your king."

I don't have a king.

A long silence engulfs them. Her jaw aches from clenching her teeth so hard. Her temples throb as her mind clouds her vision with images of kicking him in the crotch, but she locks all her muscles in place so she won't look away or scream at the top of her lungs. Ëólas bends forward, bringing his eyes closer to hers. They both refuse to look away as they will the other to blink, to flinch, to back down. Unwilling to yield, Adaline rises onto the balls of her feet. Her eyes twitch, the burning sting turning into tears, not enough to spill but enough to blur his face, to smooth his wrinkled brow, to blot out his judgment. To make him appear the way he should.

How can the same person make sure I got home safely last night, only to accuse me of harming his people the next day?

Adaline takes a long, steady breath. She won't lose her temper with him. Not again. Not in front of the others. She won't prove herself to be the problem he believes her to be. She's not here to hurt anyone. As an anthropologist, she swore to...

Shit. Adaline lowers her heels to the floor.

She broke the code of ethics. That's what Ëólas was getting at. Her exploration harmed the safety or privacy of the people she's been observing. As much as she wants to slap him, everything he's said stems from wanting to protect his people. His delivery methods may suck, but he has every right to be angry with her.

Dropping her shoulders, she leans back, and the rest of the world zooms into focus again. Behind Ëólas's ear, Magnus locks eyes with her, willing her to make the right move.

Although her mouth feels mechanical, she unlocks her jaw, forms words as calmly as possible, and speaks only the truth. "I'm sorry for being disrespectful. When I learned you caught the last attacker and because the *other* elves were so friendly, I assumed I could explore the city more. But it was dangerous for me to have made such an assumption, both for myself," she dares to look Ëólas in the eyes and lifts her chin, "and for your people. My curiosity and excitement got the better of me. I'm truly sorry for not being more aware of your people's fears and concerns."

Ëólas blinks. Several times. As he leans away from her, the tremors that had been simmering beneath the surface settle. Knitting his brows together, he looks her up and down one last time, hesitantly walks away from her, and rejoins Magnus.

With a gleam in his eye, Magnus gives Adaline a broad smile. "I'm glad we better understand each other, Adaline. I absolve you. Consider this matter closed."

All energy drains from her body while Thoren shakes his head. Whatever he's grumbling into Magnus's ear, his king shoos him away.

Merith beams, as does Hamon, who now stares only at the buffet table and licks his lips. Even though her muscles feel like Jell-O, she agrees with Hamon and wants to inhale the entire buffet. Her shaking hands must be due to her hunger.

Gesturing at the food, Magnus steps down from the raised platform. "Now that the formalities have concluded, let us eat."

While the other five head to the buffet, Magnus lingers beside her. "Join us."

At first, she thinks he's ordering her to do so. But the warmth in his eyes says he's giving her an opportunity to continue getting to know each of these guys better. As much as she's exhausted from today's trial, God only knows when next she'll have a chance to discuss her options for getting home if she were to leave now.

Better to play nice.

The guys climb over the benches and pile mountains of food onto their plates. Like Arthur's round table, no one sits at the head of the table. They mingle like friends.

Adaline grabs her skirts, ready to hike them up and clamber onto the bench next to Hamon, when a servant appears out of nowhere and places a chair at the end of the table, next to Ëólas and Magnus. She gulps but takes her seat next to them. A servant passes her a plate, and Hamon and Merith send platters down her way so she can take her pick. She piles her plate up high too.

Magnus takes a long drink of wine. "Now, you must be eager to discuss the miraculous circumstances that brought you to us."

"Yes!" She nearly knocks over her own goblet. "My colleagues must have reported me missing by now." She's been trying not to think about Cindy and Dax calling her phone over and over again, starting to worry, and eventually discovering her missing person's report on the news.

"Merith, please," Magnus says, gesturing for Merith to speak.

Merith swallows a pastry puff in one bite and peeks around Ёólas so he can better see her. "My lady, has your world managed to retain some of the magic that created it?"

"Magic?" Adaline's brain struggles to process that word and the absurdity of the concept. Since her arrival, she's pondered parallel dimensions, an anti-universe, cyclical theories, and eternal inflation. Not that she fully grasps those theories. But magic? She shouldn't rule out the possibility, but the idea feels more like wishful thinking. Magic is for fairytales.

Yet here I am, talking to an elf. A real-life elf. Who sings and dances. And who looks like he could kill me with one strike.

Adaline takes a bite of minced pie, chews slowly while she faces this new reality, and continues. "As far as I know, my world doesn't have magic. Then again, maybe it depends on your definition. Throughout history, we've had periods of people being accused of witchcraft, which never ended well for the accused. Those individuals were being used as scapegoats for things we couldn't explain back then, like drastic weather, solar eclipses, sudden disease, men who refused to take responsibility for their lust..."

Six pairs of eyes look at her.

Adaline pauses mid-bite. "What? You don't have those issues here?" She tries to keep the smirk off her face but fails miserably.

While Thoren chokes on his food and Hamon's shoulders rise up to his ears, Magnus releases a big belly laugh. "Sadly, we have, though we've seen less of that in the last ten years. You see, men who refuse to raise their own children are fined, heavily. Especially those in my service." Magnus pauses, and Hamon's shoulders can't possibly swallow his head anymore. "And the entirety of that fine goes to the mother."

Dang. Renaissance child support. Adaline puts down her drink and looks Magnus in the eye. "I'm genuinely surprised. What if the mother can't prove who the father is?"

"Then the entire town must pay the fine, which turns the citizens against the father. Neighbors talk. They know who should step forward. That pressure usually makes him do so, if he wishes to hold his head up high."

"Wow."

Magnus beams. "You have something similar? In your world?"

Adaline nods, then looks to the other side of the table. "What about the elves?"

"No" is all Ëólas offers.

Fólas elaborates. "We don't have such an issue, my lady." He smirks at Hamon and kicks him under the table. The two of them exchange glares and chuckles.

"Uh-huh." Adaline takes another bite.

"Let us move on!" Thoren hisses. "This is not a proper conversation for a lady's ears."

Adaline nearly spits out her sip of wine as she laughs internally, both at the idea of Thoren now thinking her a lady and his assumptions about ladies in general.

If he only knew what women talk about. Hell, if he knew she'd given up her maidenhood *long ago, he'd probably forbid her from ever talking to Mercia again.*

Inhaling the scent of red wine, Adaline drinks half the goblet. "Anyway, as I was saying, I don't think magic is real, at least not in my world, but we do have various scientific theories I've been pondering." And when she describes them, one by one, the guys' stares resemble that of her third-grade class when she told them that the Spanish Flu didn't actually originate in Spain, only the reporting did, and that U.S. troop deployments around the world caused the pandemic to spread quickly during the Great War. That was also the first time she learned what a know-it-all is, a label she couldn't shed until college. "To be clear, I don't have magic. There's nothing magical about me."

With a scoff, Thoren digs into the roast chicken, tears off a massive chunk of breast meat, and stuffs his mouth shut.

Magnus places his hands on both sides of his plate and ponders his next words carefully. "I'm sorry your world doesn't seem to value magic, my lady." When he looks at her, there's a gleam in his eye, a spark. "Here, we revere it, though we have not witnessed a display of magic for centuries, that is, until two nights ago."

Adaline looks around the table. She can't hide from the six faces studying her every move. She swallows. "So you think…?" She can't process what her presence might mean to them. The idea is too preposterous. "Does that mean you don't know how to send me home?"

"We're not sure." Magnus rests his hand on Adaline's. "I have brought some books from my personal library here, but they are limited on this matter. However, that does not mean we are without resources. Ëólas and his people are your best hope in this regard, given that elves have, in fact, retained connection to the magic of creation."

Adaline looks at Ëólas and suppresses the urge to vomit. Fantastic. Her fate is in the hands of the guy who barely tolerates her.

"I will continue to investigate the matter." Ëólas pays more attention to the cube of cheese on his plate than he does her.

She grinds her teeth. "How can I help? I'm not one to sit around and do nothing."

With a heavy sigh, as if breathing the same air as her is laborious, Ëólas cranes his neck to look at her. "As Magnus said, magic is our domain, though I will keep you informed about my findings. I have requested that Lameiría send either a priestess or books here. Regardless, the journey will take them at least five days."

"Five days." Adaline's high pitch voice could shatter glass. "I'll be missing for at least a week?" She pushes her chair back and jumps to her feet, tripping over her hem. Hiking up her skirts, she paces back and forth in front of the platform with the head table. Her long strides kick the bottom of her dress, and she slows down only so she won't fall out of her shoes.

Everything she just ate threatens to come back up again. "Five more days. How am I going to explain this to my boss? To the committee? To my grantor? I'm going to lose my funding. I'll lose my job. Oh god. What about Nan's property? I haven't even gone over all the paperwork with Doña Mariana. What'll happen to Nan's and Dad's stuff if I don't…"

She can't finish that thought. From the corner of her eye, Magnus rises and approaches her.

And here I am stuck with a crazy redhead and stuck-up elf who both think I represent the End of Days.

"Adaline." Magnus plants himself in front of her so she's forced to stop pacing.

"I'm fine. It's fine. Everything's fine." Gluing her hands to her sides, she faces him head on.

He takes two more steps to shrink the distance between them and speaks softly, his eyes worn and tired again. "I am truly sorry for your predicament, for being thrust without warning into a life you know little to nothing about. We cannot change what is, not at the moment. All I can provide in the meantime is safety. Perhaps a home, even if temporary. I hope, in some small way, this offers you comfort."

Adaline considers him quietly, noting that his exhaustion seems different today. Maybe it's not exhaustion per se but empathy. Moments ago, she feared his wrath, but he's never hurt or threatened her. Warned her, yes, but threatened, no. And he did promise her from day one that she has friends here.

Commanding herself to calm down, she whispers, "Thank you, Magnus."

He pats her back and guides her toward their table where the other five resume eating as if they hadn't been watching her freak out.

"No kings in your world," Magnus mumbles and laughs.

That's not quite what I said. "I'm sorry. I didn't mean—"

"Think nothing of it." He gestures toward the head of the table where a servant sets her chair upright again. She hadn't noticed knocking it over.

She smiles an apology at Magnus, who shakes his head as if all's forgotten. She's fortunate she didn't wind up with a tyrant.

What makes Magnus so understanding?

A thought flashes in her mind, the way he looked at her when he spoke about magic, about humans not having retained that connection. For a moment, she frowns, but she snuffs out that thought and chooses to listen to the voice in the far recesses of her mind that tells her Magnus is kind through and through.

She takes a seat but turns to the elves. "Lord Ëólas." She bites the tip of her tongue when he moves only his eyes, not his head, to acknowledge her. "Thank you immensely for offering to help me find a way home. But please, let me know how I can help too. After all, research is my area of expertise."

Ëólas quietly and gently rests his spoon beside his soup bowl. "Lovely. I wasn't aware you can read Elvish."

Damn. "No, but I enjoy learning other languages. I'm a fast learner."

As Ëólas purses his lips, Merith nudges his lord's shoulder and smirks. "She's tenacious."

"She still lacks decorum," Thoren says. "Your Majesty, you may have absolved her, but she should be confined to the damn castle."

The tightness building in Adaline's chest feels like someone's squeezing her neck with their bare hands.

Magnus grumbles, "There's no need for that, Thoren. She may freely roam Market and Front Street. Adaline, if you wish to explore other areas of the city, request an escort."

She releases a slow breath. But after processing what Magnus said, she scrunches her nose. *An escort?*

"Adaline, this is for your safety, too."

"I appreciate your concern, Magnus. Really, I do. But I know how to stay safe. I stick to public spaces. I'm not about to walk off with strangers or wander down creepy alleys. And most people keep their distance from me because," she looks down at her dress with its gold hem, "well, for obvious reasons."

Ëólas stares into his soup while stirring his spoon and watching the vegetables collide in a whirlpool. "So you know how to wield a sword or dagger to protect yourself?"

Do wooden swords count? She should have taken Dax up on his offer to join his long-sword fight club while he was perfecting his LARP character years ago. Joke's on her. She pushes thoughts about Dax and home out of her mind again. "No. But I know how to throw a solid punch and kick a guy where it counts."

The corner of Magnus's mouth perks up. "Well, let's make certain you never need to use those skills."

"Fair enough," Adaline says.

Resting his elbows on the table, he drops all amusement from his voice. "Even if we did, indeed, apprehend the last attacker, the damage will linger for a long while. I do not want you caught in the middle of a misunderstanding."

Adaline tilts her head. A misunderstanding. Images of the last two days flash through her mind, of Jósep's patience, Sallie's honesty, the tavern's boisterous jubilation, and the peaceful gardens. "Huh."

"What?"

"It's just—" Adaline notes Thoren's glare. "Nothing."

"Speak freely." Magnus dons an exaggerated scowl and deepens his voice. "I order you to do so."

"Humph." Adaline rolls her eyes, making Thoren curse under his breath. "It's just...I'm not saying this attack wasn't horrible, but—"

"Three citizens were murdered on our streets." Ëólas glares, pushing his bowl away from him. "For the first time, someone has dared to break our laws, and discord grows like a vine."

"Who died?" she asks.

Ëólas furrows his brows, but she can't tell if her question disturbs or surprises him.

"Two humans and one elf," says Merith. "No one recognized the attackers. Some claim a human started the fight. Others insist the elf initiated the argument."

Of course, they're blaming each other. Community violence, sadly, is familiar territory, and it's easier to focus on this than where the hell she is.

"Who were they? Guards? Townsfolk? Thieves?" she asks again.

Fólas leans over his plate, making his wavy russet hair visible next to Merith, and presses his usual wide and goofy smile into a thin line of severity. "They were newcomers to the territory, my lady. The elf was a stonemason named Galdor."

Was he Jósep's friend? If so, why was Jósep so open to chatting with me?

Hamon swallows the mouthful of chicken he tore off a wing. "And the humans were a smithy and a woodworker."

"Which is why you will not stray so far from the castle again," says Magnus. "Distrust is more prevalent at the moment."

"I don't think that's entirely true." *Shit. Why can't I keep my mouth closed?*

"What exactly did you notice during your excursions?" Magnus asks.

She studies the others' expectant faces, each waiting for her judgment, to prove she knows nothing. She'd rather present her findings in a research paper, not to the local community itself.

Magnus arches an eyebrow, cueing her to speed up.

Adaline huffs loudly. "Fine. Yes, the city is literally divided in half. The people don't feel comfortable mingling, but that's because they don't know how. The humans think the elves don't want to socialize with them, and the elves don't know how to initiate conversations with the humans. You've enabled both sides to *observe* each other, but they don't know how to *speak* to each other. But I think they want to. Everyone I spoke with was very affable, and they all admitted that curiosity brought most people to this city. They want to bridge the divide. I think they're just looking for the right opportunity. I mean, don't you feel it? There's this subtle current of hope here. It's in the air."

Everyone sucks in a deep breath, and their thoughts seem to turn inward.

Did I say something wrong? Or right?

"And you observed all of that in two days?" Merith asks.

"It's part of my job."

"Studying civilizations?" Magnus asks.

"That's part of it. I don't just research how people built their homes and arranged their cities, what forms of government they had, and which battle tactics they used. I study the people, how they used to live, what their daily lives were like at all social levels, how they expressed themselves through art and socialization, and so on. Anthropology isn't just about how groups of people survived and died; it's also about how they lived. And most of them had more in common than they'd ever acknowledge."

While everyone else thinks about what Adaline said, Thoren throws back his head and finishes his wine. "Your leaders require such frivolous studies?"

Fuck you. "Anthropology is a family hobby."

"Studying people is a hobby?" Magnus rests his elbow on the table and his chin in his hand. "Why?"

Popping a grape in her mouth, she chews slowly, assessing everyone's eyes on her to make sure she's not about to piss someone off. Except for Thoren, the rest seem curious. Maybe even eager. Well, not Ëólas; he's still staring at his soup. "Because studying the past is our best chance to not repeat our mistakes. And studying other cultures creates empathy, understanding, acceptance, and cooperation. The benefits are endless."

"Fascinating." Magnus drops his hand and hunches over his arms folded on the table. "That's similar to what we hope to achieve here in the Neutral Territory, opening the minds of humans and elves alike so they are willing to know each other. Although, as you noticed, that has proven challenging."

"Why do you think that is?"

Maintaining his stoic expression, Ëólas taps the edge of his bowl, as if counting his possible replies before choosing an answer. "Elves don't trust humans, especially those who seek power, and humans fear and resent elves for our natural abilities."

"So you're fighting against a history of bias, prejudice, otherism, and isolationism. For how long?"

"Six thousand years, at least," says Magnus.

Adaline whistles. "That's no joke. And the Neutral Territory is your attempt to bring two different cultures and ideologies together? Of course, that's going to be challenging. But it's admirable too."

"Thank you," Magnus says. "I wish all our people shared your enthusiasm."

Something about his exasperation tells Adaline this includes those closest to him, maybe even his own council members. She can't help but wonder which ones support him and which ones are biding their time.

"Few do," Ëólas says.

"Precisely." Magnus says nothing further and drops his napkin on his plate, signaling he's done eating, but a far-off look overtakes his face, revealing that his mind has drifted beyond food. Ëólas waits for him to speak his mind while the other four talk among themselves.

Finally, Magnus addresses Adaline. "Shortly, the rest of the council will join us as we venture into the city to review its development, inspect particular sections, and assess our people's needs. Given your insatiable curiosity, how would you like to join us? You could see the entire city, and I'll answer your questions."

A grin spreads across Adaline's face, and her eyes sparkle. "I'd love that. Mercia filled me in a bit, but..." Adaline gulps at Thoren's snarl.

Man, first Seira. Now Mercia. Am I not allowed any female friends here?

She leans back until Magnus's body blocks Thoren's face. "But I'm curious if your people own their own land, or do they work the land in exchange for housing? And what metal are your weapons made of? And what sort of rights do women have? And what other intelligent beings exist here? Dwarves? Wizards? Mermaids! What about—"

"A scholar, indeed." Magnus chuckles. "Then it's settled."

"Are you serious?" Thoren slams his bread down.

Crumbs scatter across the table and ping Merith's plate. Merith pointedly angles his head to the side, and Thoren mumbles an apology.

Magnus stares Thoren down. "I said, it's settled."

Fólas and Hamon rest their cheek against their fists to conceal their grins, but Adaline's uncertain which they find more amusing: Magnus schooling Thoren, or the sudden stare off between Magnus and Ëólas. When Ëólas purses his lips but resumes eating his soup, Magnus grins his victory.

How can Ëólas's nostrils flare so much? Actually, how does he keep his temper so damn level?

Magnus points to her plate still piled high. "Finish your meal. Then we're off."

"Okay." Adaline takes three large bites, focusing on her excitement instead of home. She can fret later. When she's alone. Again. "I'd love a history lesson too."

"Then you shall have one."

"Wonderful!" Maybe a history lesson will shed some light on how this world works—and how she might find the key that will take her home.

Chapter Thirteen

A History Lesson

The long stairway echoes the footfalls of their small group, led by Magnus and Ëólas with Adaline between the two. As they descend to the first floor and toward the awaiting council members, Magnus explains the history of the castle itself, his face and gestures alive with memories. When Adaline's pinkie accidentally brushes Ëólas's, they both yank their hands away. Listening to Magnus, she erases Ëólas's placid expression from her mind.

"The same day Lameiría agreed to my proposal," Magnus says, "I initiated the creation of this castle, or at least Alderton's half, to help nudge Ëólas into taking action." He whispers in her ear, loud enough for everyone to hear, "He likes to ruminate for decades at a time."

"Ha." Ëólas's slightly raised, rounded cheek warms his face. "And Magnus likes to forge ahead, forcing me to step in and course correct as quickly as possible."

Adaline watches both leaders banter, unsure if she's fallen into a different reality. From the corner of her eye, she studies Ëólas more closely as she ponders if Magnus was exaggerating or being literal. Ëólas's smooth skin and chiseled features appear to be the same age as her's, but he also bears the aura of someone older. Someone who feels weighed down with decades of responsibility. Someone who's determined, decided, and unaltered.

Many tales describe elves as immortal or at least extremely long lived. If either is true, then Ëólas could be...

Magnus's voice pulls Adaline away from her ruminations. She wiggles her shoulders and neck to loosen them and turns her attention to him and only him again.

"Ëólas, how was I to know you would prefer such a different layout? Besides, your need to oversee the foundational changes significantly sped up your arrival time, which in turn sped up the planning process for the entire city."

"Your unique perspective never ceases to—"

"Neir Nía!" Seira's shouting not only interrupts Ëólas but also causes their entire group to stop and turn around. Seira sprints down the stairs, and the guys split in half as they step back to make way for her. She runs past them and halts in front of Adaline while flailing her arms at Ëólas and Magnus until they both step aside too. Grabbing Adaline's hand, Seira tugs her closer, her pale lavender eyes dark and glazed over while her eyebrows raise and fall with her heavy breathing. "Are you injured, Neir Nía?"

A chill runs down Adaline's spine. "What? Why would I—"

Before Adaline can answer, Seira yanks up Adaline's sleeve and rotates her forearm, examining all sides.

Ëólas slowly reaches for Seira's shoulder. "No one harmed Ada—"

Repositioning herself in front of Ëólas, Seira silences him with her back. He looks to Merith, who mirrors Ëólas's concern, but no one else dares interrupt her. Using her thumb, Seira rubs circles over a birthmark near Adaline's elbow, the only visible blemish. With a wrinkled brow and narrowed eyes, Seira drops Adaline's hand, only to grab her other one and give that arm the same attention.

Adaline contemplates pulling her hand free, but Seira's sudden conviction that Adaline had been, or maybe is, in some sort of danger has hindered her ability to think clearly. She follows Seira's gaze and studies her own arm, half expecting to discover something she doesn't remember.

"My lady?" Magnus's gentle voice cuts through Seira's consternation. "I assure you Lady Adaline is safe within this castle."

"Within this castle…" Seira releases Adaline's hand and closes her eyes. She rolls her head from side to side like a metronome, then, as if time stopped, she stares at the ceiling. A moment later, she pulls herself together, stands tall, and smiles at Adaline as if seeing her for the first time today. Her eyes glow brighter too. "I, I must have been dreaming. Everyone's getting along then?" She looks hopefully at Ëólas.

For her sake, he nods. When Seira exhales, he breathes more easily himself. "Why don't I escort you to—"

"Right then." Seira tucks a rogue brown lock underneath Adaline's hairband, looks her up and down, and nods in approval. "I'll find you shoes that fit properly. Go now. Enjoy your tour."

With an about-face, Seira scampers up the stairs and prances along the balcony until she disappears out of sight. *Sometimes I wonder if Seira exists only in my dreams.* She rotates her head to Magnus, hoping he'll explain.

He nods knowingly but turns to Thoren and barks, "Why wasn't Adaline fitted with proper shoes?"

Thoren tosses his hands about. "I don't know what the ladies have on hand."

Seriously? This is what he's focusing on?

Adaline touches Magnus's arm. "I'm fine. Really."

Casting his gaze to her feet, he purses his lips and grumbles, "Will you be able to walk?"

Thoren snorts so loudly that his broad shoulders shake. "Her shoes haven't hindered her yet."

While Merith, Fólas, and Hamon snicker together, Adaline looks Thoren in the eyes, squares her shoulders, and allows a smile to stretch across her face. "Damn right."

Adaline curls her toes in her slippers so the added pressure prevents them from sliding off as she quickens her pace to keep up with the council's long strides. Even the three female elven members are taller and faster than her. Overall, the fourteen council members and the additional guards behind them have increased their party from seven to about twenty-five. Not one of them appears agitated from the low sun drying up the air.

Magnus reaches between him and Ëólas and, finding the small of Adaline's back, guides her between them again. She's grateful he hasn't forgotten her, but Ëólas's momentary grimace at the location of Magnus's hand makes her stomach twist.

I'm not a gold digger, she mentally projects at him. But Ëólas is already facing forward and keeping his distance beside her while Thoren's breath warns her from behind.

Magnus, oblivious to Ëólas's disdain and Thoren's scrutiny, points at the cluster of buildings as their group follows along the river leading toward the city's center. "Half the city, the half closest to us, is entirely new. The elves weren't thrilled with me building new structures on the Forbidden Lands, but I saw no other way to move forward and provide accommodations that would encourage elves and humans to reside within such close proximity."

Adaline's father always said to note what's not mentioned too. *So what's the history of the older portion of the city, and why isn't Magnus talking about that?*

Magnus continues, "Most humans have feared elves for hundreds of years, believing them to be dangerous and vengeful. The occasional missing person or pillaged home added to those fears."

Adaline steals a glance at Ëólas, who remains expressionless. "Vengeful about what?"

Magnus takes a deep breath. "You ask the difficult questions, don't you?"

With an apologetic shrug, she tugs on her bodice to allow a breeze to sneak inside and cool her skin.

After pausing to scratch his cheek, Magnus drops his hand and rests it on the hilt of his sword. "In short, for stealing land."

"Short, indeed," Ëólas quips.

Adaline turns her shoulders to remove him and his long, sun-warmed hair out of her peripheral vision. *If only he didn't have to be here.* "So what made you think differently, Magnus?"

"My father." He stops and points at the jagged line of forest that dissolves into the clouds along the horizon. "Led by his curiosity, he entered Lameiría when he was only seven years old," he pauses for dramatic effect, "and lived to tell the tale."

As if fondly recalling the memory himself, Ëólas chuckles. Then his brows droop as though he's remembered what's been lost. Adaline wants to hear the entire story, what Magnus and Ëólas know about that moment, but Magnus nudges her forward, and their group continues into the city.

"My father, King Rioran, recognized rumors and fear for what they were, and we had no evidence that anyone from Lameiría had ever attempted to invade our lands."

"Because we have no desire to expand our borders," says Ëólas. "An inability to accommodate enormous population growth is a human issue. Those who went missing did so only because they dared to venture into our woods."

"Isn't that a bit extreme?" She tries not to look at him, but curiosity gets the better of her.

Ëólas never misses a step and keeps his eyes forward. "Strict rules deter more humans from invading our land."

"I get that. Back home, so many civilizations, cultures, and languages have been lost throughout history because of invaders. That's one reason why I love my field of study; I don't want their stories to be forgotten. I can see why you're on your guard so much."

Ëólas stumbles over a rock and locks eyes with her. "Yes."

Why does he look confused? That I can understand?

Magnus's voice pulls their eyes apart. "Well, the only war and later skirmishes between our two peoples centered on the Forbidden Lands. My ancestors wished to absorb this territory into Alderton. Otherwise, the elves never ventured into Alderton, so I sought to foster communication between our peoples and repair the damage."

Adaline lifts the hem of her dress higher as she hops over a muddy puddle. "How did you go about that?"

"I've known Ëólas since I was a boy."

"A troublemaker to start," Ëólas snickers. "Then a persistent young man, who, like his father, dared to enter our woods, presuming we wouldn't hold a king prisoner indefinitely and risk war." Even though his words are harsh, his lips curve into a rare, unrestrained smile.

"Whoa," Adaline says, uncertain whether Magnus is extremely brave or hopelessly naïve.

"I simply wanted to prove my theories," Magnus says, "that the elves weren't so scary after all. I'd much rather have civil relations with our neighbors than constant fear of the unknown."

"So you went into Lameiría. And?" she asks.

"I kept going back. Ëólas was in charge of border patrol, so the more he saw me, the more I wore him down."

"He's relentless," Ëólas says.

"Yes, indeed." Magnus puffs up his chest and lifts his chin higher. "Well, during those trips, I began sharing my idea that we should repurpose the Forbidden Lands so elves and humans could try to live, work, and perhaps even socialize regularly once again. As a gesture of good faith, I started building this castle, and together our people have contributed significantly to repairing and building the foundation for our new city."

"I'm impressed," Adaline says. "Both sides taking a chance to break down assumptions about the other—there's that hope again. It's inspiring what you're doing here."

"Are you always so optimistic?" Ëólas asks.

"I guess." She shrugs, not thinking too deeply about that potential compliment. "What's the second half of the city? And why were the Forbidden Lands forbidden? I find it hard to believe anyone would choose to give this territory such an ominous name."

"Mmm," Magnus mumbles. "Quite right. The second half of the city is more of a restorative project." He looks ahead, as if to ward off the guilt that has taken hold of him. "Long ago, when my ancestors' ancestors ruled over Alderton, this land belonged to an elfdom known as Aeyrtol."

Aerytol. That's the name Seira said. "What happened?"

Before he can answer, if he was going to, everyone in their group stops and observes the lavender flowers Adaline noticed her first morning in the city. As if overnight, the small, star-like blossoms spread across the entire embankment now.

"There's more," Ëólas says.

Magnus nods, and they both look proud of some accomplishment that goes beyond planting wildflowers.

While they continue talking, Hamon leans forward and whispers into Adaline's ear, "Those flowers, Purple Stardust, used to grow all over Aerytol, but no one had seen them in nearly five hundred years. They began growing about two months ago. Everyone believes they mean we have the late queen's blessing."

"The late queen? Aerytol's late queen?"

Hamon nods.

They enter the city along the elven side of the river, and their group weaves through the streets and neighborhoods, crossing back and forth over the bridges and acknowledging all of their citizens. Gradually, Adaline drops back a few steps to better allow Magnus and Ëólas to discuss their observations, which new shops are flourishing, which guilds are still needed, where they'd best expand next, and so forth.

As if part of a parade, she walks past bakers, fruit and vegetable farmers, spice sellers, a fabric stall, and the metalworker. The shopkeepers, human and elven alike, stop their work and lower their heads as the king's group passes, but the people's actions are more than a display of reverence. They freely smile. Their shoulders seem less burdened, and the children giggle and bounce when they peek out from store windows or around crates to get a better look at the council members.

The further they head down Front Street, the more the traffic flows in only one direction, toward the Rialto, where a large crowd gathers. The group turns onto the bridge but stops midway, under the gazebo, where Magnus and Ëólas step up to the balustrade. Leaning forward, they project their voices over the river to address the people who have crammed together and filled the small bridges and streets to hear their leaders speak. While the crowd hushes, Adaline shimmies past shoulders, moving backward so she can hide between the council members and guards and merge with the stage extras.

An arm pressing against her shoulder blades stops her from getting too far. "Not fond of large crowds?" Hamon asks in her ear.

She wrinkles her nose at him, and his chortle punctures the expanding quiet.

Thoren cranes his neck to glower at them both, and they immediately straighten their faces into perfect portraits of decorum. But when Thoren turns around, Hamon and Adaline use a hand to stifle their chuckles.

"He's really not so bad," Hamon whispers, "once he's determined your merits."

"I'm screwed."

"Ha!" Hamon combs his fingers through his blond hair, forcing his locks to spill over the other side of his face, away from Adaline, so she can clearly see the humor rolling around in his eyes. "I highly recommend you choose another description, my lady, lest the other guards misinterpret your meaning."

"Oh god. Spare me."

Hamon chuckles again while Adaline shakes her head and rolls her eyes, but with her heart feeling less shaky, she no longer tries to disappear.

Following his lead, she faces forward as Ëólas speaks. With a clear, strong voice, the commander general shares the reports he received from his own guards, that with the increased security, no disturbances have been reported since the attack. Every face Adaline scans has given him their undivided attention. When Ëólas makes his voice lighter, friendlier, the crowd beams. When he's stern and determined, the people nod their heads and commit themselves to his objectives.

During his own turn, Magnus reveals the new reports the captains received regarding what people witnessed and the fate of each attacker, namely that the captains of the guard have secured the city's safety. Adaline glances at Hamon, who, as a co-captain, most likely sentenced someone to die this morning. His affable demeanor and Westley-like charm are nonexistent. Instead, a seasoned soldier committed to carrying out his king's laws towers beside her.

Adaline shivers. The crowd looks at Hamon and Fólas with nothing short of admiration and gratitude. As she observes the crowd again, she spies Sallie with Jem on her hip and her kids lined up in a row, the eldest son balancing the youngest sister on his shoulder. When Sallie's and Adaline's eyes meet, Adaline raises one hand in front of her chest and wiggles her fingers in a subtle wave. Sallie doesn't wave back. Shifting Jem to her other hip, she braces him with both arms to stop him from toppling forward and out of her arms. Adaline chews the inside of her cheek until Jem squeals as he waves to her. A smile spreads across Adaline's face, which Sallie returns with a quick wave that sweeps away the doubt that had settled in the pit of her stomach.

"A new friend?" Hamon nudges his chin in Sallie's direction.

"Don't you already know that, what with all the guards you have watching me?"

"Hey, I am responsible for making certain all people within this city are safe, including beautiful, headstrong foreigners with the most peculiar yet delightful accent and with no idea how this city operates, but she still insists on exploring as much as possible while she's alone and defenseless."

Adaline side-eyes Hamon while her lips twitch upward. "Don't even try using that charm on me."

A dimple appears on both sides of his mouth as he clamps down on a ballooning smile. "If I were attempting to charm you, you'd know. I'm merely being honest."

Adaline swats his arm and shakes her head, which only makes his grin grow wider.

After Magnus and Ëólas reassure the people that they will not permit further violence in the city, the crowd disperses with the city guard positioned throughout the streets to safeguard order and peace. Adaline waits off to the side, trying again to blend in, but goosebumps prickle her arms. When she looks up, one of the street guards gives her his back, his turn so sudden that Adaline furrows her brows. Subconsciously, she slips her hand into her pocket and clasps her knife. Hamon might recognize the guard, but before she can ask him, the king and commander general approach. With a slight bow, Hamon excuses himself and joins Fólas at the end of the bridge where they clear the way for the council.

Adaline hesitantly rests her hand around Magnus's offered elbow. When they cross the bridge, they enter the human half of the city with Thoren huffing behind them. "Do you and Ëólas always address the people together?"

"Yes. As long as we both are here, I establish human law, and Ëólas oversees the elves. We jointly mediate any grievances as well."

Huh. How's that work? Adaline refrains from commenting as they continue toward a forge. Along the way, Magnus points out banks, hospitals, public bathhouses, and other businesses all while answering Adaline's endless questions with mutual enthusiasm. He radiates a subtle but constant internal glow when he takes stock of the city's growth. The council members talk among themselves and take notes, but Adaline and Magnus pay them and Thoren's scrutiny little attention during the walk. If Thoren knew Adaline still carried her knife, he'd probably tackle her to the ground and rip it from her pocket.

At the human-run forge, Adaline peeks into a slack tub full of water and tests the weight of the cross peen hammer while overhearing the council inspect the building's rotting foundation, and Magnus and Ëólas assign people to handle repairs. On their way to the elves' forge, they traverse over another large bridge, where everyone's steps slow. From here, the castle resembles something a child would build on a beach.

On the opposite side, however, the ruins and columns still standing cast long shadows over the dark-green fields that stretch between the city's end and the abandoned palace where she first arrived. The sun, sagging low in the late-summer sky, highlights the curved three-story center building. Set a bit farther back, its two-story wings sweep away from both sides until they bend backward and fade out of sight. The white marble, gray-lavender roofs, arched windows, and exterior walkways must have awed visitors long ago. Now the collapsed roof of one wing, shattered windows, and smashed balconies sing the palace's lamentation. Further desecrating the palace ought to be forbidden.

Adaline presses her hand over her heart, her instincts telling her those ruins have everything to do with the Forbidden Lands being forbidden in the first place. That palace must have belonged to the late queen Hamon mentioned.

"What happened there?" she whispers.

Ëólas lowers his eyes, turns away, and hurries off the bridge.

Magnus's face wilts. "That, we do not speak about." Gently, he nudges Adaline to keep moving forward.

As she follows suit, Adaline looks at the palace one more time, committing to memory what should have been, rather than what is. A story waits there, begging to be told, and Adaline can feel her curiosity taking root deep inside her.

To peel her eyes away from the ruins, Magnus changes the topic. "What makes the Neutral Territory and this city unique is that humans and elves are forbidden from entering each other's lands. Though we have established routes for passage between the kingdoms, the routes are not the safest."

"So the other kingdoms are isolated from each other?"

"Quite."

"Doesn't that make trade difficult?"

"Very, which is why we must rely on our people and work together to ensure the success of our kingdom. And by fostering relations with Lameiría, we're creating new opportunities for the future."

"So there's a lot more riding on the success of the Neutral Territory than just your two kingdoms becoming friendly, isn't there?" When Magnus confirms her thoughts with a nod, Adaline's mind races ahead. "But if the kingdoms are so isolated, wouldn't some of them feel threatened by what you're trying to do here? Is that why those people started fighting the other night?"

"Did I not say she's perceptive?" Magnus says to Ëólas, who keeps walking, lost in his own thoughts.

"I'm not certain that's a good or bad thing," Thoren says behind her.

When they've almost made their way back to the castle, an arena the length and shape of a football field marks their arrival at the training grounds for the city guard. Instead of one large field though, a low rock wall divides the grounds into quarters, each sporting a pair of guards sparring and a handful of people observing their efforts. Squat buildings surround the arena itself, which Magnus explains are both barracks for the unwed and private indoor training rooms.

"Of course, we have more housing arrangements surrounding the outskirts of the city," Magnus says, stepping closer to her, "but this arena allows us to learn how to balance our different methods so we complement each other. It's here that Ëólas and I determined how the city guard would patrol together and report disturbances or disagreements among our peoples."

Adaline nods as she processes everything Magnus has shared, but she can't peel her eyes away from the flashes of steel against steel. Each clang echoes inside her head, warning her to turn around and head back to Market Street by herself. She's held a sword only once, when Dax threw an axe at Renn-Fest and won a sprained ankle. She vowed to keep his baby safe while he lay on the canvas-and-plank stretcher before two peasants carried him away.

Swept along with Magnus and his group, Adaline enters the arena and the sunbaked grounds. One spectator rises and hollers, and the sparring ends immediately, allowing her the chance to exhale and clear away the migraine that threatened to take hold. All guards present rise and stand at attention, facing the king and Ëólas. Two people, one wearing burgundy and the other navy, sprint over to the council. When their conversation about supplies, injuries, and schedules lasts more than thirty minutes, Adaline meanders toward the private training rooms.

The tan brick buildings with rounded oak doors are indiscernible from each other, but the sound of laughter pulls her toward the fourth building to the right. Peeking in the window, she discovers a small room with a standing rack supporting swords of various lengths, weights, and materials, including a few wooden varieties shaped like German long swords and Japanese tantou double-edged short swords. The back wall displays posters with Da Vinci-like sketches of foot stances, arm positions, and motions.

Must be for rookies.

She moves to push the door open, but before she touches the knob, the door swings open. Two sweaty teenage boys rush out, only to stumble backward when they see her. With a quick bow, they rush around her to fall in line behind the other guards still standing at attention. The boys can't be more than twelve years old—a reasonable age for them to join their local militia. But their baby-smooth faces make her heart ache.

Despite the circumstances that would've motivated them to sign up—free lodgings, daily food, a secure future, adventure, camaraderie, et cetera—she can't imagine ever making that decision herself.

Chapter Fourteen

THE GOBLET

After touring the city, Adaline excuses herself and heads to her room to wash up, relishing the cool water on her tacky skin. As she wipes away a streak dripping down her neck, she kneels on the sofa to enjoy her partial view of the human side of the city, as well as Alderton's farmlands and meadows that extend into the horizon. Folding her arms over the windowsill, she rests her chin on her wrists. She can't recall the last time she saw so much green and blue without buildings obstructing the view, but she misses the hustle and bustle of the city streets and the diversion they provide.

In her room, she's not sure what to do with her time, aside from looking out the window and attempting to record notes and sketch moments from the day. Reaching into her pocket, she wraps her hand around her phone. She could watch a movie, but that would kill the battery faster, and she needs to know she can turn it on the moment she returns home. If she returns home.

Five more days.

At least.

How desperately she wishes she could check her social media accounts and connect with a friend. She could search the castle for Mercia or Seira, but after an entire day of playing the role of Lady Adaline, she wants time to be herself. Without snide comments about impropriety. Without watching every word that comes out of her mouth so she doesn't reveal the advances of her own world.

At home, she'd most likely be grading papers or working on her next research project or curling up on Cindy's sofa while they drank wine and leaned on each other's shoulders, Cindy's chin-length hair tickling Adaline's neck. Does her best friend think she hasn't returned any texts or left a voicemail screaming congratulations at Cindy and Dax's official engagement because, once again, Adaline's chosen to bury herself in her work? Does Cindy not yet even realize Adaline's missing? Aside from her students, Beccah, and the Grump, no one would wonder where she's gone. Not for a long while. Because she has no family left back home to care she's disappeared.

Adaline jumps off the sofa and wipes her eyes.

Books. Books are always an excellent distraction, and Magnus said he has some.

Despite her throbbing feet, she makes to leave her room when a new pair of shoes resting by the vanity catches her eye. Squatting down, she picks up one shoe and turns it over in her hands, noting the light gray fabric, the hand-sewn beaded flowers on top, and the thick cushion inside. When Adaline slides one foot in, warmth and comfort cushion her sole, and the day's exhaustion and chaotic emotions drift away.

Seira. The shoes have to be from her. Adaline hugs the other half of the gift to her chest, then slips that one on as well and exits her room while humming softly as she meanders toward Magnus's private study. As much as she would love to find and thank Seira first, she doesn't want to venture to the elven half of the castle uninvited and risk disappointing Ëólas again. Besides, somehow Adaline knows Seira will show up when she's ready.

Throughout the castle, female servants pass by, carrying trays of food, dirty laundry, and buckets of water. They either don't notice Adaline or avoid eye contact for a reason, similar to the cleaning crew when they'd enter the university building after most other staff had gone home for the night.

The two guards standing beside the study doors don't stop her from knocking. Magnus's muffled voice tells her to enter. She pulls on the thick, round knocker, but the heavy door doesn't budge. One guard steps forward, pushes it open for her, and stands to the side to allow her space to enter.

"Ah, push, not pull. Thanks." When the guard doesn't speak or smile, Adaline goes inside where she finds Magnus rising from his chair and walking around his desk. Ëólas is nowhere to be seen in the dim study. All that remains of him is an empty chair and a tidy stack of papers on his desk.

"What brings you here at this hour?" he asks.

A cool breeze drifts in through an open arched window, a gift after a sultry afternoon. The days may be hot, but the evenings usher in an unrelenting chill. "Am I interrupting? You said you have books."

"I am only reviewing some old documents, nothing of importance. Come in and help yourself."

Magnus points to the bookshelves near his desk and beside the flickering fireplace. When she strolls over to the leather-bound books, he sits down and resumes his tasks, shuffling scrolls and parchments followed by the occasional grunt. Hunched over his work, he rubs the back of his neck, then rests his elbow on the desk and his cheek in his hand.

Examining one book at a time, Adaline flips through a couple of pages to discern the topic of each. The language stuns her at first, forcing her to re-read the first page a few times until she realizes everything is spelled phonetically.

"Convenient," she mumbles.

The first books focus on economics and politics. Wrinkling her nose, she puts those back. The next book is an overview of Alderton's history.

"Oh! May I read this one?"

When Magnus nods, she turns to leave, but he puts down a document, props both elbows on his desk, and steeples his fingers together. "Adaline, please, have a seat."

With her back to the door and Ëólas's desk, she sits in one of the two chairs in front of Magnus and lays the hefty volume on her lap. The fireplace to her left crackles and pops quietly. Not sure what to say, she waits while Magnus gazes beyond her, his expression vacant, his eyes heavy.

"I'm sorry I'm bothering you during off hours," she says, pulling him back to the present moment.

"Off hours?"

"When you're not working."

"I hardly ever have off hours, so do not fret. Did you enjoy today's tour?"

Adaline fidgets with the book cover, popping it open and closed with her index finger. The chair, with its rather hard surface, forces her to sit up straight. "Very much so, thank you."

Behind her, a chair scrapes against the stone floor. She cranes her neck to see Ëólas taking a seat at his desk. Their eyes meet for a moment, then look away.

Why didn't I hear him enter the room?

Magnus rubs his chin. "What are cities like where you come from?"

"Oh, um, you know. Cities are cities."

He arches an eyebrow. "If that were so, you wouldn't have been so curious today."

Again, she fidgets with the book cover, trapping and releasing her index finger. "I really shouldn't say much about my world."

"Why?"

Two eyes bore holes into her back. Would it be weird if she turned her chair sideways so she could at least see both Magnus and Ëólas? *Yes, yes, it would.* Because the latter doesn't particularly like seeing her.

Crossing one leg over the other, Adaline bounces her foot. "As an anthropologist, it's my job to observe and learn about other civilizations, not interfere, judge, or influence them."

"So you are free to study our world, but I cannot study yours?"

Ëólas harrumphs behind her. A bead of sweat drips between her shoulder blades, and the tingling sensation down her back makes her shudder. She should move away from the fireplace.

Flexing her shoulders, she picks at the corner of the book. "Yes? I know that sounds like a double standard, but it's not fair for me to introduce new ideas that the people of this world haven't discovered yet on their own. The achievements of my world took centuries of discovery, exploration, and trial and error. I can't rob this world of its own evolution."

Beneath his thick, trimmed beard, Mangus presses his lips into a thin line. "Tell me then, in what ways are our worlds similar?"

Ëólas scoffs, and his contempt rumbles through her core. The book slips out of her lap and hits the stone floor with a loud thud. The king doesn't flinch. Scooping up the book, Adaline hugs it to her chest.

"Well…" She glances about the room for inspiration, but her thoughts focus on the things she misses most: flushable toilets, toothpaste, social media, cars, and TV. When Magnus lists his head to the side and sighs, she takes a deep breath and recalls instead the moments that made her feel at home here.

While she thinks, she hugs the book tighter. "Print books haven't died. We still love a good story. I mean, who doesn't, right? Parents still work their asses off. Kids still play in the streets. Sometimes. They much prefer vid—indoor games."

"And?"

Adaline goes blank.

He drops his hands to his lap and leans back. "How about the food? Using horses? How we construct buildings? Farming? Really, all of that's different where you're from?"

Her eyes drift to the brocade curtains. "Oh, we hang curtains in our rooms too."

Magnus bursts out laughing, releasing those pursed lips. "Is that really all? Please, tell me something else, anything." When she doesn't respond, his eyes narrow, and his expression darkens. "Do you have wars in your world too?"

Again, Adaline can feel Ëólas staring at her back, staring through her. She curls in on herself and shrinks against the back of her chair. "I don't think humans will ever stop causing war."

Magnus nods, his face full of sorrow. She hears only silence from Ëólas.

Unable to stand the sadness on Magnus's face, she offers, "But we're also more vocal about protesting bad decisions and challenging our government to make better laws."

Peering up at her, Magnus asks curiously, "Your people can protest the decisions of your leaders?"

She nibbles her bottom lip. She should learn to keep her mouth shut. Who knows how leaders in this world might crack down on such an idea before it even has the chance to take root among the people?

When she doesn't answer, Magnus presses again. "Are they not imprisoned for creating unrest and defying their lords?"

"I should go," she blurts out. Placing the history book on Magnus's desk, she turns to leave, pausing for only a moment when her eyes meet Ëólas's as he ponders her words. The fire casts shades of amber on his long, dirty-blond hair that falls softly over his chest. For once, his expression appears neutral, which confuses her even more. Contempt and frustration are easy to read. But neutral?

"Adaline, sit down." The command in Magnus's voice forces her to spin around and face him. "I haven't dismissed you. And if you defy me again, I'll have you spend the night in the dungeons." Standing up, Magnus looms over her, glaring at her as he dares her to disobey him, but the corner of his mouth twitches mischievously.

She narrows her own eyes and stiffens her back to puff up her chest. He could have thrown her in jail this morning, but he didn't. Even now, she hears that voice in the far recesses of her mind, reinforcing the idea that this man is, in fact, a friend. "Fine. Do I at least get a blanket and dinner? I'm rather hungry from all that walking."

Magnus and Adaline stare at each other for a full minute. When he doesn't break his pretense, Adaline sighs and turns to leave. She's too tired to play a game of Renaissance chicken. Ëólas shakes his head as she walks past him, but she can't discern whom he's disagreeing with.

Magnus erupts into laughter as she reaches the door. "Is this how you talk to people in power?"

"To those who don't deserve respect, yes."

Both of Magnus's eyebrows shoot upward. "Your leaders must earn the respect of their people?" He laughs more when Adaline stares him down and grinds her teeth. "Alright, alright. I won't press anymore. Come, take the book." He holds it out to her while she lurks by the door, mentally cursing herself for giving away details about how democracies work.

The door opens from the outside, forcing Adaline to move out of the way. Servants enter the room, carrying large trays of food, plates, and bottles of wine.

After they place everything on a long table against the back wall, they hurry out of the study, silently tugging that heavy-ass door closed.

She tries to follow them out, but Magnus calls her over, his voice having resumed that jovial tone she came to appreciate today. "Have some food. I invite you to dine with us. And I won't ask you more about your world. At least for tonight. Come now."

Her fingers brush against the metal door handle, but she doesn't tug it open, not as she listens to Magnus and Ëólas fill their plates and reminisce about the day. Even though they touch upon a disagreement about expansion goals, the way they speak frankly shows they're friends. They're different when it's just the two of them; they're more at ease. They banter the way Cindy and Adaline do when staying up until the wee hours of the morning and getting punch-drunk. Letting go of the door handle, she walks to the table. With a wide smile, Magnus hands her a plate. Without an audience watching her or servants fretting beside her, she takes three thick slices of lamb, cuts herself thin slices of smoked gouda, and grabs a puffy sourdough roll. The guys move to the smaller, round table near the window, far opposite the fireplace, and don't take their seats until Adaline does so first. Her heart skips a beat at their chivalry.

"Would you like some wine?" Magnus asks.

What she'd really love is a gallon of cold water, but before she can ask for some, Ëólas says, "She might prefer something more *spirited*."

Is he joking? With me? Who are you? Looking at him incredulously, she shakes her head. She has zero interest in drinking tree spirits ever again. "I'm fine, thank you."

"Ignore Ëólas. He's been in a foul mood the last few days, which he better shed before tomorrow evening's celebration."

Ëólas scowls.

"What kind of celebration?" she asks.

"To mark the anniversary of the Neutral Territory coming together," Magnus says. "All of the gentry will attend, those who have helped the city to reach its current potential. It's also a chance to celebrate the city's progress at being able to not only sustain itself but also introduce new trade between our kingdoms. You're expected to be there, of course, as my ward."

"Oh, okay." She looks down at Mercia's dress. "I'm sure it'll be fun."

"Don't worry. You'll have what you need, Adaline."

"Thank you." She pokes her food with a spoon, wondering how many lords and ladies will be there. And how many will judge her. Can she keep up appearances in front of so many? She sets down her spoon, ignoring her stomach's growl. Magnus hands her a goblet of wine, which she quickly takes from him but tells herself not to guzzle the whole thing.

Not daring to see whether Ëólas is watching her, she brings the metal cup with its embossed lion face to her lips. "It's so heavy. What's this made of? Pewter?" She sips slowly and fills her mouth.

"Yes," Magnus says. "And lead."

Adaline stops herself from swallowing and stares at the cup she's still holding in front of her. *Lead? Shit.*

"Not to your liking?" Ëólas asks. "Prefer something stronger?" The corner of his mouth curls into a half smile, but her brain can't comprehend this side of him, one that teases or even hints at humor.

Trying not to swallow, Adaline shakes her head and presses her lips upward into a stiff smile, but the wine trickles down her throat. She brings the cup to her lips, and as she pretends to sip more, she slowly releases the wine back into the cup and puts it down, far away from her plate.

Magnus and Ëólas stare at her.

Pretending not to notice, she focuses on her plate and whether she must pick up the slices of meat with her fingers. In the center of the table, a large serving fork rests on a platter. And a long, sharp carving knife. Magnus and Ëólas exchange a look that Magnus shakes off.

When Magnus reaches for his goblet, she curls her toes as if she's accidentally stepped in a pile of shit. He lifts his cup to his mouth. She bites her lip. Keeping his eyes locked with hers, he takes a sip. She can't help but wince. He takes a large mouthful but doesn't swallow, waiting for her to confess something.

"Oh for the love of God, stop!" she says. "Lead is poisonous to humans."

Magnus spits the wine into his cup and uses a silk napkin to pat dry his chin. "What do you mean?"

"Please don't tell me your cookware is lined with lead too? Oh my god, your baths?"

"Wood," he says. "Our baths are wooden."

"How do you know this?" Ëólas lowers his head to his hands and massages his temples.

"History," she says. "But lead poisoning takes a long while before symptoms show." Maybe that last bit will help them feel better.

"What symptoms? How long?" Magnus presses the heels of his hands into his eyes as if to stop his head from exploding.

"Decades, I think. I mean, it depends on the rate of exposure. But it took the Romans a few decades to realize they were slowly poisoning themselves, and they bathed in lead-lined baths, so...any bowel issues lately? Severe fatigue? Abnormal irritability?"

Magnus exhales loudly. "No. Although we're all certain to be irritable tomorrow when we tell my council members that we will need to cease lead trade."

With heavy brows, Ëólas looks to Magnus. "We didn't know."

Magnus nods.

Adaline hunches her shoulders and shrinks in her seat. She doesn't dare touch her food while neither Magnus nor Ëólas move.

"I'm sorry." Her small voice sounds loud within the prolonged silence.

Magnus pats her hand. "Thank you." Then he steals a slice of lamb off her plate and waggles his eyebrows. When she glares at him like she's admonishing a child, he chuckles a long, low rumble that fills the room with an air of much needed levity.

Keeping his head down, Ëólas resumes eating his meal, but in between bites, he says, "You may have just prevented another war."

Adaline blinks at them a few times. Sitting up in her chair, she reaches for the carving knife, cuts her dinner roll lengthwise, and uses the tip of the knife to place the meat on the bread, followed by the jagged slices of gouda she cut. She uses both hands to pick up the whole thing and keep it together while the guys, eating slowly, watch her do this. After she takes a huge bite, chews, and swallows, she says, "It's called a sandwich."

"Why?" Ëólas asks. "Because the bread tastes like sand?"

"Ha, no."

In a nook tucked away from the bulky furniture, the three of them eat their meal in peace. Ëólas shares his plans for adding more vegetation to the city, while Magnus tells stories from his childhood. Although Ëólas isn't forthcoming with personal stories, Magnus talks enough for the both of them.

True to his word, Magnus doesn't press Adaline again. Instead of remaining alone in her room, she spends the evening listening to their tales and learning more about the other kingdoms surrounding the Forbidden Lands, and in the wee hours of the morning when exhaustion has turned her punch-drunk, she finally trudges back to her room where she yanks the laces loose from her bodice and sheds Mercia's dress. Collapsing into bed, she barely hears Kayla enter the room and drifts off to sleep without a single thought about home.

Chapter Fifteen

THE KOI FISH

The next morning, Adaline sprints out of the castle gates, squeezing her finger that won't stop throbbing from where she jabbed it one too many times with a needle. Seira and Mercia had met Adaline in her chambers for breakfast and brought along their current craft projects. Granted, their efforts are more about survival skills than spare-time hobbies.

While Mercia squinted over the handkerchief she was embroidering, Seira made herself at home, lounging on the sofa with her almost finished periwinkle dress draped across her lap. Given the cluster of fabric it had been the day before, the dress had come together impossibly fast—a feat Adaline mentally recorded in her list of possible, extraordinary elven talents. But, given the last few days, she wouldn't be surprised if she discovered Seira had mice helping her assemble the dress in her private chambers.

Regardless, with Seira's guidance and endless patience, Adaline began learning a new skill rather than screaming every time she had to pull out the thread and try again. The morning ended only when Lady Marzella called her daughter away for lessons and insisted Adaline return mid-day for her dress fitting, the idea of which challenged Adaline to use every ounce of her reserves to keep her eyes directly on Lady Marzella and not let them roll back in her head. After all, she's trying to help in the ways she knows how.

When Adaline pulled on her cloak and slipped her feet into her shoes, she gave Seira a big hug that she returned with a gentle yet tight squeeze, a simple gesture that left Adaline speechless, maybe even hopeful. Without giving herself the chance to hesitate, Adaline asked Seira if she wanted to venture into the city today, but her small pixie-like features crumbled into a collage of anxiety and dissociation. She shook her head fervently and scurried away, ghosting through the corridor with her new dress billowing behind her.

Shaking off the image of Seira's sad departure, Adaline pops over to Jósep's stall, eager to see if he's made progress on his own ginormous project, but his craft stands alone and untouched. With a frown, she scans the crowed street, searching for that one familiar face, and hears someone calling her name from further up Market Street. Following the male voice, she weaves between the elves coming and going, their conversations quieting but not halting as they pass her, until Jósep emerges, waving her over to a stall similar to his own. Behind the display table, wooden string instruments of various sizes hang from support beams running across the length of a shop stall.

When Adaline approaches, Jósep gestures toward the elf behind the counter, a tall stranger no older than forty with long black hair braided behind his back. "Lady Adaline, allow me to introduce to you my childhood friend, Delós. He's the one who convinced me to come here myself."

Adaline curtsies, not sure if that's how she should greet an elf, but he smiles broadly and, crossing one arm over his chest, bows. As he quickly, quietly assesses her, he rests his hands on the shell of an instrument displayed across the counter, its size similar to a violin, but rounder and wider, and its future top off to the side. Given his familiar touch as he brushes his fingers across the creamy yellow grain, Adaline suspects him to be the luthier who owns this shop, and he must have perfected his skill long ago. Only a master artisan could have achieved such smooth texture, graceful curves, and detailed stenciled designs.

I bet they all sound lovely too. Her fingers twitch at her sides as the scents of spruce and ebony draw her closer. "Your work is lovely. I can't imagine how long it's taken you to make these."

"Ah." He glances at his latest project, the hollow hourglass body nestled within a bed of sawdust and wood scrapings. "My wife did half the work. She's gone for a walk with our son."

Moving in front of the top piece, he studies the jagged shape for a split second, then scrapes a thick, rectangular file along the edge in rapid successions, the sound of grinding grain hypnotic. Shavings of wood curl and fall to join the others. "I thoroughly enjoyed your song in the tavern the other night, my lady. I had not heard music like that before."

Adaline's face grows ten degrees warmer. *Damn tree spirits.*

Glancing up, Delós adds, "Thank you for introducing me to something new. I hope you equally enjoyed our company and we'll hear you sing again."

"Oh, no." She takes a step back as Jósep and Delós stare at her. "I mean I did—have a good time, that is. I loved the tavern and the music and the dancing, but I haven't touched an instrument in years." Images of Nan and Adaline sitting side by side on the piano bench bombard her mind. She shakes them loose, only to see her father pushing his stool away from his drum kit, letting her settle between his arms, his beard scratching her cheek as he held her hands and taught her how to play "We Will Rock You" in the detached garage.

Glancing around the street to avoid her new friends' scrutiny, she clears her throat to ease its sudden tightness. *Maybe spirits would be nice. Can I get some now?*

As if reading her mind, or rather her face, Delós reaches under his counter and hands Adaline a rough, half-formed instrument and scraping tool. She's too surprised to refuse him. While she registers the weight of the handle, he explains where and how to apply pressure so she can strip away the excess. The wood, light and cool, smells like summer camp outs deep in the forest.

Adaline pushes the tool against the wood as Delós demonstrated, and a shaving flutters onto the ground, its graceful descent capturing her attention, taking her with it, making her somehow feel lighter too. She smiles at Delós, but instead of finding him and Jósep watching her or chatting together, they bow deeply with an arm crossed over their chest. Knitting her brows together, Adaline takes a step back to turn around but bumps into something solid. The faint scent of lavender permeates the air.

Her heart thumps faster, and her stomach twists in on itself. Turning her head to the side, she spies long, dark-gold hair brushing her shoulder.

Ëólas looks down, eyeing what she's doing, what she's holding, the file's length so similar to a dagger's, the tip narrow and sharp. "Enjoying yourself?" His voice is flat and lifeless, even as his breath warms her cheek.

Every muscle in her body locks in place. "Uh-huh."

She inhales deeply, taking the extra beat to remember how to use her legs. Stepping forward, she puts down the tool and faces him, but he's no longer behind her. She rises on her toes and cranes her neck, scanning every face passing by, every backside merging with the crowd, but she cannot find him or his golden eyes. Even his scent has vanished, leaving behind nothing but a void, as if he's never been more than a dream.

Ready to escape the elven side of the city, Adaline excuses herself but only after convincing Delós that instead of taking home the wood and tool, she'd rather return another day and learn from him.

A few moments later, Adaline scurries across the bridge. Helping her forget that lavender scent, the smell of fresh baked bread tickles her nose and pulls her toward the bakery. A plump woman gives up stacking crescent rolls on a tiered display table and hands them directly to each man walking past in a single-file line. Wearing overalls and supporting a pickaxe slung over their shoulders, they take turns depositing a coin into a pouch on the bakery table and taking a roll with them.

When the procession concludes, Adaline strolls closer to peer in the window and admire the different sizes and shapes of loaves and treats. Without a word, the lady offers Adaline the last roll.

"I'm so sorry." Adaline clasps her hands in front of her chest. "I don't have any money on me."

"Tell the king." With a wink, the lady pushes the toasty roll into Adaline's hands and disappears into the shop with an empty basket dangling from her hand and a heavy, bulging pouch hanging from her belt.

As Adaline bites into the soft, buttery bread, she closes her eyes and moans quietly. Now where can she find *un cappuccino*? Swallowing her last bite, she meanders toward Sallie's and admires the old man and his wife hammering soles onto shoes. She snickers at the idea of elves sneaking into the shop in the wee hours of the morning and secretly finishing the shoes, then makes a mental note to never share that story here.

When she arrives at Sallie's, the shopkeeper and her kids are running back and forth, inside and out again, fetching items for multiple customers while her husband hauls a large crate around back.

Little Jem won't stop tugging on his momma's hem until he sees Adaline and runs to her, throwing his hands into the air. "Up! Up!"

With a wide grin, she scoops him up and balances him on her hip.

Sallie drops two candles. "Oh, my lady, no. You need not—"

"I don't mind, Sallie. Tend to your customers." Once she's sure Sallie doesn't mind Adaline holding her child, she teaches Jem how to do a fist bump.

After the tenth time, he points outside and squeals, "Fishes! Fishes!"

"May I bring him to the bridge?" Adaline asks his mother.

While counting out money into a customer's hand, Sallie looks up and smiles gratefully. "Yes, thank you. My mother will be down shortly with lunch."

Adaline nods and carries Jem outside. When she sets him down, he tugs her hand toward the Rialto until they stop in the bridge's gazebo-like center, in the same spot where Magnus and Ëólas addressed everyone yesterday. Biting her cheek, she pushes thoughts about that particular elf aside. She doesn't want to think about whether he's following her. Whether he thinks she's a bad omen. Whether the carefree side she saw at dinner last night was for Magnus only. She understands why Thoren dislikes her; he's doing his job, trying to keep his king safe. But Ëólas? He's nothing but stiff around her. How can she ever get that commander general to lighten up? And help her get home.

Jem tugs on Adaline's cloak, pulling her free from her thoughts. With a half-smile, she hoists him onto her hip again so they can both peer over the railing and look for fish below.

"Jem, would you like to hear a story about the persistent koi fish?"

"Story, please!"

Adaline laughs. "Okay then. Once upon a time, in days of old and when the world was still new, a school of koi fish used all of their strength to swim upstream.

They looked like polished jewels as they swam against the powerful currents of the Yellow River and pushed themselves to climb a waterfall."

Adaline wiggles her fingers as if they were fish threading through the currents. Giggling, Jem grabs her fingers and squeals when he catches two of them.

"Fish can't climb up a waterfall," a human child says, standing at the end of the bridge. Three of his friends, or maybe siblings, run up to him. A little girl with braided pigtails pulls his hand, tugging him back onto the street.

"Are you certain about that?" Adaline calls to him.

The boy regards her carefully, assessing whether he might get in trouble for speaking up, and takes a step forward, bringing his sister with him while his friends wait on Front Street. "Well, did they climb the waterfall?"

Leaning her back against the railing, Adaline moves Jem in front of her and holds his hand to distract him from the cloak's clasp at the base of her neck. "You are correct in that some of the koi couldn't bear the challenge. They gave up and let the river carry them back downstream. But..."

She glances at the kids and arches an eyebrow. Slowly, the kids climb the bridge, encouraging her to continue.

"Local nature spirits saw the fish trying to climb their waterfall, so they made it taller and taller."

"That's not fair!" another kid says.

Adaline shrugs. "A lot of the fish must have felt the same way, because they turned around and let the river carry them downstream too."

The first boy frowns, then looks up and says, "A lot, but not all?"

"But not all. After swimming upstream for a hundred years, one koi fish finally climbed to the top of the waterfall. As a reward, the koi fish was turned into a golden dragon and became a symbol of strength and power, and the waterfall became known as the Dragon Gate."

The children smile and hop around each other. Beyond them, a few adults who had been listening jerk themselves away from the bridge and resume their work. As soon as a mother's bellow cuts through the din, the kids scatter and race home.

Before they disappear from view, the boy turns back. "Thank you for the story, my lady. Do you...do you know more?"

I'm a walking library. "A few."

"If you happen to be here again tomorrow, might you tell us another one?"

A part of her heart aches; this world probably doesn't allow much for childhood. But she doesn't let the child see that as she says, "I'd be happy to."

The boy grins from ear to ear, then sprints off.

Releasing a long sigh, Adaline takes Jem back to Sallie, who rushes over, thanks Adaline profusely, and carries Jem out the back door, gesturing for Adaline to follow. With Kian, her husband, and their oldest son managing the store just fine now, Sallie's two daughters have gathered around a log table set up in the grassy alley behind the shop. Sitting on overturned crates, they eat and kick their legs until the eldest daughter hops off her seat and takes Jem from their mother. While she feeds him, Sallie waddles over to a metal garden table positioned under a window. On top of the table rests a tray of tea and plain buttered biscuits.

"Please," Sallie says, pulling out a chair for Adaline.

Feeling slightly guilty at invading their family time, Adaline sits down and takes her cues from Sallie, who passes Adaline a full teacup along with two biscuits to start. They drink in silence, neither sure how to find the easy conversation they shared two days ago.

When Adaline bites into the biscuit, the buttery texture melts against her tongue. "Perfect."

A broad smile lights up Sallie's face. Then she winces, fluffs the pillow behind her back, and wriggles to find a more comfortable position.

Looking at Sallie's rotund belly, Adaline asks, "Do you...are you nervous?"

"Nah. I was petrified the first two times, my lady. But after that, my third and fourth popped out within seconds. I consider myself a professional now. Though, truth be told, my lady, that lingering fear never goes away completely. Not even after they're born."

They both watch the girls mothering over Jem, picking up the food he throws on the ground and wiping his mouth. Their interactions aren't that much different from the way Adaline used to dote on Cindy's little sisters. But never once did Adaline imagine being a mother herself. The concept of motherhood left her feeling...nothing. Instead, she focused on music and dance and, later, academia.

Adaline takes another bite and sip. "May I ask a personal question?"

Sallie looks Adaline up and down. She crosses her arms and rests her forearms on top of her belly. "Alright."

Is she on the defense? "What did you want when you were little? What kind of future did you dream about?"

"Oh, pretty much what I have now," she says, uncrossing her arms and drinking more tea. "A good man, steady work so we wouldn't starve, and as many kids as I could squeeze out before I'm thirty. I should be able to have one or two more before then."

"Whoa." Adaline pops the rest of the biscuit in her mouth and chews. *Sallie's close to my age, but she already has five kids and looks twenty years older. Is that due to this time period or parenthood?*

As Sallie watches her four babies, the love in her eyes makes her exhaustion melt away. "Nothing is more important to me than my babies," she pauses, pats her belly, and whispers, "and that includes you."

In between sips, Sallie either rests her teacup on top of her belly or uses a fist to push the baby away from her ribs. "I'm done with pregnancy for now though. This one needs to come out. I miss seeing my feet." She rocks forward, trying to push the tea tray closer to Adaline and offer her another biscuit. "How about you? Have you found a suitor yet?"

"Oh. No. Not in there." She gestures toward the castle.

"Hoping for love, are you?"

Adaline pauses for a moment and flashes back to Derek and the numerous yet brief relationships she had before him. She debates a vague answer but decides to return Sallie's honesty. "I'm not sure I know what love feels like."

"Oh, my lady. None of us really do until we're caught up in it. Count your blessings that no man knocked you off your feet. That's how we make mistakes, and women can't afford mistakes, not when they follow us around for the rest of our lives."

Adaline dunks her biscuit in her tea and takes a bite, but she struggles to swallow the soggy clump. She got knocked down all right, only it wasn't by love.

When the girls finish eating, Adaline takes her leave and mentally promises to repay Sallie's hospitality by bringing some sort of treat next time. She just needs to figure out where to procure that treat. As she strolls further along Market Street, more people seem to recognize her as they curtsy or tilt their hats hello, which Adaline accepts as an invitation, even if only for a few minutes, to inquire where they're going and which business is theirs.

When she turns the corner, a single column from the ruins comes into view. She takes a step toward it, but the direct route leads through dark alleyways. Pocketing her hand, she clasps her knife. If she asks for an escort, will Magnus let her explore the ruins? Just because they don't speak about them doesn't automatically mean she can't go up there and explore, right? No one specifically said so...

Adaline takes another step forward, but the ding-a-ling of the shop door next to her makes her jump. She drops her shoulders and releases the knife. *I should ask first.* She owes Magnus that much.

A lady rushes out of the shop, carrying a new bolt of fabric, and hurries down the street, stopping for no one as if she's late to meet someone, probably a client based on her level of panic.

I wonder if they're going to the king's celebration too. Adaline throws her head backward and groans loudly. "Shit!" *I fucking forgot.*

Chapter Sixteen

A CHALLENGE

Gathering her skirts, Adaline walks as quickly as she can through town, across bridges, uphill, under the gate, upstairs, and down the corridor toward her room. She's out of breath by the time she reaches her chambers where Lady Marzella paces back and forth like a mother hen defending her coop from a fox.

"I'm sorry," Adaline exhales breathlessly.

Not waiting for an explanation, Lady Marzella thrusts her finger toward Adaline as if it were her husband's sword. "After all His Majesty has done for you, the liberties he's allowed you to take with your wandering, the excuses he's made for you shirking your contributions to the castle, the luxuries he's gifted you..." She stops bombarding Adaline for a moment to gesture vehemently at the doors to Adaline's chambers, then continues her verbal assault. "I don't care where you come from, but you live here now. I will not see our king saddled with a spinster. At your age, you have no room to act like a forgetful child, and if your dress isn't finished in time for tonight, I'm the one who will—"

"What a relief that you have nothing to worry about," Seira chimes, stepping out of Adaline's chambers. "Come, Adaline. Thank you for your help, Lady Marzella, but I have everything sorted."

Seira pulls Adaline into her room and shuts the door on Lady Marzella's mouth hanging agape, thus securing Adaline's eternal gratitude and willingness to do practically whatever Seira has planned for tonight's celebration. Holding Adaline's hand, Seira leads her toward the bath filled with steaming hot water.

Behind the tub, Kayla waits with soap in her hand and a towel draped over one arm. "Good afternoon, my lady. I have lunch waiting for you, but would you prefer a bath now so your hair has time to dry?"

"That's a brilliant idea." Seira undoes the laces on Adaline's bodice, followed by the corset. "Not my choosing." Seira tsks to herself, and Adaline bobs her head in agreement.

After a bath and quick meal, Adaline sits on the edge of her bed with a towel wrapped around her body and stares at Mercia's dress that Kayla had laid across the sofa. Thanks to the camise she's worn underneath, the dress smells and looks clean—except for the dusty, somewhat-muddy hem Adaline's dragged all over the city the last three days.

She topples backward onto the bed. "Can I just not go?"

"My lady!" Kayla gasps.

With a lithe laugh, Seira flits over to Adaline, tugs her hand to pull her up to standing, and leads her around the privacy screen—from the top of which hangs Seira's periwinkle dress. "Slip this on."

Where'd that come from? "But that's yours, and what about the dress the seamstress fit me for?"

"No, it's not. And I dismissed her. She didn't understand."

"Understand? But..."

"We don't have time for buts. Kayla, help Adaline, won't you?" Seira clasps her hands together and looks dreamily into the distance. "I'll wait on the other side to see the final result."

As Seira skips away, Kayla comes around the screen, her eyes widening the moment she sees the dress. "Oh, my lady. It's perfect. Let me assist you."

With Kayla's help, Adaline shimmies easily into the dress and faces the mirror as Kayla closes the clasps along the lower back, making the dress hug Adaline's figure tightly. The soft, pleated bodice cups and crisscrosses underneath her breasts, comfortably lifting, separating, and supporting them without the need for a corset or bra. At the base of the V-neck, her décolletage looks plump and round. So long as she doesn't dance closely with anyone taller than her, the neckline doesn't reveal too much.

Turning sideways, Adaline looks over her shoulder to admire the beading that fans out along the clasps, creating a subtle butterfly-like pattern that flaunts her exposed upper back. She twirls around again, causing the full skirt that extends from her waist to swish around her toes and brush the ground. She never dreamed of wearing something so grandiose. Aside from the dress being a tad too long, her only concern now is a cool night. The cold-shoulder sleeves bare most of her upper arms before flaring outward into a short, sheer, ruffled bell shape that ends just past her elbows. Already she has goosebumps.

"Can I see yet?" Seira calls. When Adaline emerges, Seira leaps off the bed and hops up and down on her toes with glee. "Oh, I knew this would suit you best."

"It's absolutely stunning, but I can't borrow something so—"

"You're not borrowing it. This one's yours. It always was. I won't have you wearing any more hand-me-downs. Now sit while I comb your hair."

In a daze, Adaline sits in front of the vanity and folds her hands in her lap, her fingers skating over the fine fabric to admire their soft touch. Setting to work quickly, Seira combs through Adaline's curls, careful not to disturb the large waves, and hums to herself. For a moment, Adaline's back in her childhood bedroom with Nan doing the same. The memory is fleeting, but the nostalgia hits hard. Seira pauses. Placing a hand on Adaline's shoulder, the elven lady with those piercing grayish-purple eyes leans forward, wraps her other arm around Adaline, and rests her heart-shaped chin on the crown of Adaline's head.

Thank you. She squeezes Seira's arm to her chest and takes several long breaths.

In the corner of the mirror, Kayla carries a small tray but stops short, hesitant to interrupt. Adaline drops her hands again and nods at her, encouraging Kayla to walk over.

"His Majesty said you should wear this tonight, my lady." Kayla removes from the tray a simple, thin silver band that she wraps around Adaline's forehead. In the middle of her brow, the band dips with a single suspended diamond teardrop.

Not sure what to say or how she feels about being pampered in such a way, Adaline focuses on her breath and reminds herself that tonight is about the Neutral Territory. No one has any expectations of her. She's only the king's ward and practically a spinster at that.

"How about we add a flower on the side of your hair?" Kayla asks.

"Oh, yes." Seira prances over to the fireplace and pulls a white flower from the vase. After snapping the stem short, she passes it to Kayla, who slides it into Adaline's hair and secures the stem with hairpins.

Adaline looks from her curls draped around her shoulders to Kayla's glowing smile. "No snood? I thought women are supposed to keep their hair up in nets?"

"Yes, but not at a celebration such as this, my lady. Tonight, you are free to show off your assets."

A bit of Adaline's lunch comes back up and burns her throat. *How can I get out of this? Or at least make myself invisible?*

"Enough fretting." Seira taps Adaline's shoulder and waves for her to follow. "Time to go, Adaline."

Prancing to the doors, Seira picks up a pair of periwinkle shoes with a thin ankle strap and presents them to Adaline with a sweet smirk. The satin shoes match her dress perfectly. They fit comfortably too, and the heel raises the hem of her dress so that even her smaller steps allow her dress to make that swooshing sound that Adaline loves but won't admit to herself.

"Seira, how can I ever—"

"No need. Now off we go."

For the first time, Adaline notes Seira's slender white dress that hangs off her shoulders, hugs her chest with a heart-shaped neckline, and fits her like a Grecian goddess. The silver diadem circling around Seira's brow is anything but simple. Along the delicate band, intertwined branches with diamond-studded leaves alternate between pointing upward and downward. The additional three teardrop diamonds, the largest of which dips in the middle, make her look like an elven princess, and her vibrant eyes and platinum blonde hair reinforce her ethereal beauty.

Good. Everyone will admire her instead.

Kayla holds open the door to Adaline's chamber and looks upon her lady with kindness and pride. "You'll win someone's heart this night, that's for certain, my lady."

"That doesn't make me feel better," Adaline mutters to herself. She turns around to grab her cloak, but Seira catches her arm and steers her out of the room.

The castle staff have transformed the dining hall into a festive ballroom with all tables set up buffet style along the walls to reserve the majority of the floor space for dancing. From every column and arch hangs garlands, ribbons, and bouquets of flowers in shades of silver and purple. Pausing in the doorway, Adaline admires the décor, its balanced grandeur, and waits to walk in discreetly behind Seira, but she reaches behind her with a sing-song laugh and pulls Adaline along, linking their elbows together. The moment they cross the threshold, a servant at the entrance announces Lady Seira and Lady Adaline to the crowd. His voice projects over the chatter, laughter, and flirting. Everyone pauses their activities for a moment to look at them. Even though Adaline convinces herself they're all looking at Seira, the murmurs sweeping through the room tell her otherwise.

Quickly, Adaline assesses the other ladies' clothes. The humans have, indeed, forsaken their snoods, with many opting for simple headbands or necklaces. Most of them have more cleavage exposed than Adaline, which makes her mentally thank Seira again, and their extra-large full skirts have transformed them into musical bells. The elven ladies prefer slender dresses with long, cold-shoulder sleeves, wispy trains, and intricate headbands with fine chains that drape in layers down their long hair.

Spying Magnus on the other side of the room, Seira throws her hand into the air and waves with her entire arm. As they approach, Magnus excuses himself from one of his council members and a young woman with copper-colored hair, the one who had snickered at Adaline's age when she visited the ladies' parlor. She must be the treasurer's daughter. The woman curtsies deeply, bats her lashes, and smiles coquettishly only for Magnus to nod in return and leave. From over his shoulder, the lady narrows her eyes and curls her lip while staring Adaline down.

Oh, spare me.

Magnus kisses the back of Seira's hand and does the same with Adaline's. "You both look absolutely lovely." His sincerity allows Adaline to breathe again.

"Your Majesty." For once, she automatically curtsies. The crown upon his head subconsciously tells her to do so while her heels and ballgown cause her to bend her arms and legs more like that of a ballerina. When she rises, Adaline says, "You don't wear that often."

With the tip of a finger, Magnus taps one of the six grape leaves adorning his gold crown—well, technically his coronet. Pretending he doesn't want anyone to overhear them, he whispers, "It's rather heavy."

Adaline smiles at his informality, but something about the moment isn't quite right. "Where's Ëólas?"

Magnus looks toward the balcony. "He's attending to private matters."

"Oh."

"Here he comes now."

Appearing through the middle most arch, Ëólas meanders toward Magnus with an unfocused gaze as if lost in his thoughts. Occasionally, he pauses to return the jovial expressions of his people, momentarily the picture-perfect general with his fitted navy brocade jacket. The high collar, caressing the base of his neck and trimmed with gold, matches his jewel-studded diadem and his dirty-blond hair parted to the left. Standing tall, he offers his people a smile, a pat on the shoulder, a kiss on the back of a hand, all of which makes them glow and encourages them to relax and enjoy the night's festivities.

But the brief moments he has to himself, the beats in between the din, his pristine features turn slightly ashen and harden. The rosy color on his cheeks dims. His full lips tug downward, and his jawline tightens, accentuating the hard lines of his chiseled features.

The change is barely perceivable, but it's enough to make Adaline wonder if he is so much older than thirty. Regardless, something appears to be wearing him down. Actually, didn't Magnus say he had to wear Ëólas down and convince him to undertake this project? Did Ëólas then have to convince his king and queen, who aren't even here, to celebrate the Neutral Territory's success? Do they know one of their subjects died under their general's watch? The burden he carries seems to grow heavier with each step he takes.

A weight settles on Adaline's chest until a garbled voice calls her name, drawing her attention back to Magnus, who watches her with an arched brow. "Adaline?"

"Huh?"

The corner of his mouth perks up, but he suppresses it immediately. "I asked if you would entertain the idea of dancing tonight."

"Oh." She shakes her head to clear away the fog. "No. No, thank you."

"You don't dance back home?"

"She's a wonderful dancer," says a male voice full of mischief.

Adaline knows that voice. Turning around, she scowls at Merith but steps aside to make room for him to join their little circle. "Thank you, Merith. But I have zero intention of confusing anyone about my intentions here tonight, which are to blend in and disappear."

Seira giggles as if Adaline's said the funniest thing she's ever heard. When her amusement diminishes, she wraps her arm around Magnus's elbow and leans her head on his shoulder as if overcome with exhaustion. Adaline questions whether to ask if Seira's okay, but Merith doesn't give her the chance.

"Disappear? You chose the wrong dress then." The corners of Merith's mouth quirk upward, but his eyebrows soften as if he's speaking with an old friend. "Truly though, my lady, you're a vision."

"Thanks," she whispers, turning her head away from him while she searches for a change of subject.

"Am I not permitted to appreciate beauty?" Merith asks.

"Oh, just stop," Adaline pushes his arm, which has the same effect as pushing a brick wall. *If only he'd fall on his ass.*

"Stop what?" Ëólas asks, his voice approaching from behind.

Looking past Magnus, Adaline fixates her gaze on the people dancing, laughing, and talking effortlessly with each other and chews the inside of her cheek.

"Oh, Ëólas!" Seira sings and waves him over. "You look so handsome."

Adaline's eyes fall to the feet of everyone mingling around them.

"Ëólas, everything alright?" Magnus asks.

"Fine, fine. Nothing of immediate concern. And thank you, Seira. You look splendid." As he angles his body toward her, Ëólas doesn't temper the warmth in his voice and kisses the back of her hand.

Seira gifts him a sweet smile. "What about Adaline? Isn't she divine?"

No, no, no. Adaline locks her arms around her waist. *I will not let him get to me. I will not let him make me doubt myself. I will not lose my temper tonight.* Plastering a smile on her face, she faces him, grabs her dress, and curtsies again. "Good evening, Ëólas."

His brow creases, and he blinks several times. As his eyes pass over her, his chest stills until he clears his throat and readjusts his belt. "Hi. Um, good evening, that is." He gives her a slight, stiff bow before turning back to Seira.

Okay, that was odd. What did I do now?

Seira scrunches her face. "What was that?"

"What was what?" Ëólas draws his brows tightly together.

"That flimsy greeting." Seira glances at everyone, waiting for them to confirm they saw the same oddity.

While Adaline sucks in her bottom lip, Magnus stretches his hand over his mouth and massages his cheeks to hide his grin. Merith provides no diversion either; he takes one look at his commander and sidles away until he disappears into the crowd, leaving Ëólas to stare after him.

Choosing now to be more cognizant than ever, Seira yanks on Ëólas's sleeve. "Well? That wasn't right at all. Do better."

Ëólas opens his mouth, closes it, then opens it once more. "Seira, I—"

"No, no. Don't speak to me. Speak to Adaline."

With his lips clamped shut for all of eternity, Ëólas glares at her and flares his nostrils.

"So!" Adaline says, her voice ten octaves higher than usual, as she stares down Magnus until his shoulders stop shaking with amusement. "What's on the agenda for tonight?"

Mimicking her exaggerated enthusiasm, the king swings his fist in front of his chest in a hurrah gesture. "Music and dancing and speeches and food."

"Oh joy!" Adaline says, keeping her tone unnaturally upbeat. "Seira, what type of music do you—"

"How long has Adaline been with us now?" Seira tilts her head toward Ëólas, her eyes dim as she searches for clarity. "A month?"

A month! Why would she think I've been here a month?

Ëólas's voice cracks, "Three days."

Understanding breaks across Seira's face. Rolling her head backward, she stares dreamily at the chandeliers. "Oh, I see..."

What do you see?

A thunderous boom rises to a crescendo throughout the ballroom, causing all conversation to halt. The first entertainment for the night begins with the drums of Alderton, a set of wooden barrels with animal skin stretched over both ends. Their behemoth size reminds Adaline of springtime in Japan, when she listened to taiko while cherry blossoms colored the sky pink.

The thinner Alderton drums fit against the musicians' waists. With the backside of the drums left open, the men rest one hand against the drumhead, allowing them to simultaneously hold the barrel in place and control the instrument's pitch and timbre. Their continuous beats reverberate through Adaline's body, sending chills up and down her spine. Her palms itch to snatch a set of drumsticks and pound away herself, drowning out every thought, every insecurity, every fear.

When the pounding concludes, servers pass by carrying trays of wine. Adaline reaches for the first one and grabs a large goblet. As she brings it to her lips, Ëólas pulls the goblet out of her hand and slips her a different one.

"Take drinks only from the human servants." Without looking at her, he downs the tree spirits she almost drank.

A deep red flush creeps up her neck to her cheeks. "Thank you."

For the next performance, elves take to the center of the dancefloor, the same musicians and singers from the tavern. During their whimsical song, the elves dance in and out of circles while the humans observe from the sidelines. Shaking her head, Adaline stares at Magnus and Ëólas, waiting for them to join in and set an example for their people. Instead, they watch the entertainment and chat with each other. With an exasperated sigh, Adaline strolls over to a buffet table, eats some nature-themed fancy desserts, and stays in the corner, hiding her frown.

Mercia, spotting Adaline, rushes over with bright eyes, a wide grin, and her red curls bouncing behind her. "Oh, Adaline. You look beautiful! Mother said so too."

Huh. So she doesn't hate me for life. I guess that's good.

"She sent me over to tell you that those three guards near the topiary plan to ask you to dance."

"Oh god." *I'd rather she hate me.* Adaline scans the room for a quick exit. Maybe if she attaches herself to Magnus's other arm, she can escape dancing too. *Is that why Seira's so fond of him?*

Mercia giggles. "Mother gave you the highest praise. She told those guards that no one's fairer than you tonight. Which is true of course. She's so happy for you."

Someone's going to serve me a poison apple for dessert.

The musicians stop playing, and a young lady takes center stage, the one with the copper-colored hair, and Mercia whispers in Adaline's ear, "That's Lady Audney. Her father's Lord Otto, the king's treasurer."

Ha! I was right.

Following a deep curtsy, Lady Audney announces in a loud, clear voice, "I'd like to honor His Majesty with a song." The lyrical ballad she chooses perfectly suits her soprano voice, and her siren song fills the room, drawing admiration from everyone.

I give her extra credit for bravery too. Solo performances aren't easy. Adaline knows. She didn't handle the pressure well herself. Then again, that's not entirely true. Whenever she was dancing, the audience disappeared. It was the pressure and guilt from her classmates that broke her.

When Lady Audney concludes her performance, she bats her lashes at Magnus and curtsies even lower until her breasts threaten to tumble out of her crimson gown. Adaline chokes on the tart she had just bitten. Following the sound like a lioness, Audney glances up and catches the disgust written on Adaline's face.

Standing up ever so gracefully, Lady Audney clasps her hands in front of her chest. To the entire room, she asks, "Would Lady Adaline entertain us next? I've heard she's not only a master storyteller but also an accomplished singer and dancer."

Adaline's eyes snap to Merith, and he flashes his palms, flailing them back and forth to defend his innocence.

"Lady Adaline, certainly you'll share with us a song and dance from your humble foreign land? Or does your kingdom not have any grand traditions?" Again, Lady Audney bats her lashes and stretches her grin wider.

Adaline rests her plate on a nearby table and steps forward. "I'd love to, but sadly the waltz isn't a one-person dance." Thinking the matter over, she turns her back to Audney and—

"Surely one of the guards here is suitable for you?"

Fuck. She could walk out onto the balcony, leaving Audney and everyone else to their gossip, but as Lady Marzella chastised earlier, Adaline's rude behavior will reflect poorly on Magnus. *I can't do that to him.* Better to take command of the stage. Like Nan always said before Adaline's dance competitions, *Pull your shoulders back, hold your head up high, and remember everyone has their own insecurities and fears too. We're really not all that different from each other in that regard.*

Channeling Nan's undeterred strength, Adaline beams at Lady Audney. "I have taught the waltz countless times before."

"Splendid!" Lady Audney gestures toward a group of guards.

One man with a long nose, high cheekbones, and dark eyes steps forward and curls his lips into a seductive smile. Every hair on Adaline's neck and arms tingles and rises. The color drains from her face, her stomach turns sour, and her heart races.

"Oh, Ëólas! This is perfect." Seira lets go of Magnus long enough to shove Ëólas three steps onto the dance floor. "Go dance with Adaline."

No, no, no, no, no, no, no.

Chapter Seventeen

A Dance

With a stiff neck, Ëólas scans the faces of his people, of his friends. No one objects. No one offers to rescue him. No one dares to imply that elves and humans will never truly get along. He takes a step forward, his arms glued to his sides. "I'd...be delighted."

Adaline's stomach churns; the sour tarts were not a wise choice. Rather than mirroring the horror in his eyes, Adaline strides over to the elven musicians. *It's just a dance lesson.* "We'll need a triple meter song with a three-four beat, please. The first beat is long and low with the second and third short and high. I'm looking for a mmm-BAP-BAP rhythm."

Even though the musicians nod, they stare at her as if she has three eyes. Like a gift from above, Delós appears and slips in among them, allowing Adaline to exhale and her shoulders to relax.

"I'd be happy to assist, my lady. Can you provide an example?" Delós passes her his mandolin.

With a swift nod, Adaline swings the instrument strap over her shoulder, and her fingers fall onto the strings as if they'd never left. Picking out the base note with her thumb, she starts with an A5 chord on the first beat so it plays long and low. When the chord vibrates through her hand and up her spine, people like Audney vanish into a distant memory. Instinctively, she strums the higher notes on the second and third beats, keeping them short and peppy with a steady rhythm, and hums along, a new song simmering on her tongue.

As she plays, Delós's brows unfurl, and he nods fervently. "Yes, yes. I see. How interesting."

She stops playing but holds on to the instrument a moment longer. Its light weight and woody varnish smell match the mandolin she took off her father's office wall. She'd busied herself by picking out the different sounds while he finished grading papers. When she finally stopped playing around, her father had been leaning back in his chair, his eyes closed, his worries gone. For once, he seemed at peace. Why do such random memories have to resurface at inconvenient moments?

Adaline hands the mandolin to Delós. "Try to stick to a major key. A progression like A5, D, and E5 would work, but feel free to add your own variations."

Delós bows low. "I understand perfectly, my lady."

"Thank you." Ignoring the hundred or so faces staring at her, Adaline walks back to the center of the room, waits for Ëólas, and prays he's thought of an excuse to end this without jeopardizing the Neutral Territory's stability.

As persistent as ever, he presses his lips into a thin line and trudges up to her. "Now what?"

He's just like every other person I've taught lessons to. He's just another student. Granted, those students had been future husbands practicing their first dance with their fiancées. But Adaline didn't feel comfortable with all of them either: A few taught her to always wear a turtleneck during lessons.

"Okay. The waltz is meant to be a fluid and roman—graceful dance during which a couple glides around the room counterclockwise."

"Alright."

"As for steps—" Gathering her dress in her hands, she lifts the hem to reveal her feet and demonstrates how to slide forward, to the side, and together again, creating a box step. He never takes his eyes off her feet and mimics her precisely in rhythm and flow. "Well done."

He smirks. "That's rather simple."

"I'm glad you think so. Now, before we move on, you need to know something," she says with all seriousness. "A gentleman never, ever lets his partner fall. To do so is utterly shameful."

"Understood," he says.

"Good." Next, Adaline gently lifts his left arm, bending it at the elbow. "Do not drop this arm. No wobbly, limp elbows either. Show your strength, but do not let your partner's arm weigh you down either. She must carry her own weight."

He arches an eyebrow. "I agree."

Confused about why her heart skipped a beat, Adaline steps forward and slides her palm against his. The breeze dies down, making the air in the ballroom uncomfortably warm. Their breath becomes shallow and their movements small, as they stare at their joined hands, at the way her palm fits naturally in his.

Even though her mouth has gone dry and her limbs feel heavier, Adaline reaches for his other hand hanging at his side. He shudders ever so slightly at the contact. Certain he loathes being so close to her, Adaline wills herself to bury all emotions. This isn't about her. She's not that important. He's probably never danced with a human before. Nothing about this moment, about him, is personal. Nothing at all.

Steeling herself, she places his hand on her waist, and Ëólas's eyes widen. Breaking eye contact, she glances down, sucks in a sudden breath, and vehemently wishes she were wearing a turtleneck. Ëólas follows her gaze until his eyes pop upward, and his grip on her hand and waist tightens. She bites the inside of her cheek to stop herself from smiling.

The murmurs of everyone watching, their wide eyes and sudden fidgeting, help Adaline refocus and find her voice. "The gentleman is supposed to lead, but I assume you'll allow me?"

"Mm."

"Alright. We'll start with the basic step. One, two, three. One, two, three. One, two, three."

Their movements are stilted and small at first. But knowing Ëólas understands the concept, Adaline nods at Delós, and the music begins. He plays through the progression a few times while Adaline and Ëólas stay in their space, focusing more on the steps and not hurting each other. Soon enough, Ëólas has the steps down. In fact, he never misses a beat or a step. Sensing he can keep up, Adaline leads him around the circumference of the dance floor.

His light steps and strong posture help her feel more like herself, and they swirl faster and faster. The other string instruments join in, creating a quartet that fills the room with a robust, smoother sound. As the strings get more comfortable, Delós picks out a more upbeat, lively melody on top of the mellow background.

Adaline initiates a turn so that he twirls her under his open hand. Instinctively, he lets go so she can spin freely across the room, her dress swishing around her feet until she spins back to him, this time with her shoulders against his chest, their palms touching, until he releases her once more, and they return to dancing nearly cheek to cheek. His hands feel more secure. His steps are confident. He even smiles as they effortlessly glide wider and wider around the room, becoming a swirl of navy blue and periwinkle that blends into one.

Slowly, Ëólas takes the lead, and Adaline floats around the dance floor like she's participating in a competition with a partner who makes sure she feels secure and protected. She's danced the waltz so many times, but never did she lose herself, never did she succumb to the movement and music, feeling all the pieces sliding back into place again. But something else about this moment is different, with the music filling the ballroom, the candlelight casting warm globes of orange and red on the marble floor, and the occasional gust of wind that sweeps through the arches along the balcony to kiss her skin.

Toward the end of the dance, Ëólas's joy permeates the air too with his fluid, long strides and raised cheekbones. He even hums with the song and pulls her closer, their bodies moving in sync together, their breaths mingling. That faint scent of lavender envelops her, drawing her nearer. Maybe she wouldn't spend the rest of the night in the corner. Maybe she'd stick around for another dance. Maybe—

Her heel catches on something solid, something that shouldn't be on the dancefloor, and the dream shatters as she tips sideways. Her hands slip out of Ëólas's grasp. His reassurance vanishes, and the music screeches to a halt. The marble rushes up toward her face, and she extends one hand to break her fall. In a split second, she's going to break her wrist. Her face turns ashen, and her chin trembles. All breath leaves her. But an arm tugs her around the waist, and the marble becomes immobile again. Her hand hovers an inch above the ground until Ëólas pulls her up against him, his warm hand resting on her exposed upper back.

Breathlessly, he cups her cheek and turns her frozen face toward his. "Are you alright?"

Leaning into him, she rests her hand on his chest, her fingers memorizing the touch of his navy jacket. While time tries to resume its normal pace, she blinks at him and his pained gaze. "Yes. Thank you."

He takes her in one more time. Certain she's okay, he narrows his eyes and glares at someone behind them.

"My deepest apologies, Lady Adaline," purrs a cold female voice. "I was too eager to try the dance myself. I ought to have been more careful and waited for you to pass." Lady Audney curtsies at Adaline but tilts her head up just enough to flash a sly smile.

Letting Ëólas go, Adaline faces her directly. "Okay," she says dismissively, then turns and walks through the center of the ballroom with her shoulders back and head held high, not giving two shits about the drama Lady Audney wants to stir up.

"Wicked. Wicked viper," Seira hisses at Lady Audney as she takes Adaline's arm and tugs her close, tucking her friend safely at her side.

While Lady Audney fumes in the corner, Magnus fusses over Adaline's well-being and thanks her for introducing everyone to a lovely dance. He asks if she could teach him next, but when she doesn't move, he turns to Seira. "Would you honor me with a dance?"

Seira holds onto Adaline even tighter. "It's not safe."

Safe? What does that mean? "I'm fine, Seira. Completely fine. Everything's fine. Go dance with Magnus."

Seira studies Adaline carefully. "I suppose. But...she wasn't too mean?"

What does she think I'll do? "No. I don't care what someone like her thinks of me."

"Good."

As if satisfied that Adaline's not about to do something rash, Seira accepts Magnus's offered arm. Once Seira and Magnus take to the dancefloor, other couples join them and attempt similar steps. The elves are more fluid than the humans, but both sides try the new dance, and the sight of them sharing a new experience makes almost breaking her arm worthwhile.

"You need me to arrest her?" Hamon whispers in her ear.

She elbows him. "Go find a pretty lady to dance with." When he waggles his eyebrows at her, she scoffs. "Look elsewhere."

With an exaggerated frown, Hamon backs up. "You know Magnus will have words with her father about this."

"I hope he doesn't. It's not worth the trouble."

"You're something else, you know that?"

Adaline shakes her head. "Go. Dance."

"As you wish." He bows, spins on his heels, and leaves.

Oh my god, he said it! He actually said it! Go, Westley!

Shrinking away from the crowd, Adaline squeals with glee. Overall, the ball has been far more entertaining than she ever thought possible. Even that dance. And he didn't let her fall. Rising onto her toes, Adaline scans the crowd, but Ëólas has disappeared. She meanders along the perimeter of the room, hoping to thank him properly, but spies him stepping out onto the balcony. Alone.

Did he get hurt?

With everyone distracted, she follows him, slipping unnoticed between the massive arches and disappearing behind the ballroom's inner glow. She peeks around the pillar to verify he's not meeting someone and to avoid any accusations that she's eavesdropping. Releasing a hard sigh, he hangs his head low and stares at his hands resting on the balcony railing.

Adaline takes a small step forward. "Is everything okay?"

He spins around, startled to see her, then refocuses his attention on the private gardens behind the castle. When he doesn't speak, Adaline bites her lip. He's never particularly enjoyed being around her, but they've made progress, haven't they? And Magnus and Merith think highly of him. Maybe she should get one of them to come out instead. She knows so little about him. Yes, he's grumpy. A lot. But she's also seen him drop his guard, when his smile warms those around him. What's it like to be on the receiving end of that?

Step by step, she strolls over to the railing and rests her hands on the cool balustrade, its grainy surface prickling her skin. Below, nightfall and uninterrupted clouds have shrouded the trees, fountains, and paths in darkness. Anyone could lose their way down there.

The wind picks up, blowing her curls behind her, exposing her bare shoulders, and erasing what little body heat had remained from that dance. Moments pass, neither speaking. She closes her eyes and inhales in the fresh night air's earthy scent. If only she could mute the music and chatter from inside. When she opens her eyes, Ëólas is staring at her, studying her, with those golden eyes no one can hide from. She faces him, but he looks away.

She grips the railing tighter as her gaze returns to the shadows concealing the garden. "So..."

"Do you need something?" His voice is deep and his words short.

"No. I just wanted to make sure you're okay. Thank you for—"

"I'm fine."

"...Okay."

"You needn't stay out here," he says, his posture rigid and voice harsh.

"Oh." Adaline drags her hands off the balustrade, letting its imperfections scrape her palms. "Have I done something to offend you?"

He doesn't respond. She pinches her lips together and presses a fist into her hip. *Is he just going to ignore me?* Silence stretches between them, making time slow down and her blood seethe. She parts her lips to repeat herself, to demand that he answer her, acknowledge her, see her. But wherever he's gone inside his head, it's somewhere she can't follow. Even if she tried, she wouldn't be welcome. He'll never let her in.

Adaline drops her fist, and her shoulders droop. "I don't know what I did wrong," she blurts out. "How can I make amends if I don't know what I did?"

When he still doesn't respond, she crosses her arms and taps her foot. "Lovely. Great progress here." Tossing her hands into the air, she turns to leave.

"Are you always so impatient for answers?"

What? How long does it take him to respond to simple questions?

She stares him down, but he doesn't speak again. With a loud huff, she storms through the archways. It's not like she asked to be here in the first place. At that thought, she spins around one more time and demands curtly, "Any updates on why I might be here?"

"No."

"Fine. When you get the books, let me know so I can help."

"No."

What? Are you fucking kidding me? That's all I'm going to get from him? I'm the one trapped here! "Why won't you let me help? Research is what I do."

"Because magic is for elves, not humans."

"But I'm the one who went poof!"

Remembering he's a living being, he waves his arms hurriedly to shush her. Adaline's eyes bulge, and her cheeks turn flaming hot. The wind picks up, whipping their hair across their faces. Ëólas doesn't bother to pull the dark, golden strands away from his eyes. Turning away from the gusts, she takes a deep breath to stop her blood from boiling and massages her temples to soothe the tension building in her head.

When the wind dies down, she lowers her voice but refuses to be silenced. "I'm the one whom magic sent here, and if I did come here for a reason, then I need to figure out why."

"You came here because you desecrated sacred grounds," he says through clenched teeth. His eyes bore into her as if he's trying to drill holes into her secrets.

"What are you talking about? How did I do that?"

"You broke the circle."

The circle? The circular structure? "I didn't break anything. The earth broke it."

"Because you went somewhere you weren't invited."

"Says who?"

He sneers impatiently. "Elves."

"We don't have elves in my world!"

Ëólas steps toward her so quickly that her heart stops beating. He's so close, practically looming over her with those golden eyes digging into her soul. She almost takes a step back but lifts her chin and chest.

"And why do you think that is, Adaline?" he asks, his voice raspy and low. "You come from a world where humans killed all elves and took control of all lands. Do you truly think I would trust you with access to magic?"

"That's not true! Elves never existed in my world. There would be historical records and evidence and—"

"What do you think that circle was? I don't need your help. I don't want your help. And trust me, I will find out why you're here. Fae help you if your intentions are malicious."

She wills herself to find words that will fill the void, but her mind fails her. She's been here only a few days, and he's assumed the absolute worst. How can someone be so close and not see her at all?

He lingers over her, his rapid breaths warming her mouth, but she refuses to flinch. Summoning the cool night air to calm her nerves, she inhales deeply, pulling into her body scents of pine and lavender. Their mellow notes help her breathe more evenly, to see clearly. Her chest stops heaving, but her bottom lip quivers. His eyes flick to her mouth. His face blanches, and he swallows hard. Taking two steps backward, he looks at her one last time, and his gaze softens for a moment, only a moment. Then he turns away and recedes into his thoughts, to that place she's not invited.

She backs up until her shoulders brush against the chilly arches, and his silhouette blurs under a misty sheen. She blinks a few times to clear her vision and steadies her voice. "You may be someone with a high status here, *Lord* Ëólas, but you're small minded and judgmental. If you want things to change in this world, then that change has to start with you."

He loosens his grip on the railing but refuses to look at her. He's done with her.

Having said her piece, Adaline marches through the ballroom to the exit. Magnus catches her, his face creased with worry, but she reassures him she's fine. She just doesn't feel much like dancing anymore.

After Kayla helps her shed Seira's dress, she shrugs into a new silk nightgown, wraps a wool throw blanket around her shoulders, and sits at the window, looking out over the city and the people bustling about, free of castle politics. Trust does exist down there. She can feel it.

If Ëólas won't trust her, then she can't trust him either. Like Nan always said, *Whenever you're in need of answers, you should look to your own feet; usually what you need is right in front of you.* Nan's always right. The answers must be down there.

Screw him. She's good at research. Tomorrow, she'll dig up the secrets of this world.

Chapter Eighteen

THE RUINS

For the first time, Adaline rises early. With Kayla's help, she dresses quickly, but they both pause when Kayla discovers Mercia's old dress missing from the wardrobe. In its place hang five silk chemises and three new gowns, each with matching shoes. The detail on two dresses hints at Seira's perfectionism and preference for beaded flowers. For today though, Adaline chooses the third dress, a dark-green crushed velvet gown with no embellishments beyond a thin, gold scroll trim. Though simple, it fits Adaline perfectly, along with the light, sleeveless chemise, and the tight bodice enables her again to go without a boned corset underneath.

Seira, I love you.

Before Adaline can sprint out of her room, Seira and Mercia pay her a visit. Their chat goes quickly, and neither of her friends comment on Adaline's lack of conversation. Her ears tune in only when Mercia mentions Lady Audney.

"Father said she received a proposal last night from some lieutenant. She turned him down, but His Majesty told her father that she best accept the proposal and not waste time waiting for others. Lord Otto is furious."

Adaline pulls another stitch out. "How old is the king?"

"Mid-thirties, which is why everyone's growing more and more nervous without an heir."

"Why do you think he hasn't married?"

"I have no idea."

Mercia's conversation fades into the background while Adaline rests the handkerchief she's been attempting to embroider on her lap and ponders why Magnus danced with only Seira. Then again, it's not like Adaline stayed long to see if maybe he did dance with someone else. Still, she sends up a little prayer to whomever may be listening in this world that Magnus doesn't suffer from unrequited love. She doesn't want him to slowly suffocate from the inside out. No one deserves that kind of torture.

At the end of their morning routine, Adaline again asks if Seira wishes to accompany her through the city. Like before, Seira's face loses all its color, and she wanders out of Adaline's room as if her mind had drifted away from her.

Adaline watches her leave, the long hallway gobbling up her slight figure, then heads into the city carrying a basket with a large loaf of bread she wrapped up during breakfast, along with a few jars of jam and pouches of tea that no one will miss. With her messenger bag slung behind her and hidden under Seira's cloak, Adaline stops by to say hello to Jósep and Delós. Then she crosses the bridge where the children spy her and beg for a story. Leaning against the railing, she tells the children about a magic mirror and a jealous queen who relies on poison apples to get what she wants, only to lose everything. More kids show up, including one elven child too. Before she goes, they beg her to tell them a story tomorrow.

"I'll try," she promises, unable to lie.

She follows Sallie's girls back to their shop and gifts their mother the basket. "I'm terribly sorry I can't stay long, but I wanted you to have this."

Staring at the goods inside, Sallie shakes her head in confusion or disbelief, maybe both. "Surely you can stay for a bite and a cup of tea?"

Unable to deny her, Adaline follows Sallie to the grassy alleyway outside where they chat about potty training Jem, her older son's first crush, and business. After the girls bring them boiled water, cups, and plates, Sallie exhales loudly and leans back in the metal garden chair. "We've had more customers recently. I think the tension seems to be lifting, thank the fae. It's hard with those ruins looking down upon us all, and the attack didn't help matters."

Why does everyone keep mentioning fae? If only she could ask without sounding like someone not from this world. She stirs her drink, the teaspoon clanking against the ceramic cup more than once, and watches the tea leaves settle to the bottom while she debates a safer question. "What are those ruins?"

As Sallie sips her tea, darkness passes over her face. "Long ago, a horrible war took place there between elves and humans. To some of us, it's a symbol of bad omens. But to others, it's a symbol of hope."

"Why such different views?"

"I suppose it's because it's the last place known to have seen magic."

"Magic?" Adaline drops her spoon in her cup, and a splash of hot tea stings her hand. As she rubs away the mess, her mind races. *That's where I first appeared. Why didn't Magnus tell me this?* Because he doesn't trust her either. Adaline grinds her teeth. *It doesn't matter. That's exactly where I'm headed next.* She could use more info first though. "Who, what, when?"

Sallie drains her cup as if to delay answering. "The last queen of Aerytol. She cast a spell there, right before she died. Some say the spell killed her. Others say she sank into the earth and—"

Jem's screams have Sallie standing up in seconds. "Terribly sorry."

"It's okay. Of course you need to go." *I can ask more questions later, and I bet Mercia knows a lot. Doh! Why didn't I ask her sooner?*

Adaline excuses herself and weaves her way through the city. When she reaches the edge of the grass plains, she ducks behind the last building, buries her hands in her hair, and removes a handful of bobby pins. Pulling off the snood, she lets her hair flow downward, covering her ears and praying that anyone who sees her heading toward the palace will mistake her for an elf. After tucking the snood into her messenger bag, she pulls Seira's cloak tightly around her shoulders and climbs the slope leading toward the ruins of Aerytol.

At first, she keeps her pace slow. *Should I really be doing this? I mean, the elves do call it the Forbidden Lands.*

Then again, the only person she'll piss off is Ëólas. *I don't need your help*, he'd said.

His words reverberate in her head, and no matter how hard she tries, she can't drown him out. *He already thinks I'm the harbinger of death, and this might be my only chance to find clues on my own.*

Digging her heels into the ground, Adaline presses forward. With every step, the faint sound of waves calls to her in the distance. When she stands in front of the triple-story main building, her Spidey sense tingles; everyone here seems eager to bury the past, but it's her job to find the truth.

Time to get to work.

In the daylight, the palace is far more enormous than she remembered. She walks along the front, taking in the smooth white marble, the graceful craftsmanship, the flowing curved lines, and the nature motifs. Many of its towering windows have been smashed, but the intact doors are shut tight. Not wishing to climb through broken glass, Adaline makes her way toward the right wing that curves gently backward until she finds an arched tunnel that leads to the gardens.

Within that tunnel, a single door stands ajar. Adaline pauses. At the end of the tunnel, green grass shines like an emerald beacon. Inside, darkness looms, pervasive and quiet. Drawing Seira's cloak tighter around her shoulders, she slips inside. The hallway is empty except for tapestries that had long since been torn in half, burnt, or shredded. Her flat shoes echo as she makes her way through the maze of corridors and passageways, the palace's silence sinking into her bones while her curiosity guides her.

One corridor leads to a grand room with partially broken stained-glass windows that cast silver and light-purple hues across the floor. Seven curved steps lead to a platform with two thrones standing tall—but empty. Adaline stills, and the stale air settles around her, either welcoming her or warning her to leave, to let this room be. A queen used to live here. Probably a king too. Did they have a family? Friends? They must have entertained thousands of people in this room. They laughed here. Loved here. Died here. With her heart aching, Adaline bows to the abandoned thrones and whispers a prayer for the lost.

She exits through another corridor that eventually leads outside to the massive gardens. The palace wraps around the gardens in a semicircle of arches, bridges, walkways, and towers before ending at the edge of the sea. The palace itself, except for the left wing's collapsed roof, remains remarkably intact. If only she had time to explore every inch of this place, but she's already missed lunch. The walk here took at least an hour, and who knows how long she has until someone tells Hamon or Fólas where she's gone. Plus, this might be her only chance. She was lucky the last time she defied Magnus. She can't fool herself into thinking there won't be consequences after this.

Following the natural curve of the garden and its slight slope downward, Adaline clears a broken fountain, a line of shrubs, and crumbled benches on the stone patio. She pauses on that patio and looks out at the adjacent sea, just like she used to do with Nan on cool nights after they finished dinner. They'd sit together, rocking back and forth, and watch the sun set over the lake. That was a perfect view too.

In the distance to the left, a tight line of trees protects an enclosed portion of the gardens. Given that the rest of the garden is so spacious and open, the closely planted trees seem out of place.

I ran through trees the night I arrived too. That's when Thoren almost killed me. And Ëólas saved...

Not finishing that thought, she hurries down the patio steps and heads for the trees, her pace hastening the closer she gets. But a breeze rustles past her ear, dragging with it a soft female voice that whispers, "Go back."

Adaline halts and scans the gardens. "Seira?" *No, she doesn't leave the castle.*

A cough near the tree line catches her attention. A leather-clad arm appears from behind a broken statue, its bottom half resembling a horse. Seconds later, a man steps out, his face half covered in stubble.

Shit. I've been caught.

"What are you doin' up here?" The man leans against the statue, against the horse's missing torso, and hooks his thumb in his side pocket.

"Exploring."

"What's that now?"

"Exploring," she repeats louder. "I was just curious and wanted to see this place for myself."

The man stands up straighter and stares at her more closely. His eyes roll over her from head to toe, and his crooked grin causes bile to rise in her throat. "Where you from, talking like that?"

No one in the Neutral Territory has ever inquired about her accent. *He's not from here.*

When Adaline doesn't answer, the man saunters toward her. He's rather short compared to Adaline's five-foot-seven, but her height advantage doesn't make her feel better. Something doesn't feel right. Even though he's taking his time, his face doesn't show any trace of kindness.

Adaline takes a step backward. "As the king's ward, he's probably looking for me by now. I'll just be on my way."

She walks in the opposite direction, toward the exterior archway she discovered when she first arrived, and keeps Shorty within her peripheral vision. But another man approaches from that same archway, his black clothing missing the insignia of Magnus's guards. Something about his nose seems off too, but she doesn't linger to ponder why or how so.

Adaline feigns a small smile, then sprints in the opposite direction, aiming to enter the castle through the doorway that will lead back to the throne room. Without looking back, she dashes around overgrown bushes and fallen chunks of the palace roof, but she can hear their grunts chasing her. Her adrenaline kicks in as she pumps her legs and arms faster than ever before, hiking up her skirts while her bag slaps her behind. But the second man cuts her off, running ahead, drawing closer to the first, and forcing her to run back into the gardens and toward the line of trees. If she can squeeze between them, maybe she'll find safety on the other side.

As she nears the trees, a sharp, sudden tug on her cloak makes her stumble a few steps. The clasp digs into her throat, choking her, slowing her down for several long seconds, until the chain snaps, and Seira's gift falls away. Adaline keeps running, but one man yanks the strap of her messenger bag. She yelps, and her face hits the grass as she rolls over a few times with broken bits of marble scraping her cheeks and arms. She scurries onto her feet, but the man with the weird nose blocks her way and glares down at her. Taking a step back, she bumps into Shorty and cringes. She's surrounded.

The wind howls through the grass, and the sea breaks against the shore. Aside from their raspy breaths, she hears nothing else. Not a bird's chirp. Not a horse's gallop. Not a friend's voice.

"She's a pretty little thing," says the man in front of her. His grin accentuates his missing nose, which someone had cut straight off.

Oh god. What do I do now?

Shorty grabs both of Adaline's wrists. "Just hurry up and get her top off."

Adaline's heart pounds in her ears. She twists and bends and tries to wrench free, but together they wrestle her to the ground, pushing her shoulders down and kicking her feet out from under her. Thoughts dissolve into instinct. She yells and kicks, not sure what she's hitting. No-Nose yanks her arms above her head and pins them against the grass, digging his fingers and nails into her forearms. He lets up only to help roll her onto her chest. With her cheek pressed into the earth, Shorty sits on her legs and rips at her laces. As her bodice loosens, all sense of reason leaves her. She screams and fights to pull her legs under her so she can push up off the ground. She flails her arms, not caring how much harder No-Nose digs into her flesh to keep her still. Her "Nos" and "Stops" sound more like the cries of a trapped animal. Survival. All she wants is survival.

"Can't you get her to hold still?" bellows No-Nose.

"You try undoin' these damn laces."

"This is taking too long."

"Then just take her with us."

Oh god. I'll never see home again. Or Seira and Mercia and—

Shorty gets off her legs and rolls her onto her back. All that rolling around and struggling caused her skirts to twist and rise up just enough to free her legs. Before he can sit down again, Adaline knees him in the groin harder than a horse pounding a road at a full gallop. Grabbing his crotch, he freezes up, squeals, and collapses beside her.

No-Nose pauses in his confusion, not long, but enough that Adaline rips her arms free. He grabs her hair to pull her back, but she turns around and punches him in the left eye like her father taught her. As No-Nose's head snaps backward, Adaline scrambles to her feet. Leaving her messenger bag behind, she clutches her loosened bodice close to her chest and runs back inside the palace. She'll do anything to never let them get a hold of her again.

As she sprints into the throne room, pounding footsteps in the main entrance cause her to skid to a halt. Her straps fall off her shoulders.

They've cut off my exit. How many of them are there?

With sweat dripping down her exposed back, she searches for another exit, but rubble blocks the collapsed corridor to the left wing.

Fuck! She runs back the way she came, only for No-Nose to emerge from the shadows. With nowhere to run, Adaline trembles. *What can I do? What can I do?*

She dashes toward the thrones, praying she'll find a passage behind them, but No-Nose sprints after her. As she scurries up the steps, his fingers brush her shoulder. She cries out, recoils, and braces herself to keep fighting. With a raised fist, she turns around. But he's falling backward, down the stairs, his hands still in the air and reaching for her. His body tips further backward, revealing behind him a head of dirty-blond hair, flinty golden eyes, and a hardened stare full of quiet rage.

Before No-Nose cracks his head open on the floor, Ëólas drags him down the steps by his collar and tosses him aside. The man jumps to his feet and reaches for a dagger in his boot, but before he pulls out the entire blade, Ëólas smashes his fist into No-Noses temple. He collapses to the ground and doesn't move again.

At the top of the stairs, Adaline crumbles into a heap, hugging her bodice close. She can't even cry. Her breaths come out jagged and shallow as she sits there, praying her heart won't explode inside her chest.

An elf with long, wavy russet brown hair pulled back in a half bun kneels down in front of her. She knows his face, but someone has switched off his usual animated expressions, replacing them with careworn eyes as he examines the dirt on her cheeks and the bruises on her arms.

I know him. "Fólas?"

"Yes, my lady. We're here. You're safe." He slowly reaches out to her, to help her up, but a tear falls from her cheek and splashes the back of his hand. He drops his arm.

"We need to leave this room immediately," Ëólas says. "Get him out of here. Return to the castle and tell Magnus she's fine. We'll be out in a moment."

I'm fine? I, I suppose I am.

"But the lady?" Fólas doesn't move from her side.

"I have her. Go." The general keeps his voice neutral, having erased any and all feelings toward her.

She wishes he'd yell.

Adaline glances up as Fólas drags No-Nose, now bound but still unconscious, out of the throne room. Ëólas's footfalls grow louder, toward her, but she can't look at him. He sits behind her, and Adaline flinches.

"I'm going to tie your laces, alright?" He waits for her to nod, then quickly pulls the laces tight and secures a bow at the bottom. The moment he's done, he rises and moves in front of her. But he doesn't offer a hand. "We need to go."

She has no energy left to stop herself from crying, a sound this room shouldn't have to hear again, but the natural stone walls amplify her sobs. "If I'm s-so vile, wh-why did you even bother?"

One by one, the hard lines carved into Ëólas's face fade away, leaving behind a haunting emptiness.

Adaline tucks her knees into her chest. Her curls slip off her shoulders, and torn grass falls to her feet. Burying her head in her lap, she rocks back and forth, but she can't get her body to stop shaking.

A silky-smooth blanket falls over her back, its electric-like warmth enveloping her, spreading throughout her body, easing her clenched muscles. She peeks up and recognizes Seira's cloak draped over her shoulders. *How did he... When did he...*

Ëólas kneels in front of her, his head hung low but his eyes find hers. "Adaline, I..." He shifts sideways and slumps beside her. Resting his forearms on his knees, he stares at his empty hands dangling between his legs. They sit in silence for a few minutes and let the air settle. When her breathing slows, they stare into each other's eyes, mirroring their regret.

Ëólas stands up first. "Can you walk?"

She nods but doesn't move.

"Do you need help?"

Again, she nods.

Ëólas leans over and, in one quick move, scoops her up into his arms. Her heart races, and she pushes him away, but he holds firm and stays quiet. He locks his golden eyes with hers and keeps his breathing slow and steady. Soon her breath matches his, and she relaxes in his arms, sinking further against him as he carries her to the front of the palace where Merith waits. Fólas and the two men tethered to the back of his horse have already started making their way downhill toward the castle.

"She broke our laws," Merith says quietly, unable to look Adaline in the eye. "What now?"

Ëólas sets her down on her feet. For once, he doesn't move away. "We take her to Magnus."

No one says anything further. After climbing onto his horse, Ëólas pulls Adaline up behind him. Once again, she rides into the city, only this time not as a guest but as a criminal.

When they enter the castle, Ëólas and Merith lead Adaline deeper inside until they arrive at the king's private study. Again, her six benefactors watch her every move as she sits down on the sofa.

"What was she even doing up there!" Magnus slams his chair underneath his desk, rattling the books, papers, and ink bottle on top. A candle falls over.

Adaline flinches while she stares at the pleats in her dress, the green velvet as pristine as this morning. Her mind keeps racing back to Shorty sitting on her, the grass scraping her skin, the dirt filling her nose. Trying to push the memories down takes all her strength, and she doesn't have much of that now.

Keeping his voice low, Ëólas leans against his desk, his eyes cast downward. "I'd like to know why she went there as well."

Merith and Fólas stay close to their lord, each lost in their own thoughts.

While Hamon paces in front of the dormant fireplace, Thoren stomps about in circles and brandishes his arms at his king. "You've been too lenient, Magnus. You should have put an end to this the first night she tried to run away."

Magnus glances her way, his eyes narrow and dark. "I thought I could trust her."

Tears sting Adaline's eyes.

"Did I not say to keep her confined to the damn castle?" Thoren says. "You can't let her keep doing as she pleases."

Magnus growls his agreement, and Adaline's head sinks lower.

Ëólas faces Magnus but keeps his voice low while he studies the grooves in the stone floor. "The harder you come down on her, the harder she'll fight to get away."

She peeks up at him. *Does he feel guilty?*

Magnus scoffs. "Are you in earnest?"

Flicking his eyes at Magnus, Ëólas nods.

The twitching vein in Magnus's neck becomes inflamed. "You warned me not to let my guard down, but I did, and you were right. Now you're saying the opposite? How can you not be equally furious? She broke your damn laws too."

I really did. And I choose to. A dull heaviness overwhelms her chest.

Ëólas winces and looks away while Magnus clenches his fists and glowers at him. The divide between them grows wider, because of her.

Oh god. Her rash actions could destroy the trust these two have been working so hard to create. "I'm sorry." She can't look any of them in the eye but can feel their gazes turn to her. She worries her hands together. "I didn't mean to create problems for everyone. I just wanted to see if I could find a way home. I, I don't belong here. I'm not much help. No one needs anything from me. I didn't think...I didn't realize..." Shorty's words cut through her thoughts: *She's a pretty little thing.* Her voice cracks.

Everyone's quiet. The only sound in the study comes from Hamon pacing in the background until his boots appear and stop in front of her. "Alright, she chose poorly, but did anyone actually explain to Adaline about the Forbidden Lands?"

Magnus inhales sharply and drops his fists from his hips to his sides. "No," he says, closing his eyes and thinking back. "I avoided the subject."

After a long pause, the sofa dips beside her as someone sits down and places a hand on her back. Adaline stiffens. When she looks up, she finds Magnus examining her arms. Already blue and black bruises have bloomed. The tension in his neck and shoulders ebbs.

In a monotone voice, he asks, "When we first met, you said you study the past to avoid repeating it. Correct?"

Adaline nods.

"Wise words." He glances at the elves. Resting his elbows on his knees, he rubs a hand over his face. "That palace is where humans betrayed the elves."

Adaline's head shoots up. She looks at Ëólas, Merith, and Fólas, each of them lost in darker thoughts that Adaline can't even imagine. Her breath hitches. "I, I'm so sorry. I didn't mean to make things worse."

Scrutinizing the sky beyond the glass windowpanes, Ëólas murmurs, "You're forgiven." He doesn't acknowledge Merith's and Fólas's bulging eyes.

Forgiven? She stares at him, urging him to look her way, just once. Even though he doesn't, a speck of hope sparks inside her, hope that she hasn't messed up everything.

"Consider yourself fortunate," Magnus says.

She trails her fingers over No-Nose's handiwork. But she's alive. And safe. She's been lucky in more ways than one.

"But you did know my law," the king adds.

"I did," she whispers.

Ëólas steps forward, but Magnus lifts his arm to stop the general from advancing. "You said your piece, Ëólas. This is for me to deal with now." He turns to Adaline. "Tell me, what are the penalties in your world for breaking the laws of your leaders?"

She pinches her thumbs together. "Depends on the crime. For misdemeanors, it's usually a fine or community service. For more severe crimes, imprisonment."

"Execution?" asks Hamon.

Adaline's head snaps up. *Would they really execute me?* She'd never escape, not with six of them.

Instead of summoning the guards, the guys look at Hamon like he's an idiot. Magnus swings his open hand as if he's smacking Hamon from across the room, and Thoren obliges, punching Hamon in the arm.

"I was just curious. Let up," Hamon says, rubbing his bicep.

Adaline twists her torso so she can look Magnus directly in the eyes. She wants to sound confident, but her voice quivers. "We don't believe in the death penalty."

"Nor do we, except for extreme circumstances." When she exhales, Magnus continues. "As for this community service idea, I hear you've been telling the children stories."

Of course you know that. "Yes."

Arching an eyebrow, Magnus leans closer. "And making friends not only with humans but also with elves."

Adaline nods.

"Then, for the duration of your stay here, I charge you with community service. I expect you to continue encouraging humans and elves to socialize together."

She furrows her brows, waiting for him to announce her real sentencing. No king could be so lenient.

For once on the same page as her, Thoren scoffs. "Tell me you jest."

"Would you rather I assign her to your constant supervision?" Magnus asks. *Hell no!*

Thoren shoots daggers at her as if she'd made the suggestion.

"I didn't think so." Repositioning himself to the edge of the sofa, Magnus blocks Thoren from her view and rests an oversized hand on her forearm, but he keeps his touch gentle, tentative even. "Adaline, will you give me your word you will not venture beyond this city again?"

"But—" When Magnus's bright blue eyes darken, she shrinks into the cushion and carefully chooses her next words. "It's just, I heard that magic happened there a long time ago. And then I appeared there. Isn't that a clue? Isn't that something we should look into?"

"We are," Merith says as if that were common knowledge.

Ëólas fixes his gaze on his shadow. "Which you would have known. If I had told you."

"You haven't told her anything?" Removing his hand from Adaline, Magnus stares Ëólas down and waits for an explanation, but the only sound in the room comes from the king grinding his teeth. Rather than let the awkward silence continue, Magnus softens his voice and tells Adaline, "We need you to be patient."

She laughs once, and her smile fades. "Patience is one thing my world severely lacks."

Leaning forward, she hugs her legs. "I've been gone three days. Almost four. I have to go home. Cindy and Dax are the only family I have left, and..." She buries her face in the folds of her dress and lets her hair fall over her shoulders, blocking her view and blotting out the light. Her arms go limp at her sides, and her eyes close on their own accord. "I'm so tired."

Magnus rests his warm hand on her lower back and rubs small circles around her spine the way her father used to when she'd wake up in the middle of the night from nightmares. "Well, as my ward, that makes you part of my family."

Adaline turns her head to the side. Never wavering, those bright blue eyes offer her another lifeline, and this time she won't second guess it.

He must have sensed her understanding because he nods once, then shifts his tone to a firm though fair warning. "I need you to stay away from the ruins, Adaline. Our presence in the Forbidden Lands gravely offends Lameiría's people."

"I, I won't go back. Not without an escort. But if we're not allowed there, why were those, those men there?"

"An excellent question, to which Ëólas and I will seek answers when we are through here."

"Are you going to kill them?"

Magnus pats her shoulder. "Don't worry yourself with that."

"No." Adaline sits up and grabs his hand. "Please, don't put that on me."

"They'll pay for their crimes," Thoren growls.

"I'll kill them myself," Hamon says. "Attacking a lady. Deplorable."

Fólas juts his chin at his co-captain. "I'll help."

"No! Please, I don't want to be responsible for someone else dying. I'm not saying what they, what they tried is excusable. But I don't want to be tied to their deaths. Please, I have enough guilt about this already. Don't put that on me too."

Magnus sighs heavily and stands up. "I'll consider your request, but let's see what they tell us. Now, I want you to go to your chambers and rest there for the remainder of today. I'll call for you soon enough. In the meantime, you can start your community service tomorrow."

"Okay." Her limbs heavier than lead, she presses her palms into the sofa and forces herself to stand up. She uses the last of her strength to semi curtsy to Magnus, making the corners of his eyes crinkle. Dragging her feet toward the door, she suddenly stops. Not thinking about why or whether she should, she hugs Magnus tightly around the middle and inhales scents of dry red wine and holly berries.

I do have friends here. "Thank you."

Magnus holds his arms up momentarily before embracing her tightly and rubbing her back.

"You've shielded me in this castle," she mumbles into his scarlet brocade jacket, "and I've taken that for granted. I'm sorry to have been so ungrateful. I didn't mean to be. I'm used to going it alone, and I thought I could..." She shakes her head.

When Magnus pulls back, he rests his hands on her shoulders, and his ruggedly handsome face is void of anger. If anything, worry haunts his blue eyes, worry about what could have happened. "I gave you my word you'd be protected here. Didn't I?"

Adaline squeezes his hands and nods. When he lets her go, she walks toward the door, glancing at Ëólas's back. If only her brain could form words, something, anything, before she leaves. Instead, she pauses in front of Merith and Fólas but struggles to lift her chin. The memory of dancing with Merith at the tavern gives her a boost of strength, and she meets at least his gaze. "I'm terribly sorry for—"

"You already apologized. Enough of that now." Merith stoops down and reaches behind his legs to pick something up off the floor. When he stands up, he passes Adaline her messenger bag.

Her jaw drops. "How did you—"

"Get some rest, my lady," Fólas says, his voice as gentle as when he first found her in the throne room. He won't forget that day anytime soon either.

"Rest, yes. I could definitely use that now." Before exiting the room, she takes in the six people who, in such a short time, have started to become fixtures in her life, five of whom stand tall and watch her without judgment as Fólas opens the door. "Thank you," she says to all of them, but her eyes linger on Ëólas.

When he lifts his chin and meets her gaze, his golden eyes reveal a new resolve, one she can't identify but one that doesn't irritate her either.

Maybe...maybe we can understand each other now.

Chapter Nineteen

THE NIGHTMARES

Adaline trudges down the hallway, ignoring Lady Marzella's gasp as they pass each other. When Adaline reaches her room, she uses both hands to shove the door open. The moment she enters, Seira stops pacing, rushes over, and throws her arms around Adaline's neck.

"Seira?"

"Thank the fae he got there in time." Leaning back, Seira slides her hands down the length of Adaline's arms and examines her haggard face. "You're filthy. I had Kayla prepare you a bath. Go clean up, and I'll wait for you here." Seira drifts to the sofa and sits down beneath the open window and the vast blue sky.

Too tired to argue, Adaline goes behind the partition and sheds her clothes, half crying and half laughing to herself when her father's knife falls out of her pocket and slides across the floor. "Ugh."

With Kayla's help, Adaline climbs into the oversized wooden tub, her legs wobbling as she submerges herself, but once the hot water coats her muscles, she sighs and rolls her head back against the rim. Only Kayla's threat to wash Adaline herself wakes her up. Grabbing the bar of soap, she scrubs every inch of her body, twice. When she sets the bar down between her knees, her eyelids droop, her breathing slows, and Seira's voice dissolves into nothingness. Darkness swallows her whole until small circles of orange light flare awake.

Stars? No, stars don't move like that.

Ten flames bob up and down as they gather together. The closer they approach Adaline, the more their light widens, revealing the faces of—

Water cascades over Adaline's head as she sits up, gasping for air and gripping the sides of the tub. She pushes the water off her eyes and stands up.

"My lady, are you alright?" Kayla runs in, a towel over her arm.

"I'm fine. Just fine."

After toweling herself off and pulling a new nightgown over her head, Adaline dismisses Kayla, sits at the vanity, and drags her brush through her hair.

"Let me, Neir Nía." Seira takes the brush from Adaline's limp hand. "Your curls are lovely but much too short." Tilting forward until her lips hover above the crown of Adaline's head, Seira whispers in a language Adaline can't quite make out. When finished, Seira perks up quickly. "There, that will help."

Um, okay?

In the mirror, Adaline watches Seira, the way her gaze seems to loosen and drift away only for Seira to shake her head ever so slightly and refocus on Adaline's hair.

"Seira, did you know?"

"Know?" She lifts her chin, and her eyes wander toward the ceiling. When Adaline pulls up her long sleeve, revealing the line of bruises darkening along her forearm, Seira whimpers and falls to her knees. Crossing her arms over her stomach, she rocks back and forth and shakes her head as she weeps, "No, no, no, no, no."

Dropping her sleeve, Adaline swivels around on the stool and reaches for Seira, cupping her shoulders and searching for a way to end or ease Seira's anguish. No one should have to deal with so much pain, especially not alone. "I'm right here, Seira. I'm not going anywhere."

She lays her tear-stained cheek on Adaline's lap, and the wet spots dripping onto the nightgown expand in circles and darken. "Not again. Please, not again."

Her heart aching at the possibilities behind those words, Adaline combs her fingers through Seira's hair. *What have you gone through?* "We're okay, Tíer Nía. You and me. I just made a stupid decision. Because I was angry."

Sitting back on her legs, Seira wipes her eyes, scans the room as if to make sure no one will overhear her, and whispers, "Anger and regret make us weaker, Neir Nía."

"Tell me about it. I made some stupid mistakes after my grandmother died."
A mistake named Derek.

After returning the brush to the vanity, Adaline stands up and crawls onto her bed, leaving room for Seira as she lays down beside her. They both fix their gazes on the sheer canopy and the regal ceiling beyond with its sprawling, white-painted wood filigree and grape leaves. She doesn't want to think about where she might have wound up tonight if he hadn't... If only he had talked to her on that balcony.

"I hate when people think they know me." *Especially when they think the worst.* Adaline rolls onto her side, facing Seira, and tucks her hand under her pillow. "I wish Ëólas didn't hate me so much."

"He doesn't hate you, Neir Nía. He could never hate you. It's not possible."

Adaline snorts her disbelief and studies the violet outer ring that encircles Seira's light-periwinkle irises. Her eyes hold no judgment, only the kindness she has shown Adaline since the first time they had tea together in Seira's chambers. She's been looking out for Adaline since day one, from giving her a reason to avoid the ladies' parlor to gifting her new clothes to—Oh. "You told Ëólas."

Rolling onto her back, Seira closes her eyes and furrows her brows as if she's trying to remember something. Before she answers, her breathing slows, and her eyes dart back and forth as she enters the dream world, where Adaline soon follows. Even though the sun hasn't set yet, she could sleep for a week. She peeks at Seira again, just to make sure she's still there and grateful not to have been left alone. Seira must have known that's what Adaline needs right now.

Does Seira have magic? Was it her voice that warned me in the palace gardens?

Adaline's gut tells her she's onto something, but that same instinct warns her that Seira suffered something horrible, something far worse than what could have happened today. If Seira was right, that Adaline will be here for at least a month, then she needs to tread carefully. She can't go back to the ruins, not alone, not without Ëólas's support. She won't initiate another war between elves and humans.

I'm going to have to be patient.

Even with Seira keeping her company, Adaline doesn't sleep well. When she closes her eyes, she's back in the palace gardens, her feet and arms pumping to get her away from those men. As she runs for the tree line, night descends, and the moon rises high above. The tree line vanishes, replaced with a meadow, and her father runs beside her, his fear equal to her own. Distant torches converge around them, and the clang of swords and people screaming shatter the night's reverence.

No matter how hard she pushes herself, she can't keep up with her father. She reaches for his black cotton shirt as her strides shrink, but she's growing smaller, so small that her father turns back, scoops her up, and runs with her in his arms. She hugs his neck, remembering but not smelling his wooly scent, and his trimmed beard tickles her cheek. But she doesn't have time to reminisce. Death is chasing them. Her father's racing heart matches her own, but his steps never falter. Just as they're about to reach Nan's front door, her three-story mansion turns into a hut—no, a cottage—and the door is too small to let them in. When her father sets her down, Adaline searches her pockets for a sour tart that will shrink them, but her pockets are empty. Her father pounds his fists on the locked door, screaming that he can't find a way inside, that he can't find a way back home.

Behind them, the torches get closer, so much so that even in the dark she can make out the shapes of people running toward them, their swords and pitchforks drawn. Adaline tugs her father's hand and begs him to save them. As she buries her face in his side, darkness envelops them, and the world fades away.

Adaline wakes up in her bed with hair stuck to her neck and forehead, her nightgown clinging to her body. Seira's gone, and the fire in the hearth crackles and pops. The room is too hot. Throwing off the sheets, Adaline runs to the window and flings the glass panes wide open, praying she won't see those same torches coming for her.

She's still shaking when the sun crests over the horizon.

For two days, her life in the Neutral Territory runs like clockwork, beginning with Kayla helping Adaline to dress and securing her curls within a snood, followed by breakfast with Mercia, who seems unaware anything happened at all, and Seira, who seems to have forgotten. After their brief chat, she heads into the city and visits both sides of Market Street, meeting new people and learning about their lives, and tells the children a story, first *Rapunzel* and then *The Three Bears*. Her days end with her meandering through the castle gardens while Seira plants flowers and dances along the hedges.

But Adaline's enthusiasm has evaporated. All interactions and conversations feel perfunctory. When Jósep and Sallie asked if she was feeling alright, she found a smile and rocked on her feet to convince them she was fine. But the moment she's alone, her chest feels hollow.

In the garden, a firm hand touches her shoulder, and a male voice asks, "Lady Adaline?"

She leaps off the bench, her heart pounding in her chest. Her eyes dart from side to side, looking for the impending threat, until they settle on Hamon and his sad eyes.

"I'm terribly sorry, my lady. I didn't mean to startle you."

"Hamon. No, it's okay. I'm fine. What's up?"

He searches the sky, his thick blond hair falling away from his blue eyes. "What's up?"

"I mean, do you need me?" she asks.

"Ah, yes. His Majesty and Lord Ëólas require your immediate presence in the throne room. This way, please."

"Oh, okay. Seira, I'll see you in the morning." After Seira waves goodbye and prances back to their abandoned picnic dinner, Adaline lifts her hem and follows after Hamon. "Am I in trouble?"

"Not at all, my lady."

They enter the castle's throne room, a spacious circular chamber with thick white columns outlining the perimeter. Between each column, a set of guards stands at attention. A long red runner, starting at the doorway, leads to a low dais supporting Magnus and Ëólas, both sitting up straight in two oak chairs with ornate animal and nature carvings. Thoren and Merith stand beside their respective lords, whereas Hamon and Fólas wait on either side of the dais, each captain accompanied by three more guards.

Near the end of the runner, two men stand before the king and commander general. Adaline gulps as she walks past No-Nose and Shorty, their wrists and ankles bound, their faces bruised. She stops in front of her friends, her skin crawling because of who's behind her, and curtsies.

From his throne, Magnus speaks first, loud and clear, so his voice projects throughout the room. "Lady Adaline, these two insist they were wandering the region when they spied you. Did you notice anything out of the ordinary?"

She shakes her head. "No, Your Majesty."

Magnus exhales his frustration through his nose. Ëólas too.

Tilting his head to the side, Magnus looks past Adaline to the two prisoners. "So you maintain you entered the Forbidden Lands by mistake and had no intention of harming the lady?" His voice is hoarse, gravely, as if this isn't the first time he's asked them this question.

"Yes, Your Majesty. At first, we sought to ask her for directions, but when we saw the lady all alone, we knew she must be looking for company," No-Nose says. "You can't blame us for misreading her intentions. I mean, a pretty little thing like that by herself?"

A pretty little thing. Each word hammers the inside of her skull. The hollow recess of her chest sparks, then rages. She about-faces, marches up to No-Nose, and knees him in the groin. When he collapses on the ground, she says as calmly as possible, "Surely you were looking for that."

Resisting the urge to spit on him, she returns to Magnus and Ëólas, both of whom are wincing while No-Nose whimpers on the floor. When she stops in front of them this time, she squares her shoulders and lifts her head. Magnus greets her with a smile. Thoren winks at her. Merith, Fólas, and Hamon smirk, and Ëólas regains that stoic expression.

"You see how violent she is?" Shorty says. "She did the same to me and punched my friend here in the eye."

Seething, she forces herself to speak, to put into words the truth, to relive that moment. "They attacked me, Your Majesty. They sought to...to...take ad-advantage of the fact that I was alone. I was defending myself."

Fólas, with his arms crossed over his chest, silently praises her with a thumbs-up.

Magnus nods and looks at Ëólas. "You vouch for the truth of Lady Adaline's words?"

Ëólas locks eyes with her. "I do."

Her stomach somersaults at the intensity of his gaze, that he's not looking through her, not anymore.

Magnus claps his hands once, summoning two guards from beside the dais to grab a prisoner's arm. "We declare these men guilty for attacking the lady and their ill intent. Lady Adaline," the king nods at her, "will decide their fate."

"What?" Adaline clutches her skirts as if they could hold her up.

"I would order their execution, but you pleaded for their lives. Thus, you will decide what you deem to be a fitting punishment."

"She's already started," Hamon says, guarding his groin.

Magnus side-eyes him, and he shuts up.

Adaline looks over her shoulder at Shorty and No-Nose, the latter standing again but hunched over. Hurting them would be easy. But Nan taught her never to give up hoping for a better tomorrow, that people can change. These two still need to pay, and Adaline can't let them go, knowing they could hurt someone else, someone who doesn't have a king on her side and a general to protect her. As much as she'd love to break their backs—

"Hard labor," Adaline says. When the king raises an eyebrow, she explains further. "Let them work for their freedom. A year should be fair. Lord Ëólas, a friend of mine told me about the quarry near Lameiría. Would you find them working there acceptable?" *Let those two struggle to cut and hoist massive chunks of marble back to the Neutral Territory.*

Ëólas takes a moment to think, then nods, and the guards drag the two pieces of Adaline's nightmares away.

When they're gone, she exhales slowly and whispers, "Thank you," knowing her friends can hear her.

The corners of Magnus's blue eyes crinkle as he smiles. "I'm glad to see your spirit returned, my lady."

With rosy cheeks, Adaline turns to leave but catches Ëólas leaning back in his chair, and a small smile warms his face, a smile that catches her breath, a smile that means everything.

Chapter Twenty

THE TRAINING GROUNDS

When Adaline returns to the children the next day, they cheer and skip about to see her smiling again, and her audience has increased to twelve. One elven child steps forward, bows his head, and presses into her palm a flower carved out of wood. Its five pointed petals remind her of the Purple Stardust wildflowers that have been spreading across the fields. Adaline holds the carving to her chest in gratitude and whispers her thanks. At the bottom of the bridge, Delós watches his son and nods his head in approval.

During story time, Adaline tells the children—and the adults who pause their work to listen—about a woman who joined an army by pretending to be a man, all to save her father. The kids love the story, especially the idea of a friendly little dragon.

Afterward, Adaline checks in on Sallie, but she doesn't stay long. Today, she has other plans.

When she exits Sallie's candle shop, she makes her way to the end of Market Street and asks a pair of city guards to escort her to the training grounds where she should find Hamon today. During her walk, her stomach threatens to expel her breakfast, but she refuses to back down, even if Hamon turns her away.

Within the arena's divided quarters, people spar two by two, their swords clanging, challengers grunting, and spectators cheering. The air smells dusty, tinged with the scent of sweat. From this distance, she can't find the boys from her previous visit. Many of the guards from Alderton look alike with their burgundy tunics, leather breastplates, and short-bearded faces.

The arena's far more crowded now than during the city tour. Adaline swallows hard.

Her escorts quickly point out Hamon. Walking through the iron gate, she passes the lodgings and private training rooms that encircle the arena and waits at the edge of the low rock wall outlining Hamon's work area.

"Sloppy, sloppy. Look at where your feet are! Fix your elbow and—Lady Adaline?" Hamon stares at her in shock, then shouts over his shoulder for someone else to take charge of training as he jogs over to her.

"I'm sorry to interrupt," she says.

"No, not at all, my lady. Are you well? Is everything alright?" He scans her body to make sure nothing's out of place. To his credit, he doesn't let his eyes linger anywhere inappropriate.

"Yes. I mean...well..." Adaline glances back at her escorts hovering behind her and bites her lip.

"You're dismissed. Return to your posts." When the guards leave, giving them space, Hamon steps closer to Adaline. "What do you need, my lady?"

She straightens her spine and tilts her chin upward. "I want to learn how to fight, how to defend myself. I know you're busy training others, and I don't mean to take away from your responsibilities or add to them, but surely someone can teach me self-defense."

"Oh." Hamon runs his hands through his blond hair. "No, my lady. I, I can't possibly. The arena is no place for a woman. And what would His Majesty think?"

"That I'm in charge of my life?"

"But you don't need such lessons, not if you plan to keep your word and—"

"This has nothing to do with my intentions, Hamon." Adaline squeezes her fingers into fists. "I don't want to depend on others rescuing me."

"But as long as you're in the city, you have—"

"Nothing to fear? Didn't people die in the city the night I arrived?"

"Yes, and we've increased security. My men and Fólas's elves have everything under control. I assure you, you're safe here."

Adaline bites her tongue to stop herself from screaming. "Telling me I'm safe isn't the same as me feeling like I can keep myself safe. Please. I can't...I can't sleep, Hamon."

The mortification written on his face subsides. Remorse quickly takes its place as he casts his bright blue eyes downward. "I'm deeply sorry, my lady, but I can't—"

"I'll teach her," Fólas says as he approaches from the side. His big, dark brown eyes, framed with arch-shaped creases along his eyelids, lock onto Hamon.

"Fólas, such permission is needed from the king. The lady will need to ask him directly."

A wide grin overtakes Adaline's face, and her eyes light up. "Actually, Magnus commanded me to continue finding ways to bridge elf and human relations, so I consider my practice with Fólas a cultural lesson. Wouldn't you agree, Fólas?"

"Absolutely. All elven royal family members know how to defend themselves, including my queen. Lady Adaline's simply learning some of our customs."

Hamon looks from Fólas to Adaline while dragging both hands through his hair. He exhales loudly, then tells his co-captain, "If His Majesty doesn't approve, I didn't see anything. I didn't hear anything. I know nothing."

Bouncing on the balls of her feet, she playfully punches Fólas's steel arm. "Woo-hoo! Which sword can I practice with?"

All enthusiasm evaporates from his face as his skin turns pasty. "No, no. No sword, my lady. Let's start with a dagger...after you've learned some hand-to-hand combat skills."

"Yeah... Don't let Thoren find out. Have fun, Fólas." With his hands in his pockets, Hamon whistles as he walks away.

"He acts like I'm already a train wreck," Adaline says.

"What's a train?" Fólas asks.

"Never mind."

"Then never you mind him either. Come with me."

Fólas leads her to one of the tan brick buildings and opens the round oak doors. Inside, the small room has a standing rack supporting a collection of forty bow staffs. The back wall contains shelves with rags, medicinal vials, and pitchers of water, either for cleansing wounds or drinking, maybe both. Windows on both sides allow sufficient light inside the otherwise barren space. As a final touch, the simple, efficient room has held on to the musky odor of the guards who used the room earlier today.

Wrinkling her nose, Adaline stands by the door while Fólas enters and waits for her to join him. Now that she's exactly where she wants to be, her feet don't want to push her forward. "I'm not taking you away from your duties?"

"No, my lady. I'm simply training a new recruit, which would be easier to do in the center of the room."

Adaline nods, more so to herself, and gingerly strolls inside, stopping a few feet from Fólas. "Now what?"

"I want you to punch me."

"What? Now?"

"Yes."

"Um, why?"

"Because I want to see what you know."

"But what if I hurt you?"

"I guarantee you won't be able to lay a finger on me, my lady."

"Well, that doesn't do much for my confidence."

Without adrenaline and terror motivating her actions, her punch deflates mid-way, and her fist bumps Fólas's shoulder before falling to her side.

He lowers one eyebrow while arching the other. "Let's try something else."

For her first lesson, Fólas tells Adaline to widen her stance, slide one foot further back so she'll be harder to knock over, and raise her fists in front of her. He shows her how to keep her shoulders, biceps, and forearms tense so she can not only support the shock of impact when blocking someone else's blows but then also push that energy away or transfer it into her own punches. Slowly and methodically, he breaks down each move into incremental steps, much like how Adaline used to teach dance lessons. Every time she elongates her spine and closes her rib cage, Fólas reminds her to widen her stance and sink lower, to dig her feet into the earth. Whenever her torso tries to retaliate and stretch, he snaps his fingers and points at her feet.

Throughout their practice, they circle around each other, two new partners learning their own pas de deux, as they study the negative space between their bodies. Adaline automatically calculates her height and position in relation to his, watches for when he transfers his weight to the opposite foot, and anticipates his next move. When he pulls his arm back as if he's about to throw a punch, the choreography of his feet tells the truth, giving Adaline enough time to dodge and spin out of his reach.

After an hour, Fólas asks, "How do you do that?"

"Do what?"

"Spin three times, come to a stop, and know exactly where I am? You never lose sight of me. Or your balance."

Adaline shrugs. "Ballet."

A quizzical look spreads across his face.

"It's a type of dance." After so much hunkering down, she allows her body to do as it desires. Stretching her torso long and lean, she assumes fourth position, raising one arm above her and extending the other in front. Releasing the compressed tension in her arms, she allows them to feel light and buoyant again. From the waist down, she turns her feet outward, crosses her legs while keeping her knees straight, and moves one foot in front of the other. When she elongates the length of her front leg, her muscles tingle as energy flows down her hip and into her toes.

Fólas jerks his head backward at the unnatural contortion.

She bends her knees. In one swift motion, she transfers her weight to her front leg and rises onto the ball of her foot. Simultaneously, she pushes off with her back foot, touching her toes to her knee, and follows the momentum into a full turn, all the while snapping her head back to the front and using Fólas for her spotting. After doing five fouetté turns in a row, she returns her legs to fourth position with the grace and ease of a glasswing butterfly.

His curiosity lengthens into awe. "That was lovely."

Adaline bows, and from that moment onward, Fólas levels up her self-defense lessons, making certain she can read his body movements correctly and block using the left or right side of her forearm. He keeps his tone gentle, but he stays focused on the lessons and doesn't let her skimp on the number of repetitions he expects. Which are a lot. By the time they're done, Adaline's growling stomach sounds the dinner bell.

"My lady, I think that's enough for today." Aside from exhaling one deep breath, Fólas looks as if he's just spent the last few hours reading a book or taking a nap.

Adaline leans against the cool brick wall and lets her arms drop to her side. Her legs are fine, but her forearms are stiff and throbbing. She massages each one, digging her thumb into the tense knots. "I just need a moment. You can go, but thank you for everything."

Instead, Fólas walks over to her. "You did well, my lady."

She rolls her wrists forward and backward, then weaves her fingers together and pushes her palms outward so she can stretch her wrists further. "I didn't land a single punch on you. Like you said."

"But you listened to everything I told you, and you made it quite difficult for me to get a hold of you. We'll keep practicing those moves until they feel instinctual."

So I won't forget I have my knife on me again.

"Besides," Fólas says, "when I dragged those barbarians to the dungeons, I noticed one of them had a nice black eye. Ëólas swears that wasn't from him."

One of Adaline's cheeks perks up into a half smile, until her stomach cramps up.

Fólas nods at the door. "Come, my lady."

Rather than following him, she asks, "If I'm here to learn self-defense, wouldn't it have made more sense for you to have been the aggressor, rather than me trying to punch you for the last few hours?"

Placing his hand on the door handle, Fólas moves his head up and down. "I suppose. But I didn't want to remind you of..." He shakes his head. "I didn't want you to see me that way. Besides, you still learned defensive moves."

Pushing off the wall, Adaline loops her arm around his elbow and follows him outside where the evening sky darkens from shades of deep blue to purple. In the arena, a group of ten guards surrounds Ëólas. She can't discern their words, but

Ëólas says something, and the laughter that follows permeates the atmosphere, transforming this formidable fight club into a brotherhood. Resting one leg on a crate, he drapes his arm over his knee, his tight navy trousers accentuating his hard, lean muscles, and slaps the back of one of his guards. When Ëólas throws back his head to laugh louder, his grin removes all weariness from Adaline's arms and legs. She takes a step forward, wishing to hear what was so funny. His relaxed posture, the informal humor, the ease with which he talks to them, it's all so unlike the person she's met so far. Even his expressions—the fake display of disbelief, the guffaws, and the way he wiggles his nose at his friends—belong to someone else, someone who's naturally fun, maybe even charming. His entire demeanor invokes carefree fun on a cool summer night.

"I didn't know he can be silly," she murmurs. But the moment she speaks, Ëólas finds her, and his smile fades. Her heart sinks. There she goes again, draining the joy out of him.

As Adaline turns to leave, Ëólas excuses himself from his people and hurries over to her and Fólas. "Everything alright here?" he asks his captain.

"Yes, my lord. I just finished teaching the lady some defensive techniques."

Adaline grips Fólas's elbow tighter. *What if he tells us to stop? What if Fólas gets in trouble because of me?* "I convinced him."

Ëólas looks down at Adaline and narrows his eyes, zooming in on her intentions, reading her carefully. "Good."

Wait? Really? She drops Fólas's arm.

Scanning her from top to bottom, Ëólas pinches his chin while he thinks. "A dagger or short sword would work best for her frame."

A flush creeps up Adaline's neck and engulfs her cheeks.

Fólas nods. "I plan to introduce her to a dagger in the next few days, my lord."

"Well done." When he releases Adaline from his gaze, Ëólas steps closer to Fólas and angles himself so she's mostly behind him. "Now that you're done, I need you to check in with section five and report back to me. I'll escort Adaline to the castle."

After confirming her plans to return tomorrow, Fólas bows to his lord and hurries off, leaving her alone. With Ëólas. Whom she's pretty sure still hates her. Or maybe just dislikes her now.

In silence, they depart the arena, making their way back toward Market Street on the elven side of town. She keeps her hands clasped together while Ëólas walks with his hands in his pockets. Every now and again, he glances at her but says nothing.

Maybe he's waiting for me to give him an out? "I can make it from here."

"Thank you, but I need to speak with you about something. Not here though."

"Oh, okay."

What could he have to say to her? If only her heart would stop racing so she could think straight. Fólas must have exhausted her more than she thought.

As they stroll down Market Street, she spies Delós waving her over. She looks up at Ëólas, making sure he's not pressed for time. Wordlessly, he understands her visual inquiry, nods, and guides them toward Delós's shop.

The luthier's grin is contagious. "Good evening, my lord! And my lady, I hoped to see you again today. A moment, please." He disappears into his shop and returns with a mandolin. With both hands, he passes the instrument to Adaline. "I had a feeling you'll appreciate this."

Carefully placing the mandolin on the table, Adaline trails her fingertips along the grain's warm, honey-like color. Her eyes gleam. "Is the top tonewood made from spruce?"

"Very similar, my lady. This is varlothía. From Lameiría."

"Wow." She lifts the mandolin and rotates it to admire the dark stripes on the backside that alternate between shades of light brown and chocolate. "Walnut?"

"Again, similar. That's nimlas."

Miniature golden leaves painted along the sides provide the final embellishment and further prove what Adaline suspected the moment he stepped outside with the glorious work of art: Delós put a lot of time into perfecting his craft.

"It's beautiful, Delós. You're gifted, truly." With both hands, she lifts the mandolin to pass it back to him.

But Delós raises both of his hands. "It's for you, my lady."

Shock wipes Adaline's delight off her face. "What? But I, I can't. I don't have any way to pay you, and—"

"No payment necessary, my lady. However, if you feel so inclined, perhaps I'll see you at the tavern again, and you can introduce us to yet another new song? I've learned two from you already. I'd love to hear more."

Gripping the handle of the mandolin, she hugs the gift to her chest. Her father would have relished this expertly crafted instrument. He would have grabbed his guitar or bass or brought home his mandolin from work, and they would have played for hours in the detached garage, helping the new mandolin to wake up and achieve its full sound. Nan would have brought them dinner, probably grilled chicken hot off the barbeque and her specially seasoned mixed vegetables that somehow retained a bit of their crunch while also melting in their mouths. Adaline would have helped her father clean up while Nan strummed her own songs, and they would have spent the rest of the night taking turns, making up new lyrics, or playing together until Adaline fell asleep on the futon. How can a single instrument bring back the sound of her family's laughter?

Adaline lowers her chin to hide her trembling lip. Reaching out, she squeezes Delós's hand in thanks, unable to say the words aloud. If she tried, a sob would come out instead, and she doesn't want him to think he did something wrong. Worse, she doesn't want Ëólas to see her cry again.

"You're welcome, my lady. Enjoy your evening. My lord," he says with a bow.

Adaline aimlessly walks into the street, only to pause after five steps because the path and people have blurred together.

"This way," Ëólas whispers in her ear, placing his hand on the small of her back to guide her through the water-color masses.

She holds the instrument close to her heart the entire way. The further behind they leave the city, the more the din fades. A cool breeze sweeps through the meadow surrounding them, ruffling the Purple Stardust that's overtaken the fields.

When they reach halfway up the hill leading to the castle, Ëólas stops and stuffs his hands in his pockets. He looks at his boots, lifts his chin, and knits his eyebrows together in consternation. "I regret to inform you that my request for the books or priestess has been denied."

Adaline inhales sharply. "Oh."

"Repeatedly." He shifts his gaze from her to the castle to the horizon, then back to her.

She wanders off the road and flops down on the grass, resting the mandolin across her lap. She tries to breathe slowly so her lungs will resume their normal rhythm, but her chest feels hollow, as if someone knocked the wind out of her. "I just need a moment." She'd been so preoccupied with the attack and not sleeping that she'd lost track of time.

Ëólas squats beside her but doesn't speak. He waits for her.

She rests her fingers on the strings, grateful to have something solid to hold on to. "What do we do next?"

"I'll leave for Lameiría and petition the queen directly. There, I'll be better able to argue the circumstances of your situation."

He's leaving? "When?"

He brushes his palm across the top of the grass. "I hadn't planned to leave the Neutral Territory for a few more months, so I need a bit of time to wrap things up here, especially as I cannot guarantee how long I'll be gone."

"Oh." *If it would have taken five days to get the books, that means he'll be gone at least ten. Most likely, longer.* The idea of him not being in the background of her life creates another vacancy inside her chest.

"I'm making plans to depart here within a week."

She trails her fingertips randomly over the strings; the discord hums around them. "I'm sorry to interrupt your plans."

"There's no need for you to apologize." His voice is surprisingly soft.

"What if the queen rejects your request again?"

Holding his hand over the grass, he pushes down a few times, letting the pointy tips of the blades jab his palm. "Then I have another possibility we can consider."

We. "What's that?"

"You come to Lameiría with me."

Adaline locks eyes with him. "Won't I be imprisoned for life?"

"That's...a possibility...which is why I'm not suggesting that route just yet. There's also a chance the queen won't want to anger Magnus by keeping a member of his family hostage."

A member of his family. She smiles to herself, then frowns. "I don't want to be another Helen of Troy."

"Who?"

"Doesn't matter." *It's not like Magnus and I are anything beyond friends. Good friends.*

Ëólas sits down beside her, and they stare into the distance, over the city, at the ruins beyond. A thought brews in her mind, but she doesn't yet have the heart to speak it aloud. Fortunately, Ëólas doesn't rush her to get up. They watch the sun grow heavy in the sky and the clouds drift lazily by. Not a sound disrupts them, until Adaline's stomach gurgles loudly.

I need to stop skipping lunch.

Reaching into the drawstring bag tied to his belt, Ëólas pulls out a circular object wrapped in cloth and passes it to her.

"Thank you," she says, peeling back the thin fabric to discover a minced-meat pastry bigger than her hand.

With one bite, sweet yet savory spices relieve her dry mouth, and her eyes roll back in her head. Ëólas says nothing, letting her devour the entire thing in peace. When she finishes, she folds up the cloth and passes it back to him, which he returns to his pouch. He doesn't make to leave.

Adaline nibbles her bottom lip. *Be brave. He seems content right now. And if I do piss him off, I'll give him space and practice that whole patience thing.* "You said I entered a circle, that I wasn't invited. Are there more of those here?"

Drawing his legs closer to his chest, he balances his forearms on top of his knees. He keeps his face and tone neutral. "We have a few. In Lameiría."

"Ah." Adaline extends her legs and leans back on her palms, balancing the mandolin on her lap. She hesitates but tries again. "What about here in Aerytol?"

"They've all been destroyed."

"I'm sorry."

"Wasn't your doing."

"I'm sorry nonetheless."

As they sit quietly, his calm demeanor encourages her to ask the big question, the one that will remind him of her rash behavior the other day that resulted in him having to fetch and save her. But he hasn't yet made her feel guilty about it. And he forgave her.

"I appeared at the ruins though," she hedges. "Any clues we might find there?"

"I don't think so, but it's worth a chance."

She studies him carefully—those lean muscles that flex every time his long fingers play with the grass, that chiseled jawline that accentuates his irritation, and those full lips that haven't scowled yet today. He appears as relaxed as he sounds. "You mean it?"

Ëólas nods. "I'll bring you there myself. Tomorrow morning."

"Really?" *He's willing to do that?*

The corner of his mouth curls into a small smile. "Really."

Adaline squeals, and Ëólas mirrors her enthusiasm in his own quiet, reserved way. She could throw her arms around his neck in thanks, but she locks her hands together to stop herself from reaching out and terrifying him. Instead, she channels her anticipation into strumming the mandolin, playing actual notes this time but nothing in particular. Ëólas shifts onto his bottom, crossing his legs beneath him, and watches her pluck the strings delicately. They ought to return to the castle, to eat dinner, but they choose the music, its harmony drifting over the hill. With so many vibrations tingling up and down her legs, she can't help but feel more hopeful than she has been in a long time.

Chapter Twenty-One

THE WAY HOME

Pushing off the mattress, Adaline stumbles over to the vanity, picks up the pitcher with shaky hands, and pours water into the basin. After sopping up the spills, she dunks a washcloth into the bowl, wrings it out, and wipes the sweat off her brow and around her neck. When she closes her eyes, her dreams fill her mind's eye. Again she's running for her life, switching between being an adult all alone or a child with her father beside her. With the cool washcloth at the base of her skull, water trickles down her spine, and the shiver running through her body forces her eyes open. The images vanish. For now.

Ignoring her nightmares, she focuses on today's agenda. First, she's going with Ëólas to the ruins. When they get back, she'll tell the kids a story and visit her friends in town, after which she'll meet Fólas for lessons. Last, hopefully Seira and Mercia will accept her invite to have dinner with them to make up for ditching them this morning.

With an admiring sigh, Kayla pulls out a rosy-pink gown and helps dress her lady. At the vanity, she pulls the brush once through Adaline's curls, but her hand slows as she reaches the end, and she gasps, "Your hair has grown much longer, my lady."

"Huh?" Adaline stands up and twists around to see behind her. Sure enough, her long brown locks reach far below her shoulder blades with the tips nearing her lower back. *Seira!* Adaline huffs, plops back down, and purses her lips. "Don't worry about it."

After Kayla tucks all of Adaline's curls into a snood, which weighs significantly more, she clasps her cloak around her neck and races out the door, through the corridors, and down the stairs that lead to the castle's inner courtyard. In the middle of the massive space, Ëólas and Merith wait for her, along with three horses, each a different color. Passing the staff going about their work, she hurries to join the two elves but drifts toward the honey-colored horse with a long chocolate mane. She keeps a safe distance, careful not to spook the beast, but the giant steed whinnies his protest, stretches out his neck, and nuzzles her face, just like when she visited the county-run stables as a child for Cindy's tenth birthday party. Oh, and that other time with Derek, before her ass hurt for days on end.

Adaline rubs the horse's nose. "Who else is joining us?"

"Only us," Merith says.

She recounts the horses the size of freight trains. *Okay, that's an exaggeration, but not by much.* Subconsciously rubbing her rump, she takes several steps backward. "How about we walk? It's a lovely day."

"Horseback is faster." Turning away from her, Merith talks soothingly to his own midnight steed.

"Do you not know how to ride?" Ëólas's eyebrows and nose scrunch together with pointed curiosity.

Must be hard for them to fathom. She shakes her head. "They're sweet face to face, but being on top of one is a completely different story."

Ëólas walks over to the horse that chose her and pats the saddle. "Today's a good day to learn then."

Um, how about I don't? When she first started dating Derek, he took her horseback riding for her birthday, something completely different to help distract her from the fact that Nan was gone. Before they got started, that horse also nuzzled his nose under her hand, a seemingly innocent, trusting gesture that lured her in. She enjoyed the initial ride, the smell of the damp woods and the trotting, until less happy memories drowned her peace of mind. She never saw it coming, the horse rearing up on its hind legs and throwing her to the ground. Within hours, her ass had turned black and blue, perfectly outlining the rock she had landed on.

Taking two more steps backward, Adaline clutches her cloak shut around her chest. "But...walking is great exercise, and—"

"Adaline." Ëólas cocks his head to the side and studies her thoroughly. Whatever he's thinking, he doesn't push for details and doesn't make her inability to ride a big deal. "You can ride with me."

Her eyes dart between him and her horse, and she gulps.

Ëólas doesn't seem to care. With a nod of his head, an elven stableboy dashes into their circle, takes the reins of the honey-colored horse, and leads him away, his tail swishing with disappointment. Not giving Adaline the chance to protest further, the commander general strides over to his own steed, white like starlight, places his hands on top of the horse's rump, and vaults onto its back where Ëólas sits not on, but behind, the saddle.

Show off. "Am I not riding in the back this time?"

"You'll have more fun up front."

He reaches down for her, his large hand open, waiting. Like the night of the ball, she slides her palm against his, and his fingers lock around hers. He flashes a quick smile, then hoists her up onto his horse, his arm locked around her waist for only a moment. Her stomach in knots, she contemplates grabbing the horse's mane or the front knobby part of the saddle, anything that will keep her stable and not require her to lean backward, to rest against him.

I should have ridden alone. Why does he intimidate me so damn much? He's being nice, which is nice, and weird, but still nice. Settle down, Adaline. Deep breath.

"Relax. I have you." Sliding his strong, solid arms around her, he grips the reins, his mouth near her ear. "I won't let you fall."

She flashes back to the ballroom, to the floor crashing up to meet her, to his firm grip around her waist that spared her wrist. He saved her then too. "I know."

"Good then. Let's go." With a flick of his feet, the horse trots toward the castle gates with Merith following behind.

The moment they clear the gates, Ëólas clicks his heels again, and the horse charges forward into a gallop. The sudden wind cools Adaline's cheeks as they race down the hill and into the city. Because the streets are several lanes wide, the elves have plenty of room to keep to the side while their general races past, the stalls and merchants turning into a stream of blurred colors. When they exit the city, the landscape opens up into green meadows covered in wildflowers. To the left, the jagged peaks of Lameiría's forest outline the horizon, and for some reason, the world feels bigger, wider than before. She's seen only a sliver of this land, a handful of its people. So many other surprises must lie in wait, discoveries yet to be made, myths proven true. If she had the time and resources, she'd travel to every corner, tasting local cuisines, learning about their histories, studying their traditions. She could explore for decades and not run out of opportunities. But that's not what today's about.

When discomfort needles her rump and spine, she leans back, accepting Ëólas's support, and takes a deep breath of fresh air. She glances over Ëólas's shoulder, catching him smiling, and locates Merith fifty feet behind them.

Twisting forward, she turns her head so Ëólas can hear her. "Does Merith always go with you?"

His lips move closer to her ear. "Yes. He's my right hand."

"Which means?"

"Merith's been training me since I was five. He's rather protective."

"Like Thoren and Magnus." She looks up to study his face, but his mouth is too close to hers. An accidental bump could—she quickly spins around.

"Yes. After King Rioran passed, Thoren became a surrogate father of sorts, hence why he often gets away with speaking more freely than he ought to."

Adaline laughs, and Ëólas's chuckle rumbles inside her ear.

As they near their destination, they slow to a trot, giving her time to take in the expanse of the palace, the way the sun illuminates the white marble, and every architectural feat without fear of being caught. The palace must have been breathtaking in its heyday. Truth be told, it still is, a testament to a glorious past, even with the broken columns and busted balconies. But it looks so lonely now. Empty.

"Ëólas, if this place is forbidden, why aren't there guards?"

"I have them posted in a wide circumference around the grounds to prevent humans from entering."

So she'd been right. Removing her snood had, in fact, helped her to reach the palace. "But how did those two men get through?"

Ëólas growls. "It's rather generous of you to refer to them as men."

"That doesn't answer my question." She cranes her neck to peek at him, waiting for an answer.

When their eyes lock, he sighs but stares ahead. "I don't know. That's part of what's been troubling me. None of my guards saw them slip by."

"But your guards saw me? And they told you?"

"No, they thought you were an elf."

Adaline sucks in her lips, hiding the grin that wants to break free.

"I don't think that's something you ought to be smiling about," he says, with a surprisingly light tone. In place of furrowed brows and flaring nostrils, he suppresses his own smirk.

"I don't know what you're talking about." Pressing her lips tightly together, she forces the corners of her mouth to stay neutral despite them trying to tug upward.

Shaking his head, Ëólas guides the horse outside the arched gateway that leads into the gardens. He slides off first, then reaches up for Adaline. As she bracing her hands on his shoulders, he grabs her waist and guides her down, not letting go as she waits for her legs to stop pulsing.

"You good?" he asks, his face tilted down toward hers, his hands warm at her sides, his eyes gentle.

"Uh-huh." She can't seem to move her arms, to remove her hands from his shoulders. Maybe the ride numbed more than her ass.

"You coming?" Merith asks, disappearing under the archway.

Ëólas quickly steps back and follows Merith, leaving Adaline alone with the horses. Stretching and shaking her hands loose, she walks through the archway and enters the gardens. Her eyes immediately dart to the spot where Shorty and No-Nose tackled her to the ground and...

She turns away. Leaning against the cool stone wall, she takes several slow breaths. Ëólas walks up behind her but keeps his distance while she changes the images in her mind, while she recalls the sound of her fist connecting with No-Nose's eye socket and each move Fólas taught her yesterday.

"Okay." Standing tall, she points to the tree line. "I thought those looked familiar. That's where I originally appeared, right?" When they nod, she walks past them, knowing they're going to stay close by, that they won't leave her alone here.

Slipping between the thick tree trunks, Adaline holds her breath, having no idea what to expect, but nothing awaits her on the other side. No more broken bits of the palace or chunks of garden décor. No sexy fae-like being with answers. No glowing doorway home. Just a wide stretch of grass that dips downward like an empty saucer. It's a good size for an indoor pool though.

Well, this is certainly anticlimactic.

Roaming into the grove, Adaline finds the general spot where she first appeared, sits down, and waits. Waits to feel the cool, stagnant air within the cave system. Waits to see the pillars towering above her. Waits to hear the voices of her colleagues and students despite knowing they left long ago. Too much time has passed. And even though she's back where she started, the gateway between worlds is closed.

Hell, I don't even know what the gateway is. Maybe that's what I need to figure out first. Huh, maybe Seira can help me.

Adaline flops backward and lays in the grass, staring vacantly up at the blue sky. Her father wouldn't have moped around, that's for sure. He would have studied everything about this world and relished the adventure. But isn't that what she's mostly done too? Part of her wishes she could return home; missing Cindy and Dax's engagement, not being at her best friend's side, and leaving them mourning her loss tears her up inside each night before she falls asleep—when she can fall asleep. But the majority of her focus throughout this experience proves she's still her father's daughter.

Besides, if the cave did suddenly swallow her whole, she'd be leaving without so much as a goodbye to Seira, Magnus, or any of the other people whom Adaline so easily invited to take up residence in her heart. Eólas would disappear too, without her ever knowing if just maybe they too will find solid footing together.

As if reading her mind, he stands over her, his dirty-blond hair glowing against the morning sunlight filtering through the trees. Like yesterday, he doesn't rush her to get up or speak. He sits next to her while Merith looks around the surrounding gardens, not that Adaline expects him to find anything extraordinary. Truth be told, she thought just showing up here would be enough to trigger something.

Sitting up, she drapes her hands in her lap. "You might be stuck with me."

"You certainly make things interesting around here."

Even though he sounds amused, she double checks his face, making sure it doesn't reveal hints of frustration or disappointment. Not finding any, she dares to ask, "You don't hate me anymore? Aren't I still a problem?"

He pinches his lips together as his eyes roam to the dilapidated palace roof. "I never hated you. I didn't... I couldn't..." He drums his fingers on his knees. "I'm trying to do what's best for my people. They chose to follow me into the Neutral Territory, to trust me. I'm responsible for them and their safety. But I shouldn't have—"

She elbows his arm. "It's okay, really. I get it."

Ëólas smiles, not the type he gives his people when he's trying to reassure them, but rather the carefree one he shares with his friends, the one that says he's at ease, that he's comfortable, that he's himself. And he's willing to share that with her, even if just this once. Progress, indeed. When she smiles, he elbows her in return, and his playfulness dissipates half of today's disappointment.

She pulls her legs into her chest, tucking her dress around her ankles, and rests her chin on her knees. The only sounds within the grove come from the trees rustling their tresses, waves breaking against the shore, and Ëólas and Adaline's breaths. The air is warm but not unbearably so, and the steady breeze makes these old grounds feel alive. Without swords drawn and people chasing her, the palace gardens are peaceful, maybe even welcoming. And with Ëólas beside her, her intuition perks up, reinforcing what she sensed the first time they met—he is one of the good guys. How could anyone think of this place as a bad omen?

Oh, maybe Sallie meant the elves find this place to be a bad omen because their queen died here? "Ëólas, what spell did the last queen cast?"

He side-eyes her and takes his time before responding. "Inlūmras né leira."
When he speaks, his eyes have a new depth to them that makes him appear older,
wiser, perhaps even wistful, as if he's conjuring both painful memories from the
past and the wisdom one gains after moving on. "A spell of hope."

"Hope. Wait, that's what I said after you yelled at me for going to the elven
garden, that—"

"I didn't yell."

Adaline cocks an eyebrow at him. "Uh-huh. Anyway, I said there's a current of
hope in the air, and you all kind of, I don't know, froze up."

"I remember." He laughs through his nose and runs a hand through his
dark-blond hair.

"Did...did the spell really kill her?"

He glowers at the ground. "I don't know. But I do believe she cast that spell so
her vision would come to fruition. That elves and humans could live side by side
again."

Adaline nods and closes her eyes. As she inhales the salty sea air, she lets all
thoughts drift away and break against the shore. In their place, a seed of warmth
blooms inside her chest, a promise that everything will be okay.

That's got to be it, inlūmras né leira. Does Ëólas feel it too? "Does it hurt you,"
she whispers, "to be here?"

"No. What occurred in Aerytol was before my time." He pulls his legs up to
his chest, matching Adaline's posture.

"And how much time have you had?" She keeps her gaze forward, but she
witnesses him smirk out of the corner of her eye.

"Curious as ever."

"Curiouser and curiouser."

"That's not a real word."

"It's a quote from a story about a girl who falls down a rabbit hole and enters
another world."

"Huh. I'd like to hear it sometime."

"Okay, but then you'll owe me a story."

He chuckles. "Deal."

They sit together in silence until Merith comes back with no news, and they set off again at full gallop all the way home.

The next day, Adaline starts a slightly new routine. In the morning, she and Mercia make their way to the other side of the castle, no longer sneaking around corners, and join Seira on her balcony for breakfast where Mercia updates them about the comings and goings within the castle. Sometimes Adaline attempts embroidering or helping Seira add embellishments to her white gown. Adding a random sparkling bead here and there suits Adaline just fine.

According to Mercia, the other ladies are preoccupied with overseeing all aspects of making the castle run smoothly. They calculate the food and resources they'll need as autumn approaches so that everyone, including the servants, will have what they need. Mercia's mother leads the other council members' wives, which doesn't surprise Adaline. Lady Marzella definitely owns her commanding presence.

Mercia also shares that some of the wives have become more vocal about their resentment toward Magnus and his attention to the Neutral Territory. "They're concerned, I quote, that this little project of his has decreased Alderton's overall wealth."

"Is that true?" Adaline asks.

Mercia shrugs. "Father's certain that once more human and elven kingdoms feel comfortable traveling to the Neutral Territory, they'll also make their way safely into Alderton, which will create new economic prospects for us. So while we have invested quite a lot into rebuilding this city, it should greatly benefit us in the future. The trouble at the moment seems to revolve around the resources Alderton has diverted throughout the kingdom to bring here and the disputes among the local peasants, though whether those two are related, I do not know."

The word *peasants* makes Adaline cringe, but she keeps her mouth shut and focuses on her stitches.

"Lady Audney's engagement has been settled upon too." Even though she keeps her tone casual, Mercia peeks up at Adaline and pauses her needle mid-stitch.

"Why are you smirking?" Adaline asks.

"Aren't you curious to know whom she'll marry?"

"Not really."

"Oh." With a humph, the redhead goes back to her stitches.

"Why would I care? Mercia? Hey, please look at me. We're friends, aren't we? Why do you think I would care?"

With a loud huff, Mercia tosses her latest project aside, the fabric falling in ruffles into the basket at her side. "Aren't you interested in becoming queen?"

"Whaaaaat?" Adaline's eyes shoot open, and she jumps off her seat, knocking Seira's hard work to the ground.

Seira, however, doesn't notice. She continues stitching the air while she hums to herself as if she's somewhere else.

"I don't have *any* interest in being queen," Adaline says. "And Magnus knows that."

"But you're obviously close with him."

"I rarely see him."

Mercia cocks her head to the side and tosses her hands in the air as if presenting the obvious. "You're on a first-name basis with our king."

Adaline backs up until her bottom hits the balcony railing. "But, I mean, it just kinda started out that way, and he never really corrected me, and we're friends. Only friends." Yeah, he's handsome, but he's Magnus. Kissing him would be like kissing her father. She gags at the thought. They even have the same beard. "He's on a first-name basis with Seira too!"

Mercia releases an even louder harrumph as she snatches her project, shoves it into her lap, and stabs her needle into the pillowcase—or whatever she's embroidering—with additional gusto.

"You're mad at me?" Adaline walks up to Mercia and waits for her friend to speak.

After stabbing the cloth five more times, Mercia rests her work on her lap and looks up at Adaline as though she were watching her best friend throw away her entire future. "You'd make a great queen."

Damn, that's one hell of a compliment. Kneeling down, Adaline rests her hand on the arm of Mercia's chair. A flock of birds fly past, each cawing to each other as they head toward their next adventure. "I'm fond of him, yes. But I'm not in love with him."

"I don't want to see you alone."

Adaline sucks in her bottom lip. "I haven't been alone since I came here." They both look at Seira still daydreaming while her hand bobs up and down with each imaginary stitch. Then Adaline turns back to Mercia. "Don't worry about me, okay? I'll find my way. I promise."

With a sigh, Mercia squeezes Adaline's hand. "Fine. But I still think you'd make a great queen."

"Thank you. I just don't think I'm the queen type."

Seira bursts out laughing. She grips her stomach as she rocks back and forth and wipes the tears from her eyes. "Oh, that was funny, indeed."

"What was?" Mercia asks.

"What was what?" Seira stares at them with a blank face, all humor gone, as if her mind never wandered off on its own.

"Nothing," Adaline says. She kneels next to Seira, who just realized that parts of her gown lay scattered on the floor, and helps Seira collect the pieces one by one.

As Adaline makes her way into the city, past all the stalls that run parallel to the river, elves and humans alike wave hello, tip their hats, or curtsy as she passes by. Per usual, she first visits Jósep's shop where he's out front, continuing to chisel away at that enormous stone block. Leaves have emerged at the top, and Jósep has discovered some swirls and deep grooves in the middle.

He greets Adaline with a broad smile and offers her a biscuit from his plate. She sits in his chair, munches on the buttery treat, and watches him work. Each time Jósep sheds another piece of excess, she sinks deeper into her seat, and her mind slows down.

"You're rather quiet today," Jósep says, without pausing his work.

Adaline shrugs. "Yeah."

He turns his head to assess another section, giving Adaline a view of his profile. His plump cheek and crow's feet give away his amusement. Without pressing her, he continues his work, pausing only when Adaline suddenly sits forward and exclaims, "It's a tree!"

"Ah, yes. I believe so. I'm still finding it though."

Peeking around him, she peers into his mostly empty shop. She spies a few crates, a pile of tools, some chunks of stone, but nothing more. *He must still be settling in.*

"Jósep, can I ask you something somewhat personal?"

Another bit of marble falls to the ground. "Go ahead."

"I've never seen anyone else here with you. Do you have family in town?

"I do not." He never takes his eyes away from his art. "My entire family is in Lameiría."

"Oh. And you were okay coming on your own? To carve a tree?"

Jósep releases a deep, rich chuckle full of life. "No, my lady. I came here because I haven't found the one yet. I hope destiny might send my intended here as well."

"The one," Adaline repeats. "What a lovely idea." She rests her head against the back of the chair and tilts her head upward. A large puffy cloud drifts by, the only one in the sky. "You really think such a thing exists?"

A large piece of marble crashes to the ground and rolls aside. "Absolutely."

"But there are so many people in the world. How could there be just one?"

"There are indeed a lot of humans, my lady, but not as many elves. And we're all well practiced at taking our time so we can find our other half."

"But really? Just one? What if something tragic happened and you missed your chance? Oh my god, I'm so sorry! I didn't mean to worry you."

"I'm not worried, my lady. More often than not, someone we already know can become the one over time. And sometimes…" He keeps chiseling but stops talking.

"What?"

"Sometimes destiny steps in."

"What does that mean?" Hunching forward, she crosses her legs, balances her elbow on her knee, and rests her chin on her hand as she waits for his reply. But minutes pass, and it's not because he's engrossed with his work. "You're not going to tell me, are you?"

"Would you believe me?"

"I don't know. But I'd like the chance."

Setting his chisel down on his stool, he fans his hands out on top of his display table, and his brown locks neatly tied at his nape hang over his shoulder. As a human, he might be around twenty-five years old, but his patience and wisdom, plus the depth in his eyes, make Adaline think he's much, much older than that.

"Sometimes, my lady, destiny sends us the one person in all the world best suited for us, so we can become what the world needs."

His words replay inside her head, each time imbedding themselves into the cracks of her heart, wedging themselves deeper as they tear her open. What a gift. Maybe even a burden. But the thought of never having someone like that hurts far more than the fear of what payment destiny would require. "How do you know when you've found them?"

"Do you like water? Do you like breathing air? Do you like eating food? How do you know? You just do. There's no doubt. No fear. No hesitation. You just know, and you trust that knowledge unequivocally." With a wink, Jósep returns to chiseling his block.

She stares after him but doesn't see him as her mind ponders the idea, the possibility. "Well, if there is such a thing for humans, at least that explains the last ten years."

"What do you mean, my lady?"

"Just that maybe there's not something wrong with me. Maybe I just haven't found the one yet. But I don't have hundreds of years, so I'd appreciate it if destiny could speed things up."

"As impatient as ever," he says.

"Yep, definitely a defining characteristic of my species."

Usually after a visit with Jósep, Adaline also visits Delós, or she picks someone new to observe and asks them a million questions. The people of Market Street seem to expect this now. Both elves and humans are more forthcoming with answers, eager to share their methods with someone who simply listens and observes and admires their hard work.

A bit after noon, Adaline climbs up the Rialto and waits in the gazebo-like center where she usually leans against the balustrade, keeping her back to the ruins as she tells the children stories. Today, someone's placed a bench in her spot. Carved out of stone, two full-body deer support the seat, one a wide-eyed doe and the other a stag with its antlers growing into the scalloped edges of the seat itself. Sunken crisscrossed vines decorating the backrest create diamond shapes, and the vines grow into a floral arrangement in the center of the headrest. Two more animals form the armrests, one a sheep and the other a ram.

"Do you like it, my lady?" asks the first elven child to arrive. "Jósep placed the bench here this morning."

Adaline traces the smooth top of the seat with her fingertips as she nods *yes*. When she sits down, her back sings its gratitude that she doesn't have to stand for the next hour or so. More children arrive, and she shares a new story about a young woman who gives up her freedom to save her father and must live with a temperamental beast. The audience, which now includes adults munching on their lunches in the background, gasps in awe at the idea that someone so ghastly could turn into someone so kind.

After story time, Adaline runs back to Jósep's stall, where he's sat down to enjoy his own lunch. "Jósep, did the city plans designate that bridge for social gatherings? How convenient!"

With a nonchalant tone, he asks, "Did they now?"

"You, you don't know?"

He shrugs and sips his soup.

"Oh, Jósep. You didn't…I mean, did you?"

"Did you find the bench comfortable, my lady?"

"It's exquisite, Jósep. Thank you, immensely."

"Thank you, my lady, for the entertainment."

CHAPTER TWENTY-TWO

THE DAGGER

The next day when Adaline finishes telling the children a story and visiting with Sallie, she makes her way to the training grounds, with escorts of course, and follows Fólas into a different building. This private room has an entire wall dedicated to killer projectiles, from tiny star-shaped ones that would make a ninja proud to thin daggers longer than Adaline's forearm. At both ends of the room, four hay-stuffed dummies await their demise with frowns painted on their wooden stump heads.

Adaline lifts her brows as she walks past the rows of weapons. "So, I'm leveling up today?"

"Leveling up?"

"Advancing in my training."

"Ah, yes. Time for a dagger."

Scanning the wall for all of two seconds, Fólas retrieves a dagger with a small triangular scabbard no longer than Adaline's palm. When he unsheathes it, the blade is even smaller. "Alright, safety first."

"Let me guess: Don't touch the sharp edges and keep my eye on the pointy end."

Fólas arches one eyebrow and passes the weapon to her. "In short, yes."

"Nice. How sharp is it?" She brings her fingertip toward the blade, but Fólas grabs her wrist to stop her.

"Don't touch the pointy end either. It will slice through your skin like butter, and you won't feel it until your finger lies on the floor."

When he lets go, Adaline drops her hand and tries to pass the dagger back to him. "Got a wooden one?"

He chuckles once, then dons his strict teacher's face, and begins her lessons by showing her two ways to hold the dagger, either with the blade pointing up as if she were wielding a hammer or with the blade facing downward as if she were about to jab the tip of the blade into a cutting board. Next, he lists the areas of the body that will either incapacitate or kill someone, as well as which of the latter will do so slowly versus quickly.

And now I remember why I didn't join Dax's long-sword LARPer club.

"Let's start with incapacitation." Fólas points at Adaline's feet and waits for her to widen her stance and sink lower, condensing her energy into a tight-fisted ball. "Good. Extend your blade arm forward, and point the tip of the blade toward me. Using your wrist, move your hand in a circular motion. Exactly."

Fólas makes her continue this motion for several minutes until her face tightens and the movement in her wrist becomes jerky. "Alright, you can stop. To incapacitate an attacker, the goal is to cut, not stab, especially in a circular motion. Aim for the forearm or, if you have to, the thighs. If you drive your blade into the bone, you'll lose your dagger in the process. But if you cut and drag the blade around in a circle, your attacker will have to retreat and tend to his wounds. Otherwise, the blood loss will make him weaker until he collapses and loses consciousness."

Adaline winces and massages her wrist. After she bends her hand backward, pulling on her palm to stretch, Fólas offers his arm, covered in a leather armguard, and has her practice the motion on him. Every time she pulls back, he flicks his eyes at her and stares until she repeats the motion with more confidence. By the time they're done, he needs a new armguard.

"We're not going to shy away from real-life practice, my lady. That's the only way you'll have confidence to take action should you find yourself in a situation when you need to defend yourself."

Adaline nods, but the dagger feels heavier in her hand, and that's not only because of its bulky hilt or her sore wrist.

Fólas gives her a moment to recover but quickly moves on with their lesson. "With the dagger, think about soft-body target areas such as the face, the neck, the lower abdomen, and the groin. Stabbing someone at the base of the neck or in the heart or lungs will kill your attacker within minutes. For a slow death, you can slice their abdomen, just below the naval, and if their intestines fall out—"

"Stop! Please, stop. Please." Shaking her head fervently, she steps backward until her shoulders hit the wall. "I, I. Nope. I'm done for today." Dropping her dagger, she hugs her abdomen, making sure her own intestines are where they ought to be. Her head feels foggier the more she wills herself not to visualize what Fólas described.

Hand-to-hand combat, cool. Disembowelment, no thank you.

Fólas eyes her quietly. Whether he's disappointed, he doesn't let on as he picks up her dagger, sheathes it, and rests it on a shelf. Crossing his arms over his chest, he moves toward her as if he were approaching a wounded animal on the side of the road. "I'm sorry. I got ahead of myself."

"I don't think I can stomach the idea of killing someone."

He smiles to himself. "Alright. How about we focus on incapacitation?"

"Yeah. Thanks."

"Just promise me one thing, my lady. If you're ever threatened again, you won't hesitate to fight back."

She nods once. When Fólas raises his eyebrows, questioning if she's being truthful, she walks to the center of the room, widens her feet, and raises her fists in front of her. "Let's go."

He grins like a proud sensei. After about an hour, not that Adaline can check the time on her mobile phone rattling around in her pocket, a guard knocks on the door to pull Fólas away. Apparently, someone sliced their leg open.

And that is why we should be practicing with wooden weapons first.

Before Fólas rushes out, he tells Adaline to keep striking the target and practicing the moves he showed her. When he's gone, she turns back to the dummy and mimics its frown. She thrusts forward, sideways, and upward, but her movements are slower and her wrist floppier.

Ten days. I've been gone ten days. Cindy and Dax must know I'm missing now, which means so do Cindy's entire family and my colleagues. I know I can't do anything about that right now, but is telling stories and stabbing a dummy really what I should be doing here?

She stabs the dummy again but leaves the dagger embedded in its heart and slumps down next to it in the corner. Uncertainty seeps into her limbs, travels into her gut, and wrings her stomach back and forth. After high school, she knew college was next. After her bachelor's, she knew earning her master's was next. Then her PhD. Then her post-doc. Then teaching and working toward tenure. She's done all that, well, except having tenure. But it's all beginning to feel pointless. She gave up dancing to focus on her PhD. She gave up music when her father died. What's left? Who is she becoming? Or rather, as Jósep said, who does the world need her to be?

I'm stuck in limbo, and I have no clue what's going to lead me in the right direction. The best direction.

The door handle jiggles. Adaline jumps to her feet, and Ëólas enters the room. It's the first time she's seen him in two days. He looks clean and comfortable and... *Of course he looks clean. He always looks clean.*

She shakes her head, wiping her thoughts away as if her brain were an Etch A Sketch. "I was just practicing with the dagger."

"From beside the dummy?"

"I got lost in my thoughts."

Ëólas nods, then glances at the dagger lodged in the dummy's chest. "How's it feel?"

"Like I'm losing my mind?"

He tilts his chin to the side, but instead of asking for clarification, he walks over and yanks the dagger out of the dummy's chest. "The hilt. How does the hilt feel in your hand?"

"Oooooh. It's fine."

"Let me see." He extends his open palm toward her, waiting for her to give him something. When she furrows her brows, he asks, "May I have your hand?"

Something about the sight of him waiting for her, extending his hand for her, makes her heart race. "Um, yeah." She reaches for him, but before their palms connect, he wiggles his fingers, making her jump and him laugh.

"Relax, Adaline. I will not bite you."

Her cheeks feel like they've caught fire. "I know that." *I may have been drunk that night, but you made it perfectly clear that elves don't find humans attractive.*

With a smirk, he reaches for her, turns her hand upward, and lays the hilt on her palm. "Grip that for me."

She closes her fist around the long, hard handle and shifts her weight from one hip to the other and back again while she stares at her hand in his and the dagger between them.

"Hmm. Your hands are smaller than I thought. You can't even close your fingers around this one's girth. How's it feel?"

"What? Oh, um, stiff?"

"Stiff? It's solid metal. I would hope so. But does it feel heavy?"

"Heavy?"

"Yes, heavy."

"Oh, it's fine. It feels...good." Adaline swallows hard and looks anywhere but his golden eyes, full lips, and her hand in his. For someone well versed with a sword, his touch is surprisingly gentle.

"Are you alright?"

"Fine. Just fine. Perfectly fine. I mean, what girl doesn't enjoy holding hard objects in her hand for long periods of time? Whew, this has been a weird day for me. I think I need water." *And a filter for my mouth. What is wrong with me today?*

Ëólas cocks his head to the side and parts his lips, but he doesn't seem able to find words.

While he processes the situation, Adaline feels her skin flushing in patches along her arm, up her back, and down her thighs. Her hand tingles, and her body temperature keeps rising to an uncomfortable degree that makes not writhing on top of him—on top of his palm—extremely challenging. "May I have my hand back?"

"Oh." He lets her go but takes the dagger and places it back on the wall. "None of these will fit your hand right." Grabbing the pitcher and a bowl off the shelf, he pours water from one into the other and passes her the bowl. When she stares at it blankly, he says, "You said you needed water."

"Ha. I did, didn't I. Thank you." She guzzles the whole lot down and hands him the bowl, which he places in a crate in the other corner of the room, a Renaissance bus tub for dirty bowls.

"Oh, what about this?" She pulls her father's Swiss army knife out of her pocket and shows the blade to Ëólas, who frowns at the sight of it.

"If you must keep that on you, save it for emergencies. We have nothing like that in our world. It stands out too much."

"Oh." She folds the blade down and pockets the knife.

"No need to worry. We'll figure out the dagger situation later. In the meantime, show me what you've learned."

"Oh. Um."

Ëólas stalks toward her, his eyes narrow, his strides long and confident. "I don't see you taking a defensive stance yet, Adaline." He doesn't stop walking toward her, his hands swaying gently at his side, his long hair framing his square chin. "Why are you backing up?" He looks like someone who knows what he wants, like a soccer player on the pitch who sees the ball and won't stop until he's in control of the game. "Adaline," he calls quietly.

She gulps. When he's directly in front of her, that lavender scent hits her, and her stomach flutters violently. He reaches for her arms and pulls her close. Instinctively, she places her hands on his hard chest, his breath hitching as she slides her hands upward. She raises her arms higher, turns them outward, and wraps her elbows around his, forcing him to release his hold on her.

He smiles brightly. "Well done."

In a flash, he reaches for her throat. She blocks him, pushing her forearm against his shoulder, and hooks her arm around his, wedging his elbow against her side. At the same time, he traps her other arm behind her back, and they're locked together.

"Well done. But I want you to think for a moment about how you can get your wrist free. Fólas must have shown you this."

"Um." Her gaze drifts to his lips hovering a few inches from her nose. "I...um."

The longer they stay together, Ëólas's breathing grows deeper, heavier, and a slight pink takes over his cheeks. His eyes darken to a molten gold, and neither of them moves. Neither of them speaks. Neither of them backs down. The heaviness in the air settles around them, and the din from outside fades away. She lifts her chin. He tilts his face downward. Her heart pounds louder until the door swings open, ushering in the outside world and a cool breeze, and as Fólas strides into the room, Ëólas and Adaline release their holds and fly apart.

"Fólas, good timing. Adaline needs a bit more work with escaping close encounters." Rubbing his hand on the back of his neck, Ëólas takes large, quick steps toward the door.

"Ah, yes. I didn't want to make her feel uncomfortable."

"Well, she needs those lessons." Before he leaves, Ëólas turns to Adaline, his face having resumed its cold, statue-esque Grecian perfection. "You're small and fast. You can use that to your advantage so you never get locked in a corner." Without waiting for a reply, he exits the room, shutting the door loudly behind him.

"Bye," she mumbles to the dark wooden slats. She can't peel her eyes away from the brass handle, even as Fólas paces the room.

"Alright." He claps his hands together and marches into the middle of the room. "We have a lot of time left for today, so let's first practice here where you have space to, um, breathe, and then we'll move into a corner. Ëólas is correct in that you are small and—everything alright, my lady?"

"Huh? Oh, yeah. I just don't get him."

Fólas follows Adaline's line of sight to the shut door. "My lord?"

"Uh-huh. We used to fight. A lot actually."

"I know." Fólas snorts, strolling over to her.

Oh, great. Of course he told them. She's certain her cheeks have reddened again. "I thought we were finally getting along. Sometimes he's kind. But sometimes he's still cold. I was certain he hated me, but now I, I don't know."

Fólas sighs. "My lord never hated you, my lady."

"I don't believe you." She drops her gaze to her empty hands.

"Don't you dare tell him I told you this, but," Fólas leans toward her and whispers, "he convinced the king that you ought to learn how to fight, before you even asked me."

Adaline meets Fólas's dark eyes as her eyebrows slowly knit together. *But he doesn't trust me. I'm a danger.*

"My lord was quite distraught after the incident at the palace. He encouraged the king to let you sentence those pigs."

Ëólas. That was his doing? "But. But, even now, I more often than not drain the life out of him."

Fólas shakes his head and stuffs his hands in his pockets. "I think you confound him."

"In what way?" Her eyes dance back to the door.

With a shrug, he stands in front of her, blocking her view. "Time will tell, my lady."

"We have that expression back home too."

"Because it's the truth. Hmm. How about we end this session early, and we'll incorporate my lord's instructions tomorrow?"

She should argue, insist that she's capable. But her brain hurts. "Thank you."

Fólas escorts Adaline out of the training room, allowing her to leave that cramped space behind. With the sun shining brightly ahead, a fresh breeze pushes the musty air off her face, and she inhales deeply, grateful she has full use of her brain again. Maybe now, with some distance, she can think more about what Fólas said, about what Ëólas did, not that she cares. Because going home is her top priority. At least, it ought to be.

CHAPTER TWENTY-THREE

THE HEALER

On her way back to the castle, Adaline stops by to see Delós, but he's busy entertaining other shoppers, so she continues down the street, noting the lady sitting at her loom, the upholsterer loading a loveseat into a customer's cart, the jeweler hanging up necklaces with gems that gleam in the sunlight, and the ceramic couple adding their newest creations to the kiln—all people she's come to know. When she approaches Jósep's shop, he's engaged in a conversation with an elven lady, so Adaline gives him a small wave and continues on her way, only for Jósep to call her over.

"Lady Adaline, always a pleasure. May I please introduce you to my friend, Lady Loríen."

As Adaline approaches, Lady Loríen rotates her body so she mirrors Adaline's posture. Her heart-shaped lips look ready to share knowledge at any moment, while her big eyes observe when to choose the right opportunity. With her mint-green tulle dress and its pale-yellow and pink embroidered flowers, she looks ready for afternoon tea. Fine jewelry falls in layers down the back of her head and around her neck and wrists, and her tan skin has a natural, sun-kissed undertone that reminds Adaline of the toasty beaches that outline Southeast Asia.

"A pleasure to meet you, Lady Adaline. Jósep says you have the heart of an artist. For Jósep, that's quite the praise."

"Oh, well, I appreciate all forms of art, but I can't really call myself an artist anymore."

Lady Loríen blinks slowly, lowers her eyelids halfway, and stares at Adaline like a sage reading an ancient scroll. She tucks a smile into the corner of her mouth. "Not even regarding music?"

"Oh, well, yeah. I put that aside a while back. I needed to focus on…other areas of study."

"Mmm," Lady Loríen says, her voice both light and strong as she weighs the meaning of every word she speaks. "Life can call us in many directions, causing us to feel lost. Yet those very same experiences conspire to help us discover our potential. It's quite magical, I think."

Adaline's mouth hangs slightly open. *Where have you been the last ten days?*

Logically speaking, hearing another elf willingly mention magic in Adaline's presence should hoist a major red flag. But everything about Lady Loríen, her slow movements, her steady gaze, and the way she tilts her body toward those who are speaking, tells Adaline she's a kindred spirit.

Adaline rests her elbow on Jósep's table and leans toward Loríen. "Yes. Exactly. I feel like I'm ready for that next direction, but I don't know what it is yet."

Loríen blinks once and slowly.

"Well, my lady," says Jósep, resting his hands on top of his stall table, "if you're interested in carving—"

"Jósep! Your hand?" Adaline gasps at his swollen left hand wrapped like a mummy holding a baseball. "What happened?"

"Kind of you to worry, my lady, but do not fret. One of my tools broke, and, well, my hand was in the way." With his good hand, he mimics a tool piercing his injured palm.

"Oh god!" *Please tell me he won't die of tetanus. No, no, no. That can't happen, not to him.* "How do we get that treated?"

"I'm alright. Lady Loríen has just finished examining my hand again."

"He'll be perfectly fine in another day or two," Loríen says.

Adaline looks from Jósep to Loríen. "So soon?"

"Certainly." Loríen takes one step sideways, revealing a large bag with small vials and clean bandages folded into neat balls. "My treatment is working as we speak."

"You're a healer." When Loríen nods, Adaline bounces forward and clasps her hands in front of her chest. "May I come by sometime and learn more about what you do?"

"She's quite curious," Jósep says with a chuckle. "An endearing trait, truly."

Aww, Jósep.

Loríen smiles softly and lifts her arms, turning her palms upward. "Then of course you may. Though you must understand that healing humans and elves is quite different."

"Really?" Adaline asks. "In what ways? Do you mean in your methods of practice or in how the body itself heals?"

Like jingling bells, Loríen's musical laugh makes the corners of her eyes crinkle the way any teacher would when finding someone interested in their passion. "We combine treating any wound with balancing the energy within the body to speed up the recovery process."

"You mean like with chakras?"

Loríen raises her fingers to her mouth while she contemplates. "I'm not familiar with that word."

"Oh, right. Some people believe there are seven points of energy in the body, and moving that energy around can improve our mental, emotional, and physical health."

"I was not aware humans knew of such things."

Oops. "Well, back home, some do." *Please don't ask for more details.*

It's not like Adaline can explain that her father spent several years studying about India or that Adaline listened to his lectures so often that she convinced Cindy to participate in a free workshop in D.C. They both felt that energy movement her father described, only Adaline had a panic attack. Afterward, her father said that without proper instruction, the energy buildup can shock the body, and he made her promise she wouldn't try that again.

"Fascinating." Loríen collects her supplies, placing them gingerly inside her bag. "Lady Adaline, would you care to accompany me back to my shop now? Jósep is going to head upstairs and rest so that my methods work most efficiently."

When Loríen's eyes dart toward Jósep, he bows and takes his leave. "I would never dream of disregarding your advice. If you'll excuse me, good evening, ladies."

Both Adaline and Loríen wish Jósep a speedy recovery and wait until they see movement in his upstairs window. Then Loríen escorts Adaline to the apothecary located four blocks beyond Market Street. Her establishment is everything Adaline loves about metaphysical shops. The smell of incense when she walks in the door induces relaxation. Crystals hang like wind chimes in front of the windows and reflect light around the room. Shelves display glass bottles in various shades, each containing herbs and other oddities that Adaline can't quite make out, as well as more crystals, geodes, and stones. By the window, four chairs surround a table with a tray holding a teapot and two stacks of cups, just waiting for the next customers to sit down.

While Loríen goes behind the counter, puts away her medical supplies, and lights a fire in the hearth to boil water, Adaline admires the crystals lining the wall opposite the door. The assortment of reflected colors decorating and blending together on the shelves creates a painter's palette. She recognizes the clear quartz and the large peridot. In the back, behind a blue-green geode, sits a small, round broken piece of rose quartz that fits perfectly in her palm. It's warm to the touch as she turns it around and admires the milky white swirls within the pink.

Loríen appears next to her. "You like that one?"

"Rose quartz is lovely." She rolls it around in her palm once more, then reaches forward to place it back on the shelf, but she stops halfway when Loríen shakes her head.

"Keep it."

Elves sure are big on free giveaways. "That's very kind of you, but I can't. I don't have any money, and—"

"Money means little to us." With a featherlight touch, she closes Adaline's hand around the crystal. "And this one calls to you. It's yours. Keep it in your pocket, and it will bring more love into your life."

"Love?" Adaline's chest shrivels inward. "I've not been successful in that department for a long while now."

"There are many types of love, and it would appear that's what you seek most right now."

Love. She would love to get back to Cindy and Dax. Then again, Adaline would love—No. Shedding light on impossible wishes only makes the pain more visible. Best to keep those fantasies buried. Still, she pockets the rose quartz and takes a few deep breaths while Loríen pours them tea. They both sit down, and Adaline inhales hints of licorice, cardamom, and something else she can't identify, but the scent is sweet and comforting. "I love the smell of this tea."

Loríen offers her a honey pot. While Adaline rolls the dipper around and around until she can safely get the sweet, sticky substance into her cup without leaving a trail on the table, Loríen continues. "I'm glad I could share it with you. I obtained the hibiscus tea leaves only two weeks ago. When merchants travel here from Alderton, I look forward to bringing new items into my shop. The resources my grandmother used to possess have become harder to find since our neighbors closed their borders. This city has given us hope that we'll be able to travel the world freely again."

"I hope so too." Using both hands, Adaline brings her cup to her mouth and blows away the rising steam.

"You came a long way here. The journey must have been perilous." Loríen keeps her long, slender nose pointed toward the honey pot while she readies her own cup, but she flicks her eyes toward Adaline.

She sips her tea carefully. While her tongue adjusts to the temperature and relishes the flavor, she contemplates her answer. "It was surprising, to say the least. But I also appreciate the change of scenery. There's so much to discover and learn here."

"You have the heart of an explorer."

Adaline laughs. "I inherited that from my father. He relished studying history. His home office is littered with relics and replicas of whatever he could get his hands on."

As Loríen stirs her tea, she watches the leaves swirl like a whirlpool in her cup. "When did he pass?"

The knife in Adaline's pocket burns a hole in her hip. "Two years ago," she whispers.

"But that's not the only loss you've suffered?"

With her fingertip, Adaline traces the rim of her cup and shakes her head. "My grandmother passed away eight, almost nine months ago."

"And she left a hole inside you." She keeps her gaze steady, then focuses on sipping her own tea before her guest can feel uncomfortable.

With a heavy sigh, Adaline looks out the window. A few elves walk past, talking animatedly without a care in the world. They have each other. Confidants. Support. Guidance. Adaline sips her tea and closes her eyes so she can savor the taste of each herb. Resting her cup on the saucer, she looks Loríen in the eyes to gauge her reaction. "Do you read minds?"

The healer sets down her teacup and speaks with amused earnestness. "Not at all. I read the energy that all living beings emit. Sometimes that energy is as visible as the sunlight. Other times, people hold that energy close to their hearts or hide it altogether."

She's talking about auras. "And you see mine?"

"A bit. May I read deeper?"

Adaline strums her fingers on the table. Rather than overthinking this opportunity, she nods her head. Loríen leans forward. Although her expression is neutral, her pointed gaze burrows into Adaline. At first, her head buzzes with a low vibration that's barely perceivable. Then her cheeks flush as warmth settles throughout her body, thick and heavy as if she were standing in front of a bonfire, only the heat originates from inside. Her arms and chest tingle, and she closes her eyes to calm her beating heart. Pressure builds inside her limbs, her chest, her head until that pressure pops, and every odd sensation stops abruptly, leaving her muscles relaxed and her eyes droopy.

Adaline takes a sip of tea. *I hope this has a lot of caffeine.* "That was intense."

"It can be. Thank you for trusting me."

Adaline lifts her cup in a gesture of cheers. "So, what now?"

"You want the truth?"

"Always."

"I sense not only much intelligence but also wisdom, both of which have the capacity to grow stronger, but you don't know your own strength, not yet. At the moment, I'm more concerned that the energy around your heart is blocked. You have been suppressing too much, which dims your energy. And that puts you in danger."

"Danger?"

"When our energy is dim, we cannot see or judge clearly. We more easily make mistakes that further weigh down and dim our hearts, making escape that much more difficult."

Staring at her teacup, Adaline gives it a swirl. The leaves float for a few seconds before sinking to the bottom. *Derek. Dating him was a huge mistake. So was fucking him.* "I know what you mean." They sit in silence while Adaline ponders Loríen's words. *Seems like she's also a therapist.*

"Is this what you do regularly?" Adaline takes another sip.

"Sometimes."

"What else do you do?"

The door opens, and Loríen stands. "Excuse me just a moment, my friend." *Friend? Yay!*

An elf Adaline's never seen before holds the door open for a lady. After following her inside, he shuts the door quietly behind them. The elven lady's eyes are red and puffy, but when the elf places his hand on the small of her back, her body relaxes, and her face softens until they both see Adaline sitting by the window, and their eyebrows jump upward. But Loríen greets her customers with subtle grace and continues business as usual, at least Adaline assumes so, and they speak in whispers, maintaining doctor-patient confidentiality.

She debates leaving, but Loríen doesn't seem to mind Adaline's presence. She turns back to her tea, but her curiosity won't hush up. From the corner of her eye, she watches Loríen grab bottles from around her shop and pour drops from each into one small vial the size of a thumb. She also chooses a few crystals, places them in a pouch with the vial, and hands them to the lady who presses them close to her lower abdomen and tears up. Her husband rests his hand on top of his wife's abdomen too. They look at each other, their faces reflecting hope and adoration, and Adaline says a silent prayer for the couple as they leave.

After Loríen puts her bottles back in their proper places, she sits across from Adaline. Keeping her voice as clear as wind chimes, she says, "Your concern is visible."

"Mmm. A friend of mine struggled for seven years before having her baby girl. She felt so alone with her grief. I hate that I couldn't help her back then."

"I didn't know humans struggle with infertility too."

"Oh, we do. We just don't talk about it as much as we ought to."

"*That* I can understand." Loríen glances at the vials surrounding them and lowers her head. "I am fortunate though. I have one son, Edmor, who is also here in the Neutral Territory. He's joined the castle guard."

"Oh, I wonder if I've seen him? I'll ask about him."

Loríen's smile fades as she rests her hand on her own abdomen. "I confess I'd like another one. I'm ready for more."

"Well, I look forward to the day I hear your good news."

Spinning her drained cup in her hands, Loríen stares at the bottom, and her voice thickens with each word she shares. "Thank you, but that may be awhile. We elves ovulate rather infrequently."

That must hinder population growth. "I'm sorry that's so challenging."

She reaches across the table and refills their cups, her bracelets jingling loudly even though her hands remain steady, never letting a drop spill onto the table. "Well, I have faith and my own ways to assist."

"I'm glad." Sliding her cup so it sits beneath her chin, she inhales the rising aroma and lets it coat the inside of her lungs. The combination of the shop's scents and the tea's steam makes her feel like she's at a spa and enjoying a candid conversation with a close friend who will tell her what she needs to hear. "So, you help with cuts and fertility. What else?"

"Anything that requires healing the mind, body, and soul."

Hmmm, other cultures back home believe the same. But Loríen said earlier that healing humans and elves is different. "Why do you think humans might not respond to your methods?"

"Ah, that is the big question, isn't it?" Loríen raises her cup in a cheers gesture. She seems to appreciate when people know which questions to ask. "Elves are naturally in tune with the world and all its elements. Our energy harmonizes with the earth, so we can call upon the elements and use that reciprocal relationship to heal ourselves. Humans, I've heard, are individual beings and have either closed themselves off to the elements or never had access in the first place."

Setting down her cup, Adaline rests her elbows on the table, steeples her fingertips together, and taps her chin.

Oh, there's a lot to unpack here. Dr. Adaline A. Yates needs to dig into this. "If you've lived in Lameiría most of your life, then what foundation are you basing your observations on, in terms of humans?"

"History."

"Huh. History that was written by elves, I presume?"

Loríen leans forward, her necklaces chiming against the edge of the table, and her eyes sparkle. "Yes, indeed."

Adaline narrows her eyes and smirks. "You see the flaw there, don't you?"

"Yes, and it's very rare for me to converse with someone who sees it too."

"So do you think humans can learn how to gain access to the elements and this energy, if given the opportunity?"

With a sigh, Loríen leans back in her chair, glances out the window, and studies the sky turning ruby red and burnt orange. "I do not know, but the methods we use to gain that access are sacred to us."

Adaline sits back too and stares at the bottles and gems covering the shop walls. *Just like how the queen refused to let those books leave Lameiría.* "So humans have to find their own way."

Loríen nods and collects their empty teacups. "And gaining access is all the more difficult when your living energy is suppressed."

Dang. That sucks. And yet there it is again, curiosity's roots growing longer and deeper into Adaline's core.

Adaline meanders toward the castle, her heavy soul making each step more challenging. She lifts her eyes to the fourth floor where her window overlooks the human side of the city. Her bed feels like it's thirty miles away. Only her stomach keeps her moving forward.

"Adaline!" Seira's singsong voice calls, drifting over the stone path and dancing across the meadows. The Purple Stardust bristle and wave in response as the wind picks up and cools Adaline's cheeks.

Under the main gate, her toes touching the threshold, Seira waits for Adaline to enter the courtyard. When she does, Seira and Adaline hook their elbows together and walk past the guards, footmen, and horses. Magnus's page sits beside the doors to one of the lookout towers. *Magnus must be somewhere in the city today. I haven't seen him for a long while. I hope his council members haven't been giving him too hard a time.*

"The weather is so ideal I had our meal brought to the gardens. You will join me, won't you?" Seira's lavender eyes beg Adaline to walk toward the archway that leads to the private gardens.

"Sounds perfect."

Adaline sighs and leans her head on Seira's shoulder, only to halt and glance behind her. The guards seem not to pay her and Seira much mind, but whenever she turns her back to them, her skin tingles as if a spider were crawling up her spine, as if someone's watching her. Adaline hugs Seira's arm tighter and hurries her along. As they pass through the archway, someone coughs, and Adaline jumps.

"Are you alright, Adaline?"

"Mmm-hmm."

The farther they walk into the gardens and oak trees and hedges surround them, the more Adaline's breathing returns to normal. She rolls her shoulders to shake off the day and follows Seira to a burgundy fringed blanket with an assortment of large and small dishes, sweet and savory scents, and two bottles of wine.

Sitting in one corner of the blanket, Magnus brushes a few crumbs out of his thick, well-trimmed beard. "Ah, good timing!"

Starving, Adaline sits beside Seira, and they spend the evening enjoying the cool air settling around them while they nibble on an endless parade of delicacies, sip the continuous pouring of wine, listen to the crickets, and chat about anything that pops into their minds.

Seira's snickering draws Adaline's attention away from Magnus's story about his great-great-great grandfather's run in with a stone lizard. Seira points to Kayla walking down the hedged lane, carrying the mandolin Delós gifted Adaline.

"Did something happen?" After wiping her hands on a gold napkin, Adaline sits up and accepts the instrument from Kayla, who curtsies and leaves immediately with her gown swooshing around her fast strides. "Seira?"

"I asked her to fetch it. Would you sing me a song?" Seira's eyes twinkle as she bites her bottom lip and wiggles on her bum to find the perfect spot to enjoy live entertainment.

"Oh, yes." Lounging on the pillows surrounding him, Magnus rests his head in his hand and turns his face up to the billions of stars piercing the twilight. "I do believe I deserve to hear something from your home."

With a loud humph, Adaline shakes her head at Seira but strums the strings, plucking out of her memory the notes for Pink's "Cover Me In Sunshine." Magnus bobs his head, letting the music take him elsewhere. When Adaline sings about wildflowers standing still, Ëólas's head appears in the study window, his eyes locking with hers until the chorus, and he steps back quickly, the flickering light from inside swallowing him whole. Before Adaline loses herself wondering what he's thinking, Seira jumps up and spins in circles around the blanket, her arms extended and her hands dipping from side to side like she's scooping up sunshine. For Seira, Adaline continues playing, eager to help the mandolin come into its full sound. But she chose the song for herself, to remind herself that as upside down as her life has become, the world will keep spinning and, eventually, everything will be alright.

Chapter Twenty-Four

THE SWORD

For the next couple of days, Adaline visits Sallie, who spends most of her time resting in bed because she's less able to move around. With her belly protruding past her nose and her ankles swelling every time she stands, her children and husband have doubled down with handling the store. Every day, Kian rushes upstairs, bringing his wife water and fresh washcloths that her mother uses to wipe the sweat off Sallie's brow and from around her neck.

The summer seems to have come back with a vengeance the last few days, refusing to relinquish its seasonal turn without a fight, but the oppressive heat can't quiet the hum of the townsfolk talking about the harvest festival's fast approach. The human side of Market Street feels more alive when Adaline passes the perfumer restocking his collection of oils, the glassmaker waving his arms about with a half-formed vase at the end of his stick, and the fishmonger hauling his next crate of salmon off the back of a wagon.

Their enthusiasm adds a spring to Adaline's steps as she proceeds to her lessons with Fólas—and only Fólas, as Ëólas has been preoccupied with getting ready to leave. Every time Adaline remembers that he and Merith will be gone for weeks, her pace slows and her face falls. Losing two of the few people who know the truth about her feels like the stability she's found here is crumbling.

When she arrives at the arena, a guard directs her to the projectile training room. She opens the door, steps into the shade, and pulls at the neckline of her dress to peel the tacky undergarments away from her flesh and let some air flow between her breasts. "Oh, a long bath cannot come soon enough." She rolls her head back and to the side, elongating her neck to help cool her there too. When she moans, someone inside the room clears his throat, and her head snaps forward.

In place of Fólas, Ëólas stands at the back of the room as stiff as a marble statue with his back arched, thumbs hooked over his belt, and jaw clenched. Rather than looking her in the eyes, he's fixed his gaze on the hollow of her neck.

Oh, great. He's cranky again. Well, this heat's enough to drive anyone mad.

Adaline releases her neckline and wipes her sweaty palms on her bodice. "Some weather."

Ëólas nods his head, at least she thinks he does. Instead of his usual tunic and trousers, he's wearing a leather breastplate like his guards with the chest featuring those three stars high above a massive tree.

She walks further into the room, stopping in the center. "Moments like this, I really miss home."

"You don't have heat there?" His voice sounds gravelly.

He must be working long hours.

"Oh, we do." She grabs the cuffs of her sleeves and rolls them up, past her elbows. "But we wear a lot less clothing. One layer max, and my sundresses stop here." She hits her thigh with the side of her hand where she'd prefer her hem fall.

Ëólas gulps and darts his eyes around the room.

Placing her hands on her hips, she stretches her back. "Where's Fólas?"

"Oh, I wanted to see how this would work for you." He takes a long object wrapped in cloth off a shelf and walks over to her. Sticking his hand into one end of the bundle, he pulls out a sheathed sword, ignores her gawking, and lays it across her open palms.

Strips of navy and sage green leather wrap around the grip. The miniature etchings in the silver spherical pommel at the end depict people lounging in a garden, drinking wine, dancing, and playing the mandolin with vines draped above them. The same vines wrap around the small yet thick hand guard and secure a diamond in the center, and silver caps on either end of the slim leather scabbard feature more etchings of intertwined tree branches and flowers.

This belongs in a museum, not a battle. "It's beautiful."

"It's a weapon—"

"I know."

"That we use to protect what's dear to us; it should be well made. It's also lighter and smaller, more suitable for a woman's frame. Take it out of the scabbard."

Adaline draws the narrow blade out. The hilt fits perfectly in her right hand, and the scabbard feels lighter than air. She lowers the blade, pointing its tip at the ground. "Why are you giving me this? I seem to recall someone once thinking I came here to destroy all elves?"

Éólas stands perfectly still, staring at the blade in her hand. As seconds stretch into minutes, she shifts from one foot to the other. Just when she's about to sit down and let him keep thinking, his life force revives, and he says, "Hmm. Good point. Given your tenacity, I'd rather you have a means to defend yourself. And if we should meet on the battlefield one day, at least the fight will be somewhat fair."

Adaline's mouth falls open. *He still thinks we might end up enemies?* She takes a breath to speak, but when words don't emerge, she shakes her head in denial and blurts out, "That's horribly pessimistic."

Miracle upon miracles, Éólas cracks a smile, and his grumpy exterior shatters as his chest rises and falls with laughter. The robustness of his voice shifts the stuffy air out of the room. "It is, isn't it? My apologies."

Am I dreaming? I must have entered a whole other world again.

After she pinches her arm, time stands still. She's seen his broad smile before, but only from afar. Up close, a dimple appears in the corner of his mouth, and his gold irises turn a deep shade of yellow, like sunflowers soaking in the sunlight.

Grinning, he drops his hands to his sides. "Alright. Sheath that again, please. We'll keep your sword in this training room for now. Once you've had *a lot* of practice, you can carry that with you, and you won't need an escort around the city."

Adaline beams. "Sweet."

Éólas arches an eyebrow but shakes off his confusion, unties a sheathed dagger hanging from his belt, and passes it to her. Only, instead of one strap like the sword, the dagger has two, one at the top and one at the bottom. "This is for now. Keep it tied around your calf and hidden until you need it. Surprising your opponent will give you an advantage."

"Oh, okay." Again, the dagger feels as if it were made specifically for her hands, and the hilt and sheath match the color and designs of the sword, making them a matching set. When Ëólas turns away from her, she lifts her skirts and ties the sheath around her leg, but she doesn't draw the dagger. "So..."

"Let's get started," he says, facing her again. "I want a review of your hand-to-hand combat and then dagger skills. Afterward, I'll introduce you to the sword."

"Okay." Adaline slides one foot backward and raises her hands in front of her body in a defensive stance.

Ëólas doesn't wait. He strikes with his fist faster than when he showed up three days ago, but based on the few times she's seen him training others in the arena, she knows he's still moving slower. And that's okay. Speed isn't the point now. Like Fólas instructed, Adaline focuses on precision and making her reactions second nature. As Ëólas and Adaline dance around the room, with her dodging his attempts to corner her, they focus on the steps. She follows the stars on his breastplate like a constellation map and reads his intentions. When he snatches her wrist, she twists underneath and behind him, forcing him to let go. They continue moving counterclockwise around the room until he grabs her around the waist, pinning her arms at her sides. Realizing she can't wriggle free, she screams out in frustration, and Ëólas loosens his grip.

He whispers into her ear with a calm, soft voice, "You don't have enough leverage to flip me. Squat lower and—"

Before he can finish, Adaline squats, slips to one side, and spins out from under his arms. As he rises, her palm snaps into his eye, making him stagger back not one but two steps.

"Oh my god!" She covers her open mouth. "I'm so sorry! Are you okay?"

Wincing and squeezing one eye shut, he says, "That was brilliant. I thought you had given up. I never saw that coming."

With a flat voice, Adaline cheers and tosses her fists upward. "Yay? I didn't hurt you, did I?"

Ëólas stretches his face and rubs his left eye. "You stunned me. Which is perfect for aiding your escape."

Not giving her a chance to apologize again, he moves on to daggers. While Adaline attacks a hay-filled dummy, Ëólas's quiet, steady gaze on her every movement helps her to concentrate and prove, both to herself and him, that she takes these lessons seriously, that she'll never be without a self-defense strategy again, that she'll be able to take care of herself by herself.

Because when she goes home, she will be.

"You learn quickly," he comments as she plants the dagger in the dummy's neck.

She leaves it there and steps back. "Yeah, I know." She tilts her head to the side, and her vision zooms in to the spot where the dagger and dummy become one. Dummies don't bleed. They don't cry out in anguish. They don't have a life for someone else to take away.

"Adaline, are you okay?" His voice pulls her attention away from her victim.

"Yeah, I'm fine. Swords?" Ripping her dagger free, she lifts her skirts and tucks the blade into its sheath.

Ëólas nods, and Adaline retrieves her sword. *My sword? When did I ever think that would happen?*

Outside, charcoal gray clouds roll across the sky, and a chilly breeze makes everyone in the arena turn their faces into the wind as sweat trickles down their temples. The world outside grows quieter, except for a few people shouting, followed by doors and windows slamming shut. Inside, the only sound Adaline hears is Ëólas's breath. Surprised to find him so close, she turns away from the window. Her eyes drift to his muscular chest, to his leather breastplate. Lifting her hand, she touches the largest star embossed a few inches above his heart. He doesn't pull away.

"Why three stars?" she asks.

He places his hand over hers, and their eyes lock. "It's a memorial," he says, his voice low and sad.

He doesn't say anything more, and Adaline doesn't ask. She gently removes her hand, and they both walk into the center of the room where Ëólas instructs her to draw her sword. The blade shimmers, casting a reflection on the wall beside them. Its light weight and comfortable fit encourage her to swing once and effortlessly. She doesn't know if holding this instrument makes her feel powerful or like a child wearing her father's shoes. Leaning the scabbard against the wall, she turns around to see Ëólas with his own sword drawn.

Normally, the sight of someone holding a sword only a few feet away makes Adaline cringe. But she approaches Ëólas and raises her own, mirroring his stance with the sharp edge toward him and the blade angled across the center of her body. She's ready for his instruction, but he doesn't give any. When he steps forward and swings, she jumps back, leaving plenty of room between them. Studying the angle of his blade, she squints her eyes, trying to discern what she should do in return. She grips the hilt with both her hands, but her breasts hinder her ability to swing at him.

Ëólas reads her mind. "Step forward and stand your ground. Widen your feet and move one back. One hand, Adaline. Not two. There you go. Now swing at me. Let's go. Watch your wrist. No wobbly, limp elbows here either. Show your strength."

She smirks at his reference to her dance instructions, but he swings again, slowly. She raises her blade to block him, using the sharp edge to catch his and locking her wrist so she doesn't inadvertently cut herself as he pushes against her.

"Exactly," he says. "Again."

Ëólas doesn't make any more jokes. He doesn't give her breaks. He doesn't forgive her mistakes. He spends another hour with her, knocking the sword out of her hand, encouraging her to try over and over again, but never belittling her efforts. When he knocks her down, he offers a hand to help her up and waits patiently for her to resume her proper stance.

Once she's in position, he starts again and speaks only when offering technical comments that are never harsh in tone or word choice. A few dummies take a beating as collateral damage, and their heads roll around the room. By the end of their session, she can barely lift her arms. Her forearm burns, and her feet ache too. Sheathing her sword, she hands it back to him, and he places the blade on the shelf for their next practice.

Adaline presses her back against the brick wall and closes her eyes. *Dang.* But she's smiling too. They spent hours together without a moment of awkwardness or tension.

"I'm impressed, Adaline."

She opens her eyes and finds him leaning against the wall beside her, his foot kicked up behind him. "I'm surprised at your level of endurance." He turns his head sideways. "Dancing?"

"Ha! Yes. And digging up chunks of earth and hauling equipment to excavation sites and taking the stairs up to my condo, uh, my home."

Ëólas pushes his bottom lip into his top one and nods his head in approval. "You had a busy life back home."

"I did."

"Are you bored here?"

She looks at him directly, at his neutral expression and open eyes. *This. This is how things should have been from day one.* "A little. I miss having assignments due and people expecting things from me. I miss doing research and digging for answers."

She waits to see if he'll take offense, if he'll think she's attacking his own methods regarding the attacks and her mysterious arrival, but he nods his head, and she watches his Adam's apple as he swallows. *It's not fair for someone to be so handsome.*

He purses his lips as he thinks. "I confess I have no recollection of life before obligation and duty, so I can only imagine how you must feel to have had all of that removed within a single breath. Have you asked Magnus? I'm sure he can help."

Pushing herself off the wall, she paces back and forth while weaving her way around one of the dummy's burlap heads. Its eye socket bleeds hay. After traversing the room four more times, she pauses in front of Ëólas and clicks her thumbs together. "I've been thinking..."

He chuckles. "I expect nothing less."

His grin makes Adaline smirk, but her thoughts and concerns wash away her amusement. "I've been thinking about the two men who got past the palace guards and the men who attacked people the night I arrived."

"Mmm-hmm." He lifts his chin, giving her his undivided attention.

"And sometimes I feel like I'm...being watched."

He steps away from the wall, and his expression sours, but when he speaks, his tone is nothing but compassionate. "Our guards do keep an eye out for you, but they do so knowing you're the king's ward. We hoped they wouldn't make you feel uncomfortable."

"No, I get it. They're like the Secret Service." *Whoa. I have my own Secret Service.* "This watching feels different. It gives me the chills."

Concern flashes across his face. "Continue."

"What if they're somehow related?"

Ëólas goes into silent thinking mode, hooking his thumbs on his belt. The last time she saw him this pensive was on the balcony, when she hadn't patiently waited for his reply. This time, she shows him the same patience he's given her today.

Thankfully, he doesn't take forever before speaking again. "We haven't found evidence to make that conclusion."

"Okay, but you've spent years building the Neutral Territory, and everything was hunky dory until two weeks ago, right?"

Ëólas simultaneously furrows and raises his eyebrows. "Hunky? Dory?"

"Yeah. Peachy keen? A-okay?"

"Alright."

"But then everything went sideways, and I showed up, and my gut is telling me it's more than just two random incidents. Three, if you include my arrival."

Ëólas grows more pensive as he shifts from side to side. The severed dummy head draws his attention too. "The timing concerns us. And yet we have no evidence of the two, or three, circumstances being related."

"How do you know? Where have you checked?"

Ëólas runs both his hands through his hair, gathering the lot at the nape of his neck. With his elbows above his head, he paces in front of the door. "Magnus has ears in other kingdoms. No one has said anything about the attacks here. Not a single whisper. They're concerned about the Neutral Territory imploding and war ensuing between elves and humans again, but no one has indicated sabotage."

"Which kingdoms? All the human ones?"

Ëólas barks a loud laugh. "Yes. He can't have ears in the elven ones too. That'd be suicide."

"So what have your ears heard in the elven kingdoms?" Adaline glances at the tips of his own ears peeking out from his hair. *That sounds so offensive.* She smiles awkwardly as if to apologize.

He rolls his eyes and releases his hair, the silky soft layers fanning around his wide, chiseled jaw. "Adaline, I understand you've become invested in the people here. That's clear based on the way our people react to your warmth and charm."

Her stomach flips. *He thinks I'm warm and charming?*

"But," he emphasizes, making her drop her smile, "you need to leave these matters to Magnus and myself. This is our responsibility, not yours."

"Um, yeah." She turns to fetch the other dismembered dummy in the corner, only to swing around and try again. "Okay, I hear you. But you didn't answer my question."

Closing his eyes, Ëólas rubs the bridge of his nose. "Nothing."

"Nothing?"

"Nothing. We're done here for today." He walks over to the door and grabs the handle. "The new recruits will clean up the room. Let's go. Oh, I can't guarantee I'll be able to come again tomorrow, as I'm leaving the day after. Fólas will be here regardless."

Adaline stares at the floor and purses her lips outward while her nostrils flare and her heart cracks. She can't think about him leaving right now. That's not the point of this conversation.

Outside, the wind picks up and knocks over a bucket that clangs past their door. The room darkens, and thunder rumbles in the distance.

"Adaline." Sounding tired, he lets go of the door handle.

"I can't stand it when people don't answer my questions. Nothing, as in no one has said anything in the elven kingdoms. Or nothing, as in you're not even checking?" She squares her shoulders and looks him in the eye.

Flexing his jaw, he carefully controls his tone through clenched teeth. "Do you really think I'd not ask my own people? I'm not that small-minded."

Adaline flinches.

Éólas draws in slow, steady breaths and avoids looking at her.

She can't let today end like this. She just can't. She tucks her hands behind her back, squeezes the pressure point between her thumb and index finger, and lets the sharp pain snuff out all other feelings. "I didn't mean to imply you're not good at your job. I just can't let go of the idea that someone let those men enter the palace grounds. And logically speaking, if you—" The more she talks, the more he turns to stone. Another rumble of thunder sounds behind him, and a chill runs down her spine. But she persists. "If you eliminate the possibility of elves, you're eliminating fifty percent of—"

Éólas tosses his hands in the air and drops them in a huff. Kicking the dummy head out of the way, he stalks over to her, leans forward so he's less than a foot away, and stares into her eyes as if he's about to unearth some truths for himself. "Tell me, Adaline, in this human-only world of yours, does your species continue to war with each other?"

Her silence tells him enough.

Knitting his eyebrows together, he narrows his gaze. "As long as I have been alive, do you know how many human wars have occurred within my few years? Twelve. And do you know how many elves have attacked each other? Zero. *We* don't initiate war. Our history proves that. So do not presume I am ignoring logic."

He's not always an asshole. He's not always an asshole. He's not always an asshole. "I'm not trying to presume anything. I'm just trying to share my thoughts without getting shut down every five seconds. Sometimes having a third-party, an outside perspective, can—"

"Your concerns are understandable, but—"

"Stop speaking over me!" Adaline shouts, balling her hands into fists and pinning them at her sides.

His eyes go wide. He backs up and looks her up and down while she locks all her muscles in place and stares at him, unflinching. He slides his jaw from side to side but agrees, "That was rude of me."

Bit by bit, Adaline releases the tension in her body. When her chest stops heaving, she mumbles, "Thank you." *Thank you for trying.*

They both take a moment to not speak, to not provoke each other. Adaline wanders to the other side of the room and picks up a dummy's arm. The clean cut left not even a stray thread. She returns the appendage to its body, but not seeing how to reattach it, she lays it at the dummy's feet like an offering.

When she faces Ëólas again, she drops her hands to her sides. "May I express my thoughts?"

Ëólas, who has returned to the door, readying his escape at the next opportunity, nods.

"Okay. If you have no evidence, what about Seira?"

Ëólas stops breathing, and his jaw twitches.

Ha! I'm on to something here.

Leaning backward, he crosses his arms over his chest. "What about her?"

Tread carefully, Adaline. He's on the defensive again. Good thing I've been watching him.

Not like in a creepy stalker way. But the way I watch everyone. From an academic perspective. Because that's what I do. Watch people. It's not like I've watched him more than anyone else.

Focus, focus, focus! I'm going to win this argument, and I'm going to do so amicably. Because we've grown. And we understand each other better.

Everything will be alright.

One step at a time, she approaches him. "Seira has said things to me that sound like," she takes a deep breath, "like predictions. And the way she drifts off, it's like she doesn't always live in the same moment as the rest of us. And she knew I was going to be attacked. She checked for the bruises on my arm before I got them. She told you where to find me, didn't she?"

His lips press together thinner and thinner until he scrunches his nose and looks down at her as if she just proved his worst fears. "Is this why you've become friends with her? To take advantage of her? To exploit her? And here I had begun to think better of you."

He abandons all traces of patience and kindness, and within seconds, it's like they never left that balcony. All color drains from Adaline's face as she watches him revert to the asshole who couldn't give her the benefit of the doubt, who assumed the worst, who let his own pride and prejudice come between them. Because if he wasn't so stupid, she knows in every fiber of her being that he's meant to play an important role in her story. And this isn't it.

He's being too fucking stupid.

Adaline shoves his chest as hard as she can. But, damn it, he stumbles only a half-step backward.

"Stupid, stubborn asshole." She balls her hands into fists and aims to pound on his chest, forgetting every worthwhile move Fólas taught her.

Before she can land the first blows, he catches her wrists and holds them firmly while his face grows darker and his eyes look dead.

Screw him!

She wriggles and squirms to yank her wrists free, which doesn't work, but she jerks his arms a few times, her half-hearted efforts changing his expression from anger to impatience.

Don't cry, damn it. He's not worth it. He's just some stupid commander general person who constantly looks out for his people, brokered this crazy-ass deal with Magnus, built half a city, didn't let her hit the floor at the ball, saved her from No-Nose, got her out of that palace only to take her back again when she asked, and convinced Magnus to let her learn how to fight.

"I hate you," she whispers, and her heart cracks open because that's far from the truth. So very far.

As if she slapped him, he jerks backward and releases her wrists. Keeping his tone even, he says with a gravelly voice, "I'm sorry to hear that. But as an outsider—"

"An outsider," she repeats, her eyes falling to the ground. She's always an outsider. From the moment she moved to the U.S. at age seven, to dance classes because she was a fast learner, to school for being a know-it-all, to faculty meetings because she was Eddie's daughter, to here where she'll never fit in.

But she's not supposed to interfere. She's not supposed to get involved. She's not supposed to develop her own biased feelings.

Taking a trembling breath, she faces Ëólas, forces a smile, and blinks away the sting burning her eyes. "I understand. I won't be any trouble." She refuses to cower, to run away, to hide her mistakes, but a tear escapes the dam she's trying to erect.

Damn it.

Ëólas watches the tear slide down her cheek, and his breath catches. He raises his hand toward her face, only to halt his movements mid-way and drop his arm beside him. "My tone need not have been so severe. Nor my choice of words."

"Me too," she says, looking down at her hands and the space between them. "I, I don't hate you."

Using his thumb, he tilts her chin up, and a sad smile spreads across his face. "I'm glad."

Outside, the sky bursts into a downpour of torrential rain that slants slideways and blows inside the room. They rush to the window as the rain floods the arena and drains into the city streets. He pulls the wooden shutters closed and latches them tightly, blotting out most of the light in the training room. They huddle near the door and the light peeking from beneath it while they listen for the rain to lighten up.

"That came sooner than I expected," Ëólas says.

"Fun walk home."

"Home?"

"Oh, well, yeah."

Ëólas offers a smile, and the light returns to his eyes. "I'm sorry."

Adaline studies his face, the curve of his lips, his smooth brow, his flawless skin, those other-worldly eyes. *You're sorry for arguing with me or for not knowing how to get me home?* "Me too."

"I don't want to fight with you."

"Me neither."

Ëólas nods, releases a long exhale, and takes his time to choose his next words. "You're not wrong about Seira. But asking her questions, asking her to dig deeper into wherever she goes, causes her significant pain. Whether that's mental or physical or both, I don't know. But I've tried before, and she," he pauses, "she winds up screaming on the floor in agony."

Adaline covers her mouth, and her eyebrows droop downward.

"Something happened to her a long time ago. I don't know what, Adaline. She's told no one. But I promised I would keep her safe. And having her here in the Neutral Territory places her at risk, because there are those who would take advantage of her gifts."

"I wasn't trying to."

"I know. I do. But that's why she doesn't leave the castle. The world overwhelms her, and she's scared."

"Why did she come here then?"

He closes his eyes as if he's trying to make up his mind. When he opens them again, he locks eyes with her. "I think she came to meet you."

Adaline's face goes blank. "Me? Did, did she bring me here?"

"I don't know what it means. Traveling between worlds...I've never seen her display that much magic. I don't think she's the source, but I do think she's connected."

Adaline nods, unable to think of anything else to say just yet. From the first moment she met Seira, Adaline felt drawn to her, perhaps even connected. In many ways, Seira's assumed the role of a big sister, her very own tíer nía. Maybe as that connection grows, Adaline will find answers.

"Adaline?" Ëólas's voice pulls her out of her reveries. "Please, we can't let anyone else know about Seira. Only those who know about you also know about her."

"Do, do you think that first attack and my arriving relate back to Seira?"

"I believe so, which is why I need your help. Please. Will you help me keep her secret?"

Even in this dim light, she clearly sees his eyes pleading with her. "I promise. I won't let anyone near her."

As his face lightens, he uses his thumb to wipe away the stain on her cheek. "Thank you."

If only they could stay like this. But with the drums of rain reduced to a steady mist, he removes his hand and opens the door, letting the evening light pour into the room. Blue skies peek through gray clouds to announce their imminent return. Together, Ëólas and Adaline step into the shallow streams running past their door, neither acknowledging his impending departure as they make their way home.

Chapter Twenty-Five

THE PLEA

Despite yesterday's rainstorm, the sun has erased every trace of moisture, but the heat beating down on the city doesn't deter people from taking a break and enjoying another of Adaline's stories. Today, she shares the original version of *The Little Mermaid* in which the prince falls in love with the woman who nursed him back to health, and the mermaid dies of unrequited love.

When she finishes the story, she looks over the audience, terrified they'll boo at the tragic ending, but most people sigh or cry or argue about whether the mermaid should have killed the prince to save her own life.

One little girl sits down quietly on the bench next to Adaline and stares at the river on the other side of the bridge. "The prince should have loved her. She saved his life. And she's a mermaid!"

Adaline puts her arm around the child. "Would you like a story with a happy ending tomorrow?"

The little girl looks up with big brown eyes. "Oh, yes please."

"Deal."

The little girl squeezes Adaline around the waist, then runs off when her mother calls.

Taking hold of Sallie's girls' hands, Adaline walks them back to the shop. Morie, the older child, opens the door but jumps backward as Kian dashes outside, already out of breath. He skids to a halt in front of Adaline.

"Beg your pardon, my lady, but the baby's coming. I'm off to fetch the midwife." He tips his hat and sprints down the street, disappearing into the crowd.

Adaline and the girls run inside and upstairs to find Sallie in bed with sweat beading on her forehead and her bitty old mother wiping Sallie's brow with a wet cloth. Beside the bed waits a rocking bassinet and a smaller bed with two shabby, faceless dolls. The youngest daughter, Corra, retreats to the living space, a one-room kitchen and lounge with a wood-burning stove, a threadbare cushioned bench for two, and three chairs surrounding the circular kitchen table—five seats in all for a family of soon-to-be eight.

With a weak wave of her hand, Sallie motions for Morie to climb onto the bed and lets her daughter curl into the crook of her arm. "Mummy's okay, sweetheart." She kisses Morie's brow before her daughter gets down and picks up a doll to bring to Corra. Before Morie leaves their room, she blows her mother a kiss, and Sallie sends one in return.

When Morie's out of sight, Sallie clamps down on her teeth and groans as a contraction hits, squeezing her mother's hand so hard that Adaline's terrified the old woman's bones will shatter. Adaline cringes, remembering when Cindy's abuela broke her hand because of an unfortunate DIY home-improvement clamp situation.

Tilting backward to see beyond the doorframe, Adaline peers into the other room to make sure the girls are okay. They sit on the bench together, silent while Corra combs through her doll's hair. Leaving them be, Adaline sits on the other side of the bed and offers her hand in place of Abuela's. Sallie immediately accepts and squeezes, her cheeks glowing like hot coals until she stops grunting and panting and releases her friend's hand.

Reaching across the bed, Adaline grabs Abuela's bowl, wrings out the cloth, and wipes Sallie's forehead. "How far apart are the contractions?"

"Very," says Abuela, struggling to stand up. "We have a long day ahead of us."

Adaline purses her lips. "Can I stay, or is it better if I come back in a bit?"

Sallie's head flops sideways on her pillow, allowing her to better see Adaline. "You're too sweet, my lady." Within seconds, she's sound asleep, and her snores invite the girls to come back in and curl up on the edge of their mother's bed.

Abuela hobbles over to Adaline and pats her shoulder. "Go to your lessons. We'll be here when you're done, if you wish to come back, my lady."

"Most certainly."

Throughout training practice, Adaline tries to focus on Fólas's words, but being in this room doesn't feel the same today, even with the dummies reassembled so well that they make Adaline question if she imagined yesterday's practice. Her mind is scattered. Her moves are stilted, and her heart is heavy with too many what-ifs. Ëólas leaves tomorrow, and Sallie's about to give birth without an epidural, heart monitor, stainless steel tools, or whatever else accompanies modern medicine.

After Fólas calls her name for the third time, he sheaths his dagger in his boot, calls Adaline out for holding her blade upside down, and instructs her to put hers away too. "My lady, we've been at this for an hour, but you haven't been present for any of it. What's troubling you?"

"Sallie's in labor."

He scrunches his brow. "Your candlemaker friend?"

"Yeah."

"I see." He opens the training room door. "Go. Be with her then."

Flashing Fólas a big smile, she rushes out the door, only to turn and bump into Ëólas's chest. "Oh, sorry."

"Where are you off to?" he asks, bracing her shoulders. "We can get in one more session before I leave."

"Oh." She could go back inside. After all, Abuela said the baby wouldn't come for hours, and Ëólas is already here, and he took time out of his day to help her, and it would be a shame to disregard his consideration, and she does seem to learn better with him, and—

"Her friend is in labor, the candlemaker," Fólas says. "I'm terrified she'll chop off her own hand. She's too distracted."

"I, I can focus." Adaline shrugs, but concentrating is challenging with Ëólas's hands resting on her shoulders. His thumb brushes her neck, and a tingling sensation blooms beneath her skin.

He studies her face, his irises shrinking as he watches her nibble her lower lip. His thumb gently strokes her skin again. "Go. Check on your friend."

"Oh." She glances past the arena to the path that will take her to Sallie's, that will take her away from where she ought to be. Facing Ëólas, she places her hands on top of his, locking them in place. "Promise you'll find me tomorrow and say goodbye before you go?"

Tilting his face ever so slightly toward hers, he says in a husky voice, "I promise."

Her heart dances as she races off. When she enters Sallie's shop, Kian's tending to customers with a smile plastered on his face, but he fumbles and drops packages, products, and coins because his hands won't stop shaking. The kids continue their work, with their eldest son dipping candles and stacking shelves and tending to the stall outside, and the girls encourage customers to come inside with their innocent faces. Little Jem runs out from behind the counter and buries his face in the folds of Adaline's muslin pink skirts. After patting his curls, she bops his butt and sends him off to join his sisters.

"Kian, have you eaten?" Adaline asks once he has a moment of quiet.

"I have, my lady, thank you. Sallie's waiting for you."

He nods to the stairs in the backroom, and Adaline doesn't wait before dashing up the steep flights. At the top, she enters the two-bedroom home, crosses the kitchen and living space in eight steps, and pauses in the doorway to the larger bedroom. A midwife and Abuela encircle Sallie as her mother feeds her some sort of porridge or oatmeal mixture that most likely contains a numbing agent. As another contraction hits, Sallie spits the mixture out of her mouth, and the liquified chunks splatter her bedsheets.

While the midwife holds Sallie's hand, Abuela fumbles to get off the bed. Adaline's beside her in a flash, helping Abuela to a nearby chair, passing a wet cloth to the midwife to clean Sallie's face and chest, and pulling the top sheet off the bed. The midwife and Adaline work together to change Sallie's nightgown and give her fresh bedding. Once Sallie's settled, Abuela brings Adaline tea and a slice of bread and cheese, and the midwife resumes feeding Sallie and timing the contractions.

"My lady," Sallie says between bites, "you're early. How have your lessons been going?"

"Lessons?" the midwife asks, peeking up to better examine the noblewoman in Sallie's abode.

"Oh, yes. The elves have been teaching the lady how to defend her person with daggers and swords."

The midwife wrinkles her brow, takes Sallie's empty bowl, and hurries out of the room. "Peculiar, indeed," she mumbles to herself, her face a portrait of confusion and wonder.

The girls' hurried steps and chatter announce them coming upstairs to visit their mother. While Adaline combs and braids their hair, the girls take turns telling stories to amuse and distract Sallie. Every time a contraction transforms her face into that of a demon, the girls blanch but stay by her side, choosing to prepare for their own futures.

Abuela leaves her daughter only to make dinner. She reappears to feed Sallie, allowing the midwife to get some fresh air too. In the living room, Adaline serves the girls and Jem dinner and tells them stories about beanstalks and brazen mountains and magic mirrors that reflect people's flaws so the girls don't eavesdrop on Abuela and Sallie's hushed tones between mother and daughter.

After dinner, the contractions come more frequently, and Adem, Sallie's eldest boy, takes the kids downstairs and keeps them with their father. The children aren't allowed upstairs anymore, and the midwife has mentally locked herself inside that room with Sallie. From her bags, the midwife pulls out various knives, bandages, metal bowls, ointments, and threads and sets them on a table positioned beside her.

"Sallie, I need you to lie back so I can check the baby's position." The midwife supports Sallie's arms to help her reposition herself, and Adaline moves the pillows out of the way.

Shifting to the end of the bed, the midwife spreads Sallie's legs and measures her dilation. Afterward, she massages and pushes on Sallie's belly, sometimes so hard that Adaline flinches and expects to see bruises in the shape of fingers, but none appear. When Sallie groans at the ceiling, the midwife, without lifting her chin, locks eyes with Adaline and shakes her head.

No, no, no, no, no. What's wrong?

From her bag, the midwife takes out a large, corked bottle and sets it on the table next to the bed. Speaking frankly, she tells Sallie, "The baby has assumed an unnatural position. I need to assist and turn the baby."

Sallie swallows hard. "Do whatever you need to."

The midwife turns to Adaline. "We need to be ready to change the sheets at any moment. Are you staying to assist me?"

"Yes. I'm here as long as you need me."

"Very well then." She picks up the bottle and pours onto her hands an oily mixture that she rubs all over her palms, the back of her hands, and between her fingers.

"What is that?" Adaline asks.

"Wild thyme oil."

The midwife parts Sallie's legs again, and Adaline repositions herself as much as possible to block Sallie's view. "Look at me," Adaline says while Sallie whimpers and then screams.

After minutes that feel like hours, the midwife announces the baby's turned. "My lady, help with the sheets," she says.

Together, the midwife and Adaline ease Sallie into standing up, gripping her elbows and forearms. When Abuela takes Adaline's place, pulling Sallie away from the bed, Adaline and the midwife strip the mattress and curl up the sheets to hide the bloodstains.

"This is the last set," the midwife says, grabbing fresh sheets from the narrow, shelved closet.

Adaline quickly rolls up the sleeves of her white chemise now tainted with red splotches, then collects the bundle of sheets and removes them from Sallie's room, dumping them in a metal washing bin that's already full. Rushing over to the sink basin, she washes the blood off her arms and fingers. Now that she's not inside Sallie's room, the tears silently fall down her cheeks.

She said number five would pop out easily. It's been hours, and the sun's already setting.

Brushing away her tears before anyone can see them, she shakes her hands out and turns around to discover the midwife hurrying over to Adaline. In the background, Sallie lies down in bed and holds onto her mother for support.

The midwife whispers, "Her heartbeat is slowing down."

Adaline steels herself, flinging all thoughts of the children and Kian downstairs out of her mind. "What exactly does that mean?"

"She needs to start pushing, soon. I won't know more until we see how that goes. Let's pray she doesn't lose much more blood and her heart is strong. If we lose the mother, I'll need to cut the child from her womb. Sallie's mother is too tired to help much now. I need your assistance, my lady."

Bile churns in Adaline's stomach. *Cesareans are a last-ditch effort in this world, in this time.* "Tell me what to do."

Before they take one step, Adem appears at the top of the stairs. His eyes don't dare dart toward his mother's room, but a cold sweat sticks to his skin, and his voice trembles. "Forgive me for intruding, but the captain of the city guard has come to fetch the lady."

Fólas? No, must be Hamon.

With a grunt, Adaline runs to the front window, throws up the sash, and sticks her head outside where Hamon paces below. "Hamon, I'm not leaving," she whisper-shouts. "They need me here."

Hamon throws his blond head backward and gapes at Adaline. "His Majesty says to come back and—"

"No. Tell Magnus I'm not leaving. He can threaten me with the dungeons tomorrow if he wants, but I'm not budging." She pops inside to find the midwife gawking at her, then sticks her head back out one more time. "We need another set of sheets up here. I don't care where you get them so long as they're clean. Take them from my wardrobe if you have to, but I need them now."

Again, Adaline enters Sallie's room where the atmosphere grows heavier, where every terrifying what-if gathers in the shadows, incubates in unseen nooks and crannies, and strengthens as daylight fades and darkness consumes the room inch by inch. They light candles to illuminate every surface possible.

Quicker than expected, a neighbor brings up the requested sheets and helps Adaline guide Sallie to stand and squat over a birthing stool shaped like a horseshoe with a backrest. Sweat drips down Adaline's neck and chest as Sallie holds onto both women's arms like a wall barre while the midwife checks on the baby's progress. In between screams, Sallie rests her sweaty brow against Adaline's abdomen, and her body sags and droops to the side.

How the hell has the human population continued doing this!

"Get her back to the bed," the midwife tells them. "Have her lean over the mattress, belly down. We'll have to try shaking her."

Bending over, Sallie reaches across the bed. Abuela hobbles over to the opposite side, wraps her hands around Sallie's, and holds onto her daughter like an anchor.

"I can't lose another child," Sallie cries.

Weeping, her mother stretches out one hand to caress her daughter's cheek. "Shhh, baby. Everything will be alright."

The color drains from Sallie's face as she whispers, "I don't want to leave my babies."

"I need more help," the midwife says to the neighbor, who nods and runs out of the room.

Adaline backs up until she hits the wall. Sallie's chapped lips quiver. Strands of her dark hair pulled up in a messy bun stick to her brow and cheeks. Her pupils swell and swallow her light-brown eyes, and her beige skin turns gray as she whimpers and screams as another contraction hits.

Adaline bolts into the living room, down the stairs, past Kian and the kids, and out the door. She doesn't stop to speak to Hamon as she runs down the street and over the Rialto, her legs pushing themselves as if her own life depends on their speed. She never stops, never looks back. Reaching Loríen's shop, she bangs on the door until her fists ache. But no one answers.

"Adaline?" Hamon asks, his heavy breaths following her.

She runs around him and sprints toward Market Street where elves still roam and visit with friends. When she sees Jósep emerge from the tavern, she shouts his name.

He jumps backward two steps, but when he recognizes Adaline, his face shifts from fear to concern. "My lady? What's wrong?"

"Where's Loríen? Please, it's an emergency."

"Adaline, wait," Hamon calls again, trying to grab her arm.

Jósep points to the tavern. She pushes Hamon away and bursts through the door. The musicians and singer stop mid-note. As the music dies, those dancing and listening turn to Adaline. A few elves scream and scramble toward the back door where Ëólas, Merith, and Fólas had been chatting.

"She has blood on her!" one shouts.

Before panic ensues, Merith and Fólas calm the crowd.

Ëólas runs over to her, his eyes wide and mouth agape. "Adaline!"

In place of anger, he checks her over to see where she's injured. When he stops his frantic search and looks her in the eyes, his face contorts with concern. For a moment, she wants nothing more than to fold herself in his arms and not think about what the midwife is doing with those knives and no anesthesia. As if expecting her to do just that, Ëólas opens his arms. She takes a step forward, and a sob bubbles up in her throat, but over his shoulder, Loríen emerges from the corner and walks toward them.

Clasping her hands to her chest, Adaline steps around Ëólas and rushes over to Loríen. "Please, my friend's in labor, and she... The delivery isn't going well." She can barely speak those last words, not only because her chest is still heaving from running but also because uttering those words aloud feels like she's solidifying Sallie's fate. "Can you please come and help? I don't have anything to pay you with, but I'll help out in your shop. I'll do whatever you need, but can you please come now?"

"My lady," Loríen says, her voice laden with sorrow and her body unable to move. With careworn eyes, she says as delicately as possible, "I don't know how to treat humans. It's not quite the same. I don't think she'll respond to my methods."

Adaline swallows a sob, but her hitched breaths echo in the silent tavern. People set down goblets and whisper. From behind her, a gentle pair of hands rests on her arms. When she inhales that familiar lavender scent, her chest heaves. These people don't understand. She almost turns around to leave, but she keeps picturing those four children and their momma who was Adaline's first real friend here. She uses the back of her hand to wipe her cheeks dry and pushes her worst fears deep down into the abyss where her grief resides.

There's hope here. Surely there's hope here. That's what the Neutral Territory is all about.

She finds her voice, choking back another cry, and tries again, pouring her entire soul into her words, into her voice, into her need for Sallie to not be the next person she loses. "Please," she begs. "Just try something. Anything."

Loríen looks past Adaline as if searching for answers. Twisting around, Adaline finds Ëólas behind her, his warm hands still on her arms. He doesn't look at her though, only Loríen. He gives one firm nod. In response, determination settles upon Loríen's face, and a spark of hope ignites inside Adaline's chest.

CHAPTER TWENTY-SIX

THE BIRTH

Loríen turns to the elf who had been standing by her. "My love, I need you to fetch my purple bag and bring the largest amethyst and aquamarine crystals you can find. And garnet. And malachite. Bring many and meet us at the castle."

"No, not the castle," Adaline says. "Sallie's family owns the candle shop on Market Street." Her heart leaps in her chest. Standing still proves too challenging as she shifts her weight from side to side.

When Loríen's husband rushes out the back door, she hurries to the front. Before Adaline leads the way to Sallie, she squeezes Ëólas's hand, reaches up on her tiptoes, and kisses his cheek. "Thank you."

His wide eyes and mouth falling open blur behind Adaline's tears as she dashes out the door.

"Adaline, wait!" Hamon calls again, having stayed outside.

"No, fetch Magnus," Ëólas instructs, his voice fading as Loríen and Adaline run ahead.

When Loríen enters the candle shop, Kian, slumped on the floor beside his kids, barely raises his head while he fidgets with the brim of his hat. He scratches his scruffy beard and wipes his eyes with his palms. The children huddle around him, and his male neighbors pace the length of the room.

Upstairs, three of Sallie's neighbors, including the old baker's wife, scurry back and forth, fetching whatever the midwife calls for, talking to Sallie in between her panting and crying, and tending to Abuela, who's turned white. None of the women question Loríen's arrival.

"I'm a healer," Loríen says, securing her hair with a leather tie.

"Then I need you here," the midwife says.

Sallie's eyes roam the room until they settle on Loríen, and her pupils focus. "Please, help. I'm done. I don't want to do this anymore. Just get the baby out already."

"You're almost done, love," Abuela says from across the room, sitting on the girls' bed.

All the ladies work together, sharing everything they know, listening to each other's suggestions, and trying each one. Most of their conversations Adaline can't follow. Her brain simply moves from one task to the next, whether that's boiling more water or fetching ingredients from Loríen's husband, who now waits below with Kian.

When the midwife announces she can see the baby, Adaline rushes to the living room window, opens the sash, and inhales the cool night air that frees her from the rust-like stench, the alcohol, and the perfumed oils that oppress Sallie's room.

Oh god. How could anyone want to give birth? What crazy-ass instinct takes over to convince anyone to endure this?

Outside, people have gathered in the street, humans and elves alike. They wait together with their own fears pressing up against them. The door to Kian's shop is open, and people pass candles down the street. They share a flame to ignite the next wick, and quickly the street twinkles like starlight.

Adaline carries their hope back into the bedroom where the midwife reaches between Sallie's legs. Two neighbors hold Sallie's hands and coach her through breathing and pushing, and Loríen places crystals around the room. Sallie's cries sever Adaline's hope in half, over and over again, until she's on the brink of tears. When Sallie screams again, Adaline digs her fisted nails into her palm. She looks down at the crescent shapes, and the sting reminds her that none of her pain compares to Sallie's.

Toughen up, Adaline! She's going to be okay. The baby will be okay. Everything will be alright.

Holding one of her vials to her chest, Loríen tilts her face downward, keeping her words close to her heart, as she chants or prays or sings, maybe all three. When the liquid shimmers with a speck of pale-purple inner light, she hands the vial to the midwife. "This will cleanse the birth canal."

The midwife accepts the mixture and pours it on her hands, but what she does afterward, Adaline doesn't know and doesn't want to know. She switches off her emotions and curiosity so she remains out of the way while the midwife hunches over, and Sallie's legs shake from side to side. Sallie's toes curl and claw at the bedsheets, and her continuous, hoarse screams scratch Adaline's soul.

Then, all in one breath, the midwife calls, "I have her. I have her. It's a girl, Sallie."

"Thank the fae," Sallie whispers. She tries to lift her arms to accept the baby, but they fall back to her side when the midwife passes the baby to a neighbor to wrap in a brown blanket.

Adaline opens her mouth to shout her elation, but as the neighbor passes in front, Adaline glimpses the baby's blue lips. While Adaline holds her breath, the midwife proceeds with removing the afterbirth. Loríen, moving to Sallie's side, holds her limp wrist and checks her pulse again. Loríen and the midwife lock eyes, and a grave look passes between them.

Shaking her head slowly, Adaline closes her eyes. *Please, keep them both safe. Please.*

The neighbor wraps the baby but whispers to Abuela, "She's not breathing."

Abuela stands over the little one and presses her fist to her mouth, trapping her sobs inside.

"Give her to me." Rushing over, Loríen takes the baby in her arms and hurries into the living room. On the table, she lays the baby down and rearranges the blanket like a nest, exposing the little one's chest that's no bigger than Loríen's palm. "Adaline, my bag."

Snatching her belongings from the bench, Adaline hurries to Loríen's side and watches her place six crystals counterclockwise around the baby. She pulls two vials out of her bag, which she tips upside down onto her fingers and spreads their oil across the baby's forehead, chest, and abdomen. With flawless and graceful movements, Loríen works quickly without second-guessing herself. She leans low over the baby, places her hands on the child's chest, and whispers a sing-song chant in a language Adaline doesn't recognize. One by one, the crystals illuminate, forming a circle of light around the infant.

Closing her eyes, Adaline lays her hands on her chest. *Whatever greater power exists in this world, please, please, let this child and her mother live.*

A single, high-pitched, miniature cry more heavenly than a church choir pierces the silence, fills the room, and trumpets into the night air. A crescendo of cheers erupts outside, followed by whoops and hollers. Adaline's heart swells so much that she pushes on her chest to keep it from bursting.

The baby kicks her legs and stretches her chicken-wing arms outward before tucking her tiny fingers under her heart-shaped chin. Adaline and Loríen laugh and cry simultaneously while they wring out washcloths and work together to wipe the baby down before Loríen passes her to Abuela to finish swaddling her. As Abuela stares down at her newest grandchild, her old, wrinkled brow mirrors the baby's.

Adaline's arms ache to hold the little darling, to feel with her own hands that she's alive, to count her fingers and toes and kiss her pudgy, soft cheeks.

Okay, I want one.

With the baby secure and warm, Loríen sheds her smile and returns to Sallie's side, keeping one hand on her wrist to monitor her pulse. That Sallie hasn't asked to see her child sets Adaline's nerves on edge again, and every disturbing fact Adaline's read on the history of childbirth and the dangers women faced pushes to the front of her mind, making her hands shake and her legs wobble. Glancing at Sallie's body and how her nightgown sticks to every crevice of her body, Adaline prays that's not a sign of puerperal fever.

Except for her chest rising and falling quickly, Sallie lies lifeless with her eyes shut and lips parted. The midwife continues stitching, and the neighbors clean up the room. They keep their hands moving and their mouths shut, too afraid of disturbing the air, of tempting fate to choose unfavorably. Adaline joins them, collecting the midwife's tools, dropping them in the boiling water, and actively avoiding the bowl holding the placenta.

I don't need to see that. No one needs to see that.

Laying Sallie's hand gently on the bed, Loríen turns to the midwife. "Her heart is beating far too fast."

Puerperal fever? Eclampsia? A hemorrhage?

At Loríen's behest, Adaline fetches the purple bag and the items left on the table. Repeating the same process, Loríen places the crystals around Sallie's bed and anoints her body while the midwife places her needles and leftover thread on the table. With the people cheering outside, Loríen chants her song, and Adaline counts the seconds as she waits for the crystals to illuminate. But they never do. Loríen yanks the crystals away and plunges her arm into her bag, searching for other options, but nothing she tries works. Her chants falter the moment the words leave her lips.

Not giving up, the midwife pours a brownish liquid into a cup of water and holds the drink up to Sallie's chapped lips. Sallie blinks several times, but she opens her lips and sips the concoction. The midwife doesn't move until she's certain not a drop remains. Retrieving the baby from Abuela, the midwife loosens the blanket until it falls away. The baby cries in protest—a loud, strong, heavenly scream.

Carefully, the midwife lowers Sallie's nightgown and places the infant on her mother's bare chest. "Come on, Sallie. Stay with us."

As the baby snuggles against her mother and coos, Sallie rolls her head forward. Her eyes focus, enabling her to take in her baby's button nose and curled lips. Everyone else holds their breath and waits. The minutes tick by. Sallie's breathing visibly slows down, and mother and daughter settle into matching breaths as they drift off to sleep.

Loríen ushers everyone except the midwife and Abuela out of the bedroom. "The worst is past. All is well."

Finally, the ladies vocalize their own joy, matching the cheers outside, albeit quieter, as they hug each other and whisper praise and gratitude.

"You performed a miracle, Lady Loríen," one neighbor says, resting her hand on Loríen's forearm. "We'll never forget this."

Serenity warms Loríen's face as she bows her head. "Thank you for allowing me to help."

The neighbors set to work, washing sheets and tidying up the house, and reassure Loríen and Adaline they can go; the neighbors can handle the rest.

Loríen excuses herself first, having collected her belongings but leaving behind a few crystals she placed around the room. After Adaline scrubs her arms and chest and every other inch of her she can access, she descends the stairs, holding onto the railing to keep herself steady. Inside Sallie's shop, Loríen and her husband speak with Kian, who repeatedly bows his head and thanks them profusely. The children jump and run around in circles, holding each other's hands.

Smiling to herself, Adaline approaches Kian. "The midwife says you and the kids can go up now, but wait for her word before entering the bedroom."

"My lady, how can I ever thank you?" Kian takes both of Adaline's hands in his own, his hazel eyes filled with hope and admiration. "You have been a gift."

"That's how I feel about Sallie. Now, go. Be with your wife...that is, until the midwife shoos you away."

Without another word, Kian and the children hurry up the stairs. Loríen, her husband, and Adaline exit the shop to a sea of people who greet them with a round of applause and cheers that make Adaline's cheeks burn.

Through the center of the crowd, Magnus and Ëólas approach with Thoren and Merith close behind. She steps forward, but seeing Loríen curtsy and her husband bow, Adaline jerks backward and does the same. From the corner of her eye, she sees Ëólas's boots walk off with Loríen and her husband. Adaline lifts her chin to follow them, but the crowd devours them whole.

Before she can follow after them, Magnus shakes his head in wonder, cups her cheeks in his hands, and kisses her brow. "You have my gratitude."

Thoren's grin spreads across his face from ear to ear, making him look like a happy grizzly bear. "Well done, girl. Truly."

Girl? Wait, he's smiling. At me? Behind her back, Adaline pinches her hand. *Yep, still awake.* "So, neither of you are going to threaten me with the dungeons for refusing to come home?"

Magnus and Thoren release a full-belly laugh that drowns out all nearby revelries. Offering Adaline his elbow, Magnus guides her through the crowd and down the street toward the Rialto. Thoren, per usual, stays close to her other side, only he's not glaring at her or keeping his hand on the hilt of his sword. Every now and again, she sneaks a peek at Thoren. His grin never wavers, which causes Adaline to bite down on her smile and mentally hum the theme song to *The Twilight Zone*.

Craning her neck, Adaline looks for Ëólas, but she doesn't see his long dirty-blond hair and gold eyes anywhere.

Magnus points at the crowd. "I have you to thank for this."

The people streaming through the streets, many of whom Adaline recognizes from the tavern, pat each other on the back, set up barrels of wine along the sidewalks, and carry instruments to the Rialto where humans and elves take turns playing songs and test jamming together, uniting the strings and drums. The night swells with music and laughter, and once Kian returns, people drop money into his hands as his children pass out more candles. Glowing orbs of candlelight illuminate Market Street hosting an impromptu festival.

Adaline pauses and self-consciously shakes her head. "I, I can't take credit for this. If anything, Sallie, the midwife, and Loríen made this happen."

"No, my lady. This is your doing. No one would have considered asking Lady Loríen for help," Thoren booms. "His Majesty was right. You have been a gift."

When Thoren bows to Adaline, she stumbles backward and nearly falls on her ass, but Magnus's hold on her elbow stabilizes her.

"You must be exhausted, Adaline. Have you eaten?" Without waiting for her to answer, Magnus waves the baker over. Taking two croissants and two tarts from the tray, Magnus hands them to Adaline and drops a gold coin in the baker's hand. "See to it she always has what she needs."

The baker bows his head, repeatedly thanks the king, and continues on his way, luring people to him with the scent of baked goods wafting down the street.

Adaline gives Magnus the side-eye. "That's unnecessary, Magnus. But thank you."

The emotional atmosphere is as light as a cool summer night should be. Everyone's dancing, singing, and laughing in the streets with zero concerns about tomorrow, and both humans and elves are mingling together. Adaline waves to Merith and Hamon as they dance circles around each other. She searches the faces near Merith, but none of them belong to Ëólas.

"Oh my god," Adaline mumbles between bites. *I kissed his cheek. What the hell was I thinking? No, no. I did nothing wrong. The baby's alive because of him. I'm not going to be embarrassed that I was—am—grateful.*

Once Adaline finishes stuffing her face, Fólas and Jósep pull her into the dancing circles. Despite her exhaustion, the night carries her along. Mercia even comes out, along with Lady Marzella and a few other women from court. They too move about the streets with ease and appreciate the night's spontaneous celebration. Inspired by everyone, Adaline hikes up her skirts, merges with the music, and leaps around the others, all while she continues searching for one person in particular who seems to have disappeared.

As she's spinning, she uses the Rialto for spotting so she doesn't get dizzy. More faces bob and flash past her. Then far beyond the dancing circles, she spies Ëólas at the edge of the Rialto's span, still on the human side of the city. He leans his forearm against one of the spherical finials that introduces the bridge's entrance and speaks with an elven lady whom Adaline recognizes but struggles to place.

The lady's long, straight raven hair and bright blue eyes draw Adaline away from the dancing, through the crowd, and around the group of men clanging jugs. They raise their cups in cheers to Adaline as she passes. She nods in return but keeps her eyes on the raven lady and Ëólas, who throws his head backward as he bursts out laughing. His effortless jubilation is like dark chocolate s'mores in front of a late-night campfire.

The heat and exhaustion from the day slows Adaline's steps, and her chest grows heavier. The moon is high in the sky, and the adrenaline withdrawal makes her limbs weak. She doesn't even have the strength to carry a smile anymore.

I should head back to the castle and get some rest.

She turns to leave, but Ëólas rotates his head in her direction, and his golden eyes lock onto hers. A small smile pushes up the corners of his mouth, and before

Adaline can blink, she's standing beside him. He drops his arm from the finial and stands up straight.

"Lady Síena, you remember Lady Adaline," Ëólas says.

The raven beauty curtsies. "Of course, Lady Adaline, a pleasure."

The way she utters only six words, breathy and lyrical, reveals Lady Síena's elegance. Adaline, with her flushed cheeks and snood almost falling out, feels like she's three feet tall, a child among myths.

Wait, he used her title. Does that mean she has a high rank in elven society? But he doesn't use a title with Seira.

Not wanting to be rude, Adaline perks up and grins, shaking off the weariness sinking into her muscles. When a large group of people dance over the bridge and turn down Front Street, Ëólas places his hand on the small of Adaline's back, drawing her nearer and away from rogue elbows. The scent of lavender relaxes her muscles and eases the nausea festering in her stomach.

"Oh, right. Lady Síena, you're on the council. You handle," Adaline pauses to mentally scroll through the catalog of people she's filed away, "the city planning, right?"

"Correct, my lady."

Ëólas looks at Adaline, his face carefree, as if he just stepped off a plane to enjoy a two-week Caribbean vacation with all expenses paid. But there's something more in his eyes. They twinkle with a hint of excitement. "I've also placed Lady Síena in charge of Aerytol's restoration."

Adaline drops her voice an octave to stop herself from squealing. "Oh my gosh! That's amazing."

Lady Síena grins. "Indeed. I'm excited for the opportunity. Lord Ëólas just informed me that researching and preserving history is a passion of yours as well. He's convinced me you would be an asset on my team, though I confess you would be the only human. As of yet."

With her eyes sparkling and head bobbing, Adaline flaps her hands at her side as if she could take flight. "Yes. Yes. Absolutely, yes. When can I get started?"

After Lady Síena and Adaline agree to meet tomorrow after lessons with Fólas, Lady Síena excuses herself. With movements as fluid and graceful as a ballerina, she merges with the dancing circles still going round and round.

When Adaline turns back to Ëólas, his eyes trail over her body, from the stains on her dress, to her hands red from scrubbing, to the perspiration on her chest. His gaze lingers on the curls that have fallen out of her snood. The way he silently observes more than he reveals makes her heart beat faster than the drums.

"I, I don't even know what to say, except thank you." She tries to stuff her curls under her snood, but they insist on falling around her cheeks.

Smiling softly, Ëólas takes one and tucks it behind her ear. "Thank you, Adaline. You've done more in your short time here than Magnus and I have achieved in years."

Adaline sways sideways.

"You're exhausted," he says. "I should escort you back to the castle." He presses his hand firmly against her back, keeping her steady.

Biting the side of her lip, Adaline sighs and turns to watch the dancers. "Not yet. Tomorrow can wait. I want to enjoy this a bit longer." She leans against him, and every drop of anxiety drains out of her body. The night air rejuvenates her, and the jubilation of the dancing and drinking makes her want to jump and prance about too. Hamon and Merith wave her over. She steps forward but turns to Ëólas. "Let's dance."

"You can barely keep your eyes open."

"I don't care. Dance with me." She reaches her hand out to him.

He slides his palm into hers, and a warm breeze electrifies her skin. She tugs his arm, and he lurches forward, but his feet remain planted at the edge of the bridge's span. Stomping her foot, Adaline glares at him until he chuckles. Still, his feet don't budge.

"Even commander generals need a night off. Let's go!" She tugs him again, drawing his attention to his hand in hers. His smile fades, and he lets go. Like liquid metal pouring into a cast mold, doubt and regret fill every crevice of her heart. "I didn't mean to be so—"

"Let's dance," he says.

Without another word, he enters the frenzied circles. Sometimes she loses sight of him, but the music vibrates through her body, her legs and arms moving with a mind of their own. When Fólas or Magnus or Delós suddenly dance in front of her, she laughs freely. Every now and again, her dance circle and Ëólas's align. They reach for and orbit each other with one palm against the other before the music carries them away on separate paths. No matter how long the beats keep them apart, the music eventually brings them together again.

As the song ends and a group of elves engage Ëólas in conversation, drawing him across the street, he looks at Adaline and mouths *Thank you for the dance*.

She waves at him and grins until his people steal his attention. Backing up, she stands under a shop's awning so she doesn't interrupt the next dance. Leaving the fun behind, she can't ignore that her limbs feel ten times heavier at this hour. She closes her eyes and yawns. When she opens them, a goblet of wine hovers in front of her face. "Huh?"

Behind the goblet, Merith laughs. "I thought you'd be thirsty from the long night."

"Oh. Yeah." She accepts the goblet and raises the cup to her lips. When Merith moves to stand beside her, Ëólas fills her vision again. While he gestures with his hands and laughs with his people, Adaline's hand hovers in front of her face. He's doing his thing again, where he shares his warmth and ease and encourages others to do the same. But whether he allows himself to truly feel that way, Adaline's not so sure.

I think he's holding back, somehow.

"Drink, my lady," Merith says.

"Mmm." She floats the goblet below her chin. Her mind is fuzzy, and her chest feels heavy while Ëólas seems like he just woke up and the day is new. But every now and again, when he looks away from his people, a distant, empty stare consumes him.

What's going on with him?

"My lady?" Merith asks.

"Uh-huh?"

Merith follows Adaline's line of sight across the street and frowns. Slowly, he moves in front of her, cutting off her view of Ëólas yet again. With sagging shoulders and a flat voice, Merith whispers, "No, my lady."

Adaline looks at Merith, confused. *Why does he sound so sad?* "What's wrong?"

He sighs heavily. "Never mind, my lady. Never mind. Drink the wine."

This time she does, and within the span of minutes or hours, Merith transforms into Thoren.

I need to get to bed.

She sways on her feet, and Thoren, of all people, offers his elbow. "There's a horse waiting for you, my lady." He points down Front Street where a white steed swishes his blond tail.

Isn't that Ëólas's horse? He's really thoughtful, isn't he? Adaline tilts her head to the side as she looks for him, hoping to thank him. Again, she sways. For once, Thoren's behemoth size helps her feel steady.

"My lady, might I offer some advice?"

"Hmm?"

"If you might be with us for a significant amount of time, you might consider your options. Realistic options."

Adaline furrows her brow, and Thoren jerks his chin, gesturing across the street. When she looks at Ëólas, Thoren tugs her arm and turns her ever so slightly until she's facing Magnus.

Adaline swallows her anger. "Goodnight, Thoren."

She curtsies and heads down Front Street, alone. When she reaches the white horse, she realizes up close that the small mare couldn't possibly be Ëólas's. How could she make such an obvious mistake?

A city guard helps Adaline onto the horse and escorts her back to the castle. A few moments later, she dismounts in the courtyard where Seira waits by the main doors. Arm in arm, the two ladies stroll toward Adaline's chambers.

"You seem sad, Neir Nía."

Adaline rests her head on Seira's shoulder and doesn't speak until she's in her room, Kayla's helped her bathe, and she's in bed with Seira beside her. *I'm too tired to have nightmares about ruins and forests and torches.*

Seira places her hand over Adaline's, and that far-off look takes hold of her.

To help Seira relax, Adaline says, "Overall, it was a good day."

Seira stares into nothing, and her pupils swallow her periwinkle irises. "What goes up must come down."

Adaline looks toward her window. She can still hear the city's celebration while Seira repeats, "Down. Down. Down. Down."

CHAPTER TWENTY-SEVEN

THE GUARD

When Adaline ambles along Front Street the following morning, elves and humans wave not only to her but also to each other on opposite sides of the river. A few people even cross the bridges to chat, commiserating about their morning hangovers and continuing conversations from last night.

At the crest of the Rialto, a handful of youth from both sides of the city share mid-morning tea. They tip their hats and nod at Adaline as she passes them to visit Sallie and her family first. Sitting up in bed and nursing her baby, Sallie grins as Adaline enters the room. The baby hiccups once but immediately sets to work again, gulping as much milk as possible. At the edge of Sallie's bed sits Loríen.

"My lady," Sallie says with dark circles under her eyes and a deliriously radiant smile on her face. "Lady Loríen's come by to check on us too."

Loríen strokes the baby's spongy arm. "The baby's doing just fine. She'll grow up strong, like her mother."

When the baby rolls her head to the side and passes out in a drunken stupor, Sallie tucks her breast away. With Sallie's permission, Adaline tosses a rag over her shoulder and cuddles the baby while rubbing circles on the little one's back. Instinctively, Adaline shifts her hips from side to side the way she did when Cindy's sisters were babies and hums a lullaby.

"Any thoughts of motherhood?" Sallie asks Adaline.

She scoffs and turns away. "Don't you listen to your momma. You've got plenty of time, sweet baby girl."

Sallie and Loríen laugh.

"Have you chosen a name yet?" Adaline asks.

Sallie rests her hand on Loríen's. "Yes. Her name's Lori."

"Awwwww." Adaline gently presses her lip to the baby's temple.

Loríen quickly wipes her eyes dry.

Kian, carrying a breakfast tray, knocks on the door, his drowsy eyes matching his wife's and daughter's. After he deposits the tray on the bed, kisses Sallie's forehead, and pinches Lori's cheek, he bows to Loríen and Adaline and dashes downstairs.

"Does he ever get a break?" Adaline asks.

"Rarely," Sallie says.

Leaving Sallie to eat in peace, Adaline tucks a sleeping Lori into her bassinet, her fingers lingering on the little one's rising chest, and heads downstairs where she and Loríen insist Kian rest with his wife. For the next few hours, the two ladies assume responsibility for the shop, the children, and Abuela, the time flying as they make new candles and converse with customers.

Afterward, Adaline strolls to the Rialto to retell *The Princess Bride*. A fresh breeze sweeps across the bridge, momentarily easing the midday heat. Under the gazebo, she settles on Jósep's bench and folds her hands on top of her blue muslin skirts, and the little girl to whom Adaline promised a happy story sits at Adaline's feet.

When the rest of the children have settled around her, along with adults in the opposite alcove and along the sides, Adaline catches Kian holding Jem and engaging Jósep in conversation. Grinning, she turns to the children and announces the title of the story in a clear, loud voice.

A young boy sitting next to Delós's son groans and curls his lip. "Yuck, not a love story."

Adaline summons her best Peter Falk interpretation by lowering her voice and trying to sound grainy. "Yes, that's part of the story. But it also has sword fighting, torture, giants, chases, escapes, revenge, true love, and miracles."

The children's eyebrows shoot upward as they look at each other. Then they lean forward and silence themselves.

"Once upon a time, in days of old and when the world was still new, Buttercup lived on a small farm in Florin. Her favorite pastimes were horse riding and tormenting Westley, the farm boy who worked there. She never called him by his name though, only Farm Boy. And she loved ordering him about. 'Farm Boy, polish my saddle. Farm Boy, fill these buckets of water.' And he always replied the same, 'As you wish.'"

Adaline glances around the crowd, hoping to spy Hamon, but Ëólas waits at the end of the bridge's span, leaning against a finial like the night before. He's swapped his navy-blue silk tunic for dark brown and green with leather belts crossing his chest—a rogue's outfit suited for traveling for days on end.

He kept his promise. He must be leaving afterward.

Sorrow fills Adaline's voice as she tells the children about Westley leaving to seek his fortune but how he promised he'd always come back to Buttercup. No one dares cough during the story, and more people passing by stop to listen.

When Westley and Vizzini face off in the battle of wits and Vizzini swaps the cups behind Westley's back, the kids gasp. An adult further behind them screams louder, startling Adaline and the children. They shake off the surprise, and Adaline resumes the story—only a shrill scream a few bridges downriver causes her and the kids to scurry to their feet, and the adults around them crane their necks. Another scream merges with people shouting and stampeding in various directions, making it impossible for Adaline to discern where the source of concern originates. Most of the children scatter like rabbits. Ëólas leaps onto the bridge's railing and peers out of one of the arched windows.

"Everything will be alright," Adaline says to the few children crowding around her.

After scanning the city, Ëólas jumps down and maneuvers around the crowd like water. He pulls two guards aside, instructs them quickly, and points at Adaline. As people shout and circle around them, he locks eyes with her and mouths *Go with them.* The severity of his expression, the rigidity of his features, tells her to not argue.

She tries to go to him anyway.

No, he mouths again, panic written across his face. *Go with them.*

Not giving her time to argue, Ëólas runs off, toward the castle, toward the screams, toward the danger. She tries to follow him with her eyes, but he vanishes into the chaos, and his guards rush toward her. Their leather breastplates, sporting the tree of life and those three stars, block her from running to the castle. Instead, they herd her and the children off the bridge. She scans the faces of people running by. Not seeing Sallie's girls, she searches for Kian and spots Jósep, trapped on the human side of the city, following them around the corner to the candle shop. The guards lead Adaline and the remaining nine children in the opposite direction, along Front Street and further into the human side of the city.

When they turn a corner, one guard raises his arm to stop their group. The other sprints into the middle of a small square where five people, two of them elves, pound fists into each other's faces and abdomens. A human raises his dagger and thrusts it at an elf. The blade pierces the elf's jugular vein, and red flows down his neck. As the elf chokes, Adaline screams. The guard who'd been escorting her charges into the fight. Dragging the man away from her and the children, the guard twists the man's hand behind his back and wrestles him to the ground, kicking the dagger out of arm's reach. The wounded elf staggers backward and falls beside a clay oven, his elbow and side landing on a pile of tan bricks. His blood paints them red.

No, no, no. How can this be happening? Why? Why now?

Adaline runs around the guard. "Get the children out of here," she shouts while pulling up her dress. Grabbing her dagger, she rips the hem of her chemise and tears off a strip to create a bandage even though her efforts are pointless. She knows about the jugular vein. Fólas told her such a wound would cause her attacker to enter a foggy state of mind for a few minutes, that he'd be vaguely aware of what's happening as he bled out. Silencing Fólas's voice, Adaline sheaths her dagger and squats next to the elf, who tries to push her and roll away. When he falls to the ground, toppling over the bricks, she lunges forward and presses the balled-up cloth against his neck while his wide, gray eyes dart behind her as if he's searching for someone else.

"You're going to be okay." Silent tears roll down Adaline's cheeks. She's always been a horrible liar.

Two humans, flung away from the brawl, land in a heap beside her, making her jump. She turns back to the elf only to see icy, glazed-over eyes forever staring up at the sky. She sobs once, then clamps down on her teeth, and turns to the men. One's already running away.

Another man staggers to get up with blood dripping from his bicep. "Fucking elves."

Fucking ignorance.

Adaline rips another piece of her chemise free and wraps the makeshift tourniquet around his wound, pulling the knot extra tight to make the man wince.

Amid the chaos, a breeze caresses her cheek. Like a hand, the wind urges her to turn her face toward the square, toward the danger. "Adaline," a female voice whispers. The same voice from the cave. The same voice that warned her about No-Nose and Shorty. The same voice that exists outside of time and space.

"My lady, I have to get you out of here," says her assigned guard. He grabs her arm and pulls her up as more guards run into and surround the people fighting in the square.

"I have her," says another guard running over to them, a human one this time with a burgundy padded jacket and bullet-like half helm. "His Majesty sent me. My lady, I have to get you away from here. Come with me."

The elven guard glances at Adaline. When she nods, he runs back into the square, and she follows Magnus's guard away from the fighting. Unable to head down Front Street toward the castle, he leads her in between buildings with windows and doors barred shut until they find a horse hitched to a post. Without giving her a chance to ask if the horse belongs to him, he picks Adaline up and sits her on the saddle, frees the horse's reins, and climbs up behind her. He kicks his heels once, and they gallop down a wide street empty of people.

He directs the horse over a bridge and into the elven side of the city. "I'm not certain where the fighting is now. We'll have to go around the outskirts."

The horse gallops ahead, taking them beyond buildings and into open fields where farmers gather their families and workers and race inside their homes. The forest of Lameiría peeks above the horizon before the guard turns the horse to the left and they ride alongside the length of the city. Adaline searches between the buildings and streets for signs of people, but that stretch lays dormant with not a person or a fight visible.

"We should go back," Adaline says. "I want to check on my friends."

"You mean the elves," the guard sneers.

An icy chill runs up Adaline's spine, and the hairs on the back of her neck rise to attention. "And Magnus and Hamon and Thoren and Sallie and her family and the baker and—"

"Enough. I have my orders."

Orders from whom?

They pass the city, and the castle off to the side grows smaller. "Are we going around the backside?"

The guard grips her waist tighter and doesn't answer.

I'm being kidnapped. Oh god. Ëólas, what do I do?

Trees dot the meadow swallowing them as the castle shrinks further out of view. Like mile markers, the trees tell her how much further away from her friends she's being taken. She doesn't see any other horses going in the same direction. Her bones ache.

Up ahead, the river that cuts through the city and curves around the castle comes into view, along with a mast-less boat and a handful of men. She has no intention of becoming Buttercup and letting Vizzini, Fezzik, and Inigo take her downriver.

"Ëólas," she whispers like a prayer.

As the wind rushing past her carries his name away, she does the most dangerous but only thing she can think of. She elbows the guard in the gut, knocking the wind out of him. When his chest curls inward, she slides out of his grip and off the horse that thankfully doesn't run her over. After rolling a few times, she jumps to her feet and runs toward the castle even though she'll never reach her friends in time.

Adaline glances back. The guard has already turned his horse around. He chases after her again, this time with his arm out so he can scoop her up. Halting and turning away from him, she draws her dagger, keeping it close to her side and out of his view. As he reaches for her, she pauses long enough to slice his hand, then continues running as he curses her name. The castle is maybe one mile away. She's run that in gym class before. She can run a mile. She can dodge him and—

The guard jumps down and chases her on foot. With his long strides, she can hear his breath catching up to her.

But I'm small and quicker. That's what Ëólas said. Don't let him pin me down.

"You're not going anywhere," the guard hisses, his voice too close to Adaline's ear.

She dodges left and turns around to face him, gripping her dagger like an ice pick. "Why are you doing this? Just let me go! Whatever ransom you want from the king, I'll give it to you myself."

"Ransom?" The guard laughs. "Tell me, little lady, about Seira, and I'll let you go."

Adaline's hands shake, and bile churns in her stomach. Her face turns white, and her eyes dart to the side while she tries to form a plan. The only object near her is a tree. A single tree.

Can I keep that between us somehow? But no one knows I'm out here. Seira! Maybe Seira knows. Oh, please, please, please, Seira. I believe in you. Send me help. I'll do what I can until then.

The men at the boat shout in their direction, but they're too far away for Adaline to hear them.

"Who is Seira?" the guard asks. "She's not originally from Lameiría, is she?"

"I have no idea."

"Bullshit. She follows you around like a lapdog, gifting you pretty dresses, having breakfast with you every morning, and waiting for you when you return from the city."

He's been watching me. Us.

The guard and Adaline circle around each other, she with her dagger ready, the guard with his hand dripping blood on the grass. He doesn't bother to draw his sword. She's that little of a threat to him.

For every step the guard takes, Adaline moves in the opposite direction. She studies the movement of his feet and calculates. "What do you want with Seira?"

The guard lunges. She blocks his arm coming down at her, slips under his grasp, and runs in the opposite direction for the tree, following her gut even if she's not yet sure how that might help.

"Get back here, you fucking bitch!"

As Adaline reaches the tree, her skirts twist and bunch between her thighs. A long, cold blade pierces the fabric and slides between her legs. She screams as her flesh rips open, and she trips forward. The ground rushes up too fast, slamming her in the face. She drops her dagger, and it bounces away from her. Pinned to the ground, she can't pull herself free, and the blood trickling down her legs makes her feet slippery.

Fólas, how long until I lose consciousness?

The guard yanks his sword out of the ground, releasing Adaline's dress. She rolls over and lifts one foot, trying to kick his kneecaps, but he steps on her skirts, trapping her legs. He lets up only after he grabs her arm, and he drags her back to his horse, cursing the entire time.

"She better be worth the hassle."

With her free hand, Adaline pulls his pinky sideways, trying to break it, but he turns around and backhands her across the cheek, leaving her dazed for a moment.

With the side of her face throbbing, she digs her hand into her pocket, retrieves her father's Swiss army knife, and uses her captive hand to pull the blade out. Like Fólas showed her, she slices the guard's thigh in a circular motion. He screams and releases her wrist as he stumbles forward, clutching his leg.

Scrambling to her feet, Adaline runs back for her dagger, her feet slipping inside her wet, gooey shoes. Clutching her father's knife, she reaches for the dagger too, but before she can grasp it, the guard rams into her back.

He tackles her to the ground, flips her over, and spits in her face, "You're lucky my orders are to—"

He pauses and looks up.

Adaline twists her head to see what has scared him and tucks her fist, holding the Swiss army knife, under her side. From the city, a group of men or elves or both on horseback races toward them. From the rider in the lead, dark-blond hair billows in the wind. Adaline's heart swells in her chest, as does her resolve to get this brute off her.

The guard's eyes darken. He grabs her by the throat and squeezes. She claws at his face, and he punches her in the stomach.

As she gasps for breath, he pulls her up by her hair, looks her dead in the eyes, and screams, "Are you from another world?"

Adaline's body shuts down. *Why? How?* "I, I don't know wh-what you mean."

He smacks her across the face and looks up at the horses coming for him. He pulls a fist full of her hair harder and draws his own knife, pressing it against her throat.

His eyes dart wildly from the horses to her. "Answer me, and you'll live. Are you from another world?"

Her neck burns. The hand holding her father's knife trembles. She can't possibly stab him before he slices her throat, and her blade's so small. Whatever she does, she has to make it count.

"Answer me!" With the hilt of his dagger, he hits the side of her head.

Her temple throbs and her vision blurs, but the moment his blade leaves her throat, she slices the length of the hand gripping her neck. He yowls and loosens his hold just enough that she's able to slip out of his grasp. But the guard won't give up. Before she can run toward the other horses, he seizes her arm and yanks downward so hard that her shoulder snaps and pops, and her left arm hangs uselessly at her side.

As she screams in agony, he grips her jaw and pushes his face into hers. "Are you from another world?"

She tries to stab him, but he grabs her hand and crushes her fist to force her to drop her father's knife. Then he pauses and stares at her small weapon, at its shiny red plastic casing, at the flawless folds of metal stored within, at the key ring dangling at the end, until his eyes sparkle and his mouth twists up in victory.

He throws her down. She lands on her shoulder and cries out, wriggling to get off it. When she sits up, she makes out blurry shades of navy and brown urging the horses toward her.

"Adaline." Again, that voice whispers in her ear, drawing her eyes away from her refuge and toward the guard sprinting toward the boat—his fastest ticket out of here.

He can't get on that boat.

Something bigger is at play here. Something important. Something that threatens more than just the Neutral Territory. That can't happen. Reaching into the depths of her soul, Adaline screams at the top of her lungs.

The water recedes in rippling waves, tugging the boat away from the shore. The men who had been guarding the boat scramble back onto it and shout at her captor to hurry. Adaline snatches the dagger, relieved to have the larger blade again, and stumbles to her feet. Clutching her limp arm to keep it steady at her side, she runs after the guard. He's only a few feet ahead of her. She can catch him. What she'll do when she does, she doesn't know. But she can stop him from getting away and taking his secrets with him.

"Stop," she shouts. Each footfall jostles her arm, making her whimper louder.

As the guard makes a mad dash toward the river, a tidal wave rises and collides with the boat, splintering it into pieces. His friends' shouts disappear under the currents.

Adaline slows down and smiles, until the guard spins around and glares at her like she's the embodiment of evil. He stalks toward her, his eyes fuming, his escape eliminated, his fate sealed.

The horses from the castle are so close now that Adaline can just about make out Merith's and Ëólas's faces.

The guard draws his sword and sprints after her. She runs to the tree, hoping to put it between them. She just needs to dodge him long enough for Ëólas to arrive. The guard's grunts grow louder behind her, and she turns in time to raise her dagger and block his sword from slicing her stomach open.

He swipes sideways, and as Adaline blocks with the dagger, he slices the back of her hand, causing her to stumble backward against the tree trunk.

"I won't survive this," he says. "But I'll make certain neither do you. He was right. You're nothing but a blight on this world. An abomination. Everything that's wrong is your fault."

He? My fault?

Ëólas will never reach her in time.

The guard looms over her and raises his sword, the hatred on his face unmistakable.

She's going to die in this world, and Cindy and Dax will never know what happened to her. Sallie, Jósep, Seira, Magnus. Ëólas. They need to know what's going on.

"Please," she says, keeping her dagger in front of her.

The guard laughs, but she wasn't talking to him. She doesn't know whom she's asking for help, but the ground beneath her rumbles. As he takes his final step, a tree root rises up maybe an inch but enough to catch the tip of his boot. His knee buckles, and he tumbles forward, his grin falling apart, his eyes growing wider. She parries his sword to the side, aims the dagger at his chest, and doesn't know which makes her scream more—the force of his weight smashing her shoulder into the trunk or how easily her dagger slides between his ribs. Every inch he falls against her, he descends further into death.

She wriggles away from the guard, away from his gasps, but he won't stop staring at her as he's dying, her dagger lodged in his chest.

He's still alive. They, they can save him and get more information.

When she staggers away from him, toward the horses, she sees the determination on Merith's face and in Ëólas's golden eyes. Her adrenalin drains from her body, and her footsteps slow down. Feeling dizzy, she lowers herself onto her knees as carefully as possible. Ëólas doesn't wait for his horse to completely stop before jumping down and racing over to her while Merith and the other two run over to deal with the guard.

When Ëólas skids to a halt and kneels beside her, she smiles at him. "I dodged a lot."

He looks like he's about to cry, and that's the worst look she's seen from him yet. "Well done," he chokes out, cupping her cheeks in his hands, wiping her tears away with his thumbs. His eyes dart from the blood on her neck to her shoulder to the blood coating the grass around her legs. His eyes glisten like the sun under water.

Her eyelids droop, but she blinks them open. "Is Seira safe?"

"Yes." Carefully, he slides one arm around her waist and pulls her up, leaning her against him.

She rests her head against his chest, and his heartbeat reassures her she's still alive too. "He asked about Seira," she whispers. "I didn't tell him anything. I promise."

Ëólas nuzzles his cheek against the top of her head. Sliding an arm behind her knees, he gingerly lifts her off the ground and carries her to his horse. Merith's eyes moisten as Ëólas passes her to him. Once Ëólas leaps onto his horse's rump, Merith hoists her up onto the saddle. Despite their best efforts, they jostle her shoulder, and she cries out, begging them to stop, to let her lie down.

"I'm so sorry, my lady," Merith says, his voice cracking. "We'll get you help soon."

On the ride back to the castle, she clings to Ëólas, latching onto his leather belt. His breathing sounds more strained than her own, even as every trot causes pain to sear through her chest, along her arm, and down her legs. Still, she smiles as the castle grows larger.

"Stay awake," Ëólas urges, cradling her as gently as possible in his arms.

He's so comfortable, and her body folds perfectly into the crook of his arm. His shoulder is meant to serve as a pillow, and his silky hair cushions her cheek. Her eyelids droop more and more.

"Stay awake," he coaxes her again, his lips brushing her forehead.

That's too hard when your voice is so soft. It's like a lullaby.

All she wants more than anything right now, more than going home, is to sleep in his arms. If he wants her to stay awake, he shouldn't be so inviting.

"Adaline," he calls her.

Her eyes open again. In the span of a second, the castle has doubled in size.

"Adaline, please," he keeps calling her back.

She can't ignore that voice. She rolls her head back and looks up at him, his wide jawline, his dirty-blond hair blowing in the wind, those golden eyes. A fairytale come alive. He looks down at her, his eyes absent of distrust or animosity, as if any tension between them has been permanently erased. He's back to being the person she saw when she first arrived.

"Thanks for that dagger," she says, closing her eyes again.

"You never should have needed it." The pain laced through his words confuses her as he holds her tighter.

But she did need it. Because she's a threat to someone. No, an abomination. Because she brought magic back into the world? Or because the world brought her here?

"Éolas," she whispers, "he wanted to know if I'm from another world."

Even through her drowsiness, she can see how startled he is. Then his eyes cloud over, and the horse speeds up. As soon as they're galloping around the castle itself, Adaline rolls her head into the crook of his neck. She inhales that scent of pine and lavender, closes her eyes, and everything fades to black.

Chapter Twenty-Eight

A Personal Story

In her dreams, she's running through the woods again. Sometimes her father is with her. Sometimes Ëólas. The torches never stop hunting them, and this time she hears a man's voice yelling at the torch bearers to *find the abomination.*

When Adaline wakes up, her room is dark. Silence pervades the castle. Candles on the mantle have almost burned out. She tries to sit up, but her body aches, especially her shoulder. Her arm is tied against her body, and her head won't stop throbbing. If only she could get the Excedrin out of her messenger bag.

"Neir Nía?" Seira drifts from the sofa to Adaline's side. She sits on the edge of Adaline's bed, keeping her movements slight and light so she doesn't jostle the mattress, and lays her dainty hand on Adaline's forehead. "Rest, Neir Nía."

"Seira, who are you?"

She brushes a damp curl off Adaline's cheek. "A lost orphan," she says, her eyes fading and growing distant. "Like you."

Adaline rests her hand on top of Seira's and squeezes it. "Why do people want to hurt us?"

"I don't know." Her face crumbles, and her shoulders roll forward as a tear scars her perfect cheek.

Seira's face encased in sorrow, a sorrow far more aged than Adaline's, paints itself on her heart, forever marring her memory of this world. *Damn anyone who can wound someone so deeply.*

As much as she wants to comfort Seira, Adaline doesn't fight the pull toward sleep. Seira lies down beside her, and with their hands clasped, Adaline drifts off to sleep, holding Ëólas's hand as they run from the flames.

"Kayla?" The scent of cooked meat tingles Adaline's nose. Struggling to sit up in bed, she scans her room. Seira's gone, and the evening glow warms her chambers. *How long have I been out?*

"My lady." Kayla hurries over from the corner table, carrying a tray of food. "I'm so glad you're awake."

She sets the tray on the bedside table, fluffs several pillows behind Adaline's back, and hands her lady a cup of tea. Heading to the chamber door, she cracks it open and whispers to someone outside. After she shuts the door, she sits in a chair beside the bed.

Adaline sips the tea but groans as her bladder throbs. "I desperately need to pee."

Wrapping her arms around her lady, Kayla helps Adaline to the water closet. Every sway of her hips feels as though she's aged eighty years. When she returns to the bed, she prays she never has to pee again. Ignoring the tea, she uses one hand to eat those juicy thin slices of meat that she dunks in a red wine and herb sauce.

When she's eaten only two bites, there's a knock on her door, and Magnus steps into her room. Kayla excuses herself, and the king takes the seat beside the bed the way Adaline's father used to. Stooping over, he rests his elbows on his knees and runs his hand through his hair.

She smiles weakly at him. "How many people were hurt?"

"Here you lay, and you ask about our people?" Magnus takes her hand, the one not bandaged, and kisses her knuckles. "You dear girl."

"Woman," she corrects him.

Magnus chuckles. "How do you feel?"

"Like the bottom of a taxicab."

"I have no idea what that means."

"Remind me to tell you about *Ghostbusters*."

"A promise then," he says, still holding her hand.

"Where's Ëólas?"

He drops his gaze to their hands. "He is struggling with much at the moment." *His people must be so scared.*

"I would have followed after you myself," Magnus pats her hand, "but we both couldn't leave the city during the chaos, and the elves can urge the horses faster."

"You don't have to explain."

"But I owe you an apology, Adaline. And I cannot adequately express my regret at what you've suffered. I promised you safety and protection, and I failed to provide either. I don't know how one of my guards learned about you, but you are in more danger the longer you stay here. Ëólas has been unsuccessful retrieving information about magic from Lameiría, but this incident should startle the queen and king enough to grant him access to the requested resources. He feels responsible for the situation you endured."

"It's not his fault. And it's not yours either. I really do believe you and Ëólas are good people, Magnus. This world is lucky to have you two."

"You're kind, Adaline, and far too forgiving."

"But it's true. You've been nothing but good to me. Maybe a bit too stern in the beginning." She pauses, and when Magnus arches an eyebrow, they both chuckle. "Why are you so sweet?"

"I'm sweet now?"

"Shut up. Just, what's your story?"

"You just told a king to shut up."

"And you didn't order me beheaded. Seriously, what's your story?"

Magnus leans back in his seat, crossing his arms over his chest, but when he glances at her sling, he drops his arms, and his hands fall onto his thighs. "Take another bite. If you eat, I'll talk."

Adaline stuffs a large strip of meat in her mouth and chews.

Rubbing his thighs, Magnus releases a long sigh. "I was a spoiled, selfish, rotten prince, much like my grandfather. I cared nothing for my people and expected everyone to wipe my ass for me. My father had been trying to negotiate with the elves, and my attitude didn't help his cause. He met with Ëólas first, and—"

"What?" Adaline stops chewing and opens her eyes wide. "How old is he?"

"He won't tell me. But he looks the same as when I first met him. I was six then."

Holy shit. A lump forms in Adaline's throat, preventing her from swallowing the gouda she'd dropped in her mouth. But Magnus stops talking and stares at her, so she forces it down and eats more.

"My father tried speaking with me, but I refused to listen. So, one day when I was eleven, he took me on a tour of the kingdom. When we reached Meadowbrook, a small village in the middle of nowhere, he stripped me down to my undergarments. And he left me. He told Thoren not to bring me back until I'd learned some humility."

"Damn."

"Indeed. In one night, everything I knew was taken from me, and I found myself in an unforgiving world where I had to work for every bite I ate."

They share a knowing smile, and a look of camaraderie passes between them. Adaline nibbles her lip, then asks, "So, that's why you've looked after me?"

Magnus sighs heavily. Then he gets this gleam in his eye as the memories shift from painful to nostalgic, and the corner of his mouth hints at a small, sad smile.

"Who was she?" When Magnus looks at her incredulously, she stuffs three more bites of cheese in her mouth, and her cheeks puff out like a squirrel.

"Nora. And don't you dare mention that to anyone. Ever."

In between bites, she mumbles, "What happened to her?"

"Who knows? But her father wouldn't permit her to befriend a bastard child, as Thoren had introduced me, but her kindness never faltered. Shortly after I returned home, my father's illness set in. I assisted him in all his responsibilities. Then he was gone, and I was king, and years passed. I imagine she wed long ago and has a brood of kind, rambunctious, and feisty children, just like her." He balls his hands into fists and gouges them into his thighs.

"Magnus." Adaline squeezes his hand.

What a horrible fate to love someone you can never be with.

That thought alone makes breathing more difficult. She lets go of Magnus and grips her blanket, crushing the comforter in her fist, as if she can shatter the barrier of impossibility. A tear slides down her cheek, which Magnus leans forward to wipe away.

"All hope is not lost." But he doesn't sound like he's talking about himself.

"You really are amazing, you know that?"

"As I said, you're too kind. Even after all I've tried, I fear I'm not a good king. I wanted to show the elves that humanity is capable of so much more. That we don't just take what we want and seek power. That we could redeem ourselves. And when you arrived, I thought..." He looks out the window, toward the city, and shakes his head. "Thank you, Adaline, for your efforts to bring our peoples together. But I think it best if you remain in the castle for the time being."

"What? No. I need to check on my friends and—"

"They can visit you here."

"No, Magnus, I'm not hiding up here."

"It's safer here."

"Why? What happened? How bad was that fight? Who started it?"

Magnus furrows his brow. He opens his mouth to speak but stops. Shaking his head, he stands to leave. "Rest now and—"

Adaline pushes her tray off her lap and wriggles to get out of bed, wincing every time her butt scoots forward and hoping she doesn't undo the bandages around her legs.

"Adaline, what are you—get back in bed. Now."

"No. If you're not going to tell me, then—"

"Okay, okay. So damn stubborn. Back in bed first." Picking her up like a doll, he gently places her on the mattress with her back against the pillows and headboard. Then he pulls the covers up to her waist and moves the tray onto her lap. After he stares her down and she grumbles but takes a few more bites, he passes her the tea.

As she takes a sip, he continues, "The seven who started the fights were humans. They chose four locations and initiated the altercations at the same time. We believe they aimed to undermine the progress you procured the night before."

"Me? I didn't do anything. That celebration was because of the midwife and Lady Loríen."

"No, Adaline. It was yours, and everyone in the city knows it. No one would have considered the idea of asking elves or humans to help each other in such a manner."

That's what Ëólas said. "So those people tried to undo our efforts?"

"That was our initial thought. Based on what you revealed though, we fear it was also a diversion."

"To take me," she whispers.

Magnus nods and closes his eyes as if to unsee the possibilities falling into place.

She looks at her bruised shoulder and rests her hand on the sling. "He called me a blight, an abomination. He said I'm to blame for everything that's wrong in this world."

Magnus's eyes widen. Then he knits his eyebrows together and stuffs his hands in his pockets. "Why?"

"He didn't say. He asked about Seira first, then wanted to know if I was from another world. I don't think he meant to kill me, not initially. He said he had orders, but he never said from whom. Do you think you can get him to tell you?"

Magnus remains silent longer than Adaline's comfortable with.

He pinches his chin. "He didn't survive the trip back to the castle."

She closes her eyes to keep her tears hidden, but all she sees is her dagger sliding between his ribs. The look of surprise on his face. The way he gasped for breath. She killed someone. She snuffed out a life. She took away his only chance in this world. "What about the people?"

"There were casualties amid the chaos."

"Who?"

"You need to focus on rest for now, and then—"

"Who?" Adaline narrows her eyes and stares at Magnus without blinking.

He knows if he doesn't tell her, she'll push those covers off and walk into the city to find the answers herself. Hesitantly, Magnus lists the twelve names of those who died, whom the seven assailants attacked first. The last two names on the list are Jósep and Kian.

CHAPTER TWENTY-NINE

A SYMBOL

After spending almost an entire day in bed, Adaline insists on getting dressed the next morning, despite Kayla's protests. She feels like a mummy with bandages wrapped tightly around her legs. In the mirror, she can't pretend everything is fine. Her cheek sports a large bruise shaped like a sword hilt. Red lines crisscross diagonally down her throat, and bruises dot her forearm. The sling and her lavender dress look ridiculous together.

I look dreadful, like a hospital patient dressed for a ball. But I'm alive.

The guilt of that reality makes her heart ache, as if she hasn't cried enough since learning about Jósep and Kian.

He said it's my fault. Is that true? Are Jósep and Kian dead because of me?

She had gotten so caught up in the excitement of this world, in the people, that she broke the rules of anthropology. When did she stop being an observer? When Sallie and Lori's lives were in danger? When she began telling stories to the children? When she first asked Jósep about his sculpture?

But none of those moments feel wrong, and she can't regret asking Loríen for help. If remaining an observer would have meant sacrificing Lori, then fuck that. She loves this city and its people. She loves their generosity and the communities they built. And both sides were bonding. The celebration after Lori's birth encompassed everyone. No one grumbled about the noise. No one yelled at the elves to leave the human side of the city.

Whoever attacked, they were the outsiders. They're what's wrong with this world. *And I'll be damned if I'll go home before fixing this.*

Adaline glares at her wounds one more time, steeling herself. She walks over to her nightstand and picks up her dagger, which has been scrubbed clean as if it were brand new, as if she's never used it. Delicately, she sits down and ties the sheath around her calf, her shoulder and leg burning the entire time. But she won't leave her dagger behind.

Exiting her room, she nods at the two elven guards posted outside her door and heads directly to the king's study. She hasn't seen Ëólas since he found her, since he carried her home, since she passed out in his arms. He didn't even come by to check on her. Which must mean he's struggling too. His people must be in a panic.

As she trudges through the corridors that feel thrice as long as before, she avoids making eye contact with the guards. When two human guards walk past, she pauses and leans against the wall to keep herself upright. Her bones ache. Her head throbs, and patches of her body feel both hot and cold.

"My lady," someone says from behind.

She jumps away from the wall. *Never get pinned in a corner!*

Two elven soldiers stand behind her, the same two she saw when she left her chambers. *Have they been following me?*

"Shall we escort you back to your chambers?" asks one guard.

Adaline stands up tall and faces them. "What are your names?"

"Moren, my lady. And this is Idrós, at your service."

"Thank you. Did Ëólas assign you to follow me?"

"Yes, my lady. Wherever you go, we are to remain beside you."

Adaline sighs. *He assigns me guards, but he can't stop by. Ugh. This isn't about me. Then again, according to my abductor, it is.*

After ordering her body to relax, she has the guards take her to Ëólas even though they insist all the council members are engaged in conversation in the throne room and she'll be left waiting outside for hours. She doesn't care. *We'll see about that.*

The double doors to the throne room are shut tight. Even though the wood's extra thick, about a foot deep, she hears shouting on the other side.

She approaches the guards posted outside. "I'm going to wait here."

"No, my lady," says one guard. "The king said not to keep you out."

"Oh." *That's new.*

The guard cracks open the door, which is surprisingly quiet, although perhaps that's only because the shouts from inside are so loud. Confused, Adaline slides halfway through the door but pauses when one of the council members launches himself from his seat and yells across the room. From each throne in which Magnus and Ëólas sit, a semicircle of six chairs extends outward for each side's council members.

The man who jumps up brandishes his finger in Merith's direction. "Are you implying we allowed this to happen, Lord Merith?"

Oh, that's Lord Otto, Lady Audney's father. Adaline curls her lip as she remembers when Lady Audney tripped her on the dance floor.

Another Alderton council member cuts off Merith before he can speak. "Have we not done enough on our part to invest in the success of the Neutral Territory? And at the detriment of our lands, as we've pulled resources away from our estates."

"You think we'd risk our homes to see this effort fail?" says Lord Otto.

A lady from Lameiría raises her voice. "We did not ask you to divert your resources. We have no need for them."

"We all knew this opportunity included several risks," says Magnus.

Both he and Ëólas are stuck in the middle, listening to everyone's concerns. Whereas Magnus tries to interject here and there, Ëólas is in full observation mode, but whenever someone yells, he tenses a bit.

He doesn't like conflict either.

Another of Ëólas's council members stands and bows her red hair toward him. "With all due respect, our primary objective is protecting our people, not Alderton's resources. Leaving Lameiría subjected our people to vulnerability. They trusted us. They trusted this opportunity. How many more elves will we allow to be hunted? I cannot in good conscience continue to support this endeavor, my lord."

Adaline inches further into the room to better see Ëólas's face, to make sure he's okay. He glances up, and his eyes lock with hers. His jaw unclenches, and he releases a long exhale. Even though he's cemented his body to the throne, his eyes smile at her.

"I will summon more men," says Hamon, "to safeguard the city, and—"

"Because your guards can be trusted?" says Fólas.

Whoa! Fólas. Easy, friend.

Hamon's face turns red, and he makes an odd throat-clearing sound. "Then bring more from Lameiría and—"

"Reduce our own border patrol so that all of Lameiría is made vulnerable?" asks Merith.

Hey, hey, hey. I'm not okay with my friends fighting. You guys need to be on the same side. Stop this. Someone, stop this.

Ëólas raises his arm, palm out, to silence his people. "No, I'll never permit that. The elves who wish to leave are free to do so. I will not make any of our people stay, including those under my command."

Will Ëólas leave too?

Ëólas glances at Adaline. "But I will not leave, not yet. There is more at work here than we can see at the moment, and I intend to learn what that is."

"What's at work here, my lord? Is that not obvious?" Sarcasm drips from Lady Síena, whom Adaline never got to meet with about that job opportunity. "The humans continue to prove their untrustworthiness and unpredictability. The instability of Alderton itself needs to be considered as well, as they undermined the authority of their king. Abducting the king's ward? We—"

"You go too far." Thoren rises from his seat beside his king, his voice booming across the room. "Do not bring the lady into this. And the dissent of a few do not—"

"What ransom did they hope to gain by taking the lady hostage then?" asks Lady Síena. "We prayed humanity had redeemed itself, but I have not seen enough evidence. I cannot accept us sacrificing more elves. I will not stay here and watch more of our people die."

"You forget humans were injured and died as well." Hamon leans forward and points his finger at the elves. "And they did so trying to defend your people. Do you think so little of their efforts? Or are human lives so easily dismissed because we come and go so quickly?"

Shaking his head, Fólas scoffs. "Don't pretend your people mourn our losses."

"Fólas!" Adaline shouts, startling everyone. She steps fully into the room and walks toward him. "How can you say such a thing? I lost two dear friends. Two of them. I'm grieving Jósep as much as Kian." At the mention of their names, her lips tremble, and her eyes tear as she stares him down.

"I didn't mean you, my lady," Fólas whispers. He drops his eyes to the ground.

"Is this what you're going to do all day, stand here and argue with each other?" Adaline asks.

She waits for Magnus or Ëólas to silence her, but both of them nod for her to continue. Magnus looks at her with faith. Ëólas looks at her with relief, until his eyes drift to her sling, and he grips the arm of his chair so tightly that his knuckles turn white.

Adaline walks up to the circle of council members. "Why are you in here arguing about resources and shortcomings and who's grieving more?"

Lady Síena shakes her head. "I'm glad to see you're well enough to be out of bed, Lady Adaline, but your human laws prohibit you from being a member of this council."

"Let her speak." Magnus's voice echoes throughout the room. "As a member of my family, she has every right to be here."

Family. Adaline mouths *Thank you,* and he nods at her.

"Lady Adaline is here at my request," Magnus says.

The panda-like elf, however, objects. "The last thing we need right now is a curious child asking us a million questions."

Adaline's blood boils. *Great. To humans, I'm a spinster. To elves, I'm a child.*

Ëólas raises his arm again, silencing the panda. "Lady Adaline's millions of questions without judging others opened the door for elves and humans to establish friendships. You'd be wise to learn from her." He looks at Adaline and swallows hard. "I know I have."

Whoa. Adaline's heart pounds in her chest. Everyone looks at her.

But the panda refuses to yield. "One human does not make—"

"Stop! Just stop already." Adaline steps forward and bares her teeth. "You think you are so superior and infallible, but you're mistaken. Yes, humans can be selfish and shallow and power hungry, but many of you have superiority complexes and could use a good dose of humility. You can be awfully judgmental, narrow-minded, and inflexible."

The panda rises from his seat. "How dare you—"

"I am not done!" Adaline shouts. When he slinks into his seat, she lowers her voice, but her words tumble out faster than coins hitting the ground. "You do not chop down the entire tree because of a few bad apples. You have an opportunity here. You can either keep focusing on your differences and destroy what you've created, or you can highlight how you're the same and use that to bring our people together. And I mean *our* people. Stop talking about us as two separate groups. There's only one people in the Neutral Territory, and our people are scared and frightened and hurting right now. Your doubt is theirs. Your distrust is theirs. Show them the opposite."

"By getting drunk in the tavern?" says Lord Otto.

"Maybe!" Adaline throws her unbound arm up in the air and lets it fall to her side.

While Lord Otto scoffs, Magnus and Ëólas beam at her.

Merith, however, speaks up. "That was an accident. The lady didn't know tree spirits—"

"It's okay, Merith." As she remembers the fun they had that night, she grins to herself, and Merith returns her smile.

Striding into the middle of the circle, Adaline turns about so she can look at each of them. "Do you really not see the similarities? I have yet to meet a single person in this city who doesn't enjoy a good song and a cup of ale. Dancing and music connect us. Stories connect us. Uniting against a common enemy connects us. We all value life, especially that of an innocent baby. We all want this city to thrive. We all want to live good, comfortable lives. We all want to be surrounded by friends and family and not to be left alone in this world with no one to rely on or care about us."

Damn. Her heart splits open, and that loneliness seeps inside again—the loneliness that had started to recede after she arrived here.

"Sentimental, indeed. But not practical," says an Alderton council member.

"My god! What does it take to get you to stop talking and start listening?" *What would Nan do?* Her grandmother knew how to command an audience, how to turn ears her way, how to shake loose people stuck in their ways.

Despite the pain, Adaline pushes her shoulder back, raises her chin, and lowers her voice enough that everyone has to listen closely to hear her. "How is it practical to keep doing everything separately? The city is literally split in half. You have different economic systems. Different traditions. Different uniforms for the guards. For goodness' sake, you sit on different sides of the dining hall. It's time to end that."

Lord Otto puffs his chest outward. "You suggest we throw away centuries of—"

"No, I'm not saying that at all." Adaline keeps her voice low. She has their attention, and she won't lose it. "I'm saying if we want to build a city that unites us, then we need to act united. And we start by building new traditions."

Everyone's silent as they process this information, but they can't envision it. They can't see what this would be like. Because they can't feel it, she pauses in front of Magnus and Ëólas, and she tells the council a story. "Every winter, my family and I celebrated the culmination of winter with a feast. My grandmother insisted this feast could not take place without lamb, mashed potatoes, and pudding for dessert. Our dearest friends' traditions required pavo relleno, ponche, bacalao, and tamales. When our families celebrated together, which foods did we serve?" In full professor mode now, she waits for someone to answer. She arches an eyebrow. "Anyone?"

"You eat what your host serves," says one from Lameiría.

"That's one option." Adaline glances around the circle. "Anyone else?"

"You learn how to cook your guests' favorite foods," says someone from Alderton.

"Another option, though I've tried, and I cannot make tamales as good as Abuela."

"Both," says Magnus.

Adaline glances backward and nods at the king. Then she turns back to the council. "Both. Every winter, since as long as I can remember, we'd come together for dinner, and the rule was that we could always make room for more food and traditions during the festivities, but we could never take away something that mattered to someone else."

"What if the traditions conflict with each other?" asks Lady Síena.

Adaline smiles softly at her. "Then you do both, and each person can choose which one they want to observe. Neither is wrong. Neither is bad. They're just different. And our differences are what make the world interesting and colorful and dynamic and worth exploring. Our differences are what allow us to learn and grow and evolve. So, rise out of those chairs, go down into the streets, and show our people how we can get through this grief, together. When again will you be blessed with two leaders who wish to pursue this level of peace again? Don't let those who hate what we're doing stop us from doing it. This city is a miracle and full of kind hearts and generous souls. And if someone out there wants to tear this all down, I'm going to fight them every step of the way."

Ëólas and Magnus rise out of their seats and descend from their thrones. Their boots echoing down the steps and across the floor are the only sounds in the room. Magnus kisses the back of Adaline's hand, and the wrinkles and weariness on his face lessen.

He's so tired. When did he last sleep?

Ëólas stands on her other side, careful to not brush against her wounded shoulder. "What do you propose?"

Adaline exhales. "We need something that unifies us. A single person. An idea or belief. A—"

She glances around the room, at all the faces staring at her, waiting for her to propose something concrete. The last face she looks at is Ëólas's. His full lips hint at a smile, encouraging her to continue. Her cheeks glow, and she glances away. The tapestry behind him matches the elves' breastplates, three stars hovering above the tree of life.

"A symbol," Adaline concludes, her mind already racing with new ideas. "We need a unifying symbol. Grief can tear us apart, but it can also bring us together. Let's make sure it's the latter."

CHAPTER THIRTY

THE RIVER LOCKS

"I'm so glad you're all amicable to my idea." Adaline presents a wide grin to the entire council, especially to Lord Otto, who moments ago complained about her plan being a waste of resources. "While you wrap things up here, I'll get started."

Ëólas's eyes bulge out of his head. "No, that's unnecessary. Wait for the meeting to conclude, and we'll follow your lead."

"No, I need to—"

"Then we'll conclude the meeting now and join you." Ëólas looks to Magnus to back him up. When Magnus only pinches his chin and ruminates, Ëólas's eyebrows slide further up his brow.

"Ëólas, stop." Adaline steps closer to him. Less than an arm's length away, she can perceive the hints of exhaustion, or rather stress, that's weighing down his shoulders and suppressing his light. She grips his forearm, and the stifling air makes breathing difficult. A bead of sweat drips down her back, making her shudder. Batting her lashes, she peers into his eyes and makes him focus on her words, not her injuries. "I'm okay. I'm fine. Really, I am. Most of these wounds are superficial. You don't have to worry."

He grinds his teeth. He wants to say something, but he's holding back. For whose sake, Adaline's not sure.

"Besides," she adds, "I have two bodyguards following my every move now, thanks to you."

"I assigned two last time." He brushes his fingers over the knot at the top of her shoulder that ties the sling together.

But that wasn't your fault. That creep fooled me too.

She gives Ëólas the most relaxed, confident look she can muster, even though she's certain she looks ridiculous doing so with her battered body.

"Oh!" she says, swinging around to face Hamon. "Now that I think about it, it would send the wrong message for me to have only elven guards. We should maintain the one-to-one ratio. Hamon, would you assign me one of your men?" She almost adds *someone whom you trust* but stops herself. "I mean no disrespect to Moren and Idrós, but it's more important than ever that we work together."

"Adaline," Ëólas quietly implores.

Facing him and Magnus, she lets her confidence slip for just a moment and looks at both of them pleadingly. "I need to get back out there." *Not just for our people, but for myself. Please, see that. I need your support, again.* "I can't let fear trap me here."

Magnus nods. "Hamon, assign her two."

Pursing her lips, she mouths, *Seriously?*

"Perfect," Ëólas says with a smirk. Then he looks gravely at Hamon. "Which of your guards do you trust most?"

With four guards in tow, Adaline exits the throne room and heads toward the front gates. Her new assignment helps her to ignore her pulsing shoulder and the burning gashes between her legs. Every now and again, she glances back at her new bodyguards. Their sideways glares at their counterparts don't help Adaline's cause.

Just outside the main gate, she halts, pushes her good shoulder back, and softens her face as she stares at her four new friends. At least, she hopes they'll be friends. "What I'm trying to do in the city, I don't know if it will help. But I need the four of you to help me pull this off."

They nod at Adaline but not each other, so she tries a different tactic. Turning to Hamon's guards, Tumin and Orin, Adaline asks them a series of questions about their families and what they enjoy doing when they're not guarding the city, or Adaline.

Orin, who could be a Weasley with his bright orange-red tuffs peeking out of his half-helm, shares that his father makes leather armor, and his sister and mother work in one of Magnus's many vineyards. Tumin, who's short and stocky with a neck thicker than Adaline's thigh, volunteers that he and his family are potato farmers. Adaline immediately warms to him, as her bandages and slouching make her feel shorter and bulky too.

"How about you two?" she asks Moren and Idrós.

Another pair of tall, lean professional soccer players, Moren and Idrós look to the other to speak first. Not even their helms can conceal their flawless features, especially Moren's silver eyes and Idrós's height.

He must be almost seven feet tall. Dang. And why must all elves be so attractive? There has to be a plump one somewhere.

Finally, Moren clears his throat and shares that his parents grow crops in Lameiría, and Idrós's family serves in the queen's guard.

Adaline mentally notes that she has two farmers, a tradesman, and a groomed soldier. *I can work with that.*

As they trek downhill toward the city, she asks questions about plants, about working with leather, about growing juicy grapes, about anything under the sun to get them talking and to loosen up. They each answer, their knowledge comparable. By the time they reach the city, the five of them are engaged in a conversation about their favorite restaurants.

Walking along Front Street, Adaline realizes she wasn't prepared for all the stares she's receiving. Everyone keeps their distance, glancing up now and then, but the streets are quieter, and people move slowly, cautiously. The normal chitchat and banter that populates Front Street has reduced to whispers.

Adaline knows she needs to visit Sallie, but she's not ready for that quite yet. She's not really ready for any of this. How could she be? The attack was unexpected. Once again, the world has changed in less than a day.

Turning onto Market Street, Adaline stops at an abandoned shop stall. The space behind the counter is untouched. A carver's tools lay abandoned on the table. A worn, dusty apron hangs on the nail post. A goblet of half-finished wine rests on the ground near an empty chair. A sculpture memorializes its unfinished potential, an apple tree only half freed from a block of stone.

Adaline lets the tears flow down her cheeks. She bites her bottom lip to stop herself from sobbing, but her shoulders shake as she cries, and each jerking motion causes pain to sear down her left side.

"My lady?" says a soft, approaching voice.

When Adaline looks up, Delós stands beside her. She reaches out and squeezes his hand.

"I'm so glad to see you, Delós. You're okay? Your family?"

"We're all safe, thank you. But my wife and son will be returning to Lameiría tomorrow." He squeezes her hand in return. "I, however, will remain." From behind Delós's back, out peeks his son. Denós looks up at his father with eyes wide and his small hand clutching his father's tunic.

When Delós wraps an arm around his son's shoulders, Denós looks to Adaline but keeps his voice quieter than she's ever heard during story time. "Are you terribly hurt, my lady?"

She shakes her head. "Not terribly, but I am going to miss you, Denós. Thank you so much for listening to my stories, asking the most insightful questions, and giving me this." She pulls out of her pocket the wooden flower.

"My lady kept it!"

"Always. It's a treasured gift from a dear friend, and no matter what happens, nothing will make me forget that."

"Me neither, my lady," Denós says. "I will miss your stories very much. But I look forward to coming back a year from now. Perhaps then I can find out what became of Buttercup and Westley, if you'll still be sharing stories, that is."

Adaline rubs her thumb across the ridges of the wooden flower petals. *A year from now.* Could she really still be here? She hadn't allowed herself to think about that possibility, of not teaching next semester, of someone else taking over her classes, of Cindy being forced to choose someone else to be her maid of honor.

And what about the little things, like never curling up on the sofa on Friday night to watch TV? No phones ringing. No cars zooming past her window at night. No flushable toilets.

What if there are no answers to be found? If she's stuck here, what will become of her? She can't continue to mooch off Magnus, and neither he nor Ëólas stays in the Neutral Territory year-round. Plus, she's not ready to leave the Neutral Territory, not in its current condition.

Adaline looks at Jósep's unfinished work. He finally knew what the statue wanted to be. What it still wants to be.

"My lady?" Delós asks.

Adaline shakes her head, turns to Denós, and wishes she could painlessly squat down to his level. "I'd like to finish that story today, if that's possible. But I also have a project I'm starting now. I've gotten permission to build a garden where we've been gathering for our stories. A garden around and along our bridge. It's ambitious, but if we work together, maybe we can finish today."

With large, pleading eyes, Denós looks up at his father, who humors his son with a smile and turns to Adaline. "How might we help, my lady?"

Adaline beams. "I need to find the head city gardeners and bring them here. This is also at the request of Lord Ëólas and King Magnus, but I'm not sure whom I'm looking for."

"Ah, I can help with that." The old baker woman walks over to them with a slight limp and a croaky voice. "Recca's a friend of mine, and she's done lots of gardening for the city. I can fetch her, my lady."

Before Adaline can protest, Delós steps forward. "May I accompany you?" He offers the baker his elbow, and the old woman, without hesitation, places her withered hand around his lean, strong arm.

"Thank you so much, both of you. I'll be at Sallie's home," Adaline says.

Delós opens his mouth but ponders his words before speaking. "My lady, you should know...Kian died trying to save Jósep. I don't know why this happened. I don't understand it. But I'm not abandoning the Neutral Territory. And I look forward to hearing you sing again."

Speechless, Adaline takes a moment to breathe through her rising emotions. She doesn't want to cry again, not in front of the people she's trying to help today. "Thank you for telling me that, Delós."

After he tells his son to return to their shop and help his mother, the young elf with his flawless skin and clear eyes escorts the old woman, limping along on her sore leg. Seeing them together, side by side, fills Adaline with that undercurrent of hope that flows through this city. It's easy to miss when fear and sorrow grow larger, heavier, but that steady, hopeful current is ever present, which means it's stronger in the long run.

With her plans underway, Adaline walks to Sallie's home with her four guards marching behind her. As she passes the street leading to the square where her captor found her, Adaline carefully matches her breaths to the cadence of the guards' steps. Keeping her eyes on Sallie's shop, she never looks down that other street.

Horses don't come through the city often. She should have suspected something then. How naïve.

Still, this attack proved a few things. Someone's targeting the Neutral Territory to drive elves and humans apart, which is most likely why they targeted Jósep and Kian. From a logistics perspective, those who hate losing the resources Alderton's been pouring into the city could be suspect. But their motives can also be hate-based, especially if they consider Adaline in particular to be an abomination.

But the biggest piece of the puzzle is that her abductor knew she came from another world, or at least suspected, and he was trying to bring her somewhere. Why? For what purpose? If only she could have gotten more information from him. If only he had monologued his whole strategy like a James Bond villain. Instead, Adaline has to find other ways to obtain more information, which means placing herself out in the open—not that she's shared these thoughts with Ëólas. No way. As far as he's concerned, she's here to build a garden. That's all.

Adaline pauses outside Sallie's shop. The interior is dark, not a single candle lit. She knocks on the door and waits, clicking her thumbnail against her middle fingernail.

After a few moments, Adem opens the door, a miniature version of Kian's wide eyes and Sallie's black hair. His face scrunches together while the fog clears from his mind. Then he opens the door wider for Adaline and her contingent to enter the shop.

"My lady," Adem mumbles and bows. His eyes are bloated and his cheeks pale.

Adaline takes a deep breath and says the same thing everyone told her two years ago. "I'm so sorry for your loss, Adem. Your father was a good man."

The words ring hollow; nothing she says can ease the pain that's overtaken him. His mind must be preoccupied with wondering what he could have done differently to change the events that led to his father's death. He probably spends every minute of every day wishing he could reverse time and hold his father's hand once more, hold on so fiercely that nothing could take his father away again.

Adem sniffles and nods. "Mother's upstairs."

Leaving him in his well of grief, Adaline trudges upstairs, alone. Sallie sits in the rocking chair in the corner of the living room, staring out the window at the perfumer across the street as he pours different scented oils into smaller, decorative bottles. Lori's asleep on Sallie's shoulder. The girls, Jem, and Abuela are nowhere to be seen.

Even though Sallie's arms sag at her sides, her eyes are as dark as flint. The look on her face reminds Adaline of how she felt when the funeral director handed her the small box containing Nan's remains. A woman larger than life had been reduced to ash and stuffed inside a tin can.

Adaline sits on the bench next to Sallie. When Adaline rests her hand on her friend's arm, Sallie's startled to find herself not alone.

As she examines Adaline's bruises, her eyes narrow and harden, and she hisses, "My lady, what did they do to you?"

Adaline wriggles against the threadbare bench cushion and closes her eyes. Again, she sees her captor's face, the blood dripping out of his chest, those final gasps. "Some man tried to kidnap me. I did worse to him."

Sallie gives one sharp nod. "Good."

They sit together for a while longer, neither speaking. Some pains can't be verbalized.

When Adaline spots the gardener approaching down the street, she asks, "Where are the kids?"

"With my mother. Downriver. Change of scenery."

Adaline wants to ask if Sallie and the kids will be okay, if a woman can inherit her husband's business, if they plan to stay in the Neutral Territory, if she blames Adaline for hosting those story times in the first place. "When they come back, will you let them know I'll be at my spot?"

Sallie dips her chin and rubs Lori's back. The two women stare into each other's eyes for a long moment, and the spark in Sallie's flares awake. Her heart may be missing, but she's going to fight for her kids' well-being, and Adaline's going to make sure Sallie has the help she needs.

When Adaline steps outside again, streaks of sunlight between the buildings strike the perfume bottles, each reflecting a disjointed rainbow on the cobblestone street. The sight of their mingled colors eases Adaline's heart, and she silently thanks the powers that be for creating beauty on a day like today. Now, it's her turn to inspire others.

With Delós and the baker guiding her, the gardener wrings her dirt-stained hands and looks about cautiously as she approaches Adaline. "Good morning, my lady. How may I assist you?"

Is it the sling or my silk dress that makes her uneasy? "Thank you so much for coming here, Recca. I truly appreciate it. Would you please come with me?"

Adaline leads the gardener and her guards farther down Market Street, trying desperately to ignore the twinge of pain radiating down her arm, and stops outside the mason's home. She knocks, and the door opens, revealing a tall man with broad shoulders and arms as thick as tree trunks. A full beard covers his mouth so much so that Adaline can't be sure he has lips.

"My lady, how can I help you?" He looks over her shoulder. Seeing the elves, he takes a step back and closes his door a crack.

Before he disappears from sight, Adaline raises the pitch of her voice and speaks quickly. "I'm so glad you're home today. Kian mentioned you are quite skilled, and I'm hoping you can help me."

Hesitantly, he peels his eyes away from the elves and looks at Adaline's sling. "What do you need?"

Stepping back, she gestures for the mason to step outside. He clicks his tongue a few times but does so, and Adaline explains to him and the gardener that she wants to turn the dirt bank around both sides of the Rialto into a garden. "In the center of the bridge, I also want to add a garden bed in the alcoves and add potted plants in front of some of the arched windows, which means we'll need a lot of bricks, decorative stones, and plants."

Even though Recca squishes her dark-brown eyebrows together, Adaline continues, hoping they'll both pick up on the significance of her plans for discreetly building a memorial for the twelve victims. "On the bridge itself, I'd like to pot in front of the six arches on each side vameires plants that will eventually hang over the balustrade and into the water below. Lord Ëólas said they'd be light enough to not harm the structure of the bridge."

"Vameires plants?" Recca asks.

"Oh, my lady." Delós raises his hand. "Vameires is Elvish. I believe in the Common Tongue they're called river locks."

"How pretty!" Adaline says.

Recca's face brightens too. "River locks, yes, those would work. But I have only ten at the moment."

Adaline's too tired to hide her crestfallen face. "Hmm. That won't do. We need twelve. If you don't have enough, can you recommend something else? The plants need to be the same."

"I don't think I—Ah, no. I understand." Recca grinds her palms together as she thinks. "Let me see what I can do. I'll need to request assistance from others."

"Of course. And my new friends, Moren and Tumin, grew up on farms. I'm certain they'll be a big help too."

Moren and Tumin bow to the gardener, who doesn't reject the idea.

With everything falling into place, Adaline turns back to the mason. "And I'd like to commission you to build a semicircular white brick wall that will form the garden bed, one that's low enough to double as seating for pedestrians on the bridge, and we'll need more benches for the garden around the riverbank. The city council has approved this project, so the payment is covered."

Gripping the back of his neck with both hands, the mason pushes his tongue into the side of his cheek. "Alright, my lady. When should I get started?"

"Immediately. If we have enough people working together, I'm hoping we can finish this today."

The mason laughs. "It takes two days for cement to dry."

"I know someone who can help with that," Delós says.

The mason looks him up and down, then drops his arms. "Alright then."

While the mason, gardener, and Delós retreat to their shops and recruit people to assist with the plans for the bridge, Adaline heads to the Rialto. Taking a deep breath, she climbs the slope and waits in the middle, sitting on Jósep's bench and trailing her fingertips over the ram armrest. Her guards give her space as they wait in the opposite alcove.

Please, let this help.

"My lady." Idrós gestures with his chin toward both ends of the bridge where a handful of humans and elves approach from both sides.

Delós's friend looks around cautiously when he sees Adaline, but the sight of Moren and Idrós in their sage-green and navy garb helps his facial features to relax, and he crosses the bridge's span with his people.

Look at that. Elves are still willing to come to this side of town. I'm going to call that a win. "Okay, let's get to work."

The bridge becomes a cacophony of organized chaos. After Adaline, the gardener, the mason, and a few of their associates discuss her plans, the intersection of Front and Market Street fills with the sounds of people mixing cement, stacking bricks, moving dirt, and hauling plants. Despite having only one good arm, Adaline helps too, lifting one brick at a time and carrying it up the bridge's slope, but the guards insist that she sit on Jósep's bench, so she performs the only task she can at the moment: She continues telling Buttercup and Westley's story.

As she summarizes the beginning, Ëólas and Magnus emerge with Merith and Thoren behind them. With a wink and a wave, they set to work, helping their people. More citizens gather around the bridge, either to hear Adaline's story or to witness their king and commander general performing manual labor.

Regardless, the people cheer and applaud when they learn that the Dread Pirate Roberts is actually Westley. But by the time Westley's taken to Miracle Max, the throbbing in her shoulder has Adaline wincing. She leans back against the bench, but the pressure of the stone doesn't help. When she pauses her story to adjust her sling, Ëólas drops one more load of soil around the vameires plant he's been potting and brushes his hands together to dust off the dirt.

He walks over to Adaline, who sits up straighter and projects her voice around him. "Luckily, Westley was only mostly dead, and—"

"Adaline, that's enough for today." Despite his stern eyes, his tone is soft. "Head back to your chambers. Magnus and I will see to the rest of your plans. You need rest and—"

"A water feature."

"What?"

"I need a water feature, like a birdbath or decorative pond. Wind chimes would be nice too. We can add them to the gardens below."

"Noted. I'll escort you back to the castle myself to make sure you don't wander off again, and tomorrow you may—"

"Ëólas." She stands up and in two steps closes the distance between them. Peering up into his eyes, she bats her lashes and says quietly, "Trust me. Please."

He looks at her closely, as if he's waiting for her to falter, to trip, to show she's tired, anything he can use to make her go back. She doesn't budge. He bites his tongue but summons someone to discuss adding a bird bath.

Loríen, her husband, and their son also arrive and contribute to the project, but Loríen inspects Adaline's shoulder first. "These are for you." She places in Adaline's hand a variety of crystals. "The clear quartz can help amplify your own energy, and the black tourmaline might help your shoulder. I also brought you this."

She pulls out of her pocket a small sachet containing dried herbs. The smell makes Adaline gag and resort to breathing only through her mouth.

"I know it's pungent, my lady. But brew a small amount of this every day. I can't make any guarantees, but it might help you heal faster."

"Thank you, Loríen. I mean, Lady Loríen. I'm sorry. I didn't mean to—"

Loríen presses the sachet into Adaline's palm and closes her fingers around the medicine. "You're very welcome, Adaline. I hope you'll visit my shop soon, and I'll brew you something more palatable."

Adaline pockets the gifts and wraps one arm around Loríen, who hugs her back. "Thank you. I will."

As the evening wears on and the market closes, Adaline jokes they could use a fire pit in the gardens for cooking dinner. Shortly thereafter, the metalworker brings two fire pits, complete with skewers. While Merith and Hamon take turns cooking sausages, strips of steak, and eventually rotating chickens, they listen to the end of Adaline's story.

Magnus also pays Sallie for a crate of candles, which they set up along the bridge's balustrade and around the new gardens. More people arrive, having made the pilgrimage from the further reaches of the city. They enjoy a bite, a drink, and a song provided by Delós before they head off again with their hearts a little lighter.

When Sallie sees the garden illuminated with her family's work, she sits on Jósep's bench. She counts aloud the interspersed plants beneath the arches, each pot with its own short yet rounded trellis that will guide the River Lock vines to drape over the balustrade. When she counts twelve, she weeps silently. A lot of people do. But they do so together with the candles flickering and the wind chimes singing their own lament, and the net that had dropped over the entire city begins to lift.

At the end of the night, Ëólas strolls back to Adaline. Side by side, they watch the candles flicker and listen to the crackle of the fire pits. The summer heat opted not to torment everyone today, but still Adaline turns into the occasional breeze.

As the flames pop and sparks fly into the night air, Ëólas stuffs his hands in his trouser pockets and whispers, "You're making yourself a target."

"I know."

He closes his eyes and purses his lips, but he doesn't argue with her. "I can't convince you to change your mind, can I?"

She smirks but doesn't answer him. Instead, she asks him a question that has been burning in the back of her mind. "How did you know where to find me?"

At the mention of her abduction, his expression darkens while he stares at the flames billowing in the night air. Lost in his own thoughts, he doesn't blink until a candle burns out. "I don't know. My guards returned without you, and something didn't feel right. Then I heard you call me, and I..." He turns to face her and searches her eyes as if he's looking for evidence that she'll believe him. "I just knew which direction to go."

Whoa. "Like magic."

He nods his head.

Worrying her bottom lip, Adaline pushes down the panic flooding her chest and blinks rapidly to dry her eyes. Among the bridge's din, her voice is barely audible. "Does that... Do I scare you?"

Closing the distance between them, Ëólas cups her cheeks and rests his forehead against hers. His thumbs catch and brush away her tears. "No."

Chapter Thirty-One

THE DECISION

Adaline holds her palm out to the kettle and concentrates on the sound of the water rolling over itself, the bubbles popping and hissing. Steam billows from the spout, and the kettle itself begins to rattle, to shake, to vibrate, as the pressure builds.

"Adaline, the water's boiling." Seira leans over her friend and arches an eyebrow.

"Oh, yeah." Standing up, Adaline grabs the potholder resting on the hearth's mantle and removes the kettle from where it hangs above the fire. Then she returns to the hook the potholder Mercia decorated, a patch of sunflowers facing a zig-zaggy sun in the upper left corner.

"Where's Mercia?" Seira asks.

"With her mom. I'll see her in a bit." *No point mentioning that we'll be heading into the city together.* Yesterday, when Adaline and Mercia invited Seira to join them, Seira's face paled, and she disappeared inside her mind for over an hour while her breakfast turned cold.

Looping an arm around Seira's, Adaline leads them through the arch leading to Seira's balcony. The crisp morning breeze sweeps the sheer lavender curtains in front of them, blocking their path. As Adaline bats them away, she avoids knocking a dragonfly to the ground. The blue-green bug blinks at her and zips off, diving downward and disappearing into the meadows below.

Seira takes a seat at her little table on the balcony, deposits a spoonful of tea leaves into two cups, and folds her hands on her lap. While Adaline pours the hot water for them, Seira exhales her frustration. "You're not you. You're lesser."

Adaline takes a seat across from Seira and swirls the tea leaves in her cup until they unfurl and sink to the bottom. "Thanks. I'm aware."

Since the attack, her nightmares have grown more vivid, and whenever she stops thinking and zones out, that voice pops into her head. *Blight. Abomination. Could that guard have been any more melodramatic?*

But whenever Adaline wakes up in a cold sweat, Seira's beside her with a damp cloth and soothing voice that lulls Adaline back to sleep within seconds. After that, she doesn't wake up again until morning, but the constant interruptions to her rest are adding up.

Adaline yawns, then sips the tea. The scalding hot water singes her tongue and the roof of her mouth, making her wince and bang her wounded calve against the table leg. *Damn it.*

Maybe if she could actually use magic when she wants, she could cool the water a bit. But each day that passes, the idea of magic seems more and more absurd. When alone in her room, she's tried casting spells by making up rhymes. She's tried waving around a stick she picked up on her walk home. She's tried observing Seira to see if she does anything indicative of magic, but most of the time Seira seems lost in her own thoughts as she ghosts through the castle. And Adaline's tried asking Ëólas to explain the principles of magic, only for him to scrub his face, back out of the room, and run off to handle "other important matters."

And why? Because elves aren't supposed to discuss magic with humans. Fucking hypocrite. Magic is bullshit.

Adaline glances up at Seira. With her head tilted to the side, the aloof yet immensely kind blonde beauty watches a bird chirp and jump along the balcony railing. Her wide pupils give her that faraway look, and she sits so still that Adaline could mistake her for a wax figure.

"How about you, Seira? You're less yourself too, aren't you?"

Keeping the rest of her body frozen, Seira nods once. "I haven't been myself for almost as long as I can remember." Her eyes grow cloudy, and her pupils widen further, swallowing her periwinkle irises until only the violet outer circle remains.

"Do you want to talk about it?"

"No." Her eyes snap into focus, and she narrows her gaze at Adaline. With a firm tone, she says, "I want you to do something, anything, that makes you more you again."

Adaline clangs her teacup onto the saucer. "I am doing something. I'm being patient," she says, adding layers of sarcasm to her last word.

Seira slams her hands on the table, rattling both their cups, and raises her voice. "That's even lesser you! That's not you at all!"

"Thanks! You have any advice, any information you can share, anything that will help me understand what I'm doing here and why the hell someone's after the both of us?"

"I can't." Seira grabs fistfuls of her hair and pulls as if to tear them free from her scalp. "There are too many possibilities, too many variables." She leaps out of her chair and paces the length of the balcony.

With a loud humph, Adaline crosses her arms and bites her burned tongue so she doesn't exacerbate Seira's meltdown.

Mid-pace, Seira halts in front of Adaline, releases her hair, and stomps her foot. "Being patient is going to make matters more dire. You're decisive. You have strong instincts. You know what you want, and you don't wait for others. That's who we need."

"I don't know what to do!"

Seira matches Adaline's raised voice and flails her hands about wildly. "Yes, you do. You already know. You can feel it. Stop hiding behind yourself!"

Shoving her chair away from the table, Adaline springs to her feet. "That doesn't make any sense." *I'm the one hiding? Are you fucking kidding me?* "How about you do something for once, huh?"

"Fine!"

"Fine! Let me know what you come up with."

"Oh, you'll know! I won't be subtle."

"Well, won't that be a nice change of pace." Without looking back, Adaline storms out of Seira's chambers and tugs on the heavy door to slam it behind her.

"Adaline! What about these?" From the jeweler's display table, Mercia selects a pair of dangling earrings with emerald globes at the bottom and holds one up to her friend's ear. "These will bring out your green eyes, don't you think?"

"I'm okay, thanks. Besides, I don't have any money." *And this is why I've intentionally avoided strolling beyond Sallie's shop.*

Glittering rows of earrings, necklaces, circlets, and hairpins of various metals, colorful glass, and precious stones surround Adaline and Mercia. The sea of temptation tugs Mercia from item to item while Adaline attempts to stay back.

I need to find a way to earn a living wage.

But her instincts don't react to that idea. Shaking her head, Adaline massages her temples as she pushes her argument with Seira out of her mind.

"Adaline, you don't need money. You're the king's ward. Take what you want, and the shopkeepers will send a notice to the king for payment."

Mercia places the earrings in Adaline's palm. When Mercia picks up a second pair made with garnet, Adaline returns the first set, resting them in their original spot and making sure they lay straight. The glimmer in the shopkeeper's weary eyes dims, and Adaline contemplates taking them after all.

"Not to your liking, my lady? How about these?" The shopkeeper, with his twisted arthritic hands, pinches between his shaky fingers a set of diamond studs.

Adaline drifts forward, but she stops, smiles politely, and takes a step backward. "They're lovely, thank you. I'll visit again as soon as I have money in my pockets."

While Mercia oohs and ahs and flips through a pile of carpets up to her waist, Adaline glances around the market, beyond her four bodyguards watching her, to see if anyone or anything feels off, suspicious, or goosebump inducing. Nearby, a man shops for a new saddle. A child sprints after a runaway chicken. A lady tries on a small hat, or a fascinator, as Nan would say, on top of her diamond-studded snood. And a couple purchases a simple, wooden dining table and three chairs with the promise to have money next week for the fourth. The people go about their business as if the city hadn't been attacked only four days ago, which should make Adaline feel relieved. And it does, to some extent. Nothing about the city or its people feels ominous. As she pinches the pressure point on her hand, her frown deepens.

She glances at Sallie's shop down the street where the girls work the stall, their faces void of smiles. Adaline's shoulders sag, even the stiff one.

If I'd never come here, Kian and Jósep might still be alive.

A small voice in the back of her head tells her she's wrong, but her thoughts are too loud right now—as is the voice from her dreams. *Blight. Abomination.*

If I'd never started telling them all those stupid, pointless stories, those people wouldn't have attacked.

If I'd never befriended Jósep and Kian's family, they wouldn't have been together. They wouldn't have died together.

"What a lovely day!" Mercia takes a deep breath, spins once in a circle, and clutches her belly while she laughs. "What a treasure that Father said I can join you without mother following after us."

They stroll down the center of the extra-wide street so Mercia can better see the stalls at a glance and so they can avoid having every merchant summon them to test this or try that or sample a fresh batch of whatever. All of it would be enticing, but Adaline's eager to make her way to the bridge and see the children waiting for her.

After they pass three more stalls, Adaline finally registers Mercia's words. "Why did Thoren change his mind?"

"Oh, I promised him I'd subtly plant seeds for you to consider marrying His Majesty."

Adaline stops and faces Mercia. "You're kidding. He hated me when I first arrived. He wouldn't let me near Magnus without hovering over my shoulder."

Mercia hugs Adaline's arm and tugs her along to keep walking. "Father's the cautious sort, especially when it comes to His Majesty. But once Father's decided he likes someone, he's fiercely loyal and protective of them. He sings your praises to Mother too."

Adaline's eyebrows lift upward as she shakes her head. *I'm not sure what to do with that information.* "You know I'm not going to marry Magnus, right?" *There's no way that's what Seira was getting at.*

"I suppose."

Great. That sounds convincing.

"We should head back," Mercia says. "What story will you tell this time?"

"I don't know." During their walk, Adaline skims through the Rolodex of stories in her memory banks. Nothing jumps to the front of her mind. Nothing feels appropriate. Nothing inspires her.

"Oh, Adaline, when you're done, might we explore the elven side of Market Street? I've desperately wanted to see their jewelry and goods. Granted, the king and Lord Ëólas really must do something about the city's economic situation. Having two different economies will not help our people..."

Mercia's words mingle with and fade into the rest of the city's din while Adaline's mind wanders.

Maybe when I meet with Lady Síena tomorrow, I can turn that project into a job? Or I could try asking Magnus for a job, something more than telling kid stories. Oh, I could offer to teach dance lessons again. Adaline sighs loudly. *Look at me going backward in life.*

"Are you feeling well?" Mercia studies Adaline carefully, searching for signs of physical discomfort. "Is your shoulder bothering you too much?"

Her left shoulder hurts less than yesterday, and the bruises on her face have been healing rather quickly too. Almost as if nothing happened. Except for the two people forever missing in her life now. Funny how the world keeps turning.

Adaline rotates her arm in a wide circle, proving that her stiff shoulder has continued healing each day. Then she pushes a smile onto her face. "Thanks. I'm fine."

Adaline returns her sheathed sword to the shelf. After wiping her sweaty palms on her sapphire-blue bodice, she flexes both her wrists and massages the muscle throbbing along her forearm. The sword may be unnaturally light, but her wrist doesn't like the rigid, controlled posture required to wield it properly. Granted, she's been practicing with the sword for not quite two weeks. Despite Fólas's praise, using a sword hasn't gotten easier.

"Adaline?"

"Hmm?" She rotates her feet sideways, making her eyes leave the sword, and finds Fólas holding the door open to the outside world. "Are you coming?"

"Oh. You go ahead. I think I'm going to practice a bit more by myself."

He scrunches his brows. "Are you certain? I can stay and—"

"No, it's okay. I can use the alone time to practice on precision rather than speed."

"Your shoulder's still sore. I don't want you to hurt yourself."

"I won't, thank you. Go on. You have work to do."

"You're certain?"

Adaline nods. "I'll be fine."

Fólas bows slightly and backs out of the training room, closing the door behind him. With her four guards outside, she closes her eyes and takes a deep breath. Flicking her eyes open, she grabs her sword and pulls out the blade in one swift motion. Leaning the scabbard against the wall, she moves to the center of the room, widens her stance, and places one foot behind her. Her new first position.

She swings the blade, keeping her wrist locked and elbow up. She continues to practice, attacking the air, as she loses herself in the movements, in the rhythm, in the repetition. Her stomach growls, but she doesn't pause. She doesn't yield. She doesn't quit. Her precision strengthens, and the sword becomes an extension of her right arm. Every time a thought pops into her head, she slashes and shreds it to pieces. When her footfalls land her in front of a wooden target, she swings the blade downward on an angle. The stick neck snaps, and the hay-stuffed head tumbles to the ground. Only instead of a burlap sphere, Adaline sees her captor's face, his eyes forever open and staring into her soul.

She drops the sword. The blade clangs against the stone floor, its echoed protests ringing up and down her spine, as Adaline stares at her empty hands. Nothing about them is magical. Nothing about her is special. She has no purpose here. No family. No future. And no way home. She's not even sure if she wants to go home.

What's that say about me?

With her shoulders slumped, she stuffs her hands into her pockets and clutches her Swiss army knife and mobile phone, both of which feel like relics. She lets them go, pulls out her hands, and drops them at her sides.

I'm tired. So very tired.

Someone closes the door behind her, and the resulting breeze, laced with the faint scent of lavender, propels the stale air to dissipate.

She doesn't turn around. "How long have you been watching me?"

"I check in regularly."

Of course he does.

Even though his footfalls are silent, she hears him pick up her sword and slide it back into the scabbard.

Wiping her cheek dry, she picks up the dummy's head and jams it onto the splintered neck. "What's the point?"

"I thought the point was to protect yourself, which you did quite well."

"I can't do it. I can't kill someone else." *I'm completely useless here.*

"You make that sound like a bad thing." His voice is closer, and the heat radiating off his chest warms her back.

She wants to step backward, to lean against him, to close her eyes and finally rest. Without interruption. But for all she knows, he could already be gone. She's used to his sudden appearances and long absences. Isn't she? Not that it matters. Not that she matters. At least not in the grand scheme of things.

Her shoulders shake as she wills herself not to cry. Ëólas places one hand on the side of her arm and slowly, gently, turns her around.

She keeps her head down. "I'm not a soldier. I don't want to hurt people."

With the tip of his thumb, he lifts her chin. When they're this close, she can see beyond the light in his eyes, see the shadows where he hides his sorrow and regret. If only she could help him the way he's helped her.

They both ask, "Are you alright?"

Ëólas's eyebrows spring upward. "Me? Adaline, you—" He takes a step closer but keeps his arms pinned at his sides. In one fist, he grips Adaline's sword. "When you passed out, I thought you had…" He lowers his gaze and shakes his head. His jowls move from side to side as he grinds his jaw. Lifting the sword, he rests the scabbard on his palms and locks eyes with her. "I did not give you this so you would feel obligated to kill others. I gave it to you because your kindness, your open heart, and the light inside you that draws people to you are worth protecting. If anyone dares to hurt you again, I won't forgive you if you let them win."

She sucks in a sharp breath. "I, I'm sorry I haven't been myself lately."

"You're grieving. We all are. In our own ways."

"I've been grieving for two years. And every time I think I'm just about passed it, something else happens to make it heavier." She exhales deeply. "But I won't give up. I promise."

"Now that's more like the Adaline I've come to know. Would it help if you threw my cloak in my face? Should I take it off and hand it to you now?"

"Asshole!"

"There she is!"

They both laugh.

"Are you saying I'm innately rude?"

"No. You innately see people."

She takes another cleansing breath and releases the tension that has been building inside her for days. *How does he do that?*

Keeping his gaze locked with hers, he reaches past Adaline's ear, grabs her cloak off the peg, and hands it to her. She manages to not flinch when she drapes it around her shoulders and secures the clasp.

Behind him, moonlight cascades through the window, casting a silver sheen over the stone floor. *Whoa. How long have I been here?*

"Are you ready to go?"

She glances at her sword still in his hand. *Worth protecting. Seira. Sallie. Delós. Loríen. The children. This city and its people are worth protecting.*

Adaline's gut spins like a compass searching for north. Placing a hand on her stomach, she bends forward and gasps. "Oh my god. There it is."

"What?"

As the thought blooms inside her, she tests the feeling associated with it, and the compass settles. She looks at Ëólas and steels her gaze. "Somehow, I'm a part of what's been going on. I don't know why. I don't know how. But I refuse to hide behind myself. I care about the people in this city, and I want to protect what you and Magnus have been working toward. I want an active role here. I don't want to sit and wait for someone to strike next. When I want answers, I go after them. That's who I am, and that's what I want to do. I'm ready."

He leans back on his heels, his face hardening as he thinks about what she's said, but his eyes never waver from hers. She grounds her feet, willing herself to wait for his response, but he takes only a moment to decide.

"Alright," he says.

Lifting his free hand, he reaches toward her cheek, but she steps in between his open arms and wraps hers around his waist. She ignores his torso stiffening, trusting that his shock will wear off quickly. A heartbeat later, he closes his arms around her and rests his chin on the crown of her head. Every time she inhales, that pine and lavender scent further settles her mind. *Yes. This is right. Everything about this is right. I can do this. Somehow.*

"Adaline?" As she tilts her head upward, he arches his back so he can see her entire face. "You're not the only one who wants answers. I want them too. How about we go after them together?"

A broad grin spreads across her face, making her cheeks burn and her eyes gleam. "I'd like that. Very much." Hope expands inside her chest until that warmth inhabits every crevice, giving her purpose and focus.

Inlūmras né leira.

A salty breeze ruffles their hair, and the sound of waves breaking against rocks fills the training room. The shelves and dummies become colorless and translucent until they and everything in the room disappear altogether. The stars replace the ceiling. The moon transfers to the opposite side of the sky, and the silhouettes of squat buildings standing shoulder to shoulder fill in and turn solid behind them.

Still holding onto each other, Ëólas and Adaline stand at the edge of a cliff overlooking the ocean.

ALSO BY ERIN P.T. CANNING

Adaline's story is far from over!

Join her and Ëólas as they work together to escape enemy territory, learn some devastating truths that will change their worlds, and discover just how good a team they make in book two, ***Treachery and Truths***, available now.

If you enjoyed reading this, please consider leaving a review. Nothing more helps authors to keep going and encourages other readers to take a chance on a book than your reviews. Thank you again.

All of my books blend fantasy, adventure, and romance as my characters explore other cultures, make unexpected friends, and discover their hidden strengths as they fight for what they desire most.

For regular updates, bonus chapters, free book recommendations, and more, you can subscribe to my newsletter by visiting my author website.

ELVISH LANGUAGE GUIDE

Being a fan of Tolkien, I had to create pronunciation rules for my book. Here's what I came up with when I allowed myself time to fully geek out.

Names

Ëólas (ee-oh-lus)

Delós (deh-loh-s)

Fólas (foe-lus)

inlūmras né leira (in-loom-ruhs knee lear-uh)

Jósep (joe-sep)

Lameiría (la-mear-ee-uh)

Loríen (lore-ee-en)

neir nía (near knee-ah)

Seira (sear-uh)

tíer nía (tea-er knee-ah)

vameires (vuh-mear-ehs)

Vowels

A

schwa = a (as in uh)

short = ã (as in ah / apple)

long = á or eí (rarely ay)

E

short = e (eh)

long = é *

* é becomes ë or í when pronounced separately in front of another vowel

I

short = i*

long = ai

* i becomes y when used as *and* to blend two words into one

O

short = o

long = ó (as in oh)

schwa = õ (as in aw / ball)

U

short = ū (as in oo / ooze)

long = ú

Diphthongs

eir = as in ear or weird

ae = as in air

au = as in ouch / house

oi = oy as in toy

ACKNOWLEDGMENTS

To my readers, thank you immensely for reading Adaline's journey and welcoming her story into your life. Sharing this piece of myself with you is an honor and a dream I kept at bay for far too long. I can't wait to share with you her epic adventure and short stories revolving around some of these side characters. (I don't know about you, but I think Hamon needs his own mini adventure.)

I'm not certain this book would have come to fruition without the constant support and encouragement of Maria Secoy and All Write Well. Our many virtual writing sessions, our laughter over disappearing characters, and her "get it done" attitude redirected the course of my life. Thank you for making me finish my shitty first draft. I'm forever grateful for that. Also, if not for Maria's developmental edits, Seira's story would have disappeared entirely. I can't imagine this story without her.

I also have to thank Dayna and Jason Abraham and all of my Conquer & Thrive people, who helped me to find myself again, especially when I thought I had no more dreams left inside me. Thank you for teaching me that it's okay to experiment and have fun, even later in life, and that we can always keep dreaming and striving for the life we want and the person we want to be. It's hard to believe that prior to C&T, I had forgotten that, at my core, I'm a writer. Thank you, with all my heart.

To Rita Scanga, Ginny B. Moore, and David M. Brown, thank you for your help with smoothing out ideas, catching those elusive homonyms, and pointing out missing words. Editors cannot edit their own work, so thank you for taking on that role and allowing me to experience the other side of that dynamic.

I'm also grateful to each of my guests on my podcast. Listening to your journeys—how you overcame your own self-doubt, how you made time to write despite the daily chaos, and what being an author means to you now—inspired me every day to never give up. You are my heroes.

Mom, thank you for buying me oh so many books and the hundreds of Barbies that sparked my imagination from an early childhood.

To my sweet boys, I hope seeing your momma fulfill her dream to become an author shows you that you too can achieve your dreams. I'll always support and believe in you too.

ABOUT THE AUTHOR

Erin P.T. Canning has worked for twenty years as an editor, encouraging other writers' individual voices and teaching them how to hone their writing skills. She always planned to write a book. While she focused on her family, she stopped writing for six years. But something deep inside was missing. Depression, anxiety, and anger forced her to search for herself, both for her sake and her family's.

Despite fearing her skills had atrophied, Erin started writing again. For as long as she can remember, her imagination has been her safe place—a never-ending adventure where she can travel to far-off lands, find people who believe in her potential, and be the hero. By giving herself permission to be imperfect, she finished writing her own shitty first draft in 2022. *Ruins and Redemption* celebrates Erin making her own dreams come true.

Now, she spends her days helping writers become the authors they're meant to be and her evenings writing a blend of fantasy, adventure, and romance as her characters explore other cultures, forge unlikely friendships, and discover their hidden strengths as they fight for what's right and what they desire most.

She earned her BA in Literature from The American University and MA in Writing from Johns Hopkins University, and she lives with her husband and their two boys in Maryland.

You can find Erin on Facebook and Instagram (@erinptcanningauthor). You can also catch up with her regularly by going to her website, www.erinptcanningauthor.com.